BROKEN

MARA MONAHAN

authorHOUSE®

AuthorHouse™
1663 Liberty Drive
Bloomington, IN 47403
www.authorhouse.com
Phone: 1-800-839-8640

Published by AuthorHouse   02/01/2012

ISBN: 978-1-4685-5025-2 (sc)
ISBN: 978-1-4685-5026-9 (ebk)

Library of Congress Control Number: 2012902071

Any people depicted in stock imagery provided by Thinkstock are models, and such images are being used for illustrative purposes only.
Certain stock imagery © Thinkstock.

This book is printed on acid-free paper.

Editor: Kariann J. Beechler
Photographer: Jamison Frady of Quiet Art Photography
www.quietartphotography.com

Reviews of *Broken*

I loved this book! The characters are unique, and draw you in from the first page. This is a sometimes funny, sometimes serious, sometimes heartbreaking, always an easy read. A great story that illustrates our necessity for Jesus, and the experiences that bring us all to Him at some point in our lives.

- Sharia Sims, hairdresser, Sparks, NV

Mara Monahan is going places! This book will involve all your emotions.
It is a great first book, with fast moving plot involving people you'd like to know.

- Peggy West, owner of Thurston Books an award winning store in Springfield, OR

If you need to be at work soon, don't get started reading Broken, once you pick it up you will get totally lost in the story! The author knows how to spin a great narrative better than anyone I have read in years. This is a must read and you'll be very happy that you did.

- Stephen McGuire, Appraiser, Apple Valley, CA

Mara weaves an interesting and enjoyable story while tackling important issues that affect Christians today.

- Lula Adams, Faith Colors, Author and Artist, Sparks, NV

This is the most amazing, God-filled book I have ever read. Gave me chills to read it . . ."

- Myra Johansen, Customer Service Rep., Reno, NV

This book is dedicated to Yeshua Ha'Mashiach, The Lover and Keeper of my soul. Thank you for saving me.

Acknowledgements

This book would not have been possible without the encouragement of many of my closest friends and family. I want to thank my church family for cheering me on and for reading this book, chapter by chapter as I wrote.

Thank you to my wonderful family for enduring months of me babbling away about what was currently happening with my characters, and for actually seeming interested.

Thank you so much to the people who inspired my characters, you know who you are. You all have been more than generous and patient with me.

My best friend in the whole world, the Terminator, was a huge cheering section . . . often staying up late to read my book and texting me in the middle of the night with messages such as "I need more! When will you write another chapter?!" Thank you for not allowing me to slack off when I wanted to and for believing in me.

Kariann J. Beechler was the best Editor in the world. Thank you for all of your hard work and helpful advice. I never thought I would meet anyone more detail oriented than I am, but you blew me away. I truly couldn't have done this without you. My hope is that you will be available for the second book, and the third . . .

Jamison Frady, the best Photographer I have ever known, who took the cover photo as well as the author photo, and did so in the name of Jesus. How can I ever thank you? Your work is beautiful and so is your spirit. God bless you my friend.

Mara Monahan

To my husband who has stood by my side for every adventure, what would I ever do without you? For nearly twenty years you have been a gift from God in my life and I cannot imagine doing any of this without you. I love you!

Jesus, this is all done in your precious name. My prayer from the beginning is that your truth would come through in each word and that readers would find your voice in these pages. Thank you for giving me the story.

Come to me, all you who are weary and burdened, and I will give you rest. Take my yoke upon you and learn from me, for I am gentle and humble in heart, and you will find rest for your souls. For my yoke is easy and my burden is light.

~ Jesus

Prologue
Manhattan, Spring 1998

She woke, alone, to the familiar, searing pain of what she wished was only a migraine. Moaning softly, she reached for the Japanese silk kimono hanging by the side of her bed and gingerly made her way to the bathroom.

Lit by the soft glow of a nightlight, her bathroom was her only sanctuary. With stone floors, large roman columns, and more square footage than most apartments in New York, her pride and joy was the tub she had designed after the common bathing areas of ancient Greece.

She spent hours in her massive garden tub, soaking away the tension that seemed to follow her every day. The nooks were filled with exotic oils and perfumed salts that were shipped to her from around the world. Small hidden speakers in the ceiling piped in the sounds of soft acoustic guitar, and she would feel herself start to relax the moment she entered.

She had hired a local artist to paint large palm trees and tropical birds on the walls, lush flowers peeking out around her, and a vast azure sea beyond. Sometimes she could close her eyes and almost smell the pina coladas and salty ocean air.

This was where Theresa went when she needed to escape the conference calls and emails, the demanding clients, nearly constant business trips, the pagers, and the assistants following her around with bolts of fabric. As the most successful, and highest paid, fashion designer in the country, she rarely had a few moments to herself to enjoy it. The clothing line, *Her Wicked Ways*, was her baby. The only one she would ever have. She nurtured it, fed it, cared for it, and loved it like her child.

But right now, the only refuge she sought was the rows of prescription bottles on her countertop. So many pills. Long ago she had decided that it would be best to keep them out of easy reach. Too many nights, in her fear and her agony, it would be so easy, so simple to just take a handful of them and drift away. Leave behind her mistakes, her guilt, her obsessive need to be the best at everything.

Theresa Wakefield-Anderson, however, was a warrior. When she got up in the morning, she would remember that she had never lost a fight, and she wasn't about to start now. She had battled bigger wars in her lifetime than a mere disease, and she had come out strong. She didn't need or want anyone else's help. She was strong on her own.

She thought back to the day she received the diagnosis. That one word that would change her life, turn her world upside down and change it forever. Cancer. Worse, incurable and inoperable brain cancer.

She had been given six months at the most and was advised to "put her affairs in order." The physician had looked at her with no compassion, no understanding, no hope. He watched curiously for her reaction, but nothing more. She was like a lab rat to him, and because there was nothing more he could do for her, he was ready to move on to his next project. She was informed that there were things that could be done to make her comfortable, extend her life by perhaps a week or two, but that was the most she could hope for.

She fired him. Theresa had always believed in surrounding yourself with positive people. She was NOT about to put her life in the hands of a pessimist.

She was right. Eight and a half months. That's how long it had been since that horrible, clinical announcement. As she gazed briefly into the mirror, she realized that she would not have much time left before she would have to break down and get herself a wig. She took note of the last few strands of hair that no amount of styling would make appear thicker. It was the final indignity, losing her trademark luxurious hair.

Theresa was not only known for her remarkable sense of design and flawless beauty, but also for her hair. Reaching down to her tiny waist, her thick auburn wavy hair stopped men in their tracks and caused women to gape in envy. She had always been so proud of it, and now it was gone.

Sighing, she reached for the first bottle, then the second. When she had what she thought was just enough to take the edge off her pain, she tossed them back with a glass of water. Gazing into the empty glass, she thought about how simple and happy her life used to be.

She missed Sara with her twinkling aqua marine eyes and devilish sense of humor, and Coleman, the gentle giant, always willing to rescue a damsel in distress. Tears running freely now, she thought about how that had literally been the death of him.

Sliding to the cold stone floor of her bathroom, she allowed the memories to come flooding back, one by one . . . .

Part One

Part One

Chapter One
Bayfield, Iowa
March 1945

"Mister Wakefield!!" roared the aging chemistry teacher. "Is that something you would care to read to the rest of the class?"

Eugene Wakefield went white, followed almost immediately by a charming shade of pink. "Uh . . . no, sir. Sorry, sir," he stammered. He slipped the handwritten note hastily into his back pocket, flustered and embarrassed. Was it possible to literally die of mortification?

It had taken him eight weeks to get up the courage to talk to Mary Baker, the loveliest girl in his senior class at Beaumont High School. She had never spoken as much as a single word with him, but when she glanced his way, the universe stood still for Gene.

Gene was a handsome guy and he knew it. He generally worked that to his advantage with the ladies and had dated a majority of the cheerleaders at one time or another. He had his favorite lines that he liked to use with them and they always worked. This was the first time he had been intimidated in approaching a girl. It hurt his oversized ego some, but he figured she was worth it.

He spent hours practicing his smile in the mirror, hoping to get it just right, so that the next time he saw her in the hall at school, he could flash it at her, and maybe, just maybe, she might smile back. Today, after weeks of grinning awkwardly at her, trying desperately to come up with something witty to say, and arranging to "accidentally" bump into her

3

between classes, he decided to try to pass her a note in their only class together.

He thought about the note in his pocket. He had used his best handwriting, and taken his time so that the wording would come out just right. His hands had shaken fiercely when he held that paper in his hand, and tried to subtly slip it across the aisle to Mary. Then, that horrifying moment when Mr. Schuster had caught him.

Standing an impressive six feet, five inches tall, lean and rangy with jet black hair, laughing emerald eyes, and deep dimples, Eugene Wakefield had *never* had any difficulty in landing a date. He had dated so many girls that he'd ended up with a bit of a reputation as a ladies man. He had always been a perfect gentleman, though, and hadn't been serious about any of them. Until now.

He wasn't sure what it was about Mary that haunted his every waking thought, but if he didn't know better, he would have to admit that he was in love. How was that even possible? He knew next to nothing about her, save the fact that each time he laid eyes on her his heart almost pounded out of his chest. He couldn't eat, he couldn't sleep, and he *really* couldn't concentrate on chemistry with her in there.

The shrill sound of the school bell ringing startled Gene from his wandering thoughts, and he quickly grabbed his books, desiring nothing more in that moment than to make a quick getaway, before Mr. Schuster could lecture him. He made it almost to the threshold before he heard the teacher loudly clearing his throat. Dropping his head in defeat, he slowly shuffled back into the classroom to meet his fate head on.

Robert Schuster had been teaching chemistry at Beaumont High for 30 years now. He maintained a gruff exterior for the youth that he worked with, but inwardly he was a soft touch. He wanted to do more than teach them, he wanted to reach out to them and help them when he could. Truly, he thought of them more as his own kids, than students. So, when he saw the lovelorn gazes being cast in Mary's direction, he knew he might have some issues with Gene struggling to concentrate in class.

He thought for a moment about how to handle this situation. Eugene was clearly head over heels for her. Even Robert, who was heading into his golden years, remembered what that was like. There was a time when a dazzling redhead had made his school days a challenge. Oh, but she had been so worth it. He smiled fondly at Gene and chose his words carefully.

"Son, I couldn't help but notice that you have an interest in a certain young lady. Now, I understand it's not my place to say so, but if there is anything I can do to help speed things along, I'd like to help."

Gene was speechless for a moment. Surely Mr. Schuster hadn't just spoken those words. He had fully expected to be sent to detention, given extra homework, made to do 50 pushups . . . . something. But this? This seemed completely out of character for the cantankerous old man.

"Uh, sir?" he blurted out.

Robert sighed. Was he really that much of an old codger? Maybe he'd better take a different approach.

"Well, in my day if you were courting a pretty lady, you would do a little better than a scribbled note passed in class in front of God and everyone. Don't you know anything about romance?"

By now, poor Gene was almost purple with embarrassment. He never thought he would be having this conversation with his chemistry teacher. He might as well suffer through it and see what the old man had to say, and then maybe he could high-tail it out of here in time to catch Mary, before she headed home for the day.

"May I ask what was on the note?" he asked.

"I was hoping to ask her to the prom, sir, but I doubt she'll even speak to me now. I think I really blew it." He responded dejectedly.

"Nonsense! You are just going about things the wrong way. What you need to do is start with flowers."

"Flowers? You mean I should go get her some roses?" Gene was becoming a little more interested in this conversation now.

"No, that is not going to be good enough for what you want to accomplish. Does your mother have a flower bed at home?"

"Well, yeah."

"Alright then, this is what you do. You make two nice bouquets from those flowers and go over to her home at a reasonable hour tonight, before seven. Bring flowers for Mary and also for her mother. You understand? You need to be respectful, and this is just the start. I'm assuming you want something more than just a prom date? I've seen how you look at her. I've been married for 40 years, and I still look at my own wife like that," Mr. Schuster said, with a broad smile on his weathered face.

"Honestly? I've never felt like this before, and it's a little bit like being hit by a truck. I feel dazed and confused, as if I'm going crazy! All I can think about is Mary. Are you really sure this will work? What do I do after the flowers?" Gene was getting excited now. Perhaps there was hope after all.

The old man chuckled. Finally we are getting somewhere, he thought.

"Now, I can't do everything for you, but I can give you some pointers from time to time. The thing you need to remember is that ladies need to be courted, not panted after like a hound dog. This girl is special, so tread carefully. I think you'll be fine, once you settle down."

"I don't know what to say. Thank you so much! I'm going to go home right now and get started on those flowers!" With that, Gene was out the door, in pursuit of the woman who had been haunting his dreams.

As Mr. Schuster carefully gathered up the papers he would need to bring home and grade, he thought about the pot roast and baby potatoes with fresh corn on the cob his wife had talked about making for dinner tonight. Instantly his stomach started to growl. Mouth watering, he began to move a bit faster. He hurriedly put the desks back in order and wiped the chalkboard down for the next day. Grabbing his sport coat and brief case, he was startled to hear a soft knock on the door. His eyes flew to the doorway, and he found himself mystified to see Mary Baker standing in the doorway.

"I'm sorry to bother you Mr. Schuster," she began, "but I wanted to apologize for earlier . . ."

"Oh, no need dear. I had a talk with our little trouble maker after class, and it won't happen again."

"He wasn't bothering me, really! I will discuss the matter with him."

Mr. Schuster contemplated this for a moment, wondering if he should say anything or let nature take its course. As usual, he couldn't just let it go. Not if he could help . . . .

"Young lady, may I make a suggestion? I think it might be worth your while to get to know Mr. Wakefield. All things considered, he meant well."

Stunned, she stood gaping at him, mouth wide open. Realizing what she must look like, she recovered and stammered out, "I, well . . . . sure, of course."

Mary spun on her heel and hurried away.

Whistling a cheerful tune, Mr. Schuster finished gathering his belongings and headed out to his car. All the way home, he pondered the situation with these two young people. He didn't know why, but he was quite sure he saw something between them that was much bigger than a high school crush. It was the honest to goodness real thing. God's hand was at work, of that he was certain.

Several hours later, as he sat down with his wife for dinner, he took her hands in his and bowed his head in prayer.

"Father, we thank you for providing for our family, for the roof over our heads, and the food on our plate. Nourish it to our bodies, and help us to continue to seek your will for our lives. And tonight, Lord, we want to pray for a couple of youngsters. We ask that you would guide Gene and Mary in the path that you would have them to go, and that your name would be glorified in their lives. We ask that they will learn to follow in your footsteps, if they don't already know you. We pray these things in your precious name, Jesus. Amen."

Looking up, Robert saw the quizzical expression on his wife's face and explained what had happened in school that day.

"I don't know why I have such a burden for these two, but I can't stop thinking about them. Helen, I feel like we are supposed to mentor them, and pray for them, until we see them through whatever the journey is that God is beginning with them. There is something huge about to happen, and I can't wait to see what the Lord will do."

Helen smiled across the table at the dear, sweet man that had owned her heart for the last 40 years. She was particularly fond of this side of him.

"Of course, honey. And if this is what God has put on your heart for us, then that's what we will do! Now, finish up your food before it grows cold, and then I want to hear more about them."

****

Gene paced the sidewalk, in front of Mary's home, for thirty minutes. He knew that eventually someone would see him through the window and then he would feel like a jerk, but so far he hadn't worked up the nerve to knock on the door. He felt like his heart was coming out of his chest, and he was shaking from head to toe. Gulping, he strode purposefully toward the door and knocked twice, before he could chicken out again.

Mary had seen someone walking back and forth in front of their house through her lace curtains. Finally, curiosity drove her to pull the curtains aside and peer out the window. She grinned in spite of herself and waited patiently for him to knock. Even so, the pounding on the front door startled her.

Before she could open the door, however, her mother beat her to the punch.

"I saw him too sweetheart. Why don't you go on up to your room? I'll take care of this."

Obediently, but with trepidation in her heart, she headed to her bedroom, just as she heard the sound of the front door opening and the quiet murmur of voices.

Mary had been hoping he would make some sort of contact with her. All those goofy grins, and awkward stares . . . . she was beginning to think it would never happen. He was so handsome, and so charming; he made her a little nervous. She hoped that he wasn't as arrogant as he seemed. She had never seen him with the same girl twice. It was as if he were making his way through the entire female population of their school.

She was not ignorant of the reputation he had with the ladies, yet she saw something in him, that she suspected, nobody else saw. It was a deep sense of integrity, of honesty and morality. Although she didn't know him well, she already felt as if she could trust him.

Patricia Baker opened her door to the sight of a strikingly handsome young man with carefully slicked down hair (and one noticeably protruding cowlick in the back), smelling strongly of soap and dressed in a freshly pressed suit, with two bundles of sad looking daisies in his hand.

"Good evening, Mrs. Baker," he said, staring fixedly at the ground. "My name is Eugene Wakefield, and I have come to call on your daughter. These are for you." He thrust the flowers out to her self-consciously and shifted from foot to foot.

Patty couldn't help it. She was instantly charmed by this one. Oh boy, she thought, Mary is in it deep this time.

Broken

****

Gene and Mary walked slowly up the shaded sidewalk, both desperately trying to think of ways to make conversation. After five minutes of complete silence, he blurted out, "Will you go to the prom with me?" And instantly regretted it. He had worked so hard on what he would say. Why did he have to be such an idiot? What on earth would she ever see in him?

She gazed up at him for a long moment and quietly responded, "Yes, I would like that."

He had to hold back from skipping down the street and leaving her in his wake. Suddenly the two of them couldn't stop talking. The floodgates had opened, and they chatted away, eagerly getting to know one another. As the sun began it's slow descent, the two hurried back to Mary's house, realizing they had walked over five miles together and that her mother would be getting concerned.

Thus began the slow, sweet courtship of Eugene and Mary. After that first encounter, they were together every spare moment of every day. He would arrive bright and early each morning to walk her to school, and then carry her books home for her at the end of the day. She would spend hours sharing her dreams with him, of how she would one day like to have lots of children, and her own home to care for, with a little garden in the back and flowers lining the sidewalk in the front. He talked of getting a job right out of high school and going to college to become a teacher. They spent leisurely afternoons at the drug store sipping on cherry sodas, having picnics in the park with her dog, Sam, and spent many afternoons studying together in the library.

More than anything, however, Eugene had enjoyed learning about her faith. He hadn't grown up in a home where there was any kind of religious teaching and was totally unfamiliar with it. He was fascinated by her stories from the Bible, by the joy that bubbled over in her and splashed onto the people around her, and the hope that she had that couldn't be quenched. He still had many questions, and he didn't understand some things, but she was patient with him, and it was just one more thing he adored about her.

Bayfield was the perfect small town for a young couple to fall in love. Quaint little cafés popped up on main street, offering sidewalk tables to linger over lunch in the fresh spring air on a Sunday afternoon, parks with huge flowering trees to lie beneath on a blanket, and churches on almost every corner.

In the weeks leading up to the prom, Gene and Mary had begun to attend the same small church on Apple Street, that Mary's family had been members of for years. It rested at the top of a gentle slope, pristine white with stained glass windows, and was filled to the rafters each Sunday with the sounds of earnest and heartfelt praise.

It was there, on a day in early May, that Gene surrendered his soul to the One who loved him unconditionally, the One who had sacrificed all, the One who waited eagerly to spend eternity with him. With tears coursing down her cheeks, Mary watched as Gene was baptized in front of his family and her own, and she clapped delightedly with the entire congregation. The only two pairs of hands in the whole church applauding louder were those of Mr. and Mrs. Schuster.

****

Finally, the night of the prom had arrived. Mary spent most of the afternoon preparing for her big night out. She had been to the beauty parlor to have her shiny chestnut hair pinned up in rolls with a tiny sparkling tiara nestled in the curls. Her mother helped her put on makeup that accentuated her big hazel eyes. As she stepped into her champagne taffeta gown, she felt like a beautiful princess waiting on her prince. With a final mist of Chanel No. 5, she headed down the stairs just in time to hear him knock on her door.

Patty answered his knock and wasn't surprised to see Gene looking as dashing as ever in a smart white suit with a carnation pinned to his lapel. He grinned shyly at her and asked if Mary was ready to go. Then he caught sight of her standing behind her mother, and gulped so loudly that Patty started to giggle.

"Gosh Mary, you look so pretty! Every guy there is going to be pea green with envy!" he blurted out.

She blushed and thanked him, as he slipped a dainty corsage onto her wrist and gazed down at her with blatant admiration. The two eagerly headed out the door to his waiting Oldsmobile, which had been shined up just for this occasion. Patricia watched them drive away with a mixture of pain and joy. Although there had been no plans made, no proposals, she knew that she was losing her daughter, but she also understood that she would be spending her life with an honorable young man who loved her deeply and would always care for her.

Arriving at the high school, Gene and Mary could hear the sounds of the other kids laughing and enjoying the band as it played. The Cool Cats, a local band that played proms, wedding receptions and bar mitzvahs, was belting out the *Chicken Shack Boogie* as over two hundred happy seniors danced away one of their last nights together.

Entering the school's gymnasium, they were surrounded by twinkling lights, balloons and streamers in every corner. There was a festive atmosphere, and the enthusiasm was palpable, as the kids twirled and moved to the fast-paced beat.

Feeling like they were the only two people in the room, the two danced each song, only breaking once or twice for a cup of punch. As the evening wore on Gene knew that the time had finally arrived. He had asked the band to play *On a Slow Boat to China* because it was their favorite song. As the opening strains of the song began to play, he reached into his pocket and withdrew a small ring box.

Gene had been saving his money for the past three months, mowing lawns, babysitting his little sisters, washing cars, and anything else he could think of. Along with his meager savings, he had scraped together enough money to buy a small diamond engagement ring. His big moment was now.

"Mary, since the day I met you, I knew that there would never be another woman for me. I am totally and completely in love with you, and I swear to you that I will never love anyone else."

Dropping to one knee, he held the ring out in his hand. Suddenly the huge crush of kids around them began to slowly back away, until Gene and Mary were alone in the center of the dance floor.

"Make me the happiest man alive. Spend the rest of your life with me, and I will use every breath I have making you feel like you are the only girl on this planet, because you *are*. Will you marry me?" He looked into her eyes with all the love in his heart and held his breath.

Tears formed as she looked down at him, and her hands flew to her mouth. She was absolutely stunned and completely dumfounded by this man, this incredible gift from God in her life. She knew before she could even form the words that her answer would be yes. As she nodded her head in response and wiped away the tears, the entire room exploded in cheers and applause. The band played the song one more time for the newly engaged couple, and the two held tightly to one another, dreaming of their future together.

Chapter Two

It was August, and the final wedding preparations were being made. The band had been booked, the caterer met with, flowers ordered, and a reception hall found. They were to be married at the same church where Gene had been baptized, with all of their friends and family in attendance.

Gene's brothers, Matthew and Johnny, were standing up for him, while his two younger sisters Eileen and Elizabeth were her attendants. Aunts, uncles, cousins and various other family members were coming in from out of state. It was looking like it there would be at least three hundred in attendance.

The sweetest guest of all, however, was the man who would give Mary's hand in marriage. Her father had passed away many years ago, while serving his country in the war. As she had no brothers or other close male family members to give her away, she chose the one man who had been their cheering section since the very first day.

Robert Schuster had been honored and humbled by Gene and Mary's request. His reputation as a stern and serious educator was about to come into question, however, as the tears threatened to fall even now. He had been genuinely thankful to see the Lord answer his prayers for them, and he was excited to see them starting a new life together. They were young, to be sure, but they had a strong foundation in Christ, and he knew that their life would be built upon the Rock.

He paced nervously in the hallway leading into the sanctuary. Dressed in his best suit, with a fresh haircut and shave, he wanted everything to go perfectly, so he practiced his line over and over in his head. When the pastor asked who would give Mary's hand in marriage, he would respond:

"I do, on behalf of her mother and father."

In another room of the church, with the help of her mother and bridesmaids, Mary stepped into her lace gown and adjusted the veil over her face. She had chosen a simple, elegant strand of pearls that her grandmother owned for her *something borrowed*, a matching set of vintage pearl drop earrings for *something old* and a pair of satin peep toe pumps she had purchased from a local boutique for *something new*. As she hunted through her handbag for the lucky penny to put in her shoe, her mother pulled her aside and gave her a long hug.

"Sweetheart," she began, "I have something I have been holding onto for you since the day the good Lord blessed us with you."

She extended her hand, and cradled in her palm, was a beautiful antique sapphire ring, surrounded by diamonds.

"This belonged to your great-great grandmother. It has been handed down for generations to the oldest daughter. I thought you might like it for your *something blue*."

Mary gasped softly and slipped the ring onto her right hand ring finger and marveled at how it sparkled in the light.

"I'm sorry that your father couldn't be here to see you walk down the aisle, but you know he is watching from above with the biggest smile on his face. He would be so proud of you honey, and I just know he would have approved of Gene."

She hugged her daughter again, this time a little tighter, and took a deep steadying breath.

"Okay, mom, I'm ready," Mary said, her eyes watering even as she smiled with anticipation.

****

Standing with Eugene at the altar, Mary repeated her vows with a quavering voice and slipped the gold band onto his finger. As the pastor pronounced them husband and wife, they exchanged their first kiss as a married couple and turned to face a loudly applauding congregation.

They had taken their first step together on a journey that would take them to places of complete and utter joy, heartache and pain, wonder and hope. With Christ leading the way, the two of them knew that they could handle anything.

In the days that followed, Eugene worked hard at finding employment, while Mary spent hours creating the perfect home for them. Their new house was small, but in their eyes, it was a mansion. She planted her long dreamed of garden with tomatoes, peppers, and herbs of all kinds, as well as vibrantly colored flowers along the sidewalk leading up to their front step. She diligently made bright gingham curtains to hang in the kitchen, stripped and waxed the old hard wood floors, and polished the banister leading to the second floor.

Their weekends were spent haunting thrift stores, estate sales and vintage shops for furniture, china and linens. Slowly, piece-by-piece, their home was coming together. They felt like children on some grand adventure, each day holding a precious gift that the two of them would unwrap together. At the end of the day, the two lovers would sit on the floor of their living room eating picnic suppers from cardboard takeout containers and discussing, in excited tones, the amazing finds they had come across, and where they would place them in their home.

Gene found work with the post office delivering mail, earning a decent wage and he loved it. He was getting to know the people in their small community, from the youngest child playing with a ball in his front yard, to the oldest citizen in Bayfield who would sit in her rocking chair on the front porch, complaining about the oncoming storm.

They were happy, so happy. If anything marred their perfect life together, it was the months and months of frustration they faced, as they tried to get pregnant. It had been eight months with no success. Gene would hold Mary, as she sobbed her disappointment and anguish out, and the two would beseech God on their knees every night in prayer.

The months turned into years, and finally out of desperation, they made an appointment in Des Moines with a fertility specialist. After each of them went through several rounds of tests, the results had come back, and they learned that they were both medically sound. There was no reason for them not to be able to conceive, and yet after four years of disappointment, they still didn't have the child that they both dreamed of.

They finally agreed that perhaps it was time to look into adoption. Mary made some inquiries around town and found an agency that they could work with.

The Compassion Project was a Christian based organization that helped match adoptive parents with children that needed a loving home. The desperate couple had their first appointment set for the following month, and they had taken home a packet of papers to fill out in the meantime.

The massive pile of papers was intimidating, but they wanted a child so badly that it was a task they were more than willing to undertake.

One morning they discussed the situation over a breakfast of pancakes, eggs and fresh fruit, when Mary realized that the eggs had tasted a little off. She wasn't sure if they had gone bad, or if she had seasoned them with the wrong spices, but her stomach was protesting each bite.

Excusing herself from the table, she headed into the bathroom to draw herself a bath. Sinking slowly into the suds, she laid a cool washcloth over the back of her neck and willed her stomach to settle. Suddenly, she knew that if she didn't move fast enough, she would never make it to the toilet in time. Mary vomited violently, emptying herself completely, and feeling a little better, she decided that perhaps a cup of tea would restore her.

She returned to the kitchen, and Gene looked at her with concern on his face, asking if she was okay.

"I'm fine honey. The eggs just didn't agree with me, but I'll be right as rain in a little bit."

For weeks her symptoms lingered, and she became weaker and weaker. One evening, Gene came home to find her in a heap on the floor and nearly fainted himself from panic. That was the final straw, and he badgered her into seeing a doctor.

Gene and Mary waited impatiently for the doctor to return to the exam room. She swung her feet anxiously off the edge of the table and nibbled on an index finger, trying desperately to keep the tears at bay. He reached over and took both of her hands in his.

"God is with us, you know that right? Nothing is outside of His control, and He promises us in His word that He will never leave us, and He will never forsake us. Let's keep our eyes on Him, and He will get us through, ok?" Gene spoke the words of comfort to his wife, and she drew strength from them.

The doctor reentered the exam room, chart in hand, and looked at Mr. and Mrs. Wakefield. Dr. Theodore Johnson loved this aspect of his job more than anything else. He was a kind, compassionate doctor who truly cared for his patients. They were more than a paycheck to him, they were his whole life. It was well known in Bayfield that if you needed a doctor but didn't have money, Dr. Johnson would still see you. He had been known to accept home baked pies, hand picked flowers, and even a prize pig as payment. He never batted an eye at being asked to make a house call, even at 3:00 in the morning.

"Mrs. Wakefield, you are going to be just fine. The symptoms you have been experiencing are actually quite common for women in their first trimester."

Mary thought about that for a moment. Trimester. Where had she heard that term before? Suddenly, she gasped and jumped off the table, throwing her arms around the startled doctor and shrieking, "Oh my, we are going to have a baby! Thank you so much! I can't believe it! We are going to have a baby!" They embraced each other, and the tears ran freely, as they rejoiced and thanked God for His goodness.

The next few months were spent lovingly decorating and painting the nursery for their new arrival. Sunny yellow paint on the walls, crisp white curtains hung from the windows, and an old comfortable rocking chair sat in one corner next to the baby's crib. Gifts poured in from friends and family members, as well as from members of their church, who had lifted them up in prayer and been thrilled to see God answer them.

Gene would wait each night until he was certain that his wife was sound asleep, and then he would sneak out to his little workshop in the back yard. He couldn't wait to see the look on her face, when he surprised her with the hand carved cradle he had begun the day after finding out she was pregnant. Using the best maple he could find in the lumberyard, he painstakingly worked on this piece until the wee hours of the morning. Tonight, he would add the crowning touch. Retrieving the wood carving tools he inherited long ago from his carpenter grandfather, he engraved the following words into the side of the cradle:

My soul finds rest in God alone, my salvation comes from him. He alone is my rock and my salvation; He is my fortress, I will never be shaken. Psalm 62:1-2

Three nights later, when it was clear that Mary had had an extremely uncomfortable day and was complaining of wanting this pregnancy to be done and over with, Gene took her by the hand and led her to the workshop.

"Close your eyes for me," he whispered, "just for a moment." She obediently closed her eyes and when she opened them again, she saw before her an exquisite work of art. A tiny hand crafted cradle rocked gently at her feet, smelling of freshly cut wood. As she leaned in closer to inspect the myriad of details that had been carved lovingly into every inch of the cradle, she caught sight of the scripture and sighed. She could never begin to thank God enough for this kind-hearted man.

"It is beautiful sweetheart. How on earth did you find the time to do all of this? I know you have been working extra hours lately, with the baby coming and all . . . ."

He smiled sheepishly at her and replied, "Well, I can't give away all my secrets, now can I?"

****

In the early morning hours of May 14, 1949, Coleman Eugene Wakefield made his grand entrance, weighing an impressive nine pounds, 10 ounces. Face turning red as he wailed loudly, the nurses cleaned him and handed him over to his proud parents who held him, entranced by how tiny and perfect he was. They counted his fingers and toes, stroked his downy soft hair, and said a prayer of Thanksgiving for this miracle of life.

Coleman had proven to be a sweet, loveable child, if somewhat mischievous. He had his father's dimples, and his mother's shy disposition, but he was known most for his deep belly laugh. Once he started to giggle, he could reduce a crowd of people – total strangers even – to tears. It was pure and beautiful and so full of joy that it was entirely contagious. It was the sound of angels, and it drew people to him his entire life.

He was only three years old when his sister Theresa Noreen, came along, and he adored her. While he couldn't talk his parents into renaming her Coleman Number Two, he settled for begging to feed her, dress her, and hold her. He stared at her in awe and truly believed that she was a gift that his parents had given just for him. He would sing her the only song he knew by heart, *Jesus loves me*, each night when his parents tucked her into her crib and watched as she fell asleep. He promised God that he would always protect her.

Theresa was petite, like her mother, with a head full of thick auburn hair and the most amazing eyes. They were not quite green, and not quite blue. Aquamarine, that's what people called them. She had the Wakefield dimples as well, and she thought her big brother hung the moon. When she finally said her first word, it was "Coleman," and it reduced her parents to tears, as her proud older brother grinned at her and wrapped her up in his arms.

Just one year later, Sara Virginia was born to them. The Wakefields, who never thought they would even be able to have even one child of their own, had now been blessed with three. Another beautiful child with raven hair, and those remarkable sea green eyes.

They had a good life together, the five of them. Money was always a little tight, but Mary had learned to stretch a dollar, until it begged for mercy. She grew all her own vegetables, made many of the children's clothing, and spent hours clipping coupons each Sunday from the newspaper. They didn't take family vacations, but they would put the tent up in the back yard and tell stories around a small campfire that Gene would build, laying outside and looking at the stars, or they would take picnic lunches at the park and sit under the same old oak trees, where Gene and Mary had fallen in love.

They would gather the children around the fireplace in the evening and tell them about Jesus. Reading bible stories to them, answering their unending questions, and promising them that He would never leave their side no matter what life brought them. Enthralled, they were always eager to learn more. Once they were old enough, they began to attend Sunday school at their home church.

The three children were so alike in their physical appearance; all bearing the same blue green eyes and dimples, yet their personalities couldn't have been more disparate.

Coleman was a serious boy, intent on perfecting everything he set his hand to. He had been mistaken for shy or withdrawn, but that was far from the truth. He was simply taking everything in and assessing it, before he made any conclusions. He never took things lightly, rather he seemed to have a sense that life was short, and he wanted to soak up as much as he could. He actually did have a strong sense of humor; one just had to get to know him, before it was seen. He was, deep down, a clown and loved to make people laugh, and most of the time, it caught everyone completely off guard. His comedic timing was perfect, and a joke from Coleman would always make its mark.

Theresa, on the other hand, was flirtatious. She loved to laugh, to have fun with her friends, or to tease the boys in her class. She never had a serious boyfriend though, she just wanted to have fun with them. Her dreams were set on something much larger than boys. She was lighthearted and fun to be with, but those who knew her well, knew that she wasn't really *with* them. She was in another world entirely most of the time, a world that they didn't understand, so they simply thought of her as a daydreamer. She studied hard in school, because she had high hopes of attending college, the only one of the three children with that aspiration.

Finally, there was Sara. Sara had a rebellious spirit that drove her parents crazy. They would tell her that she couldn't wear a certain skirt to school, because it was too short, so she would change her clothes but bring the shorter skirt in her school bag and change once she got there. A phone call from the principle always followed. She really didn't understand why she should have to follow all these rules. Why couldn't she just be who she was?

But there was another side to Sara, a tender hearted side. While she would be the first one to punch someone in the nose for insulting her sister, she was also the first to defend a school outcast from bullies. She was constantly bringing injured birds, rabbits, or lizards home to try to nurse back to health. When they inevitably died, there would always be the long, sad funeral in the back yard, in which she demanded each member of the family give a eulogy. Their back yard was filled with tiny homemade headstones.

At the age of 16, Coleman was the first of the Wakefield children to start to question his faith. It wasn't that he doubted what he was being taught, it was just that there were so many questions that the Pastor never could seem to answer for him. He wondered about other religions too. He was an avid reader, and in his studies, he had learned much about Hinduism, Buddhism, and Islam that fascinated him. He thought they were beautiful religions and seemed to have just as much merit as Christianity. Who was to say which of these was the right way? At this point in this life, he wasn't sure what he believed, and if asked would have called himself an agnostic. He never let on to his parents that he had doubts, however. He knew it would have broken their hearts.

Theresa, now 13, was outright rebelling against the whole "church thing." It was a battle each Sunday morning to get her dressed and out the door in time. She fought her parents tooth and nail and frankly didn't see the point in going at all. It was *boring*, and it was all she could do to stay awake for the whole service! So, she brought her notepad and pencil with her and would sketch. She drew elaborate ensembles with dresses, hats, gloves, bolero jackets, and more. Her models wore dazzling spectator pumps with stockings that had seams up the back and form fitting, high-wasted skirts with buttons down the side.

She wanted desperately to become a fashion designer. She lived for the latest fashions, and although she could never afford to buy them, she loved to see what the models were wearing on the covers of popular magazines. When she was 12, her parents had purchased for her a dressmakers doll, and her very own sewing machine. It was the best birthday gift she ever had, and she made the most of it. Each afternoon, she would race home from school and get her homework done as quickly as she could so that she could work on her designs.

Theresa truly had an innate talent for it. When she wore the latest dress that she had created, she received compliments from boys and girls alike. She would try them on her sister Sara and have her model them, before making the necessary adjustments to each garment, adding a brooch here or a flounce there, until it was absolutely perfect.

The two girls would put on fashion shows for the family. Creating a runway in the back yard, with flashlights setup on each side for spotlights, Sara would strut down the catwalk in the latest designs that Theresa had created. It had become such an ongoing tradition that soon the whole neighborhood had joined in. Each would bring their own lawn chair over to sit and watch the show.

Theresa started to receive orders from some of the neighborhood ladies for her dresses, hats, and skirts, and soon her college fund had started to grow. She found a part time job, working ten hours a week after school and on weekends, in a fabric shop where she received discounts on sewing supplies.

Sara loved to help. Her aspirations were to be a model, and she certainly had the looks and figure for it. By the time she was 12, she had already blossomed into a striking young lady. She had grown her wavy black hair to her waist, and her huge aqua eyes were captivating. Her curves were already beginning to show, which made her father a nervous wreck. She shared the same rebellious streak as her sister however; it manifested itself in a different way.

She was a dreamer. Her room was filled with movie posters of her favorite actors and of songs and poems she had written. She would lay in bed at night and think of her future strutting down the runway. Sara would be rich and would own a huge apartment in New York City filled with expensive furniture and artwork.

She would have to battle the photographers that followed her around constantly. She imagined herself in large sunglasses and hats to obscure her identity. She would attend the theater and eat in expensive restaurants, draped in diamonds and fur. In these grand dreams, she jetted off to London and Paris for fashion shows and vacationed several months of the year to places like Tahiti and Rio De Janeiro. Always in these visions for her future, Spider was by her side, supporting her.

Sara, it seemed, didn't mind church so much, because it gave her extra time to write love letters and poems to the boy she was carrying on a secret romance with. She hadn't told anyone about him, not even her beloved sister, because she was sure that they would never understand. He hung with a bad crowd, and he was 18. There was an element of danger about him that drew her in, and she was completely addicted to him. Boldly covered in tattoos, including a huge spider on his bicep, which earned him his nickname, he rode a motorcycle and smoked cigarettes. Spider was a bad boy for certain. Unfortunately for Sara, she wouldn't know just how bad until it was too late.

Chapter Three

With all three kids in high school now, the days flew by.
There were parent teacher conferences to attend, basketball
and football games, PTA meetings and cheerleading
practice. It isn't surprising, therefore, that Gene and Mary
completely missed the signs of abuse that began to appear
with their youngest daughter.

Sara was completely smitten with Spider and fancied herself
in love with him. He told her what she wanted to hear. He
told her that his world revolved around her, that they would
have a future together, and that she was only girl he ever
truly loved. She would look into those big green eyes of his
and believe every word of it.

Her individuality was slowly seeping away. Every thought
she had was followed by *what would Spider think of that?* She
ran everything she said or did by him first for approval. She
changed the way she dressed, the way she acted, the jokes
she told and the food she ate, for him.

Morgan "Spider" Fitzhugh would pull up in front of the
Wakefield home on his motorcycle and whisk Sara away, not
returning her until well after midnight, so that she would
have to sneak into her second story bedroom window, by
climbing up an old oak tree limb. Theresa would leave it
open for her, but the minute she was inside the lecturing
began.

"Sara, what is wrong with you?! You know I can't keep
covering for you. One of these days Mom and Dad will catch
you. Can't you see that guy is a total loser? He is nothing but
trouble! I have heard stories about him from the other girls
in school, and I'm frightened for you."

"Oh come on, that's just gossip. Spider would never lay a hand on me, he loves me. I swear, he is different, when he is with me. Nobody else understands him like I do, and nobody wants to give him a chance. Really, if you spent any time at all with him, you would see what I see."

"I doubt that. He is 18 and is never going to graduate. He spends all of his time riding that stupid motorcycle and seducing naïve young girls like you. He is only after one thing anyway, and once he gets that, he will drop you like a hot potato."

Now Sara's feistiness was beginning to show. She didn't appreciate *anyone* telling her what to do with her life, much less her own sister, who was supposed to be supportive of her.

"Look, just stay out of my business, and I will stay out of yours, ok? I don't need you telling me how to live my life, just because you don't have one of your own. All you ever do is sit in this room with your stupid sewing machine. When was the last time a boy asked you out on a date?" Sara gritted out between clenched teeth.

Theresa was hurt. What Sara was saying was true, but it stung. All she had been trying to do was help her. Maybe she needed to tell her parents? But then Sara would never trust her with anything again, and she would never forgive her either.

If only there really was a God who answered prayers, who helped when you needed Him. If he was real, how could he allow his children to make such stupid mistakes? She just couldn't believe in him, and she probably never would.

Coleman Wakefield had grown into a handsome young man. At six feet, four inches tall, he towered over many of his classmates. With three years of football under his belt, he could take any of them down as well, but those who knew him well, knew that he didn't have a violent bone in his body. He was ever the gentleman, opening doors for the ladies, helping out after class to clean up, even volunteering at the senior center once a month by cooking and serving meals to the elderly. He was far from perfect though; he had a hair-trigger temper that few ever saw. It was only displayed when someone in his family was hurt or in danger.

His senior year he began to date a lovely young girl named Heather James. She was a tall, dark eyed brunette with incredible intellect, and she loved to debate. The two would spend hours disputing creation versus evolution, civil rights, local politics, even which came first: the chicken or the egg? He loved how she challenged him, made him think about things that had never even occurred to him, and how she could make him laugh like nobody else could.

One day, while studying in the library together, she looked up at him with a serious expression on her face and said, "Cole, there is something you should know. I'm hearing some pretty nasty rumors about your sister, Sara, seeing that creep Spider. He is absolutely no good. He dated my friend Rebecca last year and broke her jaw. She hasn't been the same since. I'm really worried for her."

Cole's stomach dropped to the floor. Nothing was more important to him than family, especially his sisters. He had always protected them, and he knew that he would have to do something about it. As they spent the rest of the afternoon studying, he had difficulty paying attention to the words on the page. They kept blurring under the red haze that had dropped over his eyes.

"I'm sorry, Heather, I gotta go. I need to go take care of a few things. I'll catch up with you tomorrow, ok?" Leaning over, he gave her a quick kiss on the cheek, before bolting out the door.

He knew just where to find Spider. He always hung out at the back of the school with the other members of his motorcycle gang. Coming around the corner of the building, he saw him leaning against the wall, a cigarette dangling nonchalantly from the corner of his mouth while he spouted off some crude story about one of his many 'conquests.'

Coleman didn't waste any time. In three long strides, he was upon him, grabbing his black leather jacket in one hand, he hauled him off his feet, so that they dangled above the ground, and slammed him hard into the wall. A look of sheer terror took over Spider's face, as he stared into the eyes of a very large, very enraged, older brother.

"I hear you have been messing around with my little sister." He ground out.

Spider struggled against his grip, but it was no use. Coleman was far superior in strength, and at the moment, he was fueled by pure adrenaline.

"Look, man, I'm just having a little fun with her, what's the big deal? I'll get what I need and move on to the next dumb broad." He tried to grin, as if it were all a big joke.

The fist that slammed into his face came so fast that he didn't see it coming. The next thing he knew he was flat out on the ground, dazed and in a world of pain, looking up through the one good eye that hadn't started to swell shut.

"You listen, and listen well *man*. You stay away from my little sister, or I'll make you wish you'd never been born. Got that?"

Spider nodded rapidly and tried hard not to wet his pants.

****

"*Coleman!!* How could you?! Spider is a nice guy, and he's never laid a hand on me. I don't need you running after him like some big dumb jock, beating him up over nothing. Now he'll probably never speak to me again, and I *know* I'll never speak to you again!"

And with that, Sara slammed her bedroom door in his face.

Theresa and Coleman tried to remain silent on the subject of Spider. Sara became adept at hiding the bruises he had begun to leave on her body. The spunky outspoken girl, who was bent on protecting her man's reputation, had transformed into a quiet, withdrawn and easily startled girl who barely said more than two or three words at the dinner table.

Her parents assumed it was just a hormonal phase that all teenage girls go through and didn't worry too much about it, but her siblings knew that something was terribly wrong. She had begun to wear baggy clothing and would leave the house without her lipstick (something she would have never even considered doing before) or even her hair done. Sara told her mother that she was self-conscious of her developing figure and didn't want to draw attention to herself, but there were other, more serious implications that nobody was aware of.

One night, Theresa realized she had left her favorite skirt in Sara's bedroom and without knocking, walked in to retrieve it. What she saw stopped her dead in her tracks and caused her mouth to drop open in outright horror. Sara had been changing into a nightgown, but not before Theresa saw the trail of massive black bruises and red welts that started at the base of her neck and led all the way down her back and across her buttocks.

"Oh, Sara!" she wailed, "What has he done to you? You have to stop it. You have to stop seeing him!" She had been brought to tears of rage almost instantly. Theresa was prepared to beg, to threaten, to lock her in her bedroom, if she had to. She felt absolutely sick to her stomach and had no idea what to do to help her.

"Shhhh! It's okay, I promise. He feels awful; he does! He swears it will never happen again. Look," she held out her right hand and showed her a tiny emerald ring. "He gave this to me; he wants to marry me! It's a promise ring. See, he loves me. Sometimes I just say or do the wrong thing, and he gets mad, but it's not his fault, it's mine. I just have to be more careful not to make him angry. I'm happy, sis, really."

Theresa just stared at her. What happened to her vivacious little sister who wanted to take on the world? The independent girl who wouldn't let anyone else tell her how to live her life?

"And besides," Sara continued with a wobbly smile, "I can't leave him now. We are going to have a baby."

****

Coleman and Theresa met at the dining room table at two in the morning to quietly discuss how to handle what was happening to Sara.

"Mom and Dad are going to freak, you know that, right? They are church people! They might even send her away to one of those places for unwed mothers. What do we do? What is the right thing?" Theresa was near panic, and she knew it. She didn't want to lose her sister, her best friend, but she was also terrified of what would happen to her, if they didn't intervene. Those bruises on her body said it all.

"Maybe I need to go have another man-to-jerk discussion with him. Didn't seem to make a whole lot of difference though, did it? I guess I need to make myself a little more clear." Coleman said, his jaw muscles bunching as he spoke. She could practically see the steam coming out of his ears.

"Why don't we both go and talk to him. Maybe we can talk some sense into him, or threaten to go to the cops if he won't stop seeing her. If that doesn't work, I say we tell our folks. I don't want to see anything worse happen to Sara."

It was agreed that they would find him together after school the next day and warn him that the consequences of any further physical harm to their sister would be dire.

The next evening, Spider roared up to the front of the Wakefield home and revved his engine. Sara came flying down the stairs and out the front door to greet him, a huge smile on her face.

He said not a word to her, as she hopped on the back of his bike, and they drove away. Spider lived alone in an apartment that had been converted from a garage in the poorer section of town. They drove up the driveway, and as he used his key to unlock the front door, he still hadn't spoken. Sara was becoming nervous. What had she done to set him off this time? She'd never known what would throw him into one of his rages; a misconstrued look at another boy, a comment that made him feel ignorant, or even something as innocent as a joke, and he would think she was laughing at him.

Before she could ask him what was wrong, he pulled his fist back and slammed it into her face. She fell hard to the floor and looked up at him in terror and confusion.

"When were you going to tell me?! When were you going to tell me that you got yourself knocked up?! What are you thinking, you stupid cow?!" he screamed at her.

The color drained from Sara's face, and she stammered out, "I was going to tell you, I was. I just wanted to wait for the perfect time. I . . . I thought you'd be happy. And we could be together and get married. You said that's what you wanted, right? Don't you see? Now they'll have to let us! It will be perfect. We can live here, and I can fix up a small area for the baby. I can make you happy, I know I can. Just give me a chance . . . ."

"*NO!* No, you are not going to have this baby. You are going to get rid of it, and that's the end of it, you hear me? I will make the arrangements, and I will give you the money, and then I want you out of my life. You were only ever good for one thing, and you weren't even smart enough not to get pregnant."

An eerie calm had come over him now, and it was far more frightening than when he screamed at her. For some reason, however, this time she wasn't afraid of him. Her maternal instincts were taking over, and she was a tigress, ready to fight for the life of her child.

Standing slowly to her feet, she looked him square in the face and replied, "You are wrong. I will *not* kill my baby. Nothing you say or do can make me do that. You have sorely misjudged me. You may have misled me, but I see clearly who and what you are now, and we will be better off without you in our lives. Goodbye Spider."

She turned and headed for the door, only to be yanked back into the room by her elbow. Spider whirled her around to face him. Grabbing her face cruelly in one hand, he slammed her head back against the wall, speaking slowly and quietly to her.

"You are going nowhere, sister. You may not have a problem with ruining your own life, but there is no way I'll let you ruin mine."

With that, he punched her in the stomach. The pent up rage and fear spewed forth like a geyser. Then, as she lay curled in a ball on the floor, he kicked her over and over again. Looking about in desperation, he grabbed the closest weapon at hand, a fireplace poker, and rained blow upon blow on her head, until the whimpering stopped.

Clyde Wilcox, Spider's closest neighbor, heard the ruckus next door and knew that punk kid was up to no good. Wasting no time, he picked up his phone and called the police and added, "Might not be a bad idea to send an ambulance as well . . . ."

****

It was 4 o'clock in the morning, when a loud pounding on the front door woke the entire Wakefield family. Quickly throwing on a robe, Mary was the first to the door. Seeing the grim faces of the two police officers, her knees immediately went weak, and her husband had to catch her, before she slid to the floor. Turning, she made a quick head count of her children, she realized that Sara was not among them.

"Ma'am, I'm sorry to wake you at such an hour, but I'm afraid we have some disturbing news. May we come in?" asked the officer.

The wailing could be heard around the block, as the entire family sobbed out their loss and anguish that early winter morning. As the stone-faced officer reported the crime of the previous evening, the facts slowly began to sink in.

Morgan Fitzhugh, known about town as Spider, had been seeing their daughter, Sara, for almost a year. He had been physically abusing her for the last seven or eight months, and last night when he found out that she was pregnant, he flew into a rage and beat her to death. When the police arrived, he pulled a gun from his waistband, but before he could aim it at them he was immobilized by an officer's bullet and taken into custody.

Sara had been rushed to the hospital by ambulance in a vain attempt to save her life, but she had lost too much blood, and there had been no way for them to bring her back. Miraculously, however, the doctors had been able to save her baby, a little girl, who was now in the intensive care unit at the hospital.

It had been too much for Mary to bear, and she had been given a tranquilizer by her physician and put to bed, where she remained for two weeks. Gene tried to hold it together for the sake of his children, but he couldn't have even told you his own name, if you'd asked. He was like an automaton, simply going through the motions.

The two remaining siblings were wracked with guilt. They had known. They had known and done nothing to stop it. They would never forgive themselves. Would their parents ever be able to forgive them? If there was a God, would He ever be able to forgive them?

In the months to come, the family walked through life like zombies. Family dinner conversation, once so lively and jovial, now consisted of polite requests to pass the corn or potatoes. No eye contact was made, it was simply too painful. They ate their supper and went to their separate areas of the house to grieve.

Meanwhile, Sara's baby thrived under the tender care of the doctors and nurses at Bayfield Memorial Hospital. Although she had been born three months premature, and under horrific circumstances, she was perfectly healthy and growing by the day.

Dr. Johnson, the physician who delivered Sara fourteen years earlier, knew it was time to place a difficult phone call. He went into his office and closed the door behind him. Picking up the phone, he dialed the Wakefield home and asked to speak with Mrs. Wakefield.

A dull and listless voice answered, one he barely recognized. *Why, Lord? Why do these terrible things happen to such good people? I don't understand.* He prayed silently.

"Mrs. Wakefield, I am so sorry to bother you at home. I am, uh, calling about the baby. She is growing healthier and soon will be discharged from the hospital. I'm afraid a decision will have to be made soon about her living arrangements. I hate to pressure you during this time in your life, and I can't possibly begin to understand what you are going through, but something will have to be worked out. Please give yourself some time to discuss it with your husband and get back to me. And Mary, my prayers are with you."

****

Gene and Mary knew that they had a hard decision to make, but they also knew that they couldn't run from it forever. They agreed to fast and pray for the rest of the week and see where the Lord would lead them on this.

After much prayer, they met the following week, and they were in agreement that the baby should be given up for adoption. They were getting older and didn't have the energy they once did for a baby. More importantly, it would be too painful. Each time they looked at that child they would think of Sara, and how she had died. It wasn't fair to the baby.

So, they called a family meeting and told Coleman and Theresa of their decision. Sobbing, the four of them held hands and prayed together, over the life of this child.

"Father, you know what it is like to lose a child, to have your own flesh and blood taken from you in such a horrifying way, so we know that you understand what we are bearing. Lord, we pray for healing for our family and that you would bring us back together, strong once again. We lift up the precious little girl that our Sara died trying to save. We know that you must have a special plan for her life, and we pray that you would find the perfect parents for her. Parents that will love you first, and her second. We ask that you would always protect her and keep her in the palm of your hand. Thank you for carrying us through this desert and guiding us, when we have no idea where we are going. We pray these things, knowing that you are just, that you love us, and that you hear our prayers. In your beautiful name, Jesus, we pray, Amen."

At that, each of the Wakefield kids went to their rooms and sobbed their hearts out, knowing that they had just lost another member of their family.

Chapter Four

It was the Spring of 1966 and Coleman was finishing up his finals, thinking about the upcoming prom. He had heard the rumors flying around the school that the government was going to start drafting young men to serve in the Vietnam War, but it didn't concern him too much. Right now, all he could think about was Heather and their future together.

He'd grown up hearing the story of how his parents had met and fallen in love, and how he had proposed to her on prom night. He would never tarnish his manly image by admitting this out loud to anyone, but he had always thought it to be very romantic. He even thought that it would be a wonderful family tradition carried on to his own son one day, proposing at prom.

He had worked evenings and weekends at the soda shop on Main Street all four years of high school and had a nice fund set aside for his future. Heather was a large part of that future, so, one afternoon, he drove by the only jewelry store in town and chose a simple, yet beautiful, diamond engagement ring. He tucked it away in his pocket and headed over to the mens store to buy a suit for the prom. If all went according to plan, he could wear it to his wedding as well.

Three weeks later, he drove over to Heather's house to pick her up, dressed in that suit. When she answered the door, his heart stopped in his chest. He had never seen a woman so beautiful in his life. She wore a lovely gown of gold with an ivory lace shawl, her hair hanging loosely around her shoulders in waves, and her eyes sparkled, as she looked up at him. He pinned the corsage to her dress, took her hand in his, and they headed out the door.

He parked his car in the school's lot and raced around to the other side to open the door for her. Tucking her hand in the crook of his arm, they walked into the prom together to the sounds of *Unchained Melody*, being played by a local band. Coleman swept Heather into his arms and held her close. How he loved this woman!

Feeling that this was the perfect song, the perfect moment, and the perfect woman, he stopped in the middle of the dance floor and took her face gently in his hands.

"Heather, this past year with you has been the most amazing year of my life. You have helped heal my broken heart. When I lost my sister, you restored me and loved me, even when I know I was unlovable. I know that you will always be there for me, and I want to always be there for you. Let me take care of you, love you, and help you to bear your burdens like you've helped me. I know that you have made me a better man, and when I look into my future, you are always there with me. Heather, I am asking you to be my wife. Please say you'll marry me."

Like so many years before, on a night just like this one, the dancing kids parted around them as Cole went down on one knee, looking up at her, with all the love that he held in his heart.

"Coleman, I've never wanted to settle for anything less than a man like you. I can't imagine a future without you in it either. Yes, yes, yes, of course I will marry you!"

He swung her into his arms and buried his face in her neck, whispering promises of love and a beautiful future together, to the sounds of loud applause and cheers. They both wept tears, this time of joy, as the band played the song once again for them.

****

On a sultry evening in July, a small but elegant wedding took place in the park where so many young couples had fallen in love over the years. Huge vases of gardenias and orchids lined the aisle, with white folding chairs set up on either side. Tiny twinkling lights and paper lanterns hung from the branches of the old oak trees, and several violinists played as the guests arrived and the groomsmen took their places.

Heather walked down the aisle on the arm of her father, her eyes fixed on Coleman, not even aware that anyone else was there.

As they took their sacred vows, exchanged rings, and were pronounced man and wife, there was no possible way they could have known that their lives were about to change dramatically. In this moment, it was just the two of them, and the outside world did not exist.

****

Newspapers began to carry stories of the action happening in North and South Vietnam, of guerrilla warfare, and most importantly of the draft. Coleman had always had a strong sense of patriotism and had slowly come to the conclusion that he would join the military branch of his choice, rather than be drafted.

When he discussed it with Heather, however, she became so distraught that she refused to even talk about it. He loved her desperately, but he felt that serving his country was a calling on his life, and he hoped that someday she would understand that as well.

One morning, before she was out of bed, he quietly left the house and drove to the Naval Recruiting Office in Des Moines. He signed the necessary papers and had the required physical. He was, of course, in peak physical condition and the Navy was thrilled to have him. He was told that he would ship out to boot camp in two weeks and that he should get his affairs in order.

He had one more stop to make before heading home, however. On the recommendation of a friend, he found a clean, well-respected tattoo parlor on the outskirts of town. He walked in and asked for the best artist in the joint, and when he left, he had exactly what he wanted.

Driving home he thought about exactly how he would tell Heather. How could he expect her to understand what drove him to do this, when he didn't really understand it himself?

He stopped for a dozen red roses and a large box of chocolate. Chocolate always seemed to soften the blow.

He walked in the front door, and she threw herself at him, arms around his neck, so tightly he could barely breathe.

"Where have you been?! I've been worried sick about you! You didn't call, or leave me a note or anything!" she wailed, tears falling from her eyes.

"I'm sorry, honey. Here, these are for you," he said, handing over the flowers and candy.

"Sit down for a moment, we need to talk."

Heather did *not* like the sound of that. People always said that when they were about to deliver bad news.

"I enlisted in the Navy today. I leave for boot camp in two weeks. I know that it's not what you wanted for us, but it's something I have to do. I know how hard this will be for you, and I am sorry for that. I promise I will write you every day and call when I can. It's only a four year tour, and I will be back before you know it. I hope you will understand."

She was speechless . . . absolutely stunned. How could he do this to her? How could she live without him? She took a deep breath and a moment to think. He was her husband, and whatever it was that was driving him to do this obviously was important to him. She would support him. She might not like it, but she would support him.

"There is one more thing. I got this for you." Lifting up the sleeve of his shirt, was a tattoo that read *"I AM COMING HOME."* With that, the tears started up again, this time in both sets of eyes.

A farewell dinner had been planned in Coleman's honor, and the two of them arrived at his parent's home, surprised to see at least fifty people in attendance. They had invited all of the extended family members, friends of his from school, even the pastor of their church.

As they gathered at small tables scattered around the yard, the Pastor led them in prayer over the meal and over Coleman and Heather as well. He prayed for Coleman's protection, peace of mind, and strength. He prayed that he would come home safely to them and that his life would be used in a powerful way to save lives and to bring glory to the name of their Lord. Finally, he prayed that Heather would know she was being watched over by the Lover of her soul, and she would be at peace.

The evening was bittersweet, and everyone in attendance felt the absence of the youngest Wakefield. The family had already suffered a tragedy that most people would never have to endure. Many prayers were offered up that night, prayers that they would not have to go through it again.

Gene pulled Coleman aside toward the end of the party and said to him, "Son, I have something I want you to take with you." Held out in his hand was an old, weathered, leather Bible, clearly loved and studied over many years. "Your mother gave me this Bible after I was baptized in 1945. I want you to have it, and I want you keep it with you when you can. The words in this book are from the hand of God and will bring you comfort, strength, peace, and wisdom. I will feel better just knowing you have it with you."

Cole tried hard not to cry in front of his Pop, but he lost the battle. He put his arms around his father and hugged him hard, telling him how much he loved him and promising to write often. "Thank you, Dad. I know this Bible means a lot to you, and I promise to return it to you one day."

The Wakefields gathered together for one last prayer, one last hug, and then they said their goodbyes and headed for home.

****

Kyle Tyrone Collins, or T-Bone as he was known to all of his friends, was more of a huge brick wall than a man. Towering above nearly every man he encountered, he was six feet, eight inches tall and weighed over 350 pounds, all of which was pure muscle. T-Bone was a proud black man, raised in the Bible belt, who lived and breathed the word of God. If T-Bone wanted to preach to you, you listened to what he said, and you listened with a smile on your face.

He had been known to grab a chair and stand in the middle of the barracks and sing *Amazing Grace* in his rich baritone voice. Everyone sang along with him, most because they knew the song, and it brought a measure of joy to their hearts to sing it, and some because they were afraid not to.

Many a soldier had been led to the Lord under the tutelage of this strong Christian man. Although massive in size, he was gentle in spirit. He had a gift for making the Bible come alive for people, for teaching and showing the love of Christ. He was a gift to the lonely men serving their country, who were scared and needed a friend.

T-Bone was the first man Coleman met, as he set foot in boot camp. As he stood in a long line to receive his uniform and the standard haircut, T-Bone sized him up.

"Well now," he said in that deep, guttural voice of his, "I see we got our work cut out for us. You fresh off the farm, boy?"

Coleman looked up at him and realized that this was the first time in his life another man had actually physically intimidated him. He was looking at a giant!

"Sir?" he managed to squeak out.

"Ha ha ha! I'm just messin' with ya boy!" He held out his hand to shake and continued, "My name's T-Bone, and I just want to help y'all get all acclimated. You let me know if you need anything, and I'm happy to help!" With that, he slapped Cole on the back and nearly sent him flying.

Over the grueling weeks to come, T-Bone had been true to his word. Training had been hard, harder than Coleman had expected, but T-Bone had always been right there, praying with him, giving him encouragement when he needed it, and space when he didn't.

More than anything, he had become Coleman's spiritual advisor. He had answered, with humility but certainty, the long held questions the Cole had. He gently explained why Jesus had to die on the cross.

"You're a good man, aren't you Cole?" he asked gently.

Coleman's chest puffed out a bit, as he nodded affirmatively.

"That's good, that's good. God only wants good people. So, let me ask you, have you kept the Ten Commandments?"

"Of course."

"Really? Have you ever told a lie?" he questioned.

"Well, sure I guess. Everyone has at one time or another."

"What do you call someone who tells lies?" T-Bone asked.

"A liar." Coleman did not like the direction this was going.

"Have you ever taken anything that wasn't yours?" he continued.

"No. I don't steal." His pride was back in place.

"I mean *anything*, Cole, even a pencil from the library, a piece of fruit in the produce aisle at the grocery store, or a paper clip from your teacher's desk?"

"I guess if you put it that way, then yes, I have," he mumbled.

"Okay, what do you call someone who steals?"

"A thief." Coleman was feeling smaller by the moment.

"Have you ever looked at a woman with lust?"

Coleman began to squirm a bit.

"Yeah, I mean, what guy doesn't?" he laughed uneasily.

"Jesus said that if you look at woman with lust, you have just committed adultery with her in your heart. So, by your own admission, you are a lying, thieving, adulterer at heart. If you were to die today, would you go to heaven or hell?" T-Bone asked bluntly.

Coleman by now was completely at a loss. He had never heard any of this before.

"I would go to heaven. I think God is fair and just, and He will overlook my mistakes."

"Listen man, if you break the law, you pay the fine. It's as simple as that. You have broken God's law."

T-Bone laughed and said that the easiest way for him to explain it was to illustrate it with something we were all familiar with in some way; a modern day courtroom.

"Alright, let's say you've been arrested for drivin' 55 miles per hour in a school zone. Not just any ol' school zone either. This is a school for blind children. You get hauled before that judge, and he throws the book at you. Gives you a fine of $250,000, and if you can't pay it, y'all gotta go to the pokey for ten years. Now, what you gonna say to the judge to get outta trouble?"

Coleman thought about that for a moment. "I supposed I'd beg for mercy. Tell the judge I'd never do it again. Ask for a second chance? If he is a just and righteous judge, he'd give me a second chance, right?"

"You right about that man! This judge IS righteous, and because he is righteous, he has to punish the guilty. So, just as he is about to sentence you, a man walks in the back door of the courtroom. He says to the judge, 'Your honor, I'd like to pay this man's fine for him.' Now you're off the hook. Somebody paid your fine for you."

Cole wasn't sure how this applied to God for a moment. Then slowly the pieces fell into place. T-Bone smiled as he saw the light dawn on Coleman's face.

"You got it now, man! God is the perfect judge. He will one day judge all of mankind for their deeds. You know those Ten Commandments we were just going over? Bible says if you break even one of them commandments, you've broken all of them, and you gotta be punished for that sin. We only went over three of them, and you had broken all of those! Nobody is without sin, nobody, but Jesus, and he went and paid the fine to the judge for you, so don't have to. He died on the cross in *your* place, and when he did that, he was thinking, 'I'm doing this for you, Coleman.'"

It made sense. It finally made sense. Now, as the weight of T-Bone's words hit him, he dropped to his knees and wept with remorse. He admitted to his friend the long held secrets he had hidden from everyone. He confessed that he could have saved his little sister from being killed, and that he had done nothing to help her. The guilt of it had been haunting him for so long, and he was weighed down with it.

Quietly, his friend spoke once again.

"Cole, you know what He did for you was a gift. A gift to all mankind, but the best part of giving someone a gift is watching them open it. That's where you at right now. You need to open that gift man, receive the gift of eternal life. You want me to pray with you?"

Wordlessly, he nodded his head, and T-Bone knelt by his side and placed his massive hand on his friend's back. "Alright then, pray along with me brother."

"Lord Jesus, I know that I'm a sinner, that I have done wrong by you. I ask you right now for your forgiveness. With your help, Lord, I will turn from my sins. I pray that you will come into my life and that you would walk by my side all the rest of my days. Thank you, Lord, for what you done for me. I pray in your Holy Name Jesus, Amen."

Boot camp training had finally come to an end. Coleman and T-Bone were going their separate ways. Cole was being transferred to an Artillery School, and T-Bone to Tank School, and then the two were to be shipped off to Vietnam, probably never to see each other again. T-Bone's influence on Coleman's life would never be forgotten.

****

Heather had received letters almost every day from her husband, just as promised. When she learned that Cole had turned his life over to Christ, she was overjoyed. She had made that decision herself, after attending church with his parents for the last several weeks, and had been waiting for just the right time to tell him.

Eagerly she reached for her pen and paper and wrote him a long letter, full of love and passion, heartbreak over missing him, and excitement over his new decision. Oh Lord, how she missed her man. She prayed daily that God would keep him safe and bring him home to her soon.

In that first year that Coleman was off serving in the Navy, Theresa was finishing up her final year of school. She had changed, no longer the carefree girl giggling with her girlfriends and flirting with boys. She had become somewhat withdrawn and did not socialize outside of school. She went straight home to do her schoolwork or to her part time job.

She was heartbroken, plain and simple. She desperately missed her sister, and now her brother was gone as well. Theresa didn't realize how close they all were, until they were gone. She had, however, drawn nearer to her new sister-in-law, Heather. They spent quite a bit of time together talking. Theresa enjoyed sharing stories from Coleman's childhood that he would be mortified if his wife knew. She was the only person that she felt like she could really be herself with. She loved everything about Heather. Everything except the whole religion thing she had recently embraced so wholeheartedly.

God had nothing to offer Theresa, nothing but pain and disappointment, and she wanted nothing to do with Him. In fact, when the subject was brought up in her presence, she simply tuned out or changed the subject.

Everything good in her life, she had accomplished all on her own. God had done nothing to help her. Her small but flourishing boutique started out of her own bedroom, with nothing but her old sewing machine and her own ingenuity. She was now taking in five orders per week from the ladies in town, orders for gowns, hats, skirts, and blouses. She hadn't needed to get on her knees and pray to some god who didn't listen.

She was, however, perfectly willing to blame this same god for the tragedy that had struck her family, for allowing her only remaining sibling to go off to this silly war, probably to come home with major injuries, if he came home at all.

Yes, she was angry. She was angry with a god she didn't believe in. If she had taken the time, and really thought that through, she would have realized how ridiculous the idea was, but right now, she couldn't really process these thoughts. She could only *feel*, and she felt furious.

****

Gene Wakefield hadn't been feeling well for several weeks now. He wouldn't mention it to his wife, but he was exhausted. It seemed that no matter how much he slept, it wasn't enough. He felt weak as well, but he was stubborn and hadn't been to the doctor or a hospital since Sara was born. He had no intention of going now. He was just feeling his age, he supposed, and tried not to think about it. He would ask Mary to pick up some vitamins at the drug store, just to be on the safe side.

Two days later, Mary walked into the bathroom to find her husband lying unconscious on the floor.

Chapter Five

Waiting in the doctor's office nervously for their results felt like déjà vu for Mary and Gene. She had called an ambulance immediately upon finding him, and they were taken to Bayfield Memorial to have tests run, under protest by Gene.

"I'm fine! Really, I think I was just hungry and got a little light-headed . . . ." he groused.

"We are going, and that's final."

After over twenty years of marriage, he knew better than to argue with this woman. He had never once won a battle with her.

Here they were, waiting once again for Dr. Johnson to come in and tell them that he was fine, and they could go home. Seemed downright silly to him, but he figured he could say 'I told you so' later on, during the ride home.

Those thoughts flew right out of his head, when the doctor entered the room with a grim expression on his face.

He explained to them, in layman's terms, that Gene had developed a mild heart condition and that he needed to start taking things a little easier. Perhaps retire early from the post office, or let the neighborhood kids mow the lawn and do the house repairs.

This particular condition would worsen slowly over time, and they needed to be prepared for that. He could recommend several reliable sources for in-home nursing when the time came, but he assured them that was several years away.

Walking back to the car, the arguing began.

"I am *not* retiring, so don't even bring it up. What would I do all day? Sit on my rear end watching television? No, that's not going to happen. I will hire one of the neighbor kids to help out with stuff, and when Coleman gets home he can help too. That is the most I'm willing to bend."

"Gene, honey, be reasonable. You've worked twenty years, and I know you have a generous pension fund. We can make it work, and there is no reason that I can't go to work somewhere part-time to fill in the gaps. Honestly, I don't know what I would do if anything happened to you. You are my whole life!" She was starting to tear up. This was the last thing that she had expected, when her day started. She couldn't even allow her mind to go in that direction.

He softened a bit, as he looked at his wife. He knew how concerned she was, but he needed a purpose in his life. He needed a reason to get up every morning. The people on his route had become like family to him, and he looked forward each day to visiting with them, as he dropped off their mail.

He knew all about their kids and grandkids, their hobbies and habits, their fears for the future and regrets from the past. He had shared their burdens in prayer, and they shared homemade pies and cookies with him. He didn't just handle their mail; he loved them as Christ would. How could he walk away from what he now considered to be a calling on his life?

"I will start taking it easier around here, I will. Just don't ask me to leave my job. You know I can't do that. If it starts to get worse, like doc said, then we'll talk about it."

Back and forth they argued. Finally, they agreed to give the matter some prayer and discuss it again in a few days.

****

Coleman had excelled in artillery school, far beyond any current or former soldier, and it had garnered him some attention. Modest as he was, it took him by surprise, when his presence had been requested in Colonel Reinhardt's office.

Entering and giving the standard salute, he tried to keep his knees from knocking together, certain he had broken protocol or done something to get himself into trouble.

"At ease soldier," said the gruff old man (whom the soldiers had secretly dubbed Colonel Cranky).

"Your skills at marksmanship, among other things, have not gone unnoticed by the United States Navy. There has been a new division of the Navy that has recently been created. It's called the Seals, and it is comprised of the best of the best. Son, we would like you to join."

Coleman was at first speechless, and then totally humbled. He wasn't even sure how to respond to a request like this.

"Sir, I would be greatly honored, sir!"

The Colonel went on to explain in great detail the duties and expectations of a Seal, and the intense training that he would be undergoing in the coming weeks. He would be shipped off to yet another training site, where he would hone his marksmanship skills, his ability to survive under extreme conditions in a jungle, desert, or arctic tundra, reconnaissance techniques, and more. It was the highest commendation the U.S. Navy had to offer at this time, and

---

he was one of only two hundred soldiers nationwide to be hand picked for this assignment.

He was told to head back to his barracks and gather his things, say goodbye to his comrades, and be ready to head out in one hour. His head spinning, he did as he was told as quickly as possible, and jotted out a quick note to his wife, explaining his transfer and asked a fellow soldier to mail it for him. With his duffel in hand, he was ready a full ten minutes early, excited to start his new adventure.

****

Gene and Mary had come to an agreement regarding his job and his medical condition. He met with his superior at the post office, explained his condition, and asked if his hours could be cut back. He was now delivering mail only four days a week, and it made his wife happy. They opted against letting the kids know, as they didn't want to worry them unnecessarily. The subject never came up with their daughter, as she was studying relentlessly for her finals and was completely oblivious to the fact that her father was home all day on Fridays.

Theresa had graduated later that year, an honor student at the top of her class. She had applied to the Pratt Institute in Manhattan. The private college was known as the best of the best, if you planned to become a fashion designer. When she received her acceptance letter in the mail, she was overjoyed and danced around her kitchen whooping and hollering at the top of her lungs. Her parents came running in, alarmed at the noise, and she hugged them both hard.

"I'm in, I'm in!" she shrieked excitedly. "I'm going to Manhattan to be a designer!"

They were, of course, thrilled for her. They knew how hard she had worked to get in to this school and couldn't have been happier for her, but it would also be a bittersweet moment for them when she left. Their home would be empty and quiet, just the two of them, once again. That was three months away though, and they planned to enjoy that time with her, while they had it.

They took her shopping and purchased for her all the things she would need to take with her to school: bedding and linens for her dorm room, a trunk and suitcases to store her things, and plenty of paper to write home with.

Neither Gene nor Mary had ever been able to attend college, and they were so proud of their girl. They promised, as the day for her departure drew near, to visit as frequently as they could. Theresa promised the same. She was starting out on a new adventure and was bursting at the seams with excitement. Her dreams were about to come true.

****

Coleman had been stationed in Vietnam for almost a month now. He never quite got past the fear of what might lurk around each corner, of taking a step and landing on a bomb, or of seeing someone he had become close to get killed. He had to remain ever vigilante, ever aware, sleeping with one eye open. He had never regretted his decision to serve, as it felt like a higher calling to him, but most days he was ready for this war to end.

As he headed back to his barracks to hit the sack, he heard the loud sounds of raucous laughter coupled with the terrified screams of a child. Fueled by adrenaline, he raced toward the sounds, which led him about 100 yards into the jungle. What he saw stopped him dead in his tracks.

Five large drunken American soldiers had captured a young Vietnamese girl of about 12, and what was about to ensue was unthinkable. His Seal training kicked into gear. He made his way quietly toward the melee and waited for the right moment to pounce. The girl made eye contact with him, and he put his finger to his lips, motioning for her to remain silent.

The laughter and crude comments continued as one soldier moved clumsily toward her, unbuttoning his pants. Coleman charged. Taking out the first soldier with the butt of his rifle to the back of his head, he moved lightning fast for the second and dispatched him as well. Before anyone realized his presence, he had dropped a third soldier. Heading straight for the child, he punched the half naked soldier squarely in the jaw and yelled at the girl to run. Then, she did something that startled him for just a moment. She yanked off the chain around her neck and placed it in the palm of his hand, before racing through the jungle. He looked down and saw a tiny, hand made wooden cross, dangling from a string of worn leather.

His pause to examine the article was his undoing. The final soldier left standing took aim and fired, hitting Coleman squarely in the chest. He fell to the ground, still clutching the cross in his hand and felt his life seeping out of him. Thoughts of Heather, his parents, and sisters flashed before him. Then, suddenly, he felt warmth like he'd never known and a brilliant light appeared before him. He heard a voice calling to him, the last thing he heard this side of heaven, "Well done, good and faithful servant! Come and share in your Master's happiness."

****

It was a sunny day in late August, and Gene was mowing the lawn. He figured that he'd already given up a day of work; he wasn't going to back down on his duties around the house.

A shiny black car pulled up to the house. A Naval officer stepped out and headed up the sidewalk to their door. Gene suddenly felt sick.

"Can I help you ma'am?" he somehow managed to blurt out.

A diminutive Hispanic woman with several bars on her and a regal bearing, Petty Officer Joyce Rodriguez, turned toward him with sympathy in her eyes.

"Sir," she responded, "are you Eugene Wakefield?"

"I am."

"Sir, is your wife at home? I would like to have a word with both of you if that is possible."

He led her into the cool of the family room and asked her to have a seat, as he went to find Mary.

When the two returned, their faces were pale and their hearts pounded.

"Please have a seat. I am here on behalf of the United States Navy to inform you that your son, Coleman Wakefield, was killed in the line of duty. I am so terribly sorry for your loss. You should know, however, that your son died saving a little girl from a gruesome attack, and he will be given a Medal of Honor at his funeral from the President of the United States."

Gene and Mary broke down and sobbed. The one thing they had prayed so hard against had come to pass.

They were barely able to see the officer to the door, when she turned to them one last time and said, "There is one more thing. When Officer Wakefield was discovered, this was found clutched in his hand. It is believed that the little girl he saved gave it to him, before she escaped. Your son," she said trying desperately not to get choked up herself, "was a truly a hero."

Gene and Mary dreaded the moment that Theresa would come home from work. She had taken the death of her sister so hard. She had been angry and bitter for years. They knew that without Christ, these kinds of burdens were nearly impossible to bear. In their pain and their anguish, they held hands and lifted all of it to the Lord.

"Father God, we are in pain! We don't understand and maybe we never will, how something like this can happen. Our hearts are broken, and yet we will continue to trust you, because we know that you have a plan in all of it. Lord please have mercy on our daughter. Use this to draw her near to you. We ask that you would help our little family to survive all of this, and that you would give us the peace that your Word says passes all understanding. We need you so desperately right now. We need your presence, your guidance, and your wisdom. We ask that you would carry us through this and that the entire situation would bring glory to your name. We pray these things in Jesus' name, Amen."

As they closed in prayer, they heard the front door open and prepared themselves for the worst. Quietly, they told their only remaining child what had happened.

"NOOOOOO!" she screamed. "Not Coleman, no! You are wrong. It wasn't him. This is all wrong. They made a mistake, don't you see? There are so many soldiers dying over there, they just have the wrong name I know it." Becoming frantic, she began to pace the room.

Her parents were at a loss. What could they do to comfort
their child, when their own hearts were breaking? They
gathered her into their arms and cried with her. They cried
until their eyes were swollen and their heads ached.

They received an official letter the next day stating that their
son's body would be shipped home for a military funeral.
It did not comfort Gene at all to realize he was the one who
had delivered the letter.

****

The funeral took place on a Saturday afternoon at the small
church on the hill, where the Wakefields had gathered on so
many occasions. They were touched to see that almost the
entire town of Bayfield had arrived to pay their respects, as
well as many of the soldiers who had served by his side.

T-Bone found Gene and Mary in the throng of people and
had given them the only gift that would matter to them. He
told them of Coleman accepting Christ, his whole-hearted
conversion and how he had spent hours diligently studying
the Bible during boot camp. He had asked his superior
officer, if he could be the one to return the family Bible to
Coleman's father. As he handed it over, he saw the old man
break down.

Tears falling onto the page, Gene opened the Bible to the first
page and found a note inscribed from his son.

Dear Dad,
How can I ever thank you for the seeds you and mom planted in
my life? Years of faithfulness to our Lord are the reason I can know
I will be with Him one day in eternity. This Bible has become my
best friend, and I'm afraid I've worn it out even more. Thank you,
Dad, for showing me what true love is. Love, Cole

Another soldier introduced himself to them and told of how he had come upon the scene too late to save Coleman, but just in time to see him take down four soldiers and save the life of the little girl. Gene and Mary listened to these stories with tears of pride and loss in their eyes, so thankful that one day they would see their son again.

The moment had finally arrived. A long black sedan with American flags waving from the front of the car arrived, as the ceremony was about to start. Secret Service agents escorted the president to his designated spot next to a podium, where he would later make his speech.

All in attendance stood to their feet and saluted, as T-Bone and a number of other soldiers who had served alongside Cole carried out the casket. It had been draped with the American Flag, which the Honor Guard then presented, folded, and handed over to Mr. and Mrs. Wakefield. Although Coleman had not yet reached a high rank, an exception had been made and a gun salute was performed in honor of his acts of bravery.

The President took his place at the podium and began to speak in a solemn tone.

"Friends and family, loved ones, I stand before you and mourn the loss of a brave and righteous soldier, who gave his life so that another might live. The word of God says, 'Greater love has no one than this, that he lay down his life for his friends.' We are humbled and blessed today to see that those words were lived out by such a courageous young man. It is an honor and a privilege for me today, to give a commendation and Medal of Honor to Coleman Eugene Wakefield for acts of bravery in the line of duty, serving the greatest country on earth, the United States of America."

A soldier in full dress uniform stepped up to the platform and began a mournful version of taps on a trumpet. Gene, Mary, and Theresa Wakefield sat numbly while the song played, and Heather, the devastated widow of the war hero, let the tears flow freely and thought of how one day she would see him again.

A private memorial was to be held once the throng had dispersed. As the casket was lowered into the ground, each member of the Wakefield family placed a red rose on top and said their final goodbyes. The grave was covered over with dirt, and a small, simple tombstone was placed at the head.

It read: "Coleman Eugene Wakefield 1949 – 1970 *I am coming home.*"

Chapter Six

Theresa slammed the trunk of her car down, after packing the last of her belongings for her move to New York. She turned to her parents, heavy hearted. She had once been so eager to leave to start an exciting new life in fashion. Now she felt nothing but guilt for leaving, fear for her future, and complete desolation over the loss of her brother.

"I'll call you when I get in," she said apologetically to her folks. Although they had repeatedly reassured her, she still felt rotten about going.

"Theresa, we want you not to worry about us. Everything is going to be just fine. We love you, honey, and we are so proud of your accomplishments. Be careful out there, ok?"

With that, she slipped behind the wheel of her Volkswagen Bug and drove out of their driveway, before she could change her mind.

Sighing, Gene and Mary walked arm in arm back to their empty house to begin a new life together, just the two of them.

****

Theresa arrived at the Pratt Institute on a sunny September morning feeling nervous and anxious to get unpacked in her dorm room. She parked her car and went to the Student Admissions office to find out where she'd been assigned. After retrieving her keys and room number, she grabbed her first load of belongings from her car and headed up three flights of stairs to room 317 and opened the door.

A petite Asian girl, wearing an outlandish hot pink and black punk outfit and sporting a spiky short hairstyle, looked up from her unpacking and gave Theresa a brilliant white, lipsticked smile.

"Hi! My name's Susie," she said, pumping Theresa's hand vigorously. "Where ya from? I'm from Los Angeles, well East L.A. technically, but that doesn't sound as cool, you know what I mean? So anyway, I know you are wondering, well my mom is Japanese and my dad is American, and they met in the war and fell in love, and the rest is history." She spoke so fast that her words ran into each other, and it took Theresa several moments to process what she was saying.

"Nothing that exciting for me. I'm from a small town you've never heard of in Iowa. I just love clothes, always have, and I've been making my own designs, since I was 13. That's about it. Oh, and my name is Theresa."

"Oh! I just know we are going to be best friends! I already know everyone on this floor, so I can introduce you, and I know the best places in town to eat and party. I've only been here for three days, but I am so excited I can't sit still, so I've been like all over the place! There's a great Chinese place that delivers 24 hours a day right up the street, and the library is open all night too! So we can be study buddies! We are going to have so much fun together!" she chirped.

Theresa was digging in her handbag for some aspirin, as Susie babbled away. It was going to be a long semester.

Susie ended up being right, though, and the two became the best of friends. They partied together, studied together, hung out with other girls in their dorms. She taught Theresa about Buddhism, and she was *fascinated*. They spent time meditating in their room before major exams, and she found that it helped center her, so that she could study. The yoga that she was learning kept her from becoming stressed out from the heavy workload she had taken on. The more she learned about the religion, the more interested and devoted she became.

Theresa gave up all meat and became a strict vegetarian. She sat in with the other kids on campus for peaceful anti-war protests, and later she would meet up with them to smoke pot and listen to John Lennon.

All in all, she would have said she was happy, but in those quiet moments, when she was alone with herself and her thoughts, she knew that something was missing. What that was she had no idea. She was wounded by the loss of her brother and sister, and that was something she didn't think she would ever be able to heal from.

Backpack slung over one shoulder; she headed into her favorite class. As she slid into her seat, someone tapped her on the shoulder and said, "Excuse me, you dropped this . . . ." She turned and looked into the bluest eyes she'd ever seen, under a mop of curly dark hair and a sheepish grin. He handed her the notepad and pen that had fallen from her bag and slid back into his chair.

Theresa felt her face turn pink. How odd. A man had never affected her that way. She certainly had seen her share of good looking guys in the three years, since she began her studies here. It was almost as if their was an electric charge that passed between them. No wait, that was ridiculous. She turned back and faced the professor who was now speaking and tried to focus on his words.

Summer was nearing again, and Theresa was spending hours studying for her finals. One more year and then she could finally start the career she had been dreaming of her whole life. Susie accused her of taking it all too seriously, but there was no way she was going to back down now.

She had gotten all of her partying out of her system that first semester. After realizing there was no possible way to keep up with Susie she would have an occasional glass of wine from time to time, but her priorities in life were ordered now: school, career, marriage (maybe), and no kids. That last part was a definite. She never wanted to experience what her parents must have gone through, when they lost their children. The only way to avoid that, in her mind, was to never have them to begin with.

It was a hot June evening in the library, and she was finishing up the last of her cramming for the finals she had to take the next day. Glancing down at her watch, she was shocked to discover it was nearly midnight. It felt like she had just arrived, yet after her studies, she thought she had a good grasp of everything and would do well on her tests the next day. Gathering her books and papers, she began to shove them in her bag.

"Want some help?" a voice startled her.

She looked up into those same startling blue eyes and said something truly brilliant.

"Uh . . . ."

He laughed. "My name is Stephen. Stephen Anderson. I don't know if you remember me or not, but I'm in one of your classes."

Yeah, she remembered him all right. She hadn't been able to stop thinking about him, although she had tried desperately to. He didn't fit into her plan. That much she did know.

"So, I've been cramming myself just a few tables over,"
he said pointing, "and I know you've been here for hours.
You've gotta be hungry. You wanna go get a pizza or
something?"

"Oh, thank you, really, but it's so late. My first class starts
at eight tomorrow. Maybe another time." She tried to
maneuver around him.

He blocked her and tried again. "Well, I know this great little
burger joint between here and the campus. Probably could
get in and out of there in about thirty minutes. Besides,
haven't you heard how dangerous it is to walk alone in New
York City this time of night?"

He finished by giving her the most mournful, pathetic,
puppy-dog expression he could muster up and was
rewarded by a laugh.

"Okay, okay. You win. We'll go get a quick burger. But I do
mean quick! I need to be on my game tomorrow for those
finals."

Stephen managed to keep a relaxed expression on his face,
but considering he had been daydreaming about her for
months, it was not an easy task. He had seen her from time
to time on campus, but he couldn't seem to come up with
an excuse to ease into a conversation with her. Thankfully,
tonight when he was studying at the library, he happened to
look up and see her a few tables over.

She had been chewing on the end of a pencil and twirling
her hair with one hand while she read. Stephen didn't think
she had any idea how beautiful she was. Long auburn hair
pulled back in a thick braid, several pieces had fallen around
her face and over her eyes. He'd been so shocked the first
time he'd made eye contact with her. Those aqua colored

eyes of hers were amazing. He couldn't even form a coherent sentence, after he'd looked at her.

She wasn't like most of the other girls he'd met in school. He had asked around and found out that she didn't date, and she didn't party. It seemed that all she really did was study. It was almost as if she was on a mission: headstrong, stubborn, and determined. Whatever you wanted to call it, she intrigued him.

Now he was actually going on a date with her. She probably wouldn't have defined it that way, but it was a *meal* together! He was going to stretch it out as long as he could, and maybe if he played his cards right, he could even weasel another date out of her.

They sat down in a corner booth and picked up the menus. He had trouble focusing on the words on his menu, however, because she smelled better than the food in the diner, almost like cotton candy.

The waitress came by to take their orders, and he asked for a cheeseburger and soda, because he knew it must be on the menu somewhere. Theresa, on the other hand, impressed him by ordering a double cheeseburger with bacon, chili cheese fries, and a large chocolate milkshake.

Grinning mischievously at him she said, "I am actually a vegetarian," she confessed, "But I don't go out often. I thought I should take advantage, and it smells so good in here, I can't help it." He had been thinking the same exact thing about her.

As the evening wore on, the two began to get to know each other. Where they were from, their dreams for the future, where they wanted to go after school was out for summer, and what their favorite classes were. The one area that she seemed to avoid discussion about was her family. He wondered if they didn't get along, or if she was just really private about them.

They enjoyed each others company though, and before they realized it, the sun was coming up. Theresa felt like Cinderella by the end of the night and knew that if she didn't get back to her dorm and get at least a small nap in, she'd flunk all those tests she had studied so hard for.

He walked her to her door and gave her a peck on the cheek. "Do you think we could do this again sometime?" he asked her shyly.

She smiled at him, those crazy aqua eyes twinkling up at him, and replied, "We'll see."

Theresa glanced at her watch on her way up the stairs and groaned when she saw that it was after five a.m.; so much for a nap. She opened her dorm room door quietly, so as not to wake her spunky roommate.

"Where have you been?!" Susie nearly shrieked at her. "I have been worried sick about you. You said you were going to the library to study and that was like, twelve hours ago!"

Chagrined, Theresa set her backpack on the floor and sat down on the edge of her bed. She was exhausted, but so wound up from her evening with Stephen that she'd never have been able to sleep anyway.

"I was sort of on a date. I ran into a classmate at the library around midnight, he took me to a greasy spoon for a burger, and we ended up talking all night. Sorry to have worried you, I thought for sure you would have been asleep this whole time."

Susie's jaw dropped open. "*You* were on date?! No way. I don't believe it! I've known you for three years now, and I've never ever seen you go on a date with anyone. Ever. Tell me all about it! I want details woman! Was he cute? What does he look like? What did you guys talk about? Did he walk you home? Oh! Did he kiss you goodnight? Oh man, this is soooo romantic!!"

She grinned and told her friend all about it. By the end of her story, Susie was predictably in awe and fanning herself, while making swooning motions. She really should have considered a school for drama rather than fashion.

****

After that first dinner, Stephen and Theresa began to see more of each other. She was reserved with him at first, scared of getting too close. She didn't want anything, or anyone, to get in the way of her plan. She knew that she really should be more focused on her studies, but the more time she spent with him, the more she found herself falling for him.

With summer coming on, they both had impulsively decided to stay on campus and spend it together, rather than going back to their home towns as planned. Theresa sat down and wrote a long letter to her folks hoping they would understand. Rushing to make it out the door in time for a date with Stephen, she crammed the letter into the outgoing mailbox, neglecting to add a stamp.

****

Gene and Mary had learned to get along without the kids around. Each had taken on new hobbies to keep them busy. She was learning to knit and crochet, and she had already made some nice winter hats and scarves for Theresa. New York was really cold in the winter, and she hoped that it would make her daughter think of her, when she wore them. Gene was now an avid bird watcher. With the lush garden his wife had tended over the years, birds of all varieties fluttered around their flowers each day, and he kept record of the ones he was able to identify in a notebook. Both took on new ministries at their church as well, Mary with Sunday school teaching and Gene with greeting and ushering. It was rewarding for them, and they enjoyed serving each week.

They kept in touch with Theresa on a regular basis and were looking forward to her coming home for the summer. Mary had already cleaned and freshened up her room in anticipation of her arrival, and she planned an extravagant dinner of eggplant parmesan (not her personal favorite, but there was that whole 'vegetarian' thing to consider now).

They knew that her train was scheduled to arrive in about an hour, so they made some final touches to the house, locked up the door, and headed out. The train station was about five miles outside the town's limits, and traffic was a little heavier than usual.

He pulled into traffic cautiously, as he always did, but this time as he made his left hand turn, he felt a sudden and heavy pressure in his chest. He glanced over at Mary to see if she'd noticed anything awry, just as his left arm began to go numb. Before he even had time to say anything or pull the car over to the side of the road, his vision dimmed, and he lost consciousness.

The car veered into oncoming traffic so quickly, Mary didn't see the big truck coming at them, until it was too late. It hit them head on, and the car flipped three times before landing on the roof on the side of the road. Both Mary and Gene died instantly, and were welcomed into the arms of their Savior.

Chapter seven

Theresa first screamed, shaking her head violently back and forth in denial, then went into a cold shock. She had been sitting in her dorm room with Stephen, when there was a knock on the door. She had been through this too many times to not recognize the look on the police officer's face.

She didn't think she could live through the pain. Stephen still didn't know all that she'd already been through. He tried to console her, to wrap his arms around her, and she pushed him away. There was no possible way he could understand, how could he when she didn't understand it herself, and she'd endured it twice already!

She suddenly realized, in a rare moment of clarity for her, that she had *no one*. No one to stand by her side and help her through this. Susie was a good friend, but a flighty one at that. She was just getting to know Stephen. Her sister, her brother, and now her parents were *gone*. Her grief would destroy her. All the chanting and meditating in the world wasn't going to make it go away. Where was Buddha, when she needed comfort?

Theresa asked Stephen to leave. He was clearly hurt, but understood her need to be alone right now. He promised to check in on her the next day. She lay down on her bed and cried until her eyes were dry and swollen, and her head throbbed.

This was her fault. She knew she should have been there. The cop had said they were apparently on the way to the train station. The letter must not have reached them. Guilt and regret overwhelming her, she screamed at the top of her lungs into her pillow.

Watching her from a realm that she couldn't yet see, was the One who could and desperately *wanted* to take her pain. His heart broke along with hers. He cried for the daughter that had been separated from Him, wanting to wrap her in His strong arms and hold her close. He would be patient, however, and He would pursue her relentlessly, because He did love her, beyond anything she could possibly imagine.

****

A loud pounding woke her late the next morning. She threw on some sweatpants and stumbled to the door.

Stephen looked at her, saw the evidence of a night of tears all over her face, and gathered her in his arms. He held her tight, kissing the top of her head, as the tears began again.

"I'm going to make us both some coffee; why don't you go take a quick shower? It will make you feel a little better. Then we can talk. I know that there are things you've never told me, and I think now is the time."

She was finally ready to give in and let some of her burden go. She simply couldn't hold it in any more, not by herself. She did as she was told and came out of the bathroom smelling of freshly shampooed hair, and that cotton candy perfume she knew he loved. Dressed simply in a tee shirt and her favorite faded bell bottoms, wearing no makeup, with eyes swollen nearly shut, and even in this moment of intense grief, he still couldn't help but think she was the most gorgeous woman he'd ever known.

He grabbed their mugs of coffee and headed to the couch. After handing hers over, he sat and gently pulled her back against him. Not saying a word, he allowed her to talk, when she was ready.

"My little sister was beautiful. Guess I never told you any of this, huh? She could have outshined the top runway models you see in Paris today, stunning, really. She had the biggest heart of anyone I've ever known. She was feisty too though. She stood up for what she believed in." She paused here, thinking of all the dead animals still buried in the back yard that she had wept so desperately over. "Her name was Sara, and if she was alive now, she'd be just a year behind me in school. She had a baby girl, and then . . . . then she was taken from us."

He sat listening, allowing her to tell him what she was ready to say. He knew the details would come in time, as the trust between them built.

"Not too long after that, my big brother Cole went off to serve his country in this war I still don't, and never will, understand. They say he died saving a little girl though. It's just like him, you know? He was always standing up for the weaker ones. He was huge, my brother. He used to sing to me, when I was a little girl, every night, and one night, I remember hearing him praying and promising God that he would always protect me. Guess he broke that promise, huh?" she whispered.

Stephen just sat and listened. Letting it all roll out of her, one story at a time, until the pieces started to fit together and all the ways that she had held back from him began to make sense. She talked for two hours, and he stroked her hair and continued to encourage her by asking questions. There was no doubt that she loved her family dearly. Now they were gone, every last one of them.

She would need him, and he wanted to be there for her. He had started to fall in love with her, not just for her beauty, but also for her standards, her intellect, her wit, and her drive. He didn't just love her, he *admired* her, and he respected her. In some ways, in fact, he wished he were more like her. It was obvious that she had been raised with principles and morals, even if she did seem to be very anti-church.

He helped her to make the necessary calls and arrangements for a memorial service and told her that he would be by her side every step of the way. Theresa, with the rug yanked out from under her, had begun to feel helpless and almost childlike in her dependence on him. She was so glad that he was in her life to help her through this. Maybe she hadn't given him enough credit after all.

They made plans to take a train to Bayfield in two days and kept in contact with the Pastor from the family's church, who had been so kind hearted and taken over almost every aspect of the memorial for her. He knew the family's history, and he knew that there was no way she would be strong enough to deal with these kinds of details. The ladies in the church were allowed into the Bayfield home to collect photos to display and to stock the refrigerator and pantry with food. They set up chairs for a reception and ordered flowers to fill the tiny home.

When Theresa and Stephen arrived at the home, they were astonished by the work that had been accomplished. Those acts of kindness reduced her to tears again. She knew in her heart that she had never been anything but impolite, if not downright nasty, to most of them over the years. She had thought that if she were ornery enough each Sunday, her folks would allow her to stop attending. Now it seemed like they were decent people after all, and she hated to admit how she misjudged them, thinking of them as hypocrites.

She turned to Stephen with pink cheeks and asked if he would mind sleeping on the couch. As modern a girl as she was, she still valued her parent's old-fashioned mentality, when it came to premarital sex. The two of them had remained chaste, and that was just fine with Stephen. In an age where sex was traded so cheaply, it was just one more thing he admired about her. He felt like this was the *real thing*, and he was more than willing to wait for her. She was a priceless treasure in his eyes, a precious gift. He wasn't about to do anything to blow his chances with her.

It had been a long day, so after a quick supper of casserole and salad they had found in the refrigerator, they said their goodnights and went to their separate rooms.

Theresa laid in bed for a long time thinking about Stephen. He was different from anyone she'd ever known. He hadn't wanted anything from her, and he'd been there for her in a way she never would have expected. A lot of men would have turned tail and run at the first sign of trouble, especially this early in a relationship. He hadn't. In fact, he had proven to have strong shoulders and was willing to help her to carry her burden. Maybe he would fit into her plan after all.

****

The service the following day was beautiful. The Pastor spoke about the years of devotion and service Gene and Mary had given the church. He told funny anecdotes, shared a touching sermon, and finished by describing what the two devoted followers of Christ saw, when they closed their eyes in this world and opened them in the next.

He spoke of heaven, of a world that was indescribably beautiful, filled with believers who had gone before us – family and friends eagerly awaiting Gene and Mary at the gates. It was a world with no pain or sickness, no fear or anger, no guilt or anxiety. He described a perfect place of peace, joy, and most of all, the love of the God of the universe. A God who not only created us, but then died to save us.

It was moving, and many in the congregation were in tears. Theresa listened, and something shook loose in her heart. The words made more sense to her now than they ever had in the past. Was this truth? She didn't know, and she was too proud to ask questions after the service. The more she pondered the matter, the more she realized that she was most likely acting on emotion anyway. Why should she believe any of this, when she never had, hearing it her whole life growing up? Why should she want anything to do with a God who eventually took from her everyone she had ever loved? No, she wanted nothing, absolutely nothing, to do with him, now or ever.

She looked over at Stephen and saw the tears glistening in his eyes, as he listened to the Pastor. What did this mean for them? Selfishly, all she could think was that if he became a religious nut that would be the end for them. She would *not* put up with it.

Following the memorial, friends and parishioners gathered at the Wakefield home for a small reception. Theresa could not wait for it to be over. All she wanted to do was be alone with Stephen and mourn in private.

With these thoughts running through her mind, she was distracted, when a bookish young man wearing round spectacles approached her. She knew she had never met him, but he had looked as if he had something important to tell her, so she gave him her full attention.

"I'm so sorry to intrude on you during this awful time, but I know that you will be traveling back to New York, and I wanted to speak with you before you went back home. My name is Thomas Allen, and I was your parent's attorney. I need to speak with you, regarding their final wishes," he explained apologetically.

This she hadn't seen coming. Her parents had next to nothing, this tiny home and perhaps a few thousand remaining in her father's pension. What on earth would they have needed a lawyer for? Especially this one. He seemed like a nice enough guy, but he couldn't have been any older than she was! Certainly, he was too young to know what he was doing.

"Can we meet tomorrow afternoon? I can come to your office if you like. Our train leaves at 5:15, so I would need to be done by 4:30 at the very latest," she replied.

He smiled in response and said, "Actually, my office is in New York as well. I traveled here to meet with you. We could meet at a café downtown, if you'd prefer . . ."

"Oh, well here is just fine then. You should know that I came with a friend. His name is Stephen, and he will be with me." She said it rather defiantly, as if daring him to challenge his presence.

"If you are okay with it, that's fine with me. Shall we say 2:00? I have several items to discuss with you."

They agreed on the time, and he left discreetly through the back door.

****

Theresa was anxious about the meeting all the next day. To keep her mind off the matter, she and Stephen began going through the rooms and boxing up the things she knew she wouldn't keep, with the intention of donating it to a charity or to the church. They followed with Sara's and Coleman's rooms. The entire process was difficult for her, but she knew she had to do it. She wouldn't be back any time soon, and she wanted to take advantage of the help that Stephen was offering her.

They took a break for lunch and were thankful for the many meals that had been left behind for them. There was one last thing they wanted to get accomplished before the attorney showed up. She boxed up all of the keepsakes, photo albums, and mementos that she couldn't bear to part with, and they drove to the post office to ship them back home.

Now all that was left was the furniture, and she was hoping the attorney could help her make arrangements to get them moved out of the house or sold. It was so hard to believe she would never see her childhood home again. She had assumed that she would inherit it, as the last remaining child, but she would end up selling it. Her future was in New York.

Promptly, the doorbell rang at 2:00. Wiping sweaty palms on her jeans, she rose to answer the door. After quick introductions were made, she ushered Thomas into the small kitchen. He laid his briefcase on the dinette and began.

"As I'm sure you are aware, your parents left a will, which was updated after the loss of your older brother, Coleman. I will leave you with a copy of their last will and testament, which you will sign with Stephen as your witness. I will summarize it for now, in the interest of time.

As for the contents of your parent's home, you are free to dispose of them as you wish. They had hoped you would donate everything that you didn't want to keep to the church they called home for more than 30 years; however, the decision is entirely yours.

The home itself was owned outright by Gene and Mary, so there is no mortgage on it. They chose to donate it to the church as well, as housing for whoever the current Pastor is."

At this last comment, Theresa was clearly stunned. Her jaw dropped open, and a small gasp escaped her. She wasn't overly concerned about the money, or hurt by their decision, it was simply that it didn't make any sense to her whatsoever. Why would they do that? Didn't the Pastor make a decent enough income to live in his own place? They certainly passed the plate enough!

He continued on, "However, your parents lived simply and amassed a reasonable savings account as well as a large life insurance policy on each of them. All of that was left to their sole beneficiary. That would, of course, be you." He smiled at her with compassion and anticipated her next question before she asked.

"Between them, they left you approximately one and a half million dollars. After Uncle Sam gets his share, you will be left with just over a million. I would be happy to offer you my services in financial planning, if that is your desire.

Let me be perfectly honest with you. I was here visiting my own folks when I met Gene and Mary for the first time. They were two of the most honest, decent people I have ever known. They led me to Christ five years ago, and I am forever in their debt. I promised them that if anything were to ever happen to them, I would do whatever was necessary to assist you. That's the real reason I am here. I know I look young, but I own my law firm with a staff of over thirty people, and I have several junior partners that I could have sent here to handle this matter. It was important to me, though, that I come and meet the daughter that Gene and Mary were so proud of, and to help you however I can."

Theresa was so moved by this, that she impulsively ran to him and hugged him hard. He was startled, but recovered quickly and hugged her back. They talked for another hour, signing papers and finalizing documents that needed to be filed in court. She asked him to please donate the furniture, along with the house to the church. He left then, handing her a business card and asking her to please get in touch with him, once she had settled back in at her dorm.

After Thomas left, she turned to Stephen. She was so taken aback by the events of that afternoon, she didn't really know how to respond or react. She gazed into his eyes and saw the uncertainty there. If she didn't know better, she would have thought it was regret.

He was filled with an anxiety he'd never known. What would she want with him now, with the world at her feet? He'd long felt that he wasn't good enough for her, but as he listened to the words of the lawyer today, his worst nightmare had been confirmed for him.

She was now independently wealthy. Why would she stay with a poor college kid like him? Worse, if he pursued a relationship with her, she might think he was only after her for her money! He was broken-hearted already, fearing the worst possible outcome.

"What is it, Stephen? Why are you looking at me like that?"

"Theresa, tell me what you are feeling right now. Right this very moment." He looked at her expectantly.

She thought about that carefully before responding.

"I'm overwhelmed by the love my parents had for me, and for the people around them. I'm in awe of their goodness. I'm scared of all that money, of blowing it on something stupid. Most of all, I miss them terribly, and if I could have anything right now, it would be to have them back instead of their money. That's what I'm thinking. I'm also a little frightened by the way you are watching me."

He sighed and pulled her over to the table to sit next to him. This was not going to be easy.

"I need to know how you feel about me. The truth. We've tiptoed around this for months now, and to be honest, I've never really known where I stand with you. I can tell you in a few simple words how I feel about you. I love you, Theresa. I want to make you my wife. You are the most beautiful woman I've ever known, inside and out. You are creative, sensitive, smart, and also, you smell *really good*," he added to lighten the moment.

"But, money changes things. This is a LOT of money. I don't want you to think that I am with you for the money, and I don't want to feel like I am bringing nothing into this relationship either. I have $142 in my bank account, and before we came here this weekend, I was awfully proud of that fact.

Theresa, you need to talk to me. I know you have had a life of tragedy and disappointment, and that has made it hard for you to grow close to anyone, but if we can't communicate, we have no chance whatsoever.

So tell me. Tell me what you see in me, what you see for our future, if we have one." He finished, looking at her with hopeful eyes.

He was so handsome, and at six feet, two inches, he towered over her. He was big and strong like her brother had been. She sometimes wondered if that was what she loved about him the most in the beginning. He felt safe to her. He had been there for her through all of this, and she could tell that was just the kind of man he was. He looked at her like she was the only woman on earth. Her mother once told her that her father had said those same words to her, when he proposed. She'd thought it corny at the time, but now she believed it possible.

She took a deep breath and replied, "I thought you knew. I do, I do love you. How could I not? You stole my heart that first night, when you got me to eat a cheeseburger!"

They both laughed, relieved.

She continued, "Please, please stay with me. Make me your wife, nothing would make me happier. I don't care about the money. Really, all it is to me is a symbol of my parents love for me. I will give it all away, if that's what you want. The only thing I want is you."

He laughed delightedly and swung her up into his arms, kissing her soundly on the mouth.

The train ride back to New York was spent excitedly making plans for a quick wedding. They didn't want to wait any longer to start their new life together.

Three weeks later at the courthouse, a justice of the peace performed their ceremony. Susie stood by Theresa's side as her maid of honor, and Thomas Allen at Stephen's side as his best man. Theresa wore a gown of her own design, a simple ivory French silk gown inspired by the 40's era; her hair up in victory rolls topped off with a fascinator. Stephen was dashing in a simple black suit and tie; his trademark curly dark hair in place for once. The entire affair was over in twenty minutes, and a limo took them to their honeymoon suite at the Plaza Hotel, where they spent a glorious week in each other's arms.

Chapter Eight

Theresa and Stephen spent the summer like kids in a candy shop. She had been so driven in school for the past three years that even her summers were spent in extra classes, studying and pushing herself. Not this summer; this summer she was going to enjoy being young and in love.

The two acted like tourists, visiting all the places in New York that she hadn't taken the time to see, since she came here from Bayfield. They took a ferry to Staten Island and spent the day picnicking in the park, basking in the sun, and playing Frisbee. They visited the Metropolitan Museum of Art and vowed to one day own a copy of their favorite Van Gogh painting, *Shoes*. They even had photos taken together at the Statue of Liberty.

In and out of Chinese and Greek restaurants, taking horse and carriage rides under a full moon in Central Park, and strolling the upscale streets of Manhattan, their love for one another deepened. They spent long Sunday mornings in bed over coffee and bagels, reading *The Times* together amidst rumpled sheets. Theresa didn't think she would ever be so content again. Indeed, a part of her feared it wouldn't last.

They found a loft in an old warehouse in the financial district. It was old and dingy and covered in a thick layer of dust and grime, and they loved it. They spent their days in and out of antique shops, estate sales, hunting through thrift stores, and attending auctions to decorate it. Wandering into hardware stores to shop for paint and wall fixtures, sandpaper and stain, they worked hard on fixing their new home up. Hours were devoted to sanding down and restoring old hardwood floors and painting the walls in each room.

Stephen was studying interior design, and she was thrilled with the choices he made to fill their loft. He had a flair for mixing the vintage with the new and hip, covering their walls in brilliant splashes of color, mixing textures in their furniture, and adding in eclectic touches here and there. They found a reproduction Tiffany lamp, a mosaic of stained glass in cobalt blue, brilliant green and gold with huge red dragonflies interspersed. Theresa discovered a groovy lime green shag throw rug for the living room, and a coffee table made from an old barn door. Her favorite piece, however, was a long white leather sofa that curved into an S shape and she found a gorgeous red mink blanket to drape over a corner of it.

They celebrated all the hard work with a small house warming party, inviting Thomas Allen and his new wife, Jenna. As the party wound down, the four sat at the sofa sipping coffee and made plans to get together again soon for dinner. Theresa really liked Jenna. She had an indefinable quality, a sweetness that she hadn't seen in many people in her lifetime. Thomas had let slip that she tended to take their clients under her wing like a mother bird. She baked them cookies, visited them in the hospital with flowers, sent long handwritten cards, and generally treated them like family.

Theresa had only just met her, but she really liked her. She wanted to know what motivated her, why Jenna didn't have any of that innate skepticism or bitterness that she herself had battled for so long. She was sweetness, pure and simple.

The two made an appointment with Thomas for the following week to discuss some financial matters, and they would be having dinner at the Allen's home afterward. Fondue was popular that year, and they agreed to bring over some cheese from the gourmet shop down the block. She was really looking forward to spending more time with

Jenna. She really wanted to know what made her tick, but more than that, she wanted her friendship.

****

"I've drawn up a five year investment portfolio for you. We are investing fairly conservatively, so I'm convinced you'll be safe with the options we've chosen. The bulk of your estate has gone into various stocks and bonds, with the remaining $225,000 into savings for your personal use. I understand that you want to someday have your own clothing line?" Thomas was asking her. "This would be a great time for you to get a head start on your new business."

"Yes! I've already put together a whole line of clothing. In fact, I've already come up with a name I'm quite proud of, *Her Wicked Ways*," she grinned. "My style is contemporary, yet sleek and sophisticated. There are also a few pieces that are a bit more provocative."

An interesting thing happened, when she made that last comment. Thomas turned red! She was startled at that.

"I'm sorry. Have I said something to offend you?" she asked.

"No, not at all. Let's continue." There were times, as a Christian man, that it was difficult to be a lawyer. There were, for instance, certain cases that he refused to take on or clients that he would not represent. He was bold in his faith and held strong to his convictions, but it was never easy. Jesus never promised him this life would be easy, though, just *worth it.*

With that, they finished up the rest of their conference and agreed to meet for dinner in an hour. Stephen and Theresa headed to the gourmet food shop and picked up Gruyere cheese, olive oil, and garlic. As an afterthought, she grabbed some dark chocolate and strawberries for dessert on the way to the register.

Their dinner was enjoyable, getting to know the Allen's on a more personal level. They were so obviously in love, just as she and Stephen were, and the way Jenna looked at Thomas nearly brought tears to her eyes. She flat out adored him. They seemed a bit old-fashioned, as Jenna had no intention of working outside of the home. She took care of her husband, and clearly submitted to him, but it wasn't in a subservient manner. She made her opinions known, and in fact Theresa was delighted to see her get a little hotheaded with him on occasion, but in the end, final decisions were left to him.

It intrigued her that a relationship like that still worked for people in this day and age. She understood this was some religious thing; her mom and dad had been that way, believing the Bible taught wives should submit to their husband as unto the Lord.

That kind of a connection would never have worked for her and Stephen. She was a thoroughly modern woman, completely sold out to the new women's liberation movement and convinced that theirs was a marriage of complete equality. Each of them was responsible for fifty percent of the work, inside the home and out. Her opinion was just as valid as his, and she didn't bow to him on *anything*. She liked things this way. She'd never asked him how he felt about it, because she didn't feel like she had to.

Fall was just around the corner, and with one more year of school left for each of them, they reveled in these last days together before hitting the books hard again. Their last two weeks were spent simply enjoying each other. They saw Broadway shows, took a trip out to the Hamptons and stayed in bed and breakfast, and slept in every morning, loving the idea of waking up in each other's arms every day.

****

Theresa was studying hard in school, but almost all of her extra time was spent on her clothing line, which she was certain would be a huge hit nationwide, when she finally released it. She would have to spend at least a year as an intern with a well-known clothing label, before she would be taken seriously by anyone, and she was prepared for that. She was still so thankful to her parents for the money they left her, so that she wouldn't have to worry about making ends meet in the beginning.

Stephen had already accepted an internship with a small interior design firm in Soho, and he was deliriously happy there. With both of them taking on all the extra work, their moments together became few and precious. They made a point of making no plans for Sundays, their one day of the week together, so that they could do whatever their hearts desired for that one day. Most times, they were so exhausted they slept 'til noon, and then made love the rest of the afternoon. There were times, however, when they would cuddle up on their couch together and talk about their future, and what they wanted.

They had been married three months by now, and Stephen was taken aback to hear for the very first time that she did not want children. He'd had no idea that she felt that way. He had seen her with children many times, and she was great with them. If they had kids, and they took after her, they would be beautiful and talented. He pursued the topic with her on several different occasions and was met with a brick wall. She simply refused to discuss it any further and would not give any reason for her decision.

He was heartbroken. Stephen had come from a large family with six siblings and lots of cousins. He'd always wanted a big family himself, and he adored kids, but they hadn't been married long. He was sure he could talk her into it, eventually.

****

Theresa was furious. Holding the little stick in her hand, she stared at the positive symbol on the end and wanted to scream with rage. *HE* had done this to her. He knew! He knew she didn't want kids. This was his fault, it had to be. She'd been so cautious. Then that one day, when she couldn't find her birth control pills, he'd been so amorous. She fumed, thinking back on it now.

They were two weeks from graduation, and now she was pregnant. She made an appointment with the clinic just to be sure. In the meantime, she was cold and resentful toward him, and he'd had no idea why. She hadn't told him yet, she wanted to wait to be positive that it wasn't a false result, but the morning sickness had already begun with a fury, so she had a good idea that it was done.

She sat in her paper gown, fanny hanging in the breeze from the open back, and waited for the doctor to come in with her results. Nibbling on her index fingernail, she worried and waited. What would she do? This would ruin everything! What about her plan? What about her internship, and her clothing line, her future?

The doctor reentered the room with a big smile on his face.

"Congratulations, Mrs. Anderson! You are going to have a baby!" he exclaimed, completely oblivious to the look of terror on her face.

She dressed hurriedly and left the clinic, in search of someone she knew that would be able to help her. Finding Susie in between classes, she grabbed her and pulled her under the shade of a tree.

"I need your help. I have a little problem I need to get rid of." Theresa was so distraught that Susie paused for a moment, thoroughly befuddled. As long as she'd known her, she'd been a strong, confident, woman, and this was unusual behavior for her.

"Well, okay. So what's up?" she asked.

Theresa explained the situation and said that she knew Susie had once had an abortion. She wanted contact info, and she wanted it now. Susie's face fell.

It was true, she'd been through it, and she loved Theresa. She didn't want to see her best friend in the world (or *anyone* for that matter) go through that. It had been beyond horrible for her, and she lived with the trauma of it every day of her life. She'd give anything to be able to take it back. She sobbed in her bed every night with regret and fear and guilt. She looked into Theresa's eyes and said very slowly, with as much compassion as she could put into her voice, "I know you are scared for your future. I know you don't want kids, but I'm *begging you* please, please don't do this. I will help you in any way I can, and I will do whatever I have to for you guys, but this . . . . this I won't do."

She hadn't expected that. What was *wrong* with her? She knew her friend was just as progressive as she was. She was a modern, strong woman too. What was the big deal? It wasn't even a child at this point, just a small blob of tissue. She knew that lots of women had it done, especially in her situation. She wasn't ready to be a mother, now or ever.

Susie wanted to pursue the conversation to explain why, and what it was really like to do this to yourself and your baby. As she opened her mouth, however, she was abruptly cut off.

"Look, I don't have time for this. I need to get this taken care of right away. Are you going to help me out or not?" she demanded. She didn't want Stephen to find out. She could be sneaky too. She felt like he had tried to trick her into this, and she wasn't about to let him win this silent war.

"No, I can't. I'm sorry. You know I love you, Theresa, you know that. I'm telling you right now, that if you go through with this, you will regret it for the rest of your life. I am speaking from personal experience, and you know that too. Think about it *please!*"

Theresa stomped off. She could find help from someone else. She wasn't sure she could forgive Susie for abandoning her in her time of need, however. She really thought she knew her, but apparently not.

The following week, she found herself on a table in a back alley clinic, tears flowing down her face, as the blood flowed from her body. It was done, and now she would forever have to live with the decision she had made. Why was she so stubborn? Why hadn't she listened? Another member of her family was gone, this one by her own hand. Another part of her heart died on that day, and the walls around her were built up higher.

The Lover of her soul watched with tears coursing down His own cheeks. "Oh Daughter, you have fallen again, but I will pick you up, and I will hold you, if only you will allow me. I will be the one to catch your tears, I will heal your heart, and I will make you whole."

****

Stephen was worried about his wife. She was so sick and so weak; he was concerned she may not even be able to make it to their graduation ceremony. She kept telling him that it was just the flu, and she'd be fine in a day or two. Then he got home from the firm early one night to find her unconscious on the floor. His heart raced, as he called an ambulance and had her taken to the emergency room.

Pacing in the waiting room anxiously, for the first time in his entire life, he said a prayer. "God, if you are real, if you are listening, save her. Please! I can't lose her. She is my whole world. I will do anything; take me instead, if you need to. God, I am *scared*." He didn't even know how to pray. He just kept repeating the same words over and over, and while his words were not eloquent, they were heartfelt.

Finally, three hours later the doctor emerged from the operating room with a grim expression on his face.

"Mr. Anderson, your wife is going to be fine. You got her here just in time, she'd lost a lot of blood and even another hour would have cost her life. I'm afraid the damage to her uterus is so severe, however, that you will not be able to have children. I am so sorry," he said with sympathy in his eyes.

Stephen wasn't sure what the doctor was saying to him. Lost blood? She had the flu . . .

"What are you saying to me? I thought she was just dehydrated from having the flu for so long?"

He looked at Stephen and chose his words carefully. "Son, your wife had an abortion. By the looks of it, it was done by some butcher in a back alley. He destroyed her. The damage

was extensive, and we almost lost her on the operating table.
I do apologize for the bluntness, but I thought you knew."

His vision started to fade to black, and he felt like the earth
was slipping out from under him. The doctor grabbed
him quickly and guided him to a chair. He offered him a
sedative, which Stephen refused, and left to check on his
other patients.
Once his head stopped spinning, he got up from his chair
and walked straight to the elevators and exited the hospital.
He was destroyed. He absolutely couldn't be with his wife
right now. He was too angry and hurt, and he was afraid of
what he would say to her. He walked for hours and found
himself standing in front of a small chapel, miles from the
hospital.

He walked in the open doors and found a seat near the front.
He sat, dropped his head into his hands and wept bitterly,
for his marriage, for his wife, for the child he had lost, and
the children he would never have. He didn't know how long
he'd been there. Time had stood still for him, when he heard
a still, small voice call to him.

*"Come to me, all you who are weary and burdened, and I will
give you rest. Take my yoke upon you and learn from me, for I am
gentle and humble in heart, and you will find rest for your soul.
For my yoke is easy, and my burden is light."*

His head snapped up and he searched the room, heart
pounding, for the voice he'd heard. There was nobody in
the chapel but him. *Where had that voice come from?* It had
sounded like something from the Bible, which he'd never
personally read. As his thoughts trailed on, he heard the
voice again.

*"Child, I say to you: Ask, and it will be given to you; seek, and you
will find; knock, and the door will be opened to you. For everyone*

who asks, receives; he who seeks, finds; and to him who knocks, the door will be opened."

It dawned on Stephen slowly that this was the voice of God. *The voice of God!* Was it even possible? God had answered his desperate prayer at the hospital, and He had somehow directed him here to a church. Was it impossible to believe that God was now speaking to him?

He wanted to give this burden to God, he thought. It surprised him. He knew that he couldn't handle it alone, his heart was so torn. He was so angry with her, and yet he loved her, and he knew her desperation. He knew that she almost lost her life tonight, but he couldn't help feeling like walking away from her.

As he cried these things out to God, a peace that he couldn't explain fell over him. He fell to his knees and prayed again, "God, I know you are here, you are with me. I don't understand any of this . . . but I know you are real now, and I want to know you. Show me who you are, and I will follow you."

At that, he heard a quiet shuffling behind him and looked up to see a tall, handsome redheaded man, wearing a clerical collar. The man simply sat behind him, placed his hand on Stephen's shoulder, and began to pray softly. After a few moments, he spoke quietly in his ear, with a thick Scottish brogue.

"You've met with Him, haven't you?"

"Yes," Stephen choked out, "for the first time. I need your help. I need to understand all of this. Nothing like this has ever happened to me." Tears ran down his cheeks unchecked, and he felt a profound love that he had never known swamp him.

Father David MacDougal sat with Stephen, explaining the
way of the cross, and what having a relationship with Christ
meant. He talked with him about forgiveness, and that he
not only needed to ask for it, but to extend it to his wife as
well. After another hour of intense discussion, he felt the
burden lift from his shoulders, and he knew it was time to
go back to the hospital and face his wife.

She was in bed asleep, white as a sheet, when he walked into
her room. Hooked up to an I.V. and several monitors, sicker
than he'd ever known her to be, she was still as lovely as the
day he'd first met her. Gazing at her, all the love he still held
for her evident in his eyes, he sat by her side, and held her
hands in his. He still wondered how they would handle this,
but now he knew that there was One who would walk with
them through it.

Eventually, she opened her eyes and looked at him, fear and
sorrow plain on her face. "Honey, I'm sorry. I'm so sorry."

"I know. We'll get through this, and I won't lie to you. It
hurt that you would do this without talking to me, but I
love you. When you are well again, we have some things
we'll need to discuss." He leaned over and kissed her on the
forehead gently.

"I was so scared today, when I thought I'd lose you. I
actually prayed for you, and I even tried to bargain with
God for you. My life without you wouldn't be worth living.
Please don't ever scare me like that again, ok?" He smiled
down at her, and her heart lifted a little.

The hospital kept her for a week, and she made it home in
time to attend her graduation ceremony. The two of them
felt like they had battled death together and won. Now
Stephen had to tell her of the new relationship in his life, and
he knew the battle had only just begun.

Part Two

Part Two

Chapter Nine

"Have another cookie, honey," Rachel's mom said, handing over a plate of freshly baked chocolate chip cookies, Rachel's all time favorite. She'd had another of her *difficult* days at school.

Rachel Marie Jenkins was five years old and had already endured more than a child of that age should have to. Overweight and homely, with mousy lank brown hair, she had no friends, only tormentors.

"You know what," her mother said, in an attempt to comfort her only child, "Jesus loves you and in his eyes you are so *beautiful!* You are a princess, because you are a child of the King."

She sniffled and took another bite of the warm gooey cookie, still warm from the oven. Her mommy made the *best* cookies!

"Really?" she asked, hope sparking in her eyes. She imagined herself as a princess, with a bright shining crown on her head, long silky blonde hair, and most importantly, she was *pretty*.

"Really," Rose replied. How her heart ached for this child she loved so! At least three times a week, her precious little girl came home with tear tracks on her face and ran to her bedroom to sob out her anguish into her pillow. She was at a loss as to how to handle this. What she really wanted to do was to go down to that school and take those malicious children over her knee for a good paddling!

Her only hope was that one day her little duckling would grow into a beautiful swan and that she would see her true worth in Christ. She wanted her to have a happy childhood with real friends, who didn't taunt her, call her names, or throw rocks at her. She had to turn her head, so that Rachel wouldn't see the anger on her face.

"Why don't you wash up and help me make dinner for Daddy, ok?" she asked.

Her little girl perked up and gobbled the last of her cookie down, heading to the kitchen sink to wash up.

This wasn't how it was supposed to be, Rose thought, as the two worked diligently on supper. They had adopted her after years of heart-wrenching infertility treatments. She was such a gift from God in their lives, and they thanked Him for her every day. She was supposed to have a happy ending, that was the way it worked, wasn't it?

Lord, my precious Jesus, what are you doing in all of this? I know you have a plan, that you never waste a hurt. I've heard it all before, but how can you allow her to suffer like this? What is your purpose? Her prayer was silent but desperate. *Show me your ways, and I will follow them. I love you Jesus, that will never change, but I need direction, wisdom, and words of comfort for my child. Help me to bring her your peace that passes understanding. Thank you, Lord.*

James walked in the door from work at precisely 6:15, just as he did each night. Dark blonde hair, twinkling brown eyes that crinkled when he smiled, and a jovial manner, he brightened a room just by walking into it. His daughter thought he hung the moon.

"Daddy!" Rachel yelped and ran at him full speed, nearly knocking him off his feet. He grinned down at her and

106

swooped her up in his arms, kissing her soundly on the cheek.

"Hi, squirrel! How was school today?" he asked, completely missing the warning glance from his wife.

She eyes shifted down to the floor, and he *knew*. "Daddy, why did God make me fat and ugly? If He says I'm a princess, why do I look like this? Princesses are supposed to be pretty!!"

He dropped her lightly on the sofa, and sat next to her with his arm firmly around her shoulders. "Darling, look at me." She looked up at him with hurt emanating from her big chocolate eyes.

"God doesn't make junk. He only makes beautiful, priceless treasures. When He looks at us, He sees nothing but His incredible handiwork. He sees the beauty in your heart, your kindness and compassion for other people and for animals; He sees someone worth dying for. He knows that you love him, but even more than you love him, He loves you . . . a LOT. Did you know that the Bible says that *you* are beautifully and wonderfully made? Did you know that he knows how many hairs you have on your head, and how many days you will have in your life? Did you also know that He carries around a picture of you in His wallet? That way he can show it off to the angels in heaven!"

At that last comment, she giggled and hugged him hard. "I love you daddy! Will you tell me a Bible story?"

These were the times that Rachel reflected on, as she grew into young adulthood. She loved her parents desperately and wasn't a typical, disrespectful teen. She didn't get into trouble or talk back, she didn't mock them behind their backs or plan to leave home the moment she turned eighteen. They were here safe zone.

She had made one friend in all her years of school, one friend that never let her down, never hurt her, and never saw her as chunky or plain in spite of her latest problem – raging acne. She was the one person in her cheering section, urging her on when nobody else even knew she was alive. Her best friend, Karen, knew the pain of being ridiculed for her looks. She had been born with a cleft pallet; surgically repaired over the course of many painful surgeries, she was nonetheless left disfigured.

Rachel had met her at church, in the fledgling youth group of a small congregation, where they had both found salvation. The two had bonded almost instantly, and considered one another a lifeline directly handed to them by God. They spent nearly every spare moment together, and when one was absent from school, the other was utterly lost.

Karen had encouraged her to apply for college, when all Rachel wanted to do was stay home with her parents for the rest of her life. She reminded her regularly that God had a big plan for her life and that she was never going to know what it was, if she didn't come out of her shell.

Likewise, Rachel urged Karen to write. She had an incredible gift for story telling. For many years, when the pain of being an outcast became too much for her to bear, she would disappear into a fantasy world of her own creation. She kept volume after volume of journals filled with fantastical stories of whimsical creatures and mysterious kingdoms, in the style of the great C.S. Lewis. Rachel loved to read her stories and was always begging for more.

During their senior year of school, each felt that there was finally a light at the end of the tunnel. They counted the days until school was done, and they could begin their lives at last. Karen as a famous author, and Rachel . . . well, Rachel had never confided to anyone, not even Karen, about her dreams. They were too far-fetched. Nobody would ever take her seriously, not looking like this. Her only hope was to come in to a large inheritance from some long lost relative and have plastic surgery.

They had debated going to the prom together, just so that they could say that they had at least attended one major school function. Of course, neither had received an invitation from a boy. It was just too depressing to even think about. *Best just to skip it,* Rachel thought.

"C'mon Rach! We can just go for a little while, sit in the corner and watch. Its "Passion in Paradise," you know . . . palm trees, Beach Boys tribute band, tropical punch, and they are carting in loads of sand. It sounds like so much fun! How can you ever have kids one day and have to tell them that you never even went to prom?!" Karen pleaded her case with a mournful cast to her eyes.

"Uh, uh. No way. You'll have to come up with a better argument than that. I don't think anyone will ever want to give *me* children."

"Oh please, let's not start with the pity party, ok? If you really don't want to go, fine, but don't you dare pull the 'I'm not pretty' card with me. We've been friends far too long for that garbage to fly."

Rachel sighed. Karen never asked her for anything like this, she simply loved her and acquiesced to her wishes. She didn't push, ever. She had always understood her pain. If this one small favor would make her only friend in the world happy, who was she to stand in the way?

"One hour. That's it. We get our punch, we watch the band from the deepest, darkest corner we can find, and we leave precisely one hour later. That's my best offer."

Karen jumped off the bed, ran to her shrieking, and hugged her hard. "Thank you, thank you! You won't regret this, I promise! Get your shoes on sister, we are going to the mall!"

She was already regretting this.

Prom night arrived right on time. They borrowed a car from Karen's dad and headed out to the prom after darkness descended (another of Rachel's conditions). Paying at the door, the two entered and headed straight for the punch bowl. The girls had found dresses that would help them to blend into the night, black and shapeless, with only a small ruffle here or rhinestone there. They wanted to see without being seen.

Grabbing their plastic cups of punch, they looked about desperately for a place to sit. Eagerly Rachel was the first to find two chairs in the corner nearest the restroom and they moved in that general direction, weaving in and out of the dancing bodies as *California Girls* blared at full volume.

They sat and enjoyed the show. The gym had been decorated perfectly, swaying palms, sand beneath their feet, and leis around the necks of each guest. After about twenty minutes, Karen said she needed to use the restroom and would be right back. Rachel started to panic, and then remembered to pray instead.
She would be back in less than five minutes. What could possibly happen to her in that amount of time?

With those thoughts still in her head, she heard a loud squealing, no, wait, that was an *oinking* sound. She looked up from her cup of punch just in time to see a large pig heading in her direction. It ran right over the top of her in its desperate attempt to escape the room, spilling her punch all down the front of her dress and knocking her, along with her chair, to the floor. But all she knew was that there was a crowd of cheering teenagers, laughing and pointing at her, and making more snorting sounds.

Mortified, she raced for the door and ran out of the gym into the fresh air. Although shaking from head to toe, she realized that they couldn't hurt her any more. She was too angry to be hurt; angry at Karen for making her come here tonight, angry at the kids for bringing a pig tonight, and angry at the school staff for allowing it to happen. Most of all, she was angry with herself for putting up with this kind of abuse for so many years. It was the proverbial straw on the camel's back, or in this case, the pig's back. After all, if she was truly a daughter of the King, why shouldn't she have a life too?

She decided right then and there, she had enough. She was done tolerating the demeaning behavior, the insults, and snide comments. She was done letting other people dictate how her life would be lived out. She was done wallowing in her self-disgust and recriminations every time she bit into a cheeseburger. Karen was right. There was no reason she couldn't go to college, and there was no reason not to fulfill her dreams.

Five minutes later, when Karen came rushing out to the car, apologizing profusely, she found a very different Rachel. Expecting to see her in tears, crumpled on the ground in a heap, or running down the street screaming hysterically, she was shocked to see her perfectly composed.

"I think it's a good night to go get a milkshake, don't you?" she said in a calm voice that frightened Karen. "Let's get out of here, please."

Sitting in a red vinyl booth at the local burger joint, the two compared notes over a heaping plate of chili cheese fries and chocolate malts. The cheerleaders had somehow found out that they were planning to attend the prom, hatched their plan of ultimate humiliation, and managed to procure the pig. Karen had seen them in a huddle, as she came out of the restroom, all high-fiving each other and holding their sides as they laughed uproariously. It didn't take a rocket scientist to figure out what they had done.

"Here's the thing Karen, I'm done. I'm not doing it any more. No more tears, no more hiding from everything and everyone. I almost feel like going back to the prom just to show them that they didn't beat me! I don't want to give them any more to talk about, or I would. From this day forward, I will hold my head high.

I have something I've been holding back from you for years, but tonight, the Lord showed me that this isn't where I belong. He wants me to reach for the stars, because He thinks I'm worth it. Not on my own merit, but because of what He did for me.

In a way, those nasty girls with their immature prank helped me out. I needed the push! Karen, I want to get into fashion. I know I could never be a model, and I'm okay with that, but I love clothes! Just because I can't wear the latest trends, doesn't mean I can't design them. Maybe I could make cute clothes for girls like me. Not everyone is created to be a size four. I think God wants me to reach out to people like me, show them that they are beautiful too."

As she spoke, tears streamed down her eyes. For once in her life, though, they were not tears of pain, but of joy. She had stumbled into her calling. Karen listened to her in astonishment. She'd never heard this tone in her voice before. It was *confidence*. Only God could do that.

"I want to thank you," she continued, "for insisting I come tonight. Believe it or not, I think this entire night was pre-ordained. You were so insistent that we go and that's not like you. You don't go for this kind of thing, never have. So why tonight? It's because God led you to talk me into it. He used you in my life tonight, Karen, in a big way.

This is a perfect example of how He uses *all* things together for good, for those who love Him and are called according to his purpose," she said, citing scripture. "Who else but God could take a raging pig and turn it into something beautiful?!"

Now Karen was crying, too, and laughing. She was suddenly realizing that there would come a day, sooner than she was prepared to handle, that the two would be parting to start their own journeys. Oh how she would miss her! She knew in her heart though, that the two would never be apart for long. Besides, they would have all of eternity to spend catching up.

****

Graduation day was upon them and the girls were giddy with excitement. Karen had published her first article in the local newspaper and been awarded with a summer internship. She would be heading off to a small private college in Indiana to study creative writing in the fall.

Rachel had been awarded a full ride scholarship to the Pratt Institute in New York to study fashion design. She couldn't believe how blessed she was, how good God had been to her. For once in her life, she had a future, something to look forward to, and she was not going to waste this gift. She had already begun to draw up designs for the full figured woman, and they were really *good*.

They road up to the high school in a caravan with both sets of parents, who beamed with pride and held hankies all throughout the ceremony, trying (and failing) not to cry. Karen was first to get her diploma, and she turned and grinned widely at her parents in the audience. Pumping her fist in the air, she whooped loudly before exiting the stage.

When Rachel walked up to retrieve her own diploma, the sounds of oinking echoed through the gymnasium, but this time she didn't even notice it. All she could hear was the still small voice of her beloved Savior whispering to her *"I can do all things through Christ who strengthens me."* She whispered back, in her heart, "Thank you, Jesus. Thank you!"

Chapter Ten

Rachel spent her entire last day at home in her room packing. Trying to decide what to bring and what to leave had been more difficult than she thought. She was so excited that she couldn't seem to think straight.

Gone was the piteous girl who hid in this room night after night, fearing the outside world. She had made a complete transformation and now felt like the world was lying at her feet. With the Lord walking beside her, she knew there was nothing that would stop her now.

She was boxing up the last of her things, when she heard her mother calling her downstairs. She placed the box by the door next to her dressmakers doll and sewing machine and headed down the stairs.

She was stunned to see the small gathering of people in the kitchen, streamers, balloons surrounding them, and a huge 'Bon Voyage' banner hung on the wall.

"Surprise!" they all shouted.

Filling her kitchen were not only her own family, but that of Karen and her family, the Pastor from her church, and her entire youth group. Tears instantly filled her eyes, as color filled her cheeks. She had been so intent on her work in her room, blasting her radio, that she hadn't heard any of the commotion downstairs and was completely shocked.

Rachel ran to her mom and dad's side and hugged them, thanking them profusely. They spent an enjoyable evening with family and friends, eating, laughing, and talking excitedly about her future in design. The camaraderie was palpable, and she felt the love from each and every person there. More than anything, she knew the love of the Lord that night in such a strong way. How blessed she was to be surrounded by all these people who cared about her and were cheering her on.

The last of the guests left around eleven, and she helped her parents straighten up the house. She had a huge pile of gifts on the table that she couldn't wait to open, but first her parents had something they wanted her to have. Taking her by the hand, they led her into the living room and sat her down. She was so overcome by emotion already that she was almost scared of what they were about to say. She just wasn't sure how much she could take in one night.
Rose looked at James, and he began quietly. "Honey, first let me just say how proud your mom and I are of you!

We would feel that way no matter what profession you chose for yourself, and whether you decided to go to college or not, but we know that you are doing what God has called you to do. Frankly, honey, there is no other way you would have felt at peace with yourself, and your life, like you do now.

You know that we tried for so many years to have a child; you've heard us talk about it all your life. Obviously God wanted us to have *you*, and that is why things went the way that they did. We have no regrets in this life, and we couldn't have chosen things to turn out any better.

The day we brought you home from the hospital, we stopped at a bank and started a savings account for you. We had no way of knowing what direction your life would take, just that we hoped it would be something that was in God's will for you. As they years have gone by, we have continued to add to that account and today, before our party, I went in and withdrew the entire balance for you."

He reached out and handed her an envelope with her name written on it. She gasped and looked from one parent to the other. She'd had no idea! Her parents nodded eagerly at Rachel, indicating it was okay for her to open it now.

She gingerly opened the envelope and gasped softly at the amount written out to her on a cashiers check. *$75,000.* She nearly fell off the sofa.

"Honey," her mother began, "We wish it were more, but we know that if you are careful and frugal, you will be fine. At the very least, you shouldn't need to work while you are in school. I know that your scholarship covers room and board as well as your books and tuition, so that money will take care of any of the little things that come up. If you decide later on that you want to take some of that money to invest for your future, I can give you contact information for a lawyer in New York that is a friend of the family and can help you."

She was beyond emotionally exhausted, happy, and thankful. She looked again at her incredible parents and spoke with all the love she held in her heart, "How can I ever begin to thank you? Not just for the money, but for the wonderful example of Christ you have always been to me. You've loved me like He does, and you've taught me how to live like Him. I love you both so much!" She was crying again, as she hugged them both tightly.

Her parents looked at one another again, and her father said, "There is one other thing we need to talk to you about."

She tried to compose herself and focus on their words, but she was so overwhelmed.

"For years we've known that God is calling us into the mission field," he continued. "We wanted to make sure you were either feeling the call to go with us, which there was never any indication of, or that you would be okay here on your own. We didn't know until the last few weeks how all of this would work out, but as usual, it worked out perfectly, in God's own timing."

Her mom finished, because he was starting to get choked up. "In about a week, we are going to be leaving for Dallas, Texas for some training, and then onto China to work with the underground church. We've rented out the house and made arrangements with the church, so that if you ever need to get hold of us, they can find us wherever we are. You will be fine, of that we have no doubt whatsoever. You've become such a strong, confident young lady.

When you get to New York, we know of a church you would love, and we have some friends that attend there. We'll give you their names before you leave. It will be so important for you to stay plugged in, especially moving into a city where you know nobody, and your family is so far away. Will you promise us you'll do that?"

Rachel nodded her head, and took a moment for all of it to sink in. *China* . . . it was so far away! Once she thought about it, however, it didn't surprise her. She'd lost track of how many people her parents had led to the Lord over the years. They had a genuine love for people, and it showed. They would make amazing missionaries.

"You know what? I'm so proud of you too! How many people can actually say 'My parents are missionaries to China?' I will be praying for both of you and saving my money. Maybe after I get done with school, I can come over for a visit before starting work."

They finished out the end of the night opening her gifts and sharing fond family memories. Life was about to change

dramatically for each of them, and they savored this last
night together.

****

The next morning, they shared a tearful goodbye at the
bus station. Rachel left with her cashiers check, and several
phone numbers for her parents, as well as contact info for
the church and the attorney in New York. This was it, her
life was beginning now. With one last hug for her parents,
she boarded the bus and left for the big city.

James and Rose watched, until her bus was a small dot on
the highway, and then left for their own adventure. They
hadn't given Rachel too much detail about what missionary
work in China would be like for them, but the truth was that
they were literally risking their lives by going. Christianity
was illegal, and churches met secretly in the homes of
believers. Christians who were found out were imprisoned,
tortured, and many times, martyred for their faith.

They drove to the church, suitcases packed in the back of
their car, for a prayer meeting. They needed to be fully
covered in prayer, before they left. They entered a packed
sanctuary and were humbled by the amount of people
who had arrived to pray for them. The church gathered,
extending hands in their direction, and prayed fervently for
their protection, for direction from the Lord, and for wisdom
in their decisions. They asked their Creator to give them
influence with the Chinese government, and that many lives
would be saved because of their work.

Before they left, the Pastor stood in front of the congregation
and announced that the money raised on their behalf had
been used to purchase 1,500 Bibles translated into Mandarin.
Because the offering had been taken in secret, the Jenkins'

had no idea. They were once again humbled and thankful for God's goodness.

After hugging and thanking every single believer, they gathered their Bibles and said one last goodbye to their dear friend and Pastor. He promised to check in on Rachel from time to time and to keep in touch with them as well, so he would always know where they were located. He walked them to the car, saying one final prayer for them, and watched as they drove away.

****

Rachel's bus arrived at the depot in New York City right on time. She picked up all of her boxes and suitcases and hailed a cab to the college. Once she arrived, she wrestled all of her things into her room on the second floor of the dormitory. So far, she hadn't seen evidence of a roommate.

Would she have one? No matter, she needed to get to unpacking her things. Choosing one side of the room, she began putting her clothing into a dresser and hanging the few nicer articles in the closet.

She was making her bed, when she heard the door open and a voice that startled her.

"Oh sure, just take the bottom bunk! Don't even bother asking *me*, which one I'd prefer," the girl snapped at her.

Rachel's face turned red, and she actually took a small step back. "Oh! I'm so sorry, I didn't know-" but the other girl cut her off.

"Let's get something straight right now, since we are going to be stuck with each other all year. This is *my* room, and I was supposed to be in it alone. I had no idea I was going to be sharing it with anyone, much less anyone like *you*." With that last comment, the girl gave her the once over.

She was a tall, thin, drop-dead-gorgeous blonde. She actually looked a lot like the princess Rachel had envisioned herself as, when she was a child, minus the nasty expression on her face, of course.

Curiously enough, however, Rachel's first reaction was one of sympathy and compassion. What must this girl's life have been like for her to be like this? Straightening, she extended her hand and introduced herself.

"Hi, my name's Rachel Jenkins. What's yours?" she asked.

The girl looked at her with a bit of shock on her face. She seemed to instantly recognize that she had acted like a jerk, because her cheeks were turning pink.

"I'm sorry I snapped at you. My name is Tiffany. Tiffany Fox. I've just had a really rotten week, and I didn't mean to take it out on you," she explained herself with a soft southern-accented voice. "I was supposed to get my own room, and I found out this morning that I'd have a roommate. I'm just not really the type of person to share. Plus, my boyfriend of the last four years just dumped me, so forgive me if I'm a little cranky today."

"I'm so sorry to hear that. You feel like talking? I'm a pretty good listener."

Tiffany looked at her curiously. What she saw was an overweight, acne scarred, unattractive girl, but upon closer inspection, she noticed large, kind, brown eyes That is, of course, as long as none of her real friends found out.

"Well, he decided that since I was moving across to the other side of the country, he wasn't much interested in having a long distance relationship. Jerk," she finished.

Rachel could see she had tears in her eyes, but beneath the tears was a barely concealed rage. She didn't think that anyone had ever denied Tiffany anything. She looked at her designer clothing, her professionally highlighted and styled hair, and her perfect manicure. Her heart went out to her; she just knew in her spirit that this girl needed the Lord. Her youth Pastor had once told them that hurting people hurt people. It made sense. We lash out at others in our pain. If anyone knew pain, it was Rachel, but she also knew the One who could heal pain.

"Well, I believe that everything happens for a reason. Perhaps the one true love of your life is waiting here, right on this very campus, for you," she replied.

It was all Tiffany could do not to roll her eyes at this pathetic chubby girl. What on earth could she possibly know of true love? She'd be willing to bet her trust fund that this dork had never even been on a date in her whole life.

"Sure," she responded noncommittally. "I'm gonna go grab my stuff from my car and start unpacking. Just try not to take up too much space, ok?" She said, looking her up and down again before heading out the door and slamming it.

Rachel smiled inwardly. It wasn't as if she'd never heard these sorts of things from haughty girls her whole life. This girl couldn't hurt her with words. She had her armor on now, and now she knew it was time to do battle. With that thought in her mind, she dropped to her knees and began to pray for Tiffany.

Father God, I know that you have brought this girl into my life for a reason and a purpose. You are the only one who truly knows her heart, and you know where she stands with you, but if she doesn't know you, I ask you to allow me to minister to her. I pray that I will be used of you in this room this year. Give me your words Lord! Show me where she is hurting in her life. Allow me to teach her what true peace is, true love that comes only from knowing you. I thank you now God, for what you are about to do here. I love you Lord! I pray these things knowing that you hear my prayers and that you are faithful and true. It is in your perfect and holy name I pray, Jesus, Amen.

She finished her prayer just as her roommate reentered the room with her first load of things.

"Tiffany, can I help you bring the rest of your things up?" she asked.

How much abuse was this girl willing to take, Tiffany thought to herself. "Okay, thanks. You probably could use the extra exercise anyway."

The two headed down to her car and back up three more times for one suitcase and trunk after another. Rachel thought she must have packed her entire house before leaving. Huffing and puffing, she struggled in the door with the last box, as Tiffany watched from the comfort of the small sofa in the corner of the room.

"Maybe we'll get along after all," she smiled maliciously at her. "Seems like you are willing to help me in my hour of need. I'll remember that."

Rachel's simply smiled at her. She knew deep down that God would continue to pursue her relentlessly. She never stood a chance.

She told Tiffany that she'd be back, she needed to go make a couple of phone calls, and left in search of a payphone.

"Whatever," was the bored response she received.

****

Twenty minutes later, she headed back to her dorm with the address and service times for church on Sunday, as well as an appointment with Thomas Allen, the attorney her parents had told her about. She was meeting with him the following afternoon at 3:00. He seemed like a genuinely nice man, and had been thrilled to hear about her parents heading to China. She was excited to meet him.

She opened her dorm room and was shocked at what greeted her. Tiffany's things dominated the room. Posters of rock stars plastered every inch on all the walls, a vanity table took up one corner and it was covered with makeup, jewelry, and perfumes. Then she noticed that her dresser and suitcases had been shoved in the closet. There was no longer a single sign that she even lived in this room. Her beloved cross had been taken down and stuffed in her dresser.

She went to the closet to retrieve it and found a tiny area of wall space by the bed that was not covered, and re-hung her cross, all the while muttering to herself, "turn the other cheek, turn the other cheek, turn the other cheek . . . ."

"What was that?" Tiffany asked.

"Oh nothing," Rachel responded with a cheery smile on her face.

It was going to be a long year. She found her well-worn Bible among her things and crawled into her bunk to read. Trying to tune out the blasting rock music coming from her roommate's radio, she turned to the Psalms for comfort. *Let all that I am praise the Lord; may I never forget the good things he does for me.* She read in Psalm 103:2, and breathed it in. Peace once again overwhelmed her. She had a feeling she would find herself in this particular book many times during the weeks and months to come.

That was just fine with her. She was up for the challenge. She knew that God had brought her to this place and time for a very specific reason. Perhaps that reason was Tiffany. She didn't know for sure, but she did know that He had brought her through many trials in the previous years so that her heart would be softened toward people like her.

She continued to read and to pray, and as she drifted off to sleep her very first night in this foreign place, she thought of her parents in Dallas, and she thought, *You know what? I have my own mission field too.*

Chapter Eleven

It was midway through her second semester in school, and
Rachel had finally made a small amount of headway with
Tiffany. When nobody else was around, she actually spoke
to Rachel as if she were a *human*. It was quite remarkable
considering how things had started out between them. She
had just flatly refused to give up on or give in to this snobby,
rude, selfish girl. She wanted to get to the core of her, to find
out who had hurt her. In Rachel's mind she was damaged in
some way, because in rare brief moments, before the walls
came back up again, she would see in her the same hurt little
girl that she herself had once been.

"So," Tiffany was saying now, "what got you into this whole
religious thing?"

Boy was that a loaded question. Where to even start? Rachel
thought. She had tried to live her life in a way that showed
her faith to others, rather than beat people over the head
with it. She wasn't shy about sharing her faith with people,
she never had been, but most people knew she was a
Christian by her modesty and integrity, her gentle spirit, and
her compassion for others. She did keep her Bible nearby
always, but she wasn't showy with it. She simply felt safe
with God's word by her side.

"First thing you should know is that being a Christian is
not about religion, it's a relationship that I have with Jesus.
Religion is merely man's attempt to follow a list of rules to be
good enough to please God. I have a relationship with Christ
just like you would have a relationship with any good friend."

Tiffany processed this for a moment. She'd had no religious
background herself. Her parents were Catholic but never

forced her to go to church, and other than Sunday, they didn't really seem to have any real interest in it, so Rachel's comment was peculiar to her.

"I was raised by parents who lived what they believed, that is, they were born again believers in Jesus Christ, and they taught me to follow him too. I know that even though we've lived together for a while, we don't really know each other that well. Let me tell you what having Jesus in my life has meant to me.
I have always been fat, and let's face it, less than attractive. I'm totally at peace with who God created me to be, but it hasn't always been that way. I grew up tortured by other kids. They made fun of me, of course, but worse, they threw rocks at me and kicked dirt in my face on the playground. They played cruel practical jokes on me.

They made it a point to single me out in a crowd whenever they could, to put me down, or make sure I knew I wasn't good enough. I had not a single friend, until I was in high school. I suffered years and years of abuse by my peers. All of this because I wasn't the cookie cutter version of who they thought I should be.

But, Tiffany, God sees me as beautiful. I am His creation, and He died to save me. I didn't really come to realize my own worth until my last year of school. Once I did though, nobody and nothing can take it away from me. He has always been there for me, and His word says that He never leaves us, and He will never forsake us.

If it weren't for Jesus in my life, I would never have left the safety of my home! I was a scared girl, hiding in my room, so that people couldn't hurt me."

Rachel went on to tell her the defining moment of her life, when God had used the pig to bring her to her senses.

Tiffany was in awe of this girl. A team of wild horses never would have gotten her to admit this out loud, but she was actually a little jealous of the peace she seemed to carry like a banner. She knew that she herself was far superior in looks, background, just about everything really, yet, she was horribly insecure. She was always certain that at any moment someone would realize that she was nothing special, that she had no *depth*.

"Tiffany, have you ever felt that way? Felt like you weren't worth anything in anyone's eyes?" Rachel asked her gently.

It was one of those rare moments when her defenses were down, and she was being honest with herself. She was sitting on her bed, worrying the blanket with nervous fingers. Her long silky blonde hair had fallen over her eyes, and Rachel could see she was using it as a curtain to hide behind. How her heart broke for this girl!

"Yes," came the quiet answer.

"Do you want to talk about it?"

There was such a long silence that followed that Rachel thought she'd lost the moment. Tiffany took a deep breath and launched into her own story.

"My parents are, well . . . rich. I mean *really* rich. A nanny, butler, maid, and personal chef raised me. They cooked for me, tucked me in at night, helped me with my homework, and bandaged me up, when I skinned my knees. They did what my parents were never willing to do themselves.

My parents would poke their head in and check on me, if they had time between business meetings or charity events. I always knew that I was an accident. I've heard them many times over the years talk about how easier things would have been, if they hadn't had me.

I was an *inconvenience* they had to deal with. Unless, of course, they were having 'important' people over for dinner. In that case, I suddenly became *very* important to them. I was dressed up and trotted out like a prize pig. I was told to be on my best behavior.

By the time I was six, I knew my place and that was in my bedroom, because children are to be seen and not heard. I grew up doing exactly what I was told to do, until I was about fourteen. Then I started to rebel, I guess you could say," she chuckled a little self-consciously.

"I would come to their fancy little dinner parties late, dressed up like a prostitute, with rings in my nose or fake tattoos down both arms, and hair dyed jet black. One time they were having a political fund-raiser for the Governor at our home. I showed up with red contact lenses in my eyes and acted demon-possessed. That got me sent off to a boarding school, where I was stranded for all four years of high school.

They had no way of knowing this, but that's where it got worse. At least for a little while, I felt like I needed to punish them for having me in the first place. I started drinking and doing drugs, hanging with a really bad crowd. They were called down to the administrator's office on more than one occasion, and on more than one occasion, they had to write a big fat 'donation' check to keep me there," she said with a hint of a smile.

"At some point during my senior year, I realized I'd better get it together, if I wanted to leave and start my future. There was no way I was ever going back to that house, so I made a more serious effort to bring my grades up, quit all the partying and here I am. Even then, my grades weren't good enough for this school . . . but my father's bank account was."

Rachel took it all in. It made sense. She had seen the supreme effort this girl had always put forth to make herself appear self-confident, beautiful, talented. She felt that nobody would love her, aside from her looks and her money.

She took Tiffany's hands in her own, and as tears filled her own eyes, she gazed at her and said, "Tiffany, you are *not* a mistake. You are a child of God! He loves you beyond anything you could possibly imagine. He knew you, before He created the earth, and He knows every bad thing you have ever done or ever will do. And guess what? He loves you *anyway!*

I'm sure at one point or another someone has told you that Jesus loves you. He demonstrated His love for us, in that while we were still sinners, He died for us. Do you know that the reason He had to die on the cross was because we are *all* sinners? The word sin simply means that we have missed the mark. We are imperfect, and we are human, and we blow it. The only perfect person in the history of mankind was Jesus, and he never once sinned. Jesus died on the cross, because there was no way for us to pay for our own sins. They are too great! His perfect life was sacrificed for us, so that we can one day be in heaven with him.

Do you understand what I'm saying to you? Once you grab onto how precious you are in God's eyes, you will never be the same. Nobody here can ever truly hurt you again, because you know that this life isn't all there is. You have a future with the Lover of your soul, if you want it."

Tiffany was now on her knees, on the floor, sobbing, with Rachel's hand on her shoulder. Nobody had ever loved her, not really. The only people in her life that ever meant anything to her had been paid to love her. Others claimed to love her but had only used her for her money or influence. Could these words be true? How could someone love her so much that he would die for her? She didn't know how she could know for certain that what Rachel was telling her was true, but it had the ring of truth. She could see the evidence of it in her friend's life as well. Rachel was the only person she knew who was real with her, who didn't want anything from her but friendship.

"I have something for you. I've actually had it for a couple of months, but I've been waiting for the right time to give it to you. It's a Bible. I'd like for you to read some of it, and if you have questions, I'm here for you. If you want, we could even do like a little Bible study together. The only way to really learn about God is to start with the love letter that He's written you."

She took it gratefully, but not before reaching out and hugging her friend. It was truly amazing to her how someone could be so homely and yet so beautiful. She grasped hard every word Rachel was telling her, and she yearned for more.

The girls made plans to start in the book of John that very night and to read together a few chapters each night, after their schoolwork was done. Rachel also offered to bring her to church the following Sunday. She couldn't wait to introduce her to the couple there that had been mentoring her and praying her through school.

****

The Pastor said his closing prayer, and the girls gathered their coats and purses and headed with the crush of people toward the back door. Rachel saw her friends on the way out and called out to them.

Thomas and Jenna Allen made their way slowly toward them. The three had become good friends over the past few months, and Rachel had learned so much from their discipleship.

Introductions were made and the Allens invited the girls to lunch at their home. Sitting at the table in the dining room, Rachel asked Tiffany what she had thought of the service and if she had any questions. She was surprised that she didn't feel self-conscious or out of place, particularly since she had never attended a church that wasn't Catholic, but she felt at home with these people.

They were kind and loving toward one another, and she was instantly comfortable with them. She asked questions about communion and baptism, why people had their hands raised in the air when they sang, and most importantly, what being "saved" meant.

Thomas answered the former questions, and Jenna took over, when it came to the question of salvation.

"We call it being saved, because we are not only saved from ourselves and what we are capable of doing to one another because of this sick, fallen world, but also we are saved by Jesus. We are saved from spending eternity separated from Him. These days people don't really like to talk about hell, but it is a reality. God created hell for the devil and his demons. It was never meant as a place for people to go. Trust me when I say that it will be awful beyond your worst nightmare. It is one of the reasons that we are constantly reaching out to people who don't know Christ. We don't want to see anyone go there!

God is pure love, but he is also righteous and just. Because of that, he must punish those who break his laws. You can accept his gift at any time this side of death, but once you step from this life into the next, it will be too late to change your mind. He is a gentleman and won't force anyone to spend eternity with Him, if they don't want to. He died so that we don't have to be separated from Him. It is His gift to us. Let me ask you Tiffany . . . have you made the decision to give your life to Him yet?"

She shook her head and replied that she and Rachel had been discussing this all week and that she had just started reading the Bible. She didn't know what she had to do to be saved, but she was more than ready.

The four held hands around the table and prayed together, with Rachel leading the prayer, and Tiffany repeating the words.

"Father God, thank you for coming into my life! I know that you died on that cross for me, to save me, and set me free. I ask you now that you would forgive me of my sins, lead me, and I will follow you. Thank you Jesus! Amen."

Tears were wiped from faces all around the table, and they rejoiced over dessert and coffee. More questions were asked and answered, while Rachel said a prayer of thanksgiving in her heart. Tiffany was completely overwhelmed by the obvious love these people had for her. She felt like she'd been given a second chance at life.

"I do have one more question," she said. "How soon can I be baptized?"

****

Months grew into years, and the girls grew closer to one another as well as to the Lord. By their third year together at

Pratt, Tiffany had led several of her girlfriends to Christ and had become quite the little evangelist. Rachel was thrilled with the way things were turning out.

If there was anything that put a damper on her rewarding new life in school, it was the fact that she hadn't been able to reach her parents in over six months. She tried to remember to convert her fears into prayers, but sometimes it was hard not to worry about them. The one thing she took comfort in was the fact that they were being watched over by the same mighty and powerful God that she herself relied on. They were doing what He had called them to do, and she knew that they would be safe in His hands.

Her summers were spent working small part-time jobs just to keep the boredom at bay. She had never had much of a social life and that was fine. She used her extra money to buy fabric and notions, and all her free time was spent sewing clothes. She still hadn't decided on a name for her new line of clothing. She figured God would give it to her, when it was time.

She kept her portfolio updated and met with Thomas on a regular basis to check on her investments. She so far hadn't needed to touch any of the money that her parents had given her. She used money from her part-time job for anything that she needed. She really didn't want to do anything to jeopardize her future, so she was overly cautious with her money.

Her plan was to spend her first few years after school interning with an established designer, and now in her final year of school, she had begun sending out her resume to various firms.

It was a rainy afternoon in late May, when she got her first letter in the mail. It was a rejection letter from one of the firms that she was most interested in working for. They thanked her for her interest, but they did not think that her line of clothing would interest the same niche of people that they sought business from. But "good luck in your future." *Great,* she thought. *Lord, have you brought me this far only to have doors slammed in my face?*

The next piece of mail she opened, however, stopped her in her tracks. She had an interview the following week with a *major* clothing line! She couldn't believe it! The letter was signed by the personal assistant of *the* Theresa Wakefield-Anderson! This was a dream come true for Rachel. She had been a huge fan of *Her Wicked Ways* for years, as long as she could remember. Her work was cutting edge, always ahead of every trend. She took chances that other designers would never dream of, and they always paid off. She was considered a renegade, and most girls would kill for an opportunity to work with her.

Jumping down from her top bunk, letter in hand, she raced out the door of her dorm in search of Tiffany. She couldn't wait to share the news!

Tiffany shared her excitement, and the two called the Allens right away with the good news. They were invited over later that night for dessert and prayer. They all agreed that this was the hand of the Lord and that He had a plan in all of it.

They prayed together over her interview the following week and asked that Rachel would be used in the life of this famous designer. They prayed for wisdom and guidance, and that in the end, the name of the Lord would be glorified. At around eleven o'clock, the girls headed back to the college to get ready for bed.

Thomas and Jenna looked at one another as the door closed. It had been so hard for them not to say anything. As an attorney, he had to maintain the strictest of confidences with his clients. He was legally obligated to keep his mouth shut, but it almost killed him. He knew Theresa, of course, had known her for years, and knew beyond the shadow of a doubt that she was far from the Lord. He knew of her past, her pain, and what her life had made her.

He and Jenna prayed quietly together for both women. They were excited to see what God was doing here, but they hoped that Theresa didn't chew Rachel up and spit her out. They were as polar opposite as two people could be. Theresa was a tough business woman, angry, skeptical, and bitter. Her life of pain had made her that way. Rachel was sweet, compassionate, generous, and loving. Her life of pain had made her that way. Only Jesus made the difference.

Part Three

Chapter Twelve

Jenna would never forget the year that changed everything for Theresa. She had woken up that first night, the night it all began to fall apart, in a cold sweat. The remnants of a horrific nightmare caused her heart of pound almost out of her chest. She only had a few small fragments of it left in her mind, but she remembered a lot of blood . . . blood, and the haunting words of her Lord urging her to go to Theresa right away.

It had been all she could do not to race over to their home at three o'clock in the morning. Instead, she woke Thomas and told him about the dream. This wasn't the first time she'd had a prophetic dream. Jesus had a way of speaking to her like this.

It was, in fact, what led to her relationship with Him. She had led a rebellious life as a teenager, dabbling in drugs, sex, and the occult. Most people would never have guessed that about her now. She had become so obsessed with witchcraft that she eventually got in way over her head. It began to twist her mind, causing paranoia, anger, and terror. She jumped at every sound, fearing demons behind every bush. She dropped all of her friendships, quit going to school, and started drinking heavily.

She was in the midst of her very own nervous breakdown the night that it happened. She had become hysterical after using her Ouija board in her room. She'd been speaking with her spirit guide, and he was predicting her death. Gone was the friendly spirit who guided her days. He told her she was worthless, a piece of garbage who didn't deserve to live. Suddenly, all the candles in the room simultaneously blew out, leaving her alone in the dark. She screamed and tried to get out of her room, but the door wouldn't budge.

After hours of screaming, begging for mercy, and crying, she passed out on her bed. She found herself in a dream with a man, dressed in a brilliant white robe, and sandals on his feet. He spoke to her, and with that first word, she knew that this was Jesus. She couldn't have said how she knew, having never set foot in a church or read a single word of the Bible. She supposed that when Jesus appears to you, there is just no question. He took her face in His nail-scarred hands, looked into her eyes, and spoke:

"I am the way, the truth, and the life. Nobody comes to the Father but by me."

She bolted upright in bed, knowing it was true. She found the nearest church and got her questions answered. The rest was history. She threw out her candles, her board, her spell books, and her talismans. She had followed him wholeheartedly since that time.

Now, God wanted to use her in Theresa's life. They were so different from one another. She was quiet and sincere, gentle and kind. Theresa was brash and intense, loud and combative, and devoutly atheistic. She wanted to debate everything, especially when it came to God.

Jenna knew that in most cases this kind of friendship would never have lasted. She also knew that it was ordained by the Lord, and there was a divine purpose in it. She prayed for Theresa, having no idea what was going on with her. She felt strongly led to pray for her protection, for God's hand to be on her, and for some reason, on their marriage as well.

When the time finally reached nine, she felt like it was safe to call, but when she did, nobody answered. She got showered and dressed and took a taxi to their apartment. She knocked loudly on the door and got no answer. Not willing to give up, she pulled out her Bible, sat on the front stoop, and waited.

Two hours later, the Andersons pulled up in front of the building. When she saw Stephen helping her out of the car, and the whiteness of Theresa's face, she was instantly panicked.

"Are you okay?! What happened?" she asked them frantically.

The two looked at one another, and Stephen started to speak. Theresa put a hand up to stop him, "It's ok. Let's go inside, and Jenna and I can visit for a bit."

Stephen put her in bed and pulled a chair in for Jenna to sit by her side. Then he wandered off to the kitchen to put on a pot of tea for them.

"I can't believe you are here. You have no idea how badly I need a friend right now," she said, the walls coming down. "I did something really stupid, and now I will have to pay for it. I don't know what's going to happen to my marriage." The tears were coming now, and all Jenna could think was that perhaps she'd had an affair. That just didn't seem possible. She knew that Theresa adored her new husband, and it also didn't explain her failing health.

"I'm here. You can tell me as much or as little as you want to tell me. You are my friend, and you know you can tell me the truth. I am not going to judge you, Theresa. I love you!"

So, she told her everything. From finding out she was pregnant, to the abortion, and finally the confrontation at the hospital. The shame on her face was evident, and her words were coming out in spurts, as she tried to overcome the sobs. She was coming to a breaking point, Jenna could see that. *Is this it Lord? Will she finally come to you?*

She chose her words carefully, trying desperately to get it right. She knew she might only get one chance, and the woman before her was in pain. The last thing she wanted to do was make it worse.

"Theresa, I am so sorry. I am sorry for what you are going through. I know that I don't have a magical formula to make all of this go away for you. I wish I did! I care about you, and I would give anything to make all of this end right now, but the only one who can take your pain and turn it into something beautiful is God. Until you come to a place where you recognize that, the pain will only get worse. We were never meant to carry these kinds of burdens alone. Jesus is waiting for you to come to Him. Allow Him to heal your heart, Theresa."

Theresa looked at her, grief evident in her eyes. "I so wish I could believe that! But all God's ever given me is more of the same: death and destruction. There is nobody that can get me out of this mess. I made my bed, and now I'll have to sleep in it. I will make it up to Stephen somehow. I will get him to forgive me, and maybe someday I can forgive myself. I don't think I need to ask some deity that I don't even believe in for forgiveness. I know you mean well, Jenna. If it makes you feel better, then by all means, please pray for me. Right now, I just need your friendship."

Jenna's heart tore a little, when she heard those words. She wasn't going to give up, not by a long shot, but for now she would just concentrate on loving her.

"Is it okay, if I pray right now?" she asked, respectfully.

She nodded her head, and closed her eyes. Jenna took hold of her hand and began.

"Lord God, we need you right now. I know how much you love Theresa, and I pray that you would allow her to feel a small measure of that everlasting love in the midst of her hurt. I pray for her, that you would allow healing to take place in her own heart and in her marriage. And I pray, right now Lord, that she would begin to soften toward you. Bring other Christians into her life to stand beside her and lift her up. I ask you Lord, that one day I will walk beside my dear friend in Heaven. Thank you, Jesus. I pray these things in your beautiful name, AMEN."

The two visited for another hour. Many tears were shared between them, and just as Jenna was about to head out the door, Stephen stopped her. He asked if he could walk her out and put her into a taxi. It was an odd request, but she acquiesced. The moment they were on the other side of the door, he told her.

"Jenna, I've given my life to Christ - just yesterday. I was so angry, so hurt, and I didn't know where to go with it. I wandered into a small church, and God met me there." He blurted out in a rush, color high in his cheeks, and joy in his eyes.

She was stunned. She threw her arms around him and hugged him, whispering in his ear, "Welcome to the family, brother!"

They chatted away while they waited for a cab, and he confessed to her that he hadn't found the courage to tell Theresa yet. They both knew what was impending. She had been fighting God all her life, and she wouldn't be happy about his decision, so he asked for prayer, and found out where they attended church on Sundays. This was all so new to him, and he wanted to get involved right away.

She was riding home in the taxi, praying for them both. They had a long road ahead of them, and it wasn't going to be an easy one. She had known Theresa for almost a year now and knew how stubborn and angry she was. *On the other hand,* she thought with a chuckle, *God is stubborn too. When He pursues you, you don't stand a chance!* She thought about how many people in Theresa's life were believers and that it wasn't coincidence, not by a long shot.

She couldn't wait to share the good news with Thomas and to join him in battle on their knees for Theresa's soul.

****

When Theresa was well again, she began looking for an internship with a designer. Everywhere she went, she heard the same thing, "Are you a model?" She knew she was attractive, but nobody wanted to take her seriously because of her looks. She would show them her portfolio, but all she heard was that she should reconsider the runway.

Finally, out of desperation, she decided she would have to start from the ground up with her own company, skipping the internship altogether. She knew she would have some barriers to break through and that, at least in the beginning, nobody would take her seriously, as she was a complete unknown.

She was working from early morning to nearly midnight every day, looking for the perfect building in a good location with an office overlooking Manhattan, the equipment she would need, and an advertising firm. She still had to hire a staff. She was distracted when Stephen tried to talk to her, and she only half-listened. She was flipping through the yellow pages looking for a sign making company. She wanted to have *Her Wicked Ways* in huge letters on the front of the building.

"And so," Stephen continued, thinking she was following him, "I've decided to follow Christ. I know I should have told you sooner, but there never seemed to be a right time. My hope is that one day you will join me . . ."

What?! What had he just said?!

"Back up a minute, can you repeat that?" she said slowly and cautiously.

So he did. He told her the whole story, about the long walk from the hospital, about how angry and hurt he'd felt, thinking of leaving her, and how he'd ended up in a chapel praying with a priest. He told her about the peace and forgiveness he'd felt, and how he wanted her to know that same peace in her own life.

Stephen had always worn his heart on his sleeve. It was an endearing quality she'd always loved about him, and he looked at her now like an eager-to-please puppy dog. It didn't help.

Her instant gut reaction to the news was rage - flat-out, intense fury. *God thinks he can take another one from me? We'll see about that!*

Trying to appear calm, she responded in a reasonable tone, "You can do what you want, Stephen. I'm not your mother, but don't you dare try to drag me into it. You know better than that. Frankly, I thought more of you than this. I never in a million years would have imagined that you'd be brainwashed by this nonsense. I will tell you this, however, don't you dare let this take over our lives or our marriage. I won't stand for it."

Her face was set in stone, and Stephen felt his heart fall. He'd known it wouldn't go well, but he had prayed that she might at least support him in it, even if she didn't agree. He knew she loved him and for that he was thankful. He could only hope that one day she would soften toward God.

He didn't bring it up again with her. He simply lived out his new life of faith and prayed fervently for her each day. He began attending church twice a week with the Allens and studying the Bible regularly. He knew that he was in this for the long haul and that now God came first in his life.

This, he also knew, was a bitter pill for Theresa to swallow. No matter how hard he tried to show his love for her, she had already started to change in her attitude towards him.

There was also the baby they had lost. She had built a brick wall around her heart that day, and he knew that she was crucifying herself for what she'd done. If only she would lay that burden at the foot of the cross! She would find forgiveness and peace for her soul. She could rebuild her life.

Instead, she kept him at arm's length and each day their marriage died a little bit. How could he bring her back from the edge, if she couldn't even forgive herself? She buried herself in her work, coming home late every night and leaving before he got out of bed most mornings. He was scared for them. She, however, had hardened her heart and was now married to her work.

****

Theresa had slowly but surely become a force to be reckoned with in the fashion industry. By the time she had been open for two years, her office was fully staffed, and she was generating a profit. She had models working the runway in Paris, regular interviews with *Vogue*, and her line of clothing was in such high demand that she had difficulty in keeping up.

Now, ten years later, *Her Wicked Ways* was a household name. Her personal assistant was her lifeline. She was smart, efficient, hard working, and dedicated. Carol was also married, and recently found out that she was pregnant. Theresa knew that meant she would only have her a precious few months, before Carol was ready to step down and hand the reigns over to someone else.

With the deadline looming, she began to peruse the resumes that were coming in from various college graduates, looking for an internship. One resume stood out, head and shoulders, above the rest. Rachel Jenkins had sent over a copy of her portfolio, a new idea for a clothing line for the plus sized woman, and the concept fascinated her. It was nothing she herself would have done, but she knew there was a market for that. How ingenious!

She asked Carol to setup an interview for the following week, but she had pretty much made her mind up to hire her already. Unless she was a total barbarian in person, she had a job at *Her Wicked Ways*.

****

Thursday morning started out as any other day, except that Rachel was up three hours early, as Tiffany did her hair and makeup for the big interview. She had gone out and bought a *Her Wicked Ways* dress at Bloomingdales and copied the pattern, sewing it into a dress in her own size. With curlers in her hair, she sat patiently while her eyeliner was applied.

When she was done, she looked in the mirror, and tried not to be disappointed. Tiffany had done her best, but she only had so much to work with. Her hair was so thin and fine that the curl fell out of it almost immediately, and the dress was clearly made to look better on someone about four sizes smaller, but even she had to admit that her eyes looked beautiful and Tiffany had managed to hide the worst of her acne scars.

They two held hands and prayed one more time over the interview, and Rachel headed out to meet her fate.

Theresa was shocked but tried to hide it. This pathetic girl would never do. She knew it right off the bat, when she saw her in the foyer. She hadn't expected this but was prepared to let her down gently. She knew how hard it was to break into this business, when nobody would give you a chance, based solely upon your looks.

Striding out confidently, she introduced herself and led Rachel to her office to be interviewed. She asked her to talk a little about herself, and once she began, Theresa took back every rotten thing she had thought about her. She was a strong, confident, educated girl and would work out perfectly. Nobody was more surprised by that than Theresa.

She recognized the dress Rachel was wearing as something she herself had created for the new fall line, but she knew that her clothes did not come in this girl's size. That meant she must have copied the pattern and made one to suit her. She had to give her credit for the lengths she was willing to go for the job.

"Well," she began, "I'm afraid I don't have an internship to offer you at this time."

Rachel's face fell. She was so sure she'd aced the interview.

"But," Theresa continued, "I am in need of a personal assistant, and it's a great way to get your feet wet in this industry. Is that something you would be interested in? I pay a decent wage, but I will be honest, it's grueling hours involving a lot of travel.

You will need to be available at all hours of the day, because believe it or not, there will a lot of emergencies that have to be tended to day and night."

Rachel stopped just short of jumping up and down. Taking a deep breath to calm herself down, she replied, "I would be honored to work for you. The long hours are fine. I don't have family here, and I'm not married, so my time is my own. When can I start?"

Theresa explained that she kept an apartment for herself and for her assistant in this building so that they could be close by in case something urgent came up. It was included as part of her compensation package. She would like her to start training with Carol on the weekends until she graduated, and then full time after that.

They concluded the interview with Rachel signing a two year non-compete and confidentiality agreement and contract. Shaking hands, she agreed to be back on Saturday to get started. On the way out, she met Carol and made an appointment to meet here at eight Saturday morning.

She hailed a cab and went directly to Thomas' office to share the good news. He congratulated her and invited her and Tiffany over for dinner the following night to celebrate. The two spent the evening praising the Lord, each for a very different reason.

Chapter Thirteen

Stephen Anderson sat on a bench in Central Park on a warm sunny day in late September and watched the children play in the falling leaves. Mothers strolled by with their infants, swaddled in pink and blue strollers, and the sounds of laughter and innocence surrounded him.

He had come here to think and to pray. The days when he couldn't stop thinking about his own child were more and more frequent. He had decided that she had been a girl with auburn hair and sea green eyes like her mother. She probably had dimples too. In the years since he'd lost her, he had come to terms with forgiving her mother and was overjoyed in the knowledge that one day they would be reunited in heaven.

Yet, the sadness of losing a child would sneak up on him when he least expected it, and he would be overwhelmed. He was experiencing so many emotions that sometimes he needed to just get away, to think, and to sort them out. He felt guilt for not protecting his child, anger with a doctor who would take an innocent life just to line his own pockets, and fear for his marriage. He knew a profound sense of loss, for not only the child that was taken from him, but also the ones he would now never have. Stephen was a broken man.

He knew that the Lord was using this in his life, and he had learned that forgiveness was an ongoing process. Every day he had to forgive again, and every day his love for his wife was renewed. He also recognized that if it weren't for the abortion, he might have never come to know Christ, but the pain was still unbearable. Even ten years later, he didn't know how to make it better.

Worse, he knew that the guilt and remorse was absolutely destroying his wife. At least twice a week she jerked awake in bed, trembling from a nightmare or sobbing in her sleep. He tried to comfort her the best that he could. He would have given anything for her to reach out to him and comfort him as well, but she just pushed him away. He had tried over the years to talk with her about it, telling her that getting it out in the open and discussing it was the only way for her to heal. He still told her every day how much Jesus loved her and that He wanted to fix her broken heart. Still, every day, she would get angry with him or become cold and distant.

Stephen signed up for counseling with his Pastor. He knew that without Christ he never would be whole. He hoped that one day his wife would go with him, but he knew that was not likely. He would continue to go to the meetings regardless and would continue to pray for Theresa.
A little boy toddled over to him and tapped him on the leg. His ball had rolled under Stephen's feet. He looked down into the sweet blue eyes of a three-year-old child with Down syndrome. He handed the child the toy and was rewarded with a brilliant smile. Tears filled his eyes once again, and he watched as the boy ran off to play. How would he ever get to a place where he could even be around kids without his heart feeling like it had been torn from his chest?

"Lord, please help me!" Stephen prayed, *"I cannot do this on my own. I need you desperately. My heart is broken and only you can heal it. I bring my child before you and lay her at the foot of the cross. You once told me to bring my burdens to you, and you would carry them. So, once again, I hand this burden over and ask you to take it from me. Help me not to pick it up again. Show me how to love Theresa in the midst of my pain. Give me the words to speak to bring healing to her. Help me to reach her Lord! I cannot stand to see such pain in her eyes and I know that it only mirrors*

my own. We need you Jesus; our marriage needs you! I pray these things, knowing and thankful that you hear my prayers. In your precious name I pray, Jesus, AMEN."

He stood up from the bench and with a heavy heart headed for home.

****

Rachel had turned out to be the best employee that Theresa had ever had. She was a hard worker, always willing to work insane hours or travel to any destination for business. She had absolutely no social life, aside from attending church twice a week. That part had become a thorn in Theresa's side. There were times that she needed her on site, but she steadfastly refused to miss Bible studies on Wednesday evenings or church services on Sunday mornings. She was so stubborn! Theresa had even offered her a raise to be available at those times, but she still refused to give it up.

Yet another Jesus freak in her life. It was like some cosmic joke that God was playing on her. Everywhere she turned, they surrounded her. First her parents, then her husband, her attorney, and now her assistant. Well, they could gang up on her all they liked, she wasn't going to close her eyes and follow meekly like they did! She actually had a *brain* in her head, and she used it.

She had to give credit where credit was due. Theresa would dish it out, but Rachel could take it. She had a short fuse and was known in the office for her hot temper, but when she snapped at Rachel, she would simply smile in return. Nothing ever seemed to bother her. In fact, if she had to put a name to it, she would have said that she had a peace about her that couldn't be touched. She almost emanated it.

People truly enjoyed being around her and, in the fashion industry, that was quite a feat. Models, photographers, fashion divas . . . . they were all superficial, only friendly with people that could further their careers. Rachel seemed to have an innate ability to touch their lives, and they flocked to her in the office. She was kind and compassionate, listening to their problems and with a sweet gentle voice she would respond with a simple, "I'm so sorry for what you are going through. I will be praying for you."

Theresa had seen the hardest, most cynical photographer she knew reduced to tears in a matter of minutes in Rachel's presence. She was the real deal, and Theresa was thoroughly pleased to have her as an assistant.

Over the ensuing months, she'd gotten to know her better. They spent long hours together in planes, or on road trips, and in business lunches, chatting and laughing. She'd learned a lot about Rachel's painful childhood, her faith, and her family. She'd also learned something that surprised her a little. She had been adopted as an infant and had no idea who her birth parents were. In fact, she had never even had a desire to find out!

That was so foreign to Theresa. She couldn't imagine having such a huge blank slate in your life and not wanting to fill it in. Being inquisitive by nature, she never stopped asking questions. One of the main issues she had with the Christian faith was that her questions were never answered to her satisfaction. How could a loving God allow disease, famine, suffering, child abuse, and murder in this world? How could he rip a family apart like he had done with hers? How could he say he loved you in one breath, and in the next tell you that if you don't believe in him, you are going to hell? It had never made sense to her that this was the largest religion in the world. What was wrong with people?!

Theresa had secretly decided to hire Thomas Allen to look into her past and try to find her birth parents. She wanted to surprise Rachel and maybe even arrange a reunion. She knew it would most likely be a long process, but she had the money, and it was like a treasure hunt for her, so she was excited by the prospect. That thought in mind, she reached for her phone and dialed his number. She had an appointment with him for the following week, and she couldn't wait to catch up with her old friend.

****

Jenna stared at her doctor in shock. "Really?!" she barely managed to squeak out.

"Really," he replied with a huge grin on his face. "I'll need to see you once a month for the next few months, and then as you get closer to delivery, you'll need to start coming in once a week. Congratulations, Mrs. Allen!"

She sat on the table a full five minutes after he stepped out and just stared at the wall in total befuddlement. When it finally sank in, she was giddy with excitement. Jumping down off the examination table, she dressed quickly and ran out the door.

Outside she hailed the first cab she saw and gave the driver directions to her husband's office. She couldn't wait to tell him!

Thomas and Jenna had been trying for years to have a child. They finally started fertility treatments just last year and cried together each month, when she would find out that once again she wasn't pregnant. Then, about three weeks ago, she started feeling really sick. At first she thought it was just a nasty stomach bug or food poisoning, but it didn't go away, so finally she gave into her husband's concern and went to the doctor.

The cab pulled to the curb in front of the firm, and she flew out the door, only realizing she hadn't paid the cabbie, when she heard the loud cursing in Spanish. She apologized profusely, as she threw a twenty-dollar bill at him through the window and rushed into the building. Jenna waited impatiently for the elevator and finally gave up, running up the four flights of stairs.

She ran straight past the startled receptionist and his secretary, who tried in vain to stop her, and flew through his door. She was completely oblivious to Theresa's presence in his office, as she blurted out, "We are going to have a baby!" and threw her arms around his neck.

Thomas smiled widely at her and hugged her back, picking her up until her feet dangled above the floor. The two began crying softly together, thanking the Lord for his goodness and mercy. She quickly shared the details with him and exuberantly told him all the names she had come up with on the way to his office. Neither of them saw the anguish on the face of the client in the office chair.

****

Theresa slammed the front door closed and stalked to the kitchen in a huff to pour a glass of wine. She couldn't have said why she was so angry and bitter, if she were asked. She drank the expensive cabernet down in two big gulps and poured herself another.

"Rough day, huh, honey?" she heard from the sofa.

"Yeah. I don't want to talk about it."

"Theresa, you never want to talk about it. That's the problem. You know, you hold everything in, and one day you are just going to explode. It's not healthy," Stephen replied.

She spun and glared at him. "I really don't need one of your little sermons tonight. Do you have any idea what kind of pressure I'm under at work? No. You don't. That is because you are too busy with your head in the clouds, watching for Jesus to come riding along in a chariot to rescue you." Contempt for him dripped from every word.

She strode into the bedroom suite to change into her robe. He was right on her heels.

"Look," he continued, "all I wanted to do was open up a line of communication with you. You are angry *all* the time. I never know what's going on with you, because you come home in a huff and head straight to bed. I don't even feel like we have a marriage any more. Talk to me, please."

She tied the knot on her robe tightly and walked into the bathroom to begin her nightly routine. Stephen watched her as she scrubbed her makeup from her face. She looked once again like the college girl he'd fallen in love with. If only he could go back to those carefree days with her again, before all the damage had been done to them.

"I don't want to talk to you. Don't you get that? I will work this out on my own. I'm a big girl."

Stephen sighed and looked at his feet. Taking a deep breath, he tried again.

"We both lost a child that day, Theresa. I know it's killing you, but if we can't talk about it, how will we ever survive this? Please, please talk to me, or if you won't talk to me, talk to God. He loves you, and He wants to help you through this."

She looked steadily into his eyes, and every time she did, she saw the future that died on the table that day with her. It was so painful to see what she'd done to him, to them, so she had buried herself in her job and avoided him as much as she could. She loved him, and she had single handedly destroyed him. Now she felt like there was no hope for them. Perhaps if he hadn't gone off the deep end with all of the God stuff, they may have stood a chance.

"Fine. You want me to talk, here it comes. I think it's time we face the fact that we made a huge mistake and go our separate ways. You will never forget what I did that day. You bring it up all the time, you try to push me toward God, you won't give me a moment's peace about it. How can I move on when you won't *stop*? You say you've forgiven me, and I think that you honestly believe that, but I don't feel an incessant need to talk about it!"

Tears were falling off her face now, and Stephen felt his heart stop in his chest. *No! Please, God, no!*

"Theresa, we can work through this. I promise. Just give us a chance; give me a chance! I love you so much. Please don't push me away."

He reached for her and tried to put his arms around her, to control his own sobs, to grasp at the life that was slipping away from him. She held onto him for just a moment, one last time, and then shoved him away brutally. She had to do it now, before she lost her nerve. She felt deep down like she was doing this for him, to save him. She knew it was too late for her, but perhaps he could still have a life without her. Perhaps he could start over with someone who would appreciate him and give him children. *You can do this, Theresa,* she thought to herself. *Do the right thing and set him free.*

"I am going to move out, Stephen. I have that apartment in the office building, and I can stay there until we make some decisions. It's over."

The anguish threatened to overtake him, but he would not give up without a fight. He begged and pleaded with her to try marital counseling; to give them more time. He told her he would do anything for her; he loved her so much. She was his entire life. He had looked into his future, and she had always been there, but the words fell on deaf ears.

He didn't know that her heart was breaking right alongside his. He only saw the bitterness, the anger, the unforgiveness, and he dropped to his knees. He wept until his eyes were painful and swollen. He prayed until his voice was hoarse, and he fell asleep finally after three in the morning, in a heap on the floor, outside their bedroom door.

On the other side of that door, a voice whispered into the dark, "You can have him now, God. I hope you are happy." Another layer of bricks went up on the walls around her heart.

****

The following week movers came to take all of Theresa's things which had been boxed and ready to go. Stephen had continued to try and talk her out of it, but she had made up her mind to go, and there was nothing he could do to stop her.

She went to see Thomas Allen again, this time to talk to him about a divorce.

"You know I don't practice that kind of law, Theresa. Is there nothing that can be done to save your marriage? I know he loves you, and if I may speak frankly, I know you love him too. I've seen you together too many times over the years to not be aware of how you two feel about each other. God can overcome any obstacle, if you give it over to him. Please, please try to work it out."

Theresa felt her face turn red, and her anger begin to boil up. Where did he get off talking to her like that? Yes, they might be friends, but she was still a paying client!

"I am so sick of hearing about God! Is that all you people can talk about? Please, just give me the name of another lawyer who can help me. It's going to happen with or without your help."

Sighing, he wrote a name down on a piece of paper. He wouldn't apologize to her, but he would pray for her. He still believed they stood a chance, if she would just swallow her pride and agree to get help or at least try to talk about it. He knew her well by now and knew how stubborn and arrogant she could be.

She put her coat back on and slung her purse over her shoulder. As she headed out the door, she aimed one last parting shot at him, "You missed your calling Thomas. You should have been a Pastor!" With that, she slammed his office door.

Chapter Fourteen

Rachel had settled into a comfortable pattern. Her alarm went off at 4:45 a.m. each weekday, and she allowed herself fifteen minutes to lie in bed and gather her thoughts, before she hit the ground running. Today, God had brought some friends and loved ones to mind and she felt led to pray for them. She prayed for old college roommate, Tiffany, and chuckled at the thought of where God had landed her. Never in a million years would she have pictured this for her, and it tickled her silly to know what a wild imagination God had.

Tiffany had met, fallen madly in love with, and married a devoted missionary to South America and was now living in a mud hut in the middle of the jungle. The girl who once would never have been caught *dead* leaving her dorm room without her lip gloss firmly in place and hair perfectly coifed, was now caught up in a new life that was devoid of running water, electricity, or even indoor plumbing. She was deliriously happy though, and wrote to Rachel regularly of her adventures with the children that she ministered to, the giant bugs she ran screaming from, and the beautiful sunsets that God had painted just for her and her husband.

Rachel was in complete awe of what God had done in her friend's life. It was as if she had been living in a world of darkness, and He had come along and flipped on the light switch for her, and she had never turned back. She felt so thankful that she had been a part of His plan for her.

Rachel also prayed for her boss and dear friend. She knew that Theresa was devastated by her recent divorce, regardless of the fact that she refused to discuss it. She prayed for God's peace and that He would use it to reach her. She asked that she could be a blessing to Theresa in every way and that God would show her how to minister to her with love and compassion.

Hopping out of bed, she took a quick shower and got dressed. Her custom was to be out of her apartment by six so that she could grab coffee, fresh bagels, and several newspapers and fashion magazines that Theresa was addicted to. She was in the office by 7:30 each morning and had the breakfast and periodicals arranged on her desk, before she arrived each day.

Rachel made friends wherever she went, and her morning routine was no exception. She breezed into the coffee shop and was greeted by a perky Latina barista named Carmen who smiled and waved her over.

Rachel weaved her way between the masses of people and made it to the counter, where Carmen had her standard fare waiting in a white paper bag for her.

"Mija! I have your regular order of two French vanilla non-fat, low foam lattes and two pumpernickel bagels with cream cheese. I swear I could set my clock by you Rachel!" she giggled, her accent heavy.

"Carmen, you are a life saver! This rush hour traffic seems to get a worse every day. Hey, before you ring that up, can you please add one more cup of coffee and another bagel? I'm going to stop by and visit with a friend really quick on the way to work, and I think he'll be hungry."

"Es no problema, mama," she chirped. Rachel handed over a twenty-dollar bill and Carmen bopped off to get her change. As she went, it was hard to miss the admiring gazes of the men in the room. Rachel couldn't help but think that one day, she would like a man to look at *her* that way.

Ten minutes later, she was out the door with her goodies in hand and in search of another friend. She glanced quickly at her watch and saw that she had about another thirty minutes, before she needed to be in the office. Increasing her pace, she looked about for the kind homeless man she had befriended several weeks ago. When she caught sight of him, her face lit up with a brilliant smile.

"Kevo!" she called out to him.

Sergeant Kevin Monacucci had lived on the streets for almost twenty years. He was no bum begging for change or alcoholic sleeping off a stupor each day. He was homeless, because he had lost both of his legs serving his country in the Vietnam War. He had inadvertently stepped on a land mine while in full retreat, and it was the last thing that he ever walked on. It had destroyed him physically, as well as mentally, and subsequently, he'd lost everything. He lost his wife and children because with his pride and anger firmly in place, he'd been unable to face them and had walked away. He'd lost his job, when he'd been discharged from the military. He lost his home, when he was too depressed to find work. Now he spent each day looking for cans to sell, so that he could buy a warm meal, and sometimes, he was lucky enough to find space in the shelter to sleep each night.

Rachel had walked into his life and suddenly a ray of light had pierced his darkness. She talked to him like he was a real person, an important and contributing member of society, instead of a cast off. She taught him the love of Christ and told him that his life had purpose and that God wasn't finished with him yet. He surprised himself by believing her.

"Kevo, I brought you a little breakfast. Hope you're hungry!" she greeted him warmly and handed over a warm white bag that smelled like heaven.

"Why thank you young lady! Aren't you just a breath of fresh air this morning?" he responded.

Rachel took one of the newspapers from her pile and placed it next to him on the sidewalk, where she plunked down to chat. He was utterly in awe of her. She was so unpretentious, so humble. Most people walked by like he was invisible, trying not to see him or, at most, tossing a quarter in his general direction to ease their guilty consciences. She actually seemed to care.

Over the weeks since he'd met her, he'd opened up to her about his time in Vietnam. He told her of the flashbacks he suffered, of how he lost his legs, and of what his life had been like since losing his family. He felt safe with her.

She looked at him with compassion, not pity, and told him that he was not a throwaway; he was precious in the eyes of God. She sometimes brought along her Bible and read to him or prayed with him. Today she had a passage marked in her Bible, and she pulled it out and turned to the book of Psalms.

When my heart was grieved and my spirit embittered, I was senseless and ignorant; I was a brute beast before you. Yet, I am always with you; you hold me by my right hand. You guide me with your counsel, and afterward you will take me into glory. Whom have I in heaven but you? And earth has nothing I desire besides you. My flesh and my heart may fail, but God is the strength of my heart and my portion forever.

Rachel closed the book and glanced over at Kevin, not at all surprised to see silent tears running down his cheeks. God's word had always affected her that way as well.

He sighed contentedly and spoke softly from the depths of his pain, "It's like He is reading my mind. How does He *do* that?"

She smiled at him and replied, "He's God. He just does. My favorite thing about reading the Bible is that you can read the same passage at different points in your life, and it always seems to speak to you. It speaks to your spirit, because it is more than mere words on a page. It is alive! This is the very breath of God; His love letter written in blood for you."

Rachel reached into her briefcase and withdrew a brown paper package. She handed it over to him and said, "This is for you. As many times as I've sat here with you, reading scripture and watching you soak it up like a starving man, I thought you ought to have your own."

Kevin accepted it gratefully, pulling the paper off like a child on Christmas morning and began to read hungrily. She stood to her feet and said her goodbyes, but he was in a world all his own and didn't respond.

****

Theresa charged through the front door, as she did each morning, like a woman with hell nipping at her heels. She barreled into her office, barking orders at everyone in hearing distance and cursing under her breath about the incompetents she was surrounded by. She thought most of them were idiots, and if she weren't so busy all the time, she would have fired them all and started over.

All but Rachel that is. Rachel had been the best business decision she'd ever made. She was so detail oriented that it never failed to surprise her. She arrived each morning to breakfast and coffee, as well as the magazines and newspapers that kept her up to date. As she settled in behind her desk, Rachel would go through her daily itinerary with her and ask what was required of her that day.

She never had to worry that Rachel would drop the ball or forget anything. She could simply hand over whatever project needing attending to, and Rachel was off and running. It would be done quickly, accurately, and without any further input needed on Theresa's part. She worried that someday Rachel would be snapped up by another designer who had heard of her reputation, as the best assistant in the business, so Theresa made a point of treating her *very* well.

Rachel knew that she was being treated like royalty. She received a generous raise every quarter, huge bonuses at Christmas, free living quarters, and a company vehicle. More importantly, the most talented designer in the industry was mentoring her. She felt like she was living out her wildest fantasies and kept expecting someone to pinch her and tell her it was all a dream.

Not all was perfect, of course. Rachel still worried about her parents, not having heard from them in over two years. The last letter she had held ominous news of them living in hiding from the communist authorities. Her gut tightened each time she thought of them, and she prayed fervently for their protection. Rachel maintained constant contact with their Pastor back home and hoped that each time she called, he would have good news for her.

Quite frankly, she was lonely, too. Each day she went home alone to her huge apartment, made a solitary meal, watched television, and went off to bed. She prayed that God would teach her to be content with the life He'd given her. If Rachel were going to be alone, she needed to adjust to the fact, but when she lay in bed at night, and she was completely honest with herself and God, she would admit that she wanted a husband. She wanted someone to love who would love her back. She knew that she wasn't beautiful or charming or funny, but she did have a big heart, and she felt that there must be someone out there who could love her for who she was. Perhaps God would bring him into her life.

For now, she kept herself as busy as she could so that she didn't have to think about it. Aside from working nearly sixty hours a week, and attending church on Wednesdays and Sundays, she had begun to exercise whenever time and weather allowed. She started slowly by going for simple walks, just a few blocks, until she got too winded to continue. Then, as she gained strength, she signed up for an exercise class once a week at the gym Theresa had recommended to her.

She knew that Theresa practiced yoga religiously, and Rachel had enjoyed the stretches and poses, but the meditation that went along with it made her uncomfortable, so she switched to a spinning class. It was all the rage and everyone was talking about what a great workout it was. The first time she tried it, she tipped her bike over in front of a class of thirty students who laughed uproariously. The second time she tried it, she only lasted five minutes before having to leave, because she was gasping for breath.

In the end, she opted for the treadmill and found that she loved walking. She had met a friendly personal trainer one day who had given her some tips on resistance training and offered her one free session. She took him up on it, and the two developed an easy friendship that grew stronger each week. She really liked Greg, who was unconventionally handsome with chestnut dreadlocks covered in beads, big brown eyes, and several tattoos. Suddenly, she had more motivation to make it to the gym each week.

Rachel had asked for, and been given, permission to get a dog, so she had gone to the local Humane Society and adopted the ugliest mutt in the place.

He was a scruffy little black terrier with a curled up tail, giant eyebrows and beard, and the saddest eyes she'd ever seen. She instantly identified with him, and named him Henry.

She leashed him every Saturday and took him on long walks in Central Park, allowing him off his leash periodically to swim in the lake and chase the ducks. Rachel spoiled and lavished all her love on her new little man, allowing him to sleep at the foot of her bed and even heating his food up in the microwave each day. Since she lived in the office building where she worked, it was convenient for her to take breaks during the day and take him out for walks. She introduced him to Kevo, and the two were best buds instantly.

One Sunday morning as she was putting her makeup on for church, she suddenly realized that her loneliness had begun to lift. God had placed people in her life that loved her, that needed her, and that appreciated her for who she was. She had a furry little friend who thought she hung the moon, a man in her life that she felt completely comfortable with in spite of his good looks, and a boss who treated her with dignity and respect. Tears of gratitude filled her eyes, as she said a silent prayer of thanksgiving. God was so good!

As she stepped out of her apartment, locking up behind her, she was struck with an idea that wouldn't leave her alone. She knew that God had planted this seed, and her heart pounded with excitement.

She hurried down the sidewalk in search of her friend, and when he caught sight of her, his eyes lit up.

"Rachel! I didn't expect to see you today. Hey, I've been reading the Bible you gave me, and I have a lot of questions for you . . ." he started to say before she cut him off.

Broken

"Kevin, will you please come to church with me?" she asked him quietly, with hope shining in her eyes.

He paused and looked down at the sidewalk. He had been worried about this very thing. He knew Rachel had the biggest heart and that she cared for him and truly wanted to see him come to know God. He also knew that logically there would come a point in time that she would want him to come to church with her. He hadn't been in a setting with regular people like that in over twenty years. The very thought scared him to death. He knew he was dirty, his clothes were ragged, and he probably didn't smell so good. How could he let her down gently? The last thing he wanted to do was hurt his friend.

"Rachel, I know you mean well, but let's be honest here, ok? None of your friends are going to want me there. I know what I look like, and I know what I probably smell like. I can learn all about God right here on the street with the Bible you have given me. I don't need to go to church."

Rachel resisted the urge to defend her brothers and sisters in Christ, knowing full well that they not only would accept him, they would *embrace* him. Instead she turned once again to the word of God.

"Get out your Bible, please," she responded. "Find the book of Proverbs. It's going to take you awhile to memorize where all the books are found. In the meantime, just use the table of contents, that's what we all have to do in the beginning."

He held his Bible reverently and slowly flipped to Proverbs. He looked at her expectantly, as she gave him the address.

"It's chapter 27, verse 17. Will you please read it out loud?" she asked.

"As iron sharpens iron, so one person sharpens another," he read. He looked up at her quizzically.

"That means that as believers we gain wisdom, when we are surrounded by other believers. We need one another, we learn from one another, we rely on one another's strengths in our own weaknesses. I can't be the only Christian in your life, Kevin. You need a godly man that you can learn from. You need to be surrounded by others who will lift you up. I know you are comfortable with me, but I think you will find that if you give others a chance, they will surprise you. We don't judge people, we love them. It is what Jesus meant when he said, *'They will know you by the love you have for one another.'*

Please, just give it one shot. Come with me this morning and prove me wrong if you can. If you absolutely hate it, I won't ask you again, I promise." She looked him steadily in the eye, and he couldn't refuse her.

"Alright. Do we have time to stop by the shelter first? I can take a shower and shave . . ."

She said that if they hurried, they could still make it. She gave him a lift in the company car and avoided the disapproving looks directed at her by her driver. She would deal with him later.

They dropped him at the shelter, and she promised to be back in twenty minutes to pick him up. As he wheeled himself towards the entrance to the building, she directed her driver to take her to the nearest department store. She raced inside and quickly purchased several changes of clothing, underwear and socks, and an expensive bottle of cologne. She couldn't wait to see the expression on his face!

****

They entered the sanctuary together, Rachel pushing his wheelchair and Kevin looking dapper in his new clothes. She paused in the entryway and looked down at him. Seeing the outright fear in his eyes, she leaned down and hugged him hard, whispering words of comfort and encouragement in his ear.

He sat and took it all in. The songs of praise and worship touched him deeply, and he soaked in the words, as they floated up around him. Kevin gazed around the room and saw the people reaching up to the heavens with their arms outstretched, looks of adoration and devotion on their faces. He didn't know that anything like this even existed. He had not seen stares of condemnation aimed in his direction, but of love and acceptance. These people had reached out to him and had shown him compassion. It was all he could do not to cry.

After the service he was introduced to the Pastor and several members of the congregation who sincerely seemed interested in getting to know him. He suddenly realized that what he was feeling was *hope*. He hadn't known that emotion in so long that he hadn't recognized it at first.

Kevin was quiet and introspective on the drive back to the shelter, and Rachel was concerned that the whole experience had been too overwhelming for him. Cautiously, she asked him if he was feeling okay.

He took a deep breath to steady himself and responded, "Rachel, will you please bring me again next week?"

She was so overcome with joy that she hugged him tightly and said, "Of course I will! You enjoyed it then?"

He smiled sheepishly at her and nodded, not trusting himself to say another word. He didn't want to cry in front

of her, but he knew that it would come later. He couldn't
wait to get back to his regular spot on the sidewalk and curl
up with the good book. He still had many questions, but for
once, things seemed to fall into place for him. He felt like he
had a future, filled with good things.

****

The following Monday, Rachel called Thomas Allen's office
and scheduled an appointment with him. God had planted
another seed in her heart, and she needed his help. She had
spent the night before wrestling with this decision, but in the
end, knowing that it was something God wanted her to do,
she gave in.

She planned to ask for his help in tracking down Kevin's
family. She was scared of how he would react, but she knew
that God was a God of restoration and that the only way he
would ever fully heal was if he were to be reunited with his
wife and children. If they rejected him outright, they would
deal with that as it came. She trusted her Lord, however, and
knew that if this were the direction He was taking Kevin,
it would bring about only good things for him. It would be
a difficult and painful journey to be sure, but in the end, it
would be worth it.

She had no way of knowing that Thomas was already in the
process of tracking down her own family for a reunion, or
how very agonizing it would turn out to be.

Chapter Fifteen

Caitlyn Woodhouse had only recently arrived in the United States. She was a transplant of Jolly Old England, Attleborough in the county of Norfolk to be precise. Her entire life she had dreamed of moving to the U.S. and after graduating from the university, she made her dream a reality.

Tall and willowy, with light brown hair streaked with blonde and big grey-green eyes, Caitlyn was lovely and intelligent. She was a trained private investigator at the top of her field, when she accepted the position with Allen and Associates. She had just found her very own flat in downtown Manhattan. She hadn't grown accustomed to calling it an apartment or loft. To her it would always be a flat.

She was trying to squeeze in time to decorate on the weekends, but Thomas was keeping her busy with tracking down the long lost loved ones of his clients. For now, she slept on a mattress on the floor, and her dining room set consisted of a chair and cardboard box with a plank on top for a table. She hoped to slow down enough to make her little place into a home soon, yet she was content to be in this country working hard at making a new life for herself.

For the most part, Thomas had left her to her own devices, checking in with her once or twice a week to see how her progress was coming along. The search for the wife and children of Sergeant Kevin Monacucci was going to be much easier in the end than trying to find the biological parents of Rachel Jenkins. Adoption records were permanently sealed, as were the lips of the adoption agency's employees. She had tried bribing them with cash, threatening legal action, and even outright begging. She would have to switch tactics, if she had any hope of success. It was time to knuckle down and conduct an in person investigation.

She contacted Thomas in his office to request a travel advance, and then booked a flight to Des Moines, Iowa, where Rachel had been adopted by the Jenkins family. She packed her meager belongings quickly and rushed out the door to hail a cab. She hoped that when she arrived, she would find some answers.

Her flight landed at eleven p.m., and she was exhausted. She took a shuttle to the nearest hotel and checked in, falling asleep almost the second her head hit the pillow.

****

Theresa hadn't been feeling herself lately. She couldn't quite put her finger on it, and it didn't seem serious. She was just feeling a little off. She was tired all the time but that was nothing new. Her job required much of her, and she had little time to do things to relieve her stress.

She hired a contractor to redesign her massive apartment. At the top of her list was a bathroom where she could escape her thoughts and fears. She wanted nothing less than a sanctuary for her soul, and at this point in her life, money was no object. She put together a list of what was important to her.

She preferred an extravagant room with a huge tub that could hold 10 people, if she desired. She wanted to be able to *float* in the darned thing! She pictured the ancient bathing pools of Rome and added in tall marble columns. While she was at it, she asked the contractor to find an artist to paint tropical plants, flowers, and birds with a deep blue sea beyond. Theresa imagined soaking in the serenity and was anxious for them to get started. She needed a place to find peace of some sort.

The headaches began shortly after her construction started. At first she contributed them to the added stress of the workers in and out of her home at all hours. Then she chalked them up to the layers and layers of dust accumulating. Finally, after they persisted for more than a month, she broke down and made an appointment with her physician.

Theresa had always been as healthy as a horse. It was unlike her to be feeling so weak and unstable. The last time she had been to a doctor of any sort had been the disastrous week, after she'd had her abortion. Perhaps that was why she had put it off for so long: bad memories.

"Hi, Theresa," her doctor began, "what brings you in to see me today?"

"I just haven't been feeling myself lately. I'm so rundown, and I've been getting these awful headaches lately that aspirin doesn't seem to touch. I don't know if I'm just battling the flu, or stress, or what, so I figured I'd come in and see if you could help me figure it out."

He looked closely at her and saw the dark circles that had begun to form under her eyes, and the pale cast to her face. He'd only met her once before for a routine physical she'd had to obtain life insurance, but glancing quickly at her chart, he gathered that she didn't have a need to see a doctor. She hadn't been seen for anything other than that physical in almost ten years.

"Well, let's have a look." He started his examination, checking her vitals and probing her abdomen. He looked in her eyes and her ears and found no signs of infection. Her temperature was normal and so was her blood pressure.

"It doesn't look like the flu to me. I'm going to send you down to get some blood work done. For now, let's just keep an eye on it. I'll give you a prescription that should help with the headaches, and perhaps you can do your part by cutting back on your hours at work. Let's schedule you to come in next week to go over your results and see how things look then, shall we?"

She nodded, knowing there was no way she could cut back her hours. She was too much of a perfectionist control freak to allow anyone else to step in, and do her work for her. She would go to the herbal store, and pick up some vitamins to boost her immune system, and ramp up her exercise routine to relieve some of her stress. Add to that more meditation, and she was sure she'd be fine. In fact, now that she thought about it, that was probably all she needed. She'd skip the blood tests for now.

****

Caitlyn overslept and was cursing herself for not asking for a wakeup call at the front desk. Thankfully she was such a natural beauty that her morning routine was quick. She didn't need makeup and her hair dried naturally curly around her face, so she was able to shower, dress, and be out the door quickly.

Her first stop was the Compassion Project, the adoption agency the Jenkins' had used when they adopted Rachel. She breezed through the door and asked at the reception desk to speak with the agency's adoption coordinator.

The crisp and proper British accent that had served her so well in the past had become her downfall, however, as the receptionist instantly recognized her voice, and her eyes quickly narrowed.

"You're that investigator that keeps calling aren't you?" she demanded.

Caitlyn flushed and tried to come up with a witty response. Luckily she was quick on her toes and thought of a reasonable way out of the situation.

"I'm here to discuss adoption options. Is she available?" she retorted.

"Oh, uh, I'm sorry ma'am. You sounded like someone who has been calling and pestering us. I'll buzz her now." Caitlyn was enjoying rattling the girl a little.

She smiled and sat in the nearest chair to wait.

"Hello. My name is Evelyn Myers, how can I help you today?" A diminutive woman in a severe dark suit entered the room and held out her hand. She was professional in every way but kindness shone in her eyes.

"Is there a place we might speak privately?" Caitlyn asked demurely, hoping the woman wouldn't recognize the accent.

"Certainly, this way please." She opened the door to the hallway and led her to an office around the corner.

The two settled into chairs across from one another with a large mahogany desk between them. Caitlyn saw multiple framed photos of happy families hanging on each wall. Clearly this woman loved her job and her clients. Perhaps that was a door she should walk through . . .

"I do apologize for the deception, Mrs. Myers, but I've come out of desperation. My client is seeking to find her biological parents, and my phone calls have gone unheeded. I need to do everything I possibly can to help her be reunited with her family. I can see by the pictures on your walls that family is very important to you and that you would do anything for your clients, so, I'm prepared to make a deal with you. If you will just give them my contact information, and ask them to call me, I promise I will let that be the end of it. If they sincerely do not wish to be contacted, I will respect their wishes and let this go."

Evelyn pressed her lips firmly together and didn't say a word. Caitlyn could see the consternation on her face and almost hear the argument mounting in her head. Before she could present her case again, however, the woman took a deep breath and spoke.

"I wish it were that easy. I hesitate to inform you of this, but considering you do not know their actual names, I suppose it won't matter. Rachel's biological parents have both passed away. I'm sorry. I don't know what else can be done to help you. I wouldn't even have told you that much, but it seems to me that you simply will not go away otherwise."

Caitlyn's heart sank at the news. It wasn't what she had been expecting. She'd come with a considerable sum of money, ready to bribe her way into an address, a phone number, or a contact of some sort. She tried again.

"Surely there is extended family? A brother or sister? Aunts, uncles? Please, I've come so far. I assure you that money is no object if that is what it will take."

Evelyn was insulted and didn't pause to soften her words, "Young lady! I assure you that I have never once taken a bribe from anyone, and I'm not about to start now! If you will leave me your information, I will make some phone calls and see what, if anything, I can do to help you. Now, please excuse me, I have a huge workload to attend to."

With that Caitlyn had been dismissed. She thanked the woman and headed back out to her rental car. She was at a loss as to what to do next, so she headed to the library out of habit.

The Des Moines Public Library was a massive stone structure with three stories of shelved books, periodicals, and filing cabinets. One entire floor was dedicated to computers for research and microfiche machines loaded with local newspapers dated from the late 19th century. Caitlyn dropped her purse by her feet and dove into the articles beginning in 1965.

She found an article entitled *Mr. and Mrs. James Jenkins named Board Members of the Year by local Assemblies of God.* Caitlyn perked up instantly, as she read the short news piece and jotted down the name of the Pastor and address of the church.

Grabbing her purse and jacket she raced out the doors of the library, the words of the librarian trailing behind her, "Ma'am! There's no running in the library!"

****

Rachel was becoming very concerned with the health of her boss. Each day she seemed to drag herself to work and more than once she'd caught her massaging her temples at her desk. She had asked her multiple times if she were feeling ok, and each time she received a curt response. "I'm fine. Now, don't you have work to do?"

One Tuesday morning in early December she walked into Theresa's office to find her in the midst of a full-blown seizure. Terrified, she ran to the phone and dialed 911. Paramedics showed up a mere five minutes later with a stretcher. Theresa argued that she was fine and protested the trip to the hospital, but Rachel could be just as stubborn. With the full support of the rest of her staff, she won the argument, and Theresa was taken to Mount Sinai hospital for treatment.

"I'm right behind you," Rachel promised her. "I'll meet you at the hospital."

She arrived within moments of the ambulance and made her way straight to the emergency room. She asked at the nurse's desk for the name of the attending physician and told them that she was the personal assistant to Theresa Wakefield-Anderson. She also gave the nurse the name of her doctor, and his phone number so that he could be contacted right away. With that, she found a chair and waited for news.

Three hours later a fatigued looking doctor walked into the foyer and asked for Rachel. He told her that they had ordered some tests to be done, and in the meantime, Theresa was asking to see her.

She walked hesitantly into the hospital room not sure what sight would greet her. Theresa could be so temperamental, and she knew that the events of today would certainly have upset her apple cart. She was surprised, however, to see her sitting up in bed talking on the phone and issuing orders to her staff.

"I know!" she was barking. "Just get it done! I don't appreciate being questioned on this, and my health is no concern of yours. Now, do your job, or you'll be looking for a new one!" She slammed down the phone and turned to Rachel. As soon as her eyes settled on her, she began to calm down. What was it about this girl that always seemed to settle her nerves?

"How are you feeling?" she asked cautiously. "Have the doctors told you anything yet?"

Theresa sighed impatiently. She just wanted to go home. This whole thing was ridiculous. It had to be a fluke, and if she thought she could get away with it, she would have removed every monitor, gotten dressed, and taken herself back to the office.

"I'm fine. I keep telling everyone that it was just a result of being stressed and tired. If you will just let me go home, I will. I promise to take the rest of the day off to relax, really."

"No, you need to find out what caused this. Let them do the tests that they need to do to find out what's going on with you. Hide it from everyone else if you like, Theresa, but we've known each other long enough that you can't hide it from me. I've seen the fatigue on your face and the headaches that have been chasing you for weeks. What happened today was a warning that you need to get help! I'm a lot bigger than you, and I'm prepared to bar the door to prevent you from leaving, if I need to."

She couldn't help but admire Rachel's spunk. She tried not to show it, but she was so thankful that at least one person in her life really cared for her. She didn't want to cross the professional boundaries she had put in place, but this girl had crept into her heart and set up camp there. She honestly felt like this girl was the only family she had now.

"Alright, alright, you win. I'll stay and get the tests done if only to prove you wrong. After today though, once they decide there's nothing wrong with me, I don't want to discuss it any more. Understood?" she smiled softly at her assistant.

"Fine. I can agree to that. How about something from the cafeteria? A cup of coffee perhaps?" Rachel was having a difficult time with all of this and needed something to occupy her, as they waited.

"Sure, that would be nice. Thanks."

She hurried out of the room, and in her absence, the doctor came and took Theresa to get a cat scan and MRI.

****

"I'm here to see the Pastor, if he's available."

Caitlyn had found the little church on the outskirts of town, nestled in the hills. She wandered around until someone pointed her in the direction of the church offices. Now she stood before the church secretary and hoped that she hadn't wasted a trip out here.

"One moment," she smiled up at Caitlyn and buzzed the Pastor in his office. As the phone rang, she put her hand over the mouthpiece and asked for her name.

"Pastor, there is a Caitlyn Woodhouse here to see you. Do you have a few minutes? Certainly I will let her know."

She turned to back to Caitlyn and let her know that he'd be out shortly to meet with her.

Pastor Afrika Bol stepped into the foyer, and Caitlyn tried to hide her shock. She had expected something entirely different than the tall, handsome, African man standing before her.

He laughed out loud and said, "Don't be embarrassed. I get that reaction a lot. I'm Afrika, but most people just call me Pastor. It's nice to meet you. Shall we go into my office to chat? I hope you don't mind, but church policy dictates that we leave the door open for propriety sake."

Caitlyn followed him into his office and took a seat opposite him. He told her a little about himself, clearly trying to make her feel at ease.

"I am from Kenya, and I came to this country as a missionary. I fell in love with the people here and attended a small Bible college to obtain a degree in theology. Now here I am, far from my home, but always with the people of God. It has truly been a blessing. I am not the first Pastor of this church. I am preceded by several other wonderful men and women who served this body, but enough about me. Please tell me what brings you here my friend."

She was startled from her reverie. Pastor Afrika's melodious voice had lulled her into a faraway land of desert sands and exotic animals. She had found herself oddly attracted to this man, with his rich ebony skin and brilliant white smile. He fairly oozed peace and joy, and she was simply enjoying his company.

She told him of her trip here from New York in search of the birth parents of Rachel Jenkins. How she had discovered, much to her dismay, that they had both died years earlier and how she had come to him to learn more of her adoptive parents, Rose and James.

He looked pensive as she spoke, listening intently to her every word and nodding. Finally, he spoke, and what he said caught her off guard.

"Do you, my friend, know Jesus?" he asked her pointedly.

"Uh . . . I know who he is, if that's what you mean," she stammered out.

"I wonder if you do. Do you know of His rich blessings, or of how He laid down His life for you? Are you aware that He has numbered the days of your life, that He has never forgotten you, and that He waits eagerly for you to come to Him? Do you know that you are here by divine appointment?" he challenged her.

She had never met anyone like him in her life. She was young, but she had been preached at before on many occasions. This was different somehow. She didn't feel like she was merely a potential convert for this man. She was entranced by his words, and they held the promise of truth in them.

"I don't really know what you mean . . ." she managed.

"Caitlyn, allow me some time to share with you the greatest story every told, written in blood by the Lover of your soul, and I, in return for your patience, will answer any questions you may have regarding the Jenkins family, as long as it is in my power to do so."

She found herself nodding in agreement, and thus began a three-hour session that turned into a week of meetings every day. This initial contact with the Pastor eventually evolved into a courtship, as she found herself not only falling in love with the Savior but also with His servant.

Chapter Sixteen

Sweat poured down her face as she ran at a pace of four miles per hour. Trying to outrun her demons, she supposed. She flew past the dog walkers, the children playing in the grass, and the leisurely couples enjoying a late fall picnic in Central Park. Theresa had come to a point where she was desperately seeking a peace that had escaped her.

Feet pounded the pavement, as her heart pounded in her chest. She had an appointment the following afternoon with yet another specialist. During her hospital stay, her doctor had found a tumor on her brain. He immediately had her undergo a biopsy, and Theresa had told no one. He then set up an appointment with an oncologist to go over her results. Knowing that an oncologist was a cancer specialist, she had instantly gone into full blown denial.

She'd been unable to sleep, to work, to even hold a conversation with anyone, so she took the rest of the week off from work. For a woman who had never missed a day of work, since the inception of *Her Wicked Ways*, this was unheard of. Theresa simply needed a reprieve, time to think, and to be alone.

Was she finally coming to a point of restitution for her sins? Was God in his heaven going to strike her down now? She couldn't escape the thoughts of what she had done to her life, her marriage, her child. All her money, fame, and success couldn't save her. It didn't bring her the joy she had thought it would. She would give every penny, every article in *Vogue*, and every flashing light bulb at every fashion show to have a chance to start over and do it right.

She kept hoping this was some awful nightmare and that an angel was going to wake her and tell her she'd been given an opportunity to go back and do things differently. She wondered where Stephen was, and if he was okay. She hoped desperately that he'd fallen in love with a good girl who would give him the life that she had stolen from him. She had thought about calling him and ultimately rejected the idea. Although she was frantic for someone to talk to that understood her and knew her, it would have been selfish to call him, when her life was falling apart. She had destroyed their life together, and she knew she had to move on.

She took a deep breath as she ran and made a firm decision not to think about all of this again, until after she met with the doctor. Perhaps the tumor would be benign after all. She turned her thoughts to the hunt for Rachel's parents. To date, Thomas had informed her that his private investigator had hit a brick wall. Rachel's biological parents had passed away. She was diligently searching for any remaining relatives but hope was diminishing that they would be found.

Theresa devised a plan to subtly draw details about Rachel's adoption from her. She might even hold clues that she was not aware of. Surely her parents had told her something of her adoption, where she'd been born, or even the circumstances that led her parents to give her up.

She made a mental note to invite Rachel to dinner and get her talking about her life growing up. The thought cheered her. Theresa loved to cook and with Stephen gone, she no longer had anyone to cook for. That, coupled with the fact that Rachel's presence always calmed her, gave her something to look forward to.

She had been a vegetarian for so long, but with her very existence hanging in the balance, her heart and soul was suddenly craving a filet mignon. How long had it been, since she'd eaten meat or even seafood? Suddenly her stomach growled, and she laughed out loud. She slowed her pace to a quick jog and started to jot down a grocery list in her mind.

****

Rachel dressed in her nicest cocktail dress, which was a gift from Theresa last year for Christmas. It was the same deep chocolate brown of her eyes and had ivory lace edging, falling at her knees in creamy swirls of silk. She didn't normally wear dresses, as she was very modest and most dresses created by *Her Wicked Ways* were extremely revealing. This one didn't show too much skin and discreetly covered her décolletage. She thought that perhaps Theresa had this gown designed just for her. It wasn't her normal style, and she hadn't seen it in any of the catalogs. She added a sparkling pearl and crystal necklace with matching earrings and a touch of lip gloss.

When she looked in the mirror, she was actually quite pleased with her appearance. Her daily trips to the gym, and the constant encouragement from Greg, had helped her to lose almost 40 pounds. She had realized in the last two months that she was following so hard after God, and his will for her life, that food was no longer a stronghold for her. Instead of loving food and serving God, she loved God and enjoyed food only when she was physically hungry for it, and she enjoyed it in much smaller quantities.

Once again Rachel turned back and praised her God for his goodness. She couldn't remember a time in her life, when she was happier. She had a life filled with His blessings: a job she adored, good friends and fellowship, an interesting and attractive man who seemed to really like her, and all of her financial needs were met.

Although she had been working for *Her Wicked Ways* for
nearly five years now, this was the first time she'd been
invited to dinner with her boss. She couldn't help being a
little apprehensive as to the reason for the invitation. Was
she doing something wrong? Was she about to be let go?
She said a quick prayer on her way out the door, asking
for God's protection and wisdom. She knew that she could
easily find work elsewhere, if she needed to, but she had
come to truly love and respect her boss and looked forward
to a long career with the company.

She took the elevator to the top floor of the building. Theresa's
home could hardly be called an apartment. At nearly 6,000
square feet, it took up the entire floor of the building. Still in
the midst of ongoing construction, Rachel was in awe of the
work that had been done already. She made excuses to use
the bathroom constantly, because it was extravagant and so
lovely that she hated to walk out the door. She stared in awe
at the columns, the lavish tub, and the hand painted artwork
on the walls. She thought she would like to have something
like this in her own apartment one day.

That thought was immediately followed by dollar signs in
her head. How much money could she give to missionaries
instead? Why spend that much on yourself when the things
of this world are so temporary? The money would be better
spent trying to share the love of God with a lost and dying
world. With a sigh, she turned off the light and headed back
into the kitchen.

Theresa was pouring herself a glass of wine. Rachel noticed
her hands trembling as she poured. She thought back to that
awful day at the hospital and wondered about Theresa's
health.

"Water is fine, if you don't mind," she responded to the offer
of the intoxicating beverage.

The ladies took their drinks and sat on the luxurious mahogany leather couches. Theresa could see that Rachel was a little nervous and tried to make her guest feel comfortable. She turned on some soft jazz music and lit a few candles on the hearth. She began to talk about her childhood, and what it had been like growing up in a small town in Iowa.

She noticed Rachel perking up and a spark of interest in her eyes. Good. She was hoping it would get her to open up about her own life. She continued, sharing the pain of losing her siblings and her parents. She talked about her dreams of becoming a designer and of meeting Stephen in college. The one thing she didn't talk about was her baby, and how that fateful decision had shattered her marriage.

Rachel was a thoughtful, inquisitive girl with a natural love for people. Her heart broke for Theresa and for all the things she'd been through.

"I had no idea you were from Iowa! You live such a glamorous life here in Manhattan that I guess I just assumed you came from Los Angeles or maybe Chicago. You know I was raised in Des Moines, so we were practically neighbors growing up! What a crazy coincidence," she smiled at Theresa, thrilled in the knowledge that they had something in common.

"No, Bayfield is nowhere near L.A. It's just a tiny little township in the middle of nowhere, filled with good people though. There are churches on every block and everyone knows each other there. I miss it sometimes. I get nostalgic once in awhile and I think about going back, but my life is here. What about you Rachel? Tell me about your childhood, your family. We work together every day, and I know so little about you."

Rachel thought about her parents and felt that familiar pang in her chest. She blinked the tears away rapidly and set her glass on the coffee table. She had prayed for an opportunity to share Christ with her friend and mentor. Perhaps this was her moment.

"I've told you I was adopted. My parents tried for years to have children and were never able to, so they signed up with an adoption agency and within six months were told they had found a little girl that had been given up. Apparently my biological parents are both gone. I don't know much about them, other than some sort of tragedy happened, and they were forced to give me up.

I had no siblings, but I had two parents who loved me desperately, and they raised me in a Christian home. They taught me the love of a Savior who died for me. They lived it out in every area of their lives. In fact, they are now missionaries to China. They smuggled in Bibles because the Chinese government has made it illegal to be a Christian. They live in hiding and meet in secret. I don't know where they are now, and it breaks my heart, not knowing if they are even alive. I pray for them constantly and have to trust God that He is doing what's best for them."

Theresa was fascinated in spite of herself. She had known many Christians, including her own parents. They had always made her at the least very uncomfortable and sometimes downright angry, yet Rachel had never had that affect on her. She was simply living out her faith. Theresa felt safe with her and for the first time in her life, actually wanted to know more. There had never been a time when she wanted to express her concerns or questions, because her pride had always gotten in the way.

Rachel continued to speak about her life, sharing her painful stories of childhood abuse by her peers and how ultimately

God had used it to prod her into action. She explained that she had forgiven those who had hurt her years ago and that she had come to accept herself and become comfortable in her own skin. She told Theresa that she was a child of the King, and she believed firmly that she was beautiful in his eyes.

Theresa thought she was indeed beautiful, inside and out. She had managed to convince her to start taking some care with her appearance and credited herself with nudging her in the direction of the gym. She still intended to get her to a dermatologist and a salon for much needed hair help, but she sensed she had to work slowly on these issues. She was content seeing her lose some weight for now.

Her thoughts turned back to the comments Rachel had made, almost in passing, about her biological parents. She spoke up in pursuit of that very topic.

"So how did you come to know that your birth parents had passed away? Did your mom and dad tell you about them?"

"Yeah, I found out I was adopted when I was about seven years old. I was flipping through a photo album and came across a picture of them holding me in front of an adoption agency. I may have been young at the time, but it didn't take long for me to put two and two together, so I confronted them and they told me the whole story, or at least what they knew. I guess my birth mom was killed at a very young age, and my father was responsible. He was sent to prison but died in an attack by a fellow inmate about ten years later. That's all I know."

Theresa stared at her in stunned silence. Goose bumps broke out on her arms, and she shivered involuntarily. It couldn't be. No, it had to be just a strange coincidence. She tucked the information away to analyze at a later date. She would follow up with Thomas on this information, and perhaps it would turn up a lead.

They continued to chat amiably, while dinner cooked, and Theresa found herself asking more about how Rachel had come to believe in Christ. She must have been such a pathetic little thing, chubby and homely, with other kids picking on her. How could she not blame God for her troubles?

Rachel spoke of a God who had given her hope for a future, who had made her feel lovely in spite of her acne scars and large frame, and who had whispered of his faithfulness in her ear. She told Theresa about her friend, Tiffany, and the transformation that had overcome her, and about her homeless friend, Kevin. She talked about how God had given her a confidence that this world, no matter how it tried to kick her while she was down, couldn't take from her.

The timer on the stove chimed, and the women moved to the table to eat. Rachel's stomach growled loudly at the sight and smell of the feast set before her. She was completely astounded to see not only filet mignon, but also jumbo garlic sautéed shrimp, linguine tossed with sun dried tomato pesto, crispy garlic bread, and a fresh tossed salad topped with olives and cracked pepper. She dug in with wild abandon, but not before stopping to ask if she could pray over their meal. Theresa whole-heartedly agreed and for the first time, felt completely at ease with another praying in her presence.

"Lord God, thank you so much for this incredible bounty you have given us. I thank you for the friendship with Theresa that you have given me. I pray, Father, that you would keep her safe in the palm of your hand and that you would breathe your breathe of life into her. Bestow upon her your peace that passes all understanding and

show her who you truly are. Thank you, God, for loving us so! We pray these things in your magnificent name, Jesus, Amen."

As Theresa lay her head on the pillow that night, her mind wouldn't stop racing. Was this the girl that Sara had died to save? Could she have worked with Rachel all these years and not known they were related? What about God? Was she wrong about Him all this time? Rachel had painted a very different picture of Him than she had ever known. She had a difficult time sleeping, but once she finally surrendered, she found a peace settling over her heart.

****

Rachel was sitting on the concrete with Kevin, reading the Bible. He had found a passage that had captivated him and was reading it to her now.

"This is found in John 15:13. "Greater love has no one than this: to lay down one's life for one's friends." That's what Jesus did for me? It is so incredible to think that thousands of years, before I was born, this was the plan to save me. I have read the account of the crucifixion as well. Jesus didn't just die, he died unjustly, after being wrongly accused and convicted. He was tortured, beaten, and scourged, the beard literally ripped from his face, while they spit on him and mocked him, yet he was God in the flesh and could have called down millions of angels to rescue him and destroy his accusers. He faced it all, knowing it was the only way to save us from an eternity separated from him. It breaks my heart, and at the same time gives me this incredible hope."

As he spoke, tears ran freely down his cheeks, and he looked at Rachel with pure wonder. She thought back to the moment, when she had accepted Jesus as her savior and goose bumps rose on her flesh. This was his day of reckoning, and once again, God was allowing her to take part in his incredible plan for Kevin. What an honor!

"Kevin, you have had the truth revealed to you. Jesus said that we would know the truth, and the truth would set us free. He also said that He is the way, the truth, and the life and that nobody gets to the Father except through Him. That literally means that He wants to set you free. He wants to set you free from your sin, all the bad decisions you have ever made, your guilt, and your shame. He wants to give you a new life now and an eternity with Him in heaven later. You just need to take another step toward him, Kevin. Are you ready to walk with him? You simply need to pray and repent, thank him for saving you, and ask him to show you how to follow him."

She looked steadily at him and saw no hesitation whatsoever. He nodded eagerly and held his hands out to her. She grasped them firmly in her own and said, "Ok, repeat after me . . ." She prayed with him and felt the presence of the Holy Spirit in their midst. Crying tears of joy, she wrapped her arms around him and hugged him hard.

They sat chatting awhile longer, and he told her stories of his time in Vietnam, explaining that since he began reading the Bible, God had showed him all the times He had intervened in his life. The land mine he stepped on should have killed him. In fact, there were many episodes of bullets whizzing by, inches from his head, or booby traps that he narrowly missed stepping on. He was recalling a story for her of a brave young soldier he'd once known that had taken over his guard duty in camp one night so that he could get some much-needed rest.

"This has haunted me for years, but God is giving me a peace about it. He was just a young private, quiet, but sincere and dedicated. His name was PFC Coleman

Wakefield, and he was always willing and eager to do what was required of him. So, one night when I was so exhausted I couldn't think straight, he offered to keep watch for me.

A bunch of young marines had gotten drunk and out of control, and Private Wakefield stepped into a situation that he never could have been prepared for. He happened upon those cretins attacking a Vietnamese girl that couldn't have been older than twelve or thirteen. He managed to take down three or four of them, before one of them took his life, but he died to save her! I found out later on that he died with her small handmade wooden cross in his hand.

Even though I never considered Jesus before now, I always knew he died a man of God. Now, reading this scripture about a man laying down his life for his friends is so bittersweet for me," he finished.

Briefly the name Wakefield flitted through her mind and jolted her. Then she dismissed the thought immediately. It was a fairly common last name, and although Theresa had mentioned losing her older brother in the war, she was almost positive that it must be a coincidence.

She said her goodbyes to her friend and headed back to her apartment. Henry must be pacing by now and would need a nice brisk walk. Then, she thought with a happy smile, she would go see Greg.

Chapter Seventeen

Caitlyn was sitting under a massive oak tree with Afrika, eating a turkey sandwich and watching the leaves as they fell to the ground. He was talking to her about rebirth.

"Look at the leaves as they change colors and drift to the ground. The tree becomes dry and brittle in the fall, losing its beautiful leaves and becoming barren. That's what we are like before Christ comes into our lives. We are like walking dead men, until He comes along and breathes new life into us. Then, just like the tree sprouts beautiful fresh green leaves in the spring, we come alive with Him. We are reborn! That is what he wants to do in your life, Caitlyn.

Do you ever think what life would be like for you if you didn't have to live a dull existence? Can you imagine not fearing the end? I tell you that I can stand in the face of death and not be afraid. I know that my Savior waits for me and that He has built a beautiful mansion for me in heaven with His nail scarred hands. I know that there is a place where I will feel no pain, no guilt, and no shame. I walk in this freedom now even! I want you to know what that is like."

She looked into his kind, beautiful eyes and saw evidence of his words there. She had never known a man to exude such peace and joy. It was so intoxicating that she wanted it for herself.

"Show me how," she responded.

The two prayed together quietly, and Caitlyn knew that she had found the new life Afrika had spoken of so eloquently.

It had been hard for her to focus on the job at hand, once she had met him. She had in fact spent two days with him, reading the Bible and asking every question she had ever had about Christianity. It wasn't until the third day that she reluctantly admitted, she needed to get back to work.

She called Thomas and reported that she'd been unable to find out anything more about Rachel's biological family. He insisted she stay for another two weeks, telling her that he would deposit another $5,000 into her bank account to cover all of her expenses.

Afrika had explained that while he had heard of the Jenkins missionaries, he hadn't had the pleasure of meeting them. They were a part of the church for many years, before he came along, and they had left for China three years before he became Pastor there.

He did, however, receive very infrequent letters from them due to their extreme circumstances. He agreed to write them and ask if they would be willing to help Rachel find her birth family. He warned Caitlyn that the likelihood of a letter coming back any time soon was not good. It had been two years since he heard any word from them at all. To be perfectly honest, he didn't know if they were in prison or even still alive at this point.

She thanked him, and they made plans to get together again soon for more study. Caitlyn really hoped that he shared the feelings that were starting to grow in her. She was too scared to bring it up, because he could so easily crush her. She knew next to nothing about him, really, but somehow she was completely in awe of him. He was so beautiful. He loved deeply and showed it to the people around him with no hesitation. She had watched him with his congregation and knew that it was sincere.

He surprised her one day by telling her that he didn't believe in dating. Before she could object to the ridiculous statement, he continued.

"Dating is a modern concept that makes no biblical sense. When you date, you are just trying people out like you would try on clothes. You try first one, then another, to see which one fits best. The Bible endorses what's called courting.

We as believers know that sex outside of marriage is not what God wants for us. You see, when most people talk about dating, it almost inevitably leads to sex. Courting inevitably leads to marriage. You go into it with the thought that this person you are spending time with is the one you plan to marry.

You remain friends and get to know one another. You learn to keep yourselves out of compromising positions, and you keep Christ at the center of your relationship. Then, once you know that this person is the one you want to marry, you declare your love - not a moment before. In doing this, you glorify God, because you acknowledge that He alone brings people together for the purpose of marriage.

Since coming to this country, I have noticed that people throw the word love around too much. 'I love this movie!' or 'I love pizza,' or 'I love my boyfriend.' It is all so meaningless!"

Her head was spinning at his words. She'd never heard anything like that. She herself was a virgin, but it was only because her schooling, and then her career, had always come first. Until now, she hadn't ever met anyone that gave her any pause to slow down enough to consider a relationship.

"So, why are you telling me all this?" she asked him slowly.

His big beautiful smile was her answer. "Because, dear one, I want to court you."

Her heart was pounding in her chest at his words, and she smiled back at him. He was her teacher, she his pupil. He talked about spending time together, doing things that would glorify God. She asked him questions about courting, and he gave her several books to read. This was all like an exciting new adventure for her. She had found God, and she had found a man of God, when all she'd been looking for was a family for Rachel.

The Lord works in mysterious ways, she thought.

****

Greg was acting really strange today, Rachel thought. He would start to say something to her, then close his mouth abruptly and turn beet red. It was odd behavior for him to say the least. He was normally the most mellow, easygoing man she'd ever met.

Finally she blurted out, "What is wrong with you today? It seems like you really need to tell me something. I don't bite you know."

He grinned sheepishly back at her and took a deep breath.

"I was, um, wondering if I could, uh . . . take you to dinner or something," he muttered, while staring fixedly at his feet.

Taken aback, she gaped at him in stunned silence.

"Never mind. Forget I said anything. Let's do another set of curls, and then you are done for the day."

"No! Wait! Of course I would love to go out with you. You just caught me off guard. I mean, I just didn't think that you could be interested in someone like me," she hastily amended.

"Someone like you? Are you kidding me? Someone funny and intelligent? Someone with a big heart and gorgeous eyes? Why wouldn't I want to go out with you?"

Her heart sang at his words. They made plans for dinner that Friday night, and she literally skipped out of the gym, heading for home. The moment she walked in the door, she picked up the phone to call Theresa.

"Hey, you know how you've been bugging me to get my hair done at that fancy upscale salon of yours? I think I'm finally ready. You won't believe this, but I have a date on Friday, so I need your help!"

"YES!" came the shrieked reply, "Oh, I've been waiting for this day to come. Please, let me do your makeup and put together an outfit for you?"

She laughed at the enthusiasm and they agreed to head over to *Vain*, Theresa's salon, right after work the next night. She was about to become Cinderella, and she couldn't wait!

****

Afrika was sold out for God. Caitlyn was learning what that meant, as she got to know him more. He ate, drank, and breathed the word of God and invited Christ into every area of his life. When she would speak to him of her worries for their future because of the distance between them, he told her that God says they should not worry about anything but instead pray about everything.

So that's what they did. They prayed that God would overcome any obstacles they had, while they were getting to know one another and that he would open doors for them to be together if that was His will for them.

She continued to search the newspapers at the library for stories about the Jenkins family or any hint of Rachel's parentage. She had started searching newspapers of outlying areas as well. There were a multitude of small towns around Des Moines, and they all had their own small paper. It was a daunting task to be sure, but it gave her an excuse to stay in town for a while longer.

She had been in Des Moines for nearly two weeks, when she received a call from Thomas with some interesting news for her. It seemed that Theresa, his client, had been pumping Rachel for information on her birth parents. She had told Thomas that Rachel's birth mother had died in some sort of tragic accident and that the father had been jailed as the perpetrator.

Excitement surged in her veins now as she searched the newspapers for articles from that time frame. Surely a story like this had to have made the paper! She spent four hours reading article after article to no avail. Wearily wiping at her tired eyes, she gathered her things and headed to find the librarian.

"Hi, I'm an investigator from New York in town, trying to track down the birth parents of a client. I've been searching your newspaper database for articles on an incident that happened approximately 25 years ago in which a pregnant young girl was killed in some sort of tragic incident and her boyfriend sent to jail for the crime. Can you tell me if that database includes every local newspaper?" she asked the petite bookish librarian, already fearing bad news.

"Well, all but one. The Bayfield Press burned to the ground in 1989, and with it, went most of their archived newspapers. Other than that, it's a most complete collection," she replied crisply, obviously proud of their work.

"I see. Thank you so much for your time. I'm sure I will be back at some point for more research."

Caitlyn frowned in consternation, as she drove back to her hotel. She called Afrika to ask for his advice, knowing what he would probably say, even as she asked the question.

"Let us devote the matter to prayer, shall we?"

The two of them prayed together over the phone and made plans for a trip to Bayfield that weekend. Afrika had shown so much interest in her work that she thought he might enjoy the process of tracking people and information down. It was about a three-hour drive from Des Moines, and they decided to make a day of it.

She pulled in front of the church offices at 8:00 a.m. sharp, and he jogged out to the car, with his brilliant white smile flashing at her. *Wow,* she thought, *the mere sight of him makes my heart jump almost out of my chest!*

They pulled out onto the highway headed for Bayfield and a wonderful, leisurely day together. The two of them made several stops on the way at roadside fruit stands and flea markets. They ate lunch at a tacky little diner called *Betty's Bistro*. Arriving in Bayfield at noon, they headed straight for the chamber of commerce.

"Hi, I am in town trying to track down the owners of the Bayfield Press. I understand the building burned down several years ago, but I'm hoping you might be able to tell me where to find them, if they are still around?" Caitlyn asked the kind elderly man behind the desk.

"Certainly can young lady! Why, that's my own nephew, Saul. Let me jot down his address for you, but, you should know that the years have been hard on him. He's suffering from Alzheimers," the old man said sadly. "I just don't know how much he remembers about his days at the paper."

Dejected at the news, Caitlyn and Afrika made their way back out to the car. Caitlyn was beginning to wonder if she would ever find anything on Rachel's parents. It almost seemed as if the project had been doomed from day one.

They pulled into the driveway of a dilapidated old mobile home and parked the car. Caitlyn knocked loudly on the door and was surprised to see a man of no more than 45 answer the door. This couldn't be Saul. He was nowhere near old enough to have Alzheimer's.

"Yes?" he looked from Caitlyn to Afrika, puzzled by their presence.

Caitlyn explained why they were there and asked if he might recall the incident that had happened so many years before. He thought hard and said that it sounded familiar.

"Where are my manners? Won't you come in?" He opened the door wider and invited them into his tiny home. They stepped over and between stacks and stacks of old yellowing newspapers and around the myriad of cats that lounged in every nook and cranny of the house.

"Now, let's see. I have papers that go back some forty years, to a time before I was even old enough to hold a job," he chuckled. "It might take awhile for me to look through them all. I just haven't gotten around to cataloging them."

Caitlyn and Afrika offered to help, and the three of them got started on the massive task at hand. Two hours later, Afrika held a newspaper out to her with a title on the front page in all capital letters, "LOCAL YOUTH JAILED IN SUSPICIOUS DEATH OF GIRLFRIEND."

Her heart jumped in her chest, as she clutched the newspaper. She turned to Saul and asked if she could take it to the nearest copy store and get some copies made. He looked at her in confusion and asked who she was.

Caitlyn and Afrika looked at one another in amazement. They had been in his home for hours now, and suddenly he was completely fearful of them. She spoke to him slowly and with a soothing voice.

"Saul, we met a few hours ago. I'm here doing some research to find the birth family of a client who has been adopted. You said we could look back through your old papers."

"Oh, yeah right. I remember you now," he said without much conviction. Clearly he was embarrassed and trying to cover it up.

Thinking quickly, Caitlyn wrote her name down on a piece of paper with a bit of information on herself and what she had borrowed from him. She added the phone number at her hotel and an estimated time that they would be back with the paper, just in case he forgot who they were again after they left.

They departed in short order and headed for the Kinkos up the street. Afrika read the details in the article to her, as she drove.

"Police arrested eighteen-year-old Morgan Fitzhugh, a.k.a. 'Spider,' this morning at his home on Brinky Avenue, after being treated at a local hospital for injuries sustained during the altercation with officers. He is being charged with murder in the suspicious death of a minor whose name is not being released at this time.

The police spokesman did report that the victim was seven months pregnant at the time of her death. She was rushed to the hospital, and at this time, her infant child is in critical condition at Bayfield Memorial Hospital.

Fitzhugh's parents were not available for comment, but the neighbor, John Williams, who reported the incident, had much to say. 'I heard a loud commotion and went outside to see what was going on. I just kept hearing muffled screams and a loud thumping sound coming from next door and figured I better call the cops. I told 'em they better bring an ambulance too.'

The police refused to comment further on an ongoing investigation but promised that a press conference would be held later on this week."

Caitlyn replied that it sounded promising, and if they could track down hospital records, they might be able to find out how old the girl was, when she'd been adopted. She also planned to make a trip to the local police department or maybe the courthouse to see about finding Fitzhugh's arrest record.

They quickly made copies of the newspaper and headed back to Saul's house. He answered their knock again, holding her handwritten note in one hand, and acted like he recognized them.

They thanked him profusely for his help and drove quickly to the police department to see what else they could learn, before they had to head back home. Afrika had to make some last minute adjustments to his sermon notes for the next morning, so they couldn't stay too much longer.

The Sergeant behind the front desk was polite but clearly not interested in helping them. He redirected them to the courthouse and told them to have a nice day. It was four o'clock by now, and the two were exhausted by the day's events. One more stop, and they'd head back.

"Oh sure, I remember that," the clerk said. "I went to school with Spider. He was so cute but such a bad boy. All the girls were either in love with him or terrified of him. Glad I kept my distance, let me tell you! He was a bad seed from the get go but that business with the Wakefield girl was awful. She was so young and so pretty! She could have been a model, you know. Let me go see if I can find those records for you." She waddled off to the back of the storage room and was gone for nearly thirty minutes before reappearing with her supervisor in tow.

Caitlyn sensed there was a problem of some sort immediately by the look of humiliation on the clerk's face. She was beet red and staring at her feet.

"I'm so sorry, but our closing time is four o'clock and Gertrude here seems to forget herself sometimes. I'm afraid you'll have to come back another time. Thank you." The staunch older woman looked down her nose at the young couple, and they realized they had been dismissed.

Caitlyn was so disappointed and tried in vain to persuade her to make and exception in this one instance, but she was up against a formidable foe that was apparently a stickler for the rules. Sighing, she gave up, and they headed back for Des Moines.

She had so enjoyed spending the day with Afrika. On the drive home, he had told her stories from his childhood growing up in Kenya and of his parents and sixteen siblings. Her head spun with the knowledge that he had such a large family, but he assured her that was completely normal where he was from. He talked of his customs and spoke to her in his native tongue. She was enthralled with him, and he with her.

He asked her about her own upbringing in England and wanted to know every detail of her life. He told her that he thought she was beautiful and that she had a sweet and gentle spirit. When he spoke, his words were almost poetic or lyrical. She felt like the luckiest woman alive.

She pulled back into the church parking lot, and he gave her a hug goodnight, before walking back to the tiny parsonage where he lived on the property. She had begun to understand that courtship was more about getting to know one another, learning about their strengths and weaknesses, and growing together in Christ, than it was about any kind of physical intimacy. Afrika taught her that it would keep them safe from temptation, and should they decide in the end to marry, it would make the wedding night even more precious.

He even confessed to her that he had waited for the woman that God wanted for him, and he had never been with anyone. She was amazed that in this day and age two people could both enter a marriage as virgins. She thought about it, though, and was deliriously happy to know that they would experience love the way that God had originally intended, and that she wouldn't have to compete with the memory of another woman.

****

Rachel stared at her own reflection in amazement. Theresa had not allowed her to open her eyes for the entire process, which took two hours. She'd had her hair cut, colored and styled. While her color processed, her makeup was expertly applied by Theresa and supervised by a professional makeup artist. When she was finally allowed to open her eyes, a completely different woman stared back at her.

Her hair had been cut into a sleek, sexy, shoulder length bob with golden blonde highlights. It shimmered brightly and swung about her shoulders like silk. Her big brown eyes popped with the subtle shades of brown and beige that had been applied. Somehow they'd worked their magic on her and been able to cover the worst of her acne scars. Coupled with her new weight loss, the hair and makeup made her feel like a fairy princess waking from a bad dream.

"Wait! We aren't done yet. If you head back into the restroom, there is a surprise waiting for you in the garment bag."

She hopped out of her chair and headed to the back of the salon. Her head felt lighter without the long dank hair holding her down. She even caught a few admiring gazes cast in her direction, as she walked by. *Well, that's a first!*

Entering the restroom, her heart banged in her chest, as she recognized the familiar insignia of the *Her Wicked Ways* trademark on the bag. Slowly she pulled the zipper down and held her breath.

It was a silky black, off-the-shoulder blouse, with metal studs on the cuffs, and a pair of dark wash jeans with rhinestone embellished pockets. Inside the bag she also found long dangly earrings, a leather cuff bracelet, and a pair of black leather high-heeled boots. Never in her life had she been able to wear a normal pair of jeans.

She had always been forced to wear what her mother called "big girl pants." They had elastic on the waist and no pockets. They were so ugly that she had resorted to skirts and dresses years ago or, at the very least sweat pants. These jeans looked way too small to her. She tried them on anyway and was surprised to see that they fit like a glove!

Rachel put the rest of the ensemble on excitedly, and when she was done, she closed her eyes, took a deep breath, and opened them in front of the mirror. She gasped out loud. Gone was the frumpy little wallflower that hid from cameras and mirrors. In its place was a gorgeous young woman about to start a new journey and not afraid in the least.

The outfit was perfect. It was attractive without being revealing, and it showed off her new and hard won assets. She had to admit that she really looked good! When she left the restroom, she didn't just walk, she *strutted*.

As she approached her team of experts, applause broke out throughout the salon, and the proud owner of the establishment bemoaned the fact that she hadn't thought to take before photos.

"Theresa, how can I ever thank you? I feel incredible tonight, and I owe it all to you!"

"Nonsense. I have always known you to be a beautiful girl, Rachel. You were just too afraid to show it. I'm really proud of you! I only wish I could be there to see the look on Greg's face! He's going to fall out of his chair!" she giggled.

Before leaving, Rachel took notes on how to recreate the look at home with her hair and makeup. She'd never had an actual hairstyle before and would need to purchase a blow dryer and some other styling tools. Theresa offered to take her by the makeup store where she shopped and help her pick out some other colors that would accentuate her magnificent eyes.

When she finally arrived home at ten that evening, she was exhausted but happy. She told Henry all about it, and he wagged his tail in approval. She went to bed, praising God once again for his goodness and thinking about Greg. She wondered what he was doing right now, and if he was thinking about her.

She added another prayer, asking God for grace and wisdom, as she wasn't sure where Greg stood with God. If he weren't a believer, she would have to keep their budding romance a simple friendship after all. As much as she liked him, God came first in her life, yet she sensed something different about him and wouldn't be at all surprised to find that he already knew the Lord. She prayed for her friend and asked for God to watch over and guide their relationship. She closed her eyes, and with a smile in place, drifted off to sleep thinking about God, Greg, and her first pair of real jeans.

Chapter Eighteen

Theresa sat across the desk from her oncologist, wringing her hands nervously. This was it. The moment of truth. Was she ready to face it?

"I'm afraid the news isn't good," he began with a grim expression on his weathered features. "Your test results indicate an advanced glioblastoma, which is an almost always fatal, cancerous brain tumor. Unfortunately, it is located deep within the brain, and we will not be able to remove it surgically. Your options are few. We can start radiation and chemotherapy immediately, but at the most, your life expectancy at this point is approximately six months at best."

He watched her closely, curious to see her reaction. There was no compassion in his voice, no kind or gentle demeanor. He was simply doing his job, and since there was nothing really he could do for her, he was preparing himself mentally for his next case.

Theresa, meanwhile, was feeling a wide range of emotions. Denial at first. He must be wrong! She would get a second opinion, a new doctor! Someone who would know what he was actually talking about. This quack looked like he'd been practicing medicine since the dark ages.

Then she was terrified. Her whole body trembled, as the thoughts tumbled through her mind. She had nobody in her life to help her get through his. What about her career and all those people who depended on her? What about Rachel? She wasn't ready to face something like this, not now.

Finally, she was angry, furious actually. Feeling the rage boiling up inside of her, she grabbed her coat and purse and stood to leave the room. Turning back to the doctor she retorted hotly, "Go find yourself another guinea pig to experiment on. You're fired."

She walked the fifteen blocks home to her apartment, snow falling lightly all around her. She was in another world altogether, dreaming of the days when life was simple, when it was just her and Stephen against the world, living in their cozy little loft, sleeping in together in the mornings, and drinking coffee while they read the paper. It seemed like a million years ago, but oh how she would love to go back and find that happiness again.

What had she done with her life? She had been given the same number of hours in a day as any one else. She had the same opportunities to show kindness and love to those around her, yet she had been driven by her dreams of making it big in the fashion industry and of becoming a household name. Now she had all that, all the money she could ever spend in a lifetime, and she was alone facing a death sentence. She had no true friends, no husband or child, and no love to sustain her. All of a sudden, these facts hit her hard and the fear, anger, guilt, and shame accumulated in her heart.

She began to sob. She cried and cried her pain and aguish out in huge wracking wails, until the people on the street stared at her as if she were a wild deranged animal. She didn't care, and in fact, she didn't even know there *were* people on the street. Her future had become as bleak as it had ever been. She felt no hope for her future, only disappointment for what she had done with her past.

When she made it home at last, she walked into her apartment and headed straight for her sanctuary. She poured the hottest water she could stand into her massive tub and added in her vanilla scented bath oil. Candles were lit and the lights dimmed by the time she lowered her aching body into the water. She settled back against the full bath pillow and sighed.

There were so many things to think about and decisions to make. She felt like Scarlett O'Hara from *Gone with the Wind*. She didn't want to think about all of this today. She'd think about it tomorrow.

****

Rachel woke with a big smile on her face. Today was the day of her big date with Greg. She bounced out of bed and got started on her morning routine, whistling a happy little tune, as she got herself ready. She hoped that Theresa wouldn't mind if she took off a little early from work that afternoon to get ready.

Just as the thought entered her mind, the phone rang. She rushed to answer it and glanced at the clock. 6:15 a.m. Who on earth would be calling her this early?

"Hello?"

"Hello, Rachel. It's Theresa. Listen, I'm going to take a day or two off from work to attend to some personal business. Can you hold down the fort for me? Just look on my calendar on my desk to see what all needs to be done."

"Oh, sure. Is everything alright?" Rachel asked her, concern in her voice.
"Yes, I'm fine. I just need to run some errands and such. I should be back in the office on Monday."

"Would you mind terribly if I left about an hour early? I have that date for dinner tonight and all the new hair and

217

makeup stuff is so new for me. I need a little time to get used to putting it all together," Rachel asked.

"Go ahead. You have fun tonight, kiddo. You deserve it."

They said their goodbyes, but Rachel's earlier enthusiasm had waned considerably. Theresa just didn't miss work for any old reason. She was really worried about her. She had never confided to Rachel the final diagnosis after her seizure and trip to the hospital. She hoped it wasn't anything serious. She took a moment to sit down and pray for her friend.

She realized she had some extra time this morning, considering she wouldn't have to pick up her boss's coffee and periodicals, so she leashed up Henry and took him for a brisk walk. Kevin's beaming smile greeted her, as she walked up with her happy little pooch.

He had slowly begun to change over the months that she'd known him. Gone was the scruffy three-day growth of beard he'd always sported. In its place was not only a clean-shaven face, but a handsome one at that! He was wearing clean clothing and cologne. He sat in his wheelchair, fondly holding his Bible, but the bags of garbage he'd kept always beside him were conspicuously absent.

He reached out for her customary hug, and she naturally obliged him.

"So, you look awfully spiffy this morning. What's going on?" Rachel asked, excited to see the new life in her friend.

"Well, I got me a job this morning at the local Veteran's Administration. Last week, I ran into an old navy buddy from way back at a Bible study I've been going to, and he offered me a place to stay. I've been living there, trying to get my act together. He helped me to write a resume and find some jobs to apply for. Today I interviewed and was hired on the spot! They said that I would be an asset working with all of the other vets in the city, considering I know what they go through from personal experience.

I just came down here to the street, because I knew you'd be looking for me, and I wanted to share my good news with you. My life is turning around and that is largely because of you. Thank you so much, Rachel. You have been such a blessing to me."

Rachel couldn't believe her ears. Her homeless friend was no longer homeless! God had changed his life just like He'd changed her own. She was thrilled for Kevo and reached down to hug him again.

"Does this mean I won't see you any more?"

"Heck no! I would really like to keep attending church with you, if you don't mind. I can meet you here, if you don't want to drive to where my friend lives, but you were right, Rachel. I need other godly people in my life. I have been going to this intense Bible study, and I am learning so much and meeting a lot of really great people."

"I have a car. I can come pick you up every Sunday. I really value your friendship, and I don't want to lose it. Neither does Henry, apparently." They both laughed at the little dog that had unabashedly climbed up into Kevin's lap and was now snoring softly, as they spoke.

"I have to get to work. I will see you Sunday, ok?" She hugged him once more and made a mental note to follow up with Thomas on the progress of the search for his wife and kids.

****

Theresa was curled up in her bed, pillows propped up behind her, and a coffee mug in her hand, as she searched the yellow pages for another doctor. Sometime during the night, she had made the decision to fight. She had never been one to take anything lying down, and she wasn't about to start now.

She made one phone call after another in search of the best oncologist in the business. Finally, after two hours and with a tired voice, she had found a doctor with an impeccable reputation not only for being up on the latest cancer treatments but also for being a caring and compassionate doctor.

Her appointment with Dr. Terry Cobb was for the following Monday morning, and she actually felt a little better just having accomplished that. She was much more comfortable now that she was back at the helm. She promised herself that when she met him, she wouldn't waste any time with pleasantries. She would tell him that it was her body, and she would be making all decisions. He was there to merely help her though it, and she would not tolerate any condescension.

She next called Thomas Allen to get an update on the hunt for Rachel's biological family and to make an appointment with him to discuss putting together a will.
"My investigator is still in Iowa doing her research. She's hit a few snags, but I should be hearing from her this afternoon. She thinks that she has found the extended family but doesn't want to give me details, until she has confirmed it. I will contact you as soon as I hear from her."

"Good. I need to set up a time to come in with you and go over some other business items, if you have the time this week?" Theresa asked him vaguely. She didn't want to tell him anything one way or another, until she'd met with her new doctor and had a better picture of her situation.

"Sure, how does Tuesday of next week sound?" he asked.

"That will work. Thank you so much. See you then." She hung up and contemplated her plans for the rest of the week.

She made the decision to have her carpenters and electricians finish up whatever their current project in her home was, and there would be no more construction. She wasn't conceding defeat yet, but she knew she needed to focus on getting better, and she just couldn't do it with the nonstop sound of hammers and drills in her home.

She also made plans to visit her herb store for a complete workup, her yoga studio to sign up for even more classes, and her organic whole foods market. She was done splurging on dead animals, wine, and dessert! She was going to clean out her cupboards and refrigerator or all unhealthy or non-organic foods. She was absolutely not going to allow this disease to gain a foothold in her life. It was time she took back control!

****

Rachel answered a multitude of questions about Theresa from the staff that day. Where was she? Why wasn't she in? When was she coming back? Was she sick? Do we still have jobs? She was thoroughly worn out by the time she locked up Theresa's office and left for the day.

Once she set foot in her apartment though, her energy was renewed, and she began to feel the anticipation build for her evening out. She leashed Henry up for a quick jaunt in the park, rushing the poor little guy, so she could get home and start getting ready.

She paused in her bathroom in the midst of applying her makeup to say a quick prayer over her evening.

Lord, you know how I am starting to feel about Greg. Please, please don't ever let me put him before you! This is the first time I've ever been out to dinner with a man, and I don't want to get caught up in the excitement. I want to remain in your will for my life and my future, so I ask you tonight to stand guard over my heart and keep me where you want me. I ask that you would guide my words and not allow me to make a misstep here. And Father, I pray for Greg. I ask that if he doesn't know you like I do, that you would allow me to minister to him this evening. Give me your words and your heart for him. Thank you for tonight and for what you are going to do, no matter what that may be. I love you, Jesus! Amen.

Putting the finishing touches on her hair and with her heart stuck in her throat, she headed to the closet to find a coat. Just as she reached for it, she heard the doorbell ring. Instantly, her hands started to shake. Would he like her new look? Would she make a fool of herself tonight? What if she tripped in these high-heeled boots? She'd never worn them and wasn't the most graceful of people.

She reached for the door, took a deep breath, and answered it. The look on Greg's face when he saw her was worth all of the trepidation she had felt. His mouth fell open, and he looked from the tips of her toes to the top of her head.

"Rachel . . . I, uh . . . Wow! You are so beautiful. I mean, not that you weren't before, but tonight you are just breathtaking!" he blurted out.

She turned pink at his words. This was an evening of firsts for her: her first pair of real jeans, her first real date, and now her first compliment from a man. Her head was spinning and her heart singing, as they left the building and headed out to dinner.

The taxi pulled up in front of an elegant Italian Bistro in midtown Manhattan. Greg ran around to her side of the car, opened the door, and held his hand out to her. She took it and looked up into his eyes. He was so handsome. He'd dressed in a sharp black suit with a silk tie in a cobalt blue geometrical pattern and black alligator shoes. He smelled wonderful too. Rachel was so used to seeing him in old t-shirts and shorts at the gym that she was speechless at the sight of him.

As they walked into the restaurant, a heavily accented Italian man in a tuxedo greeted them and immediately ushered them into an intimate corner table near the window. She was delighted to see the fresh cut roses and candles on the table and to hear the soft sounds of opera music wafting from the speakers. This night was becoming like a dream, almost too good to be true, and Rachel kept expecting to wake up at any moment.

They each ordered an iced tea with lemon and laughed at the expression of the waiter who rarely served anything but wine to his guests.

"I really don't drink," Greg confessed to her.

"Me either," she said with a smile.

"I don't really know much about you, Rachel. I mean we work out together a few times a week, and you've talked about how much you love your job, but we usually just focus on the workouts. I want to know everything about you, where you are from, your family.

I can't tell you how much I've been looking forward to this evening! You'll probably laugh when I tell you this, but I actually went shopping and got some tune-up work done at a salon. I've been as nervous as a schoolboy," he confessed unabashedly.

Rachel was immediately charmed by his candor. She had hoped that he wouldn't be the type to beat around the bush. It wasn't her style, and she didn't care for the artifice. She herself had been accused many times in her life of being too blunt and too direct in her approach with people. She felt instantly at ease and relaxed in his presence.

"You have no idea how happy I am to hear that! I had a little tune-up myself," she laughed with him. "I want to know everything about you too."

She told him about her life growing up, about her adoption, and her monumental decision to go to college. She shared her faith with him and watched closely to see how he would respond. She was curious to see the wide smile growing on his face at her words.

"Rachel, I guessed that you were a believer long ago. Your joy is nearly contagious, and your compassion for others is obvious. I just never seemed to find the right time to ask you. Jesus is my reason for living. He saved me from myself years ago, and I don't normally date, because I don't want to allow anyone to come before Him in my life. You just seemed different. I somehow knew you would feel the same way."

Greg Kendall began to share the story of how God had come into his life, and what hell he'd been saved from. She listened in awe to his words and realized that she was already starting to fall for him.

"I grew up in Missouri in a small, depressed town where drugs were abundant. My mom was single and worked constantly, so she was never home. It was just the two of us, because my dad took off when he found out she was pregnant. I have a learning disability and struggled in school my whole life. Other kids made fun of me, calling me cruel names or taking turns beating me up.

Then I met another kid who had a hard home life like me. We started hanging out together, when I was about twelve, and he introduced me to pot. After awhile we started skipping school together, so we could get stoned in his basement. It wasn't long before it just didn't do the trick for us any more, and we moved on to methamphetamines. Meth eventually took over my whole life, Rachel.

I started to steal things to pay for my habit. It was small things at first, shoplifting from the drugstore, which I would later sell on the street. I knew I'd never be good at lifting the big-ticket items, so I began breaking into homes and taking TVs or jewelry.

Sooner or later I was bound to get caught and arrested, and I did. I was arrested when I was 16 and sent to a juvenile detention center. By then I was a pretty rebellious kid, and I refused to obey the rules. Believe it or not, those places have solitary confinement.

I was sent to the hole on three different occasions. I think I had just given up on life and on myself so anything I could do for attention, I did. I picked fights with the other inmates, I refused to shower, and I even grabbed the female officer's rear end one day." At this he paused, clearly ashamed of himself all these years later. He composed himself and continued.

"That last trip to the hole something changed for me though. The Chaplain was allowed to come in and visit. He brought me a Bible and told me that there was one who loved me in spite of myself, who died to save me, and was waiting patiently for me to come to Him. He told me that Jesus thought I was worth dying for. There was just something in his words that led me to believe he was telling the truth.

Those words were like a light piercing the darkness for me. After he left, I started reading the Bible, and I had plenty of time. I had been sent to the hole for six months because of the incident with the officer. I consumed the word like a man dying of hunger. When I finally emerged, I was a completely different person.

Jesus gave me a new life, and I took it gratefully. The Chaplain was also a tutor, and he helped me to get my G.E.D. He taught me how to overcome my dyslexia and that I wasn't any less of a man just because I struggled to read. He encouraged me to make the most of my new life and to dedicate it to living for God.

Once I was let out, I signed up for college and took some courses on human anatomy, nutrition, and physical education, so I could become a personal trainer. The rest, as they say, is history."

Rachel had been watching his eyes while he spoke, and she hadn't missed the glow that came into them when he spoke of his Savior. She was thinking about the prayer that she had spoken long ago, asking the Lord to bring her a man, because she was lonely. She hadn't even known what to ask for, but God had known her heart, and He was answering this prayer in his usual way with more than she would have ever dreamed of asking for herself.

She looked down quickly, so Greg wouldn't see the shimmer of tears in her eyes. She fussed with her napkin to gain a moment to compose herself.

Clearing her throat, she said, "That's quite an amazing story. God is so good to us isn't he?"

The waiter returned to take their order, and they were both startled to realize they hadn't even looked at the menu. They quickly scanned it and placed their order. Rachel was going to try the eggplant parmesan, and Greg the fettuccine alfredo.

After he left, the conversation resumed, and the two chatted away as if they'd known one another for years. They had an easy rapport and found that they had much in common. They listened to the same Christian artists, enjoyed many of the same authors, and even had similar goals in life. Greg wanted to own his own gym one day, and Rachel wanted her own fashion line.

By the time they had finished with their coffee and tiramisu, they were both reluctant to see the evening come to an end. They decided to take a long leisurely walk to burn off some of the calories they'd consumed. They found themselves talking long into the evening and, at one point, Greg had glanced at his watch. He was stunned to find it was nearly three a.m.

"We'd probably better call it a night. I have an appointment with a new client in the morning at eight," he said regretfully.

They hailed a cab, and he walked her to her front door. He took her hand and kissed the top of it lightly. Taking a deep breath, he spoke from his heart the words he'd been trying to formulate all night.

"Rachel, I had an incredible time with you tonight. I would really like to get to know you more, but I want to make sure we do it right. I don't really believe in dating in the traditional sense. Knowing that you are a believer, I'm sure you are already familiar with a biblical courtship. I guess what I'm asking you is how you would feel about allowing me to court you?" he asked somewhat sheepishly.

Her face lit up, and she looked at him through a veil of tears.

"Oh I was hoping you'd ask me that!" she blurted out.

He gave her a hug good night, and they made plans to have brunch the following morning between his appointments. They had finally realized that while they wanted to spend time getting to know each other, they also to spend time getting to know their God better. So they were each going to bring their Bibles with them tomorrow, and they would be starting in the book of 1 Corinthians.

Rachel let herself into her apartment and made a pot of tea, while she changed into her pajamas. She scrubbed her face clean of makeup and thrust her feet into her fluffy pink slippers. She padded out to the kitchen and poured a cup of chamomile tea, settling into her easy chair.

She wanted just to sit and reminisce of her night with Greg. She was exhausted but still on an adrenaline high, and she needed to simply bask in the goodness of God. She sipped her tea, closed her eyes, and sang a song of worship until her eyes were so heavy that she knew she'd fall asleep, if she didn't head off to bed. Her last waking thought before drifting to sleep was of designing her own wedding gown.

Chapter Nineteen

Caitlyn woke to the shrill ringing of the phone in her hotel room. She pushed the hair out of her eyes and glared at the clock, discouraged to see it was only 7:00 a.m.

"This better be good," she mumbled as she switched on the lamp.

"Hello?" she gritted out.

"My, my, we aren't a morning person, are we?" A deep melodious voice spoke in her ear, and she instantly perked up, embarrassed at her tone.

"Sorry, Afrika. I was up late doing some research at the library. I'm usually up by now," she responded.

"I'm afraid I have some bad news for you. I know you planned to head out this morning for Bayfield first thing, but I don't think that's going to happen. Please set the phone down for a moment and go look out your bedroom window," he instructed.

With trepidation, she set the phone down and walked to the window. Drawing the curtains aside, she gasped at the sight before her. Sometime during the night, a massive snow storm had hit Des Moines, leaving behind at least six feet of snow in its wake.

She went back and picked up the phone.

"Afrika! What happened?! I don't recall seeing this on the forecast. I'm going to be trapped in my hotel room, aren't I?"

The panic rose in her voice, and she tried unsuccessfully to stifle it.

"Calm yourself, little one. The snowplows will eventually clear the roads. In the meantime, I want to start thinking like the eternal being that you are. There is a purpose in everything that God allows to happen. Have you considered, for instance, that perhaps it is not the right time for you to find the answers that you are seeking? God might want you to wait. Or is it possible that He wants to keep you here a little longer so that you might have time to get to know me a little better?" he asked her pointedly.

She stopped and considered his words. Of course! He was right, as usual, and she relaxed immediately. She thought back to her childhood and recalled how delighted she had been when the snow was so heavy they had to cancel school. She decided right then and there that she was going to enjoy the reprieve from work and let things happen they way that they were meant to.

"Let me make a few phone calls, Afrika. I will call you back in a few minutes, ok?"

She called the airlines to reschedule her flight home, the car rental company to extend the rental of her car another week, and finally left a message with Thomas Allen's answering service.

"Hi, Thomas, it's Caitlyn. Apparently God has decided he wants me here a little longer. A huge snowstorm has hit Iowa, leaving six feet of snow on the ground. I'm not going to be able to leave my hotel room, much less travel back to Bayfield, for at last a couple of days. Judging by the looks of the clouds outside, I think we are expecting more snow as well. I will call you and let you know when I have an ETA.

Please call when you have some time to chat, I have other things to tell you. Good news, I promise!"

She hung up and made herself a pot of tea before snuggling back under the covers and calling Afrika back.

"Hi!" she chirped into the phone.

They spent the rest of the day on the phone, getting to know one another better, interrupted only by room service knocking on the door with her meals. She was shocked to realize they had literally been on the phone with one another for eight hours. When he begged off to get back to writing his sermon for Sunday, she was disappointed but understood.

"I have a brother in Christ in my congregation that drives a huge four wheel drive truck. May I have him come fetch you on Sunday so that you can come to fellowship with us?" he asked her.

"That would be wonderful. I was hoping I wouldn't miss it. Perhaps we could have lunch afterward? My treat this time and no argument. When I was driving out of town, I found an adorable little English pub that serves traditional fare. I would like you to experience a little bit of my culture for a change."

"That sounds wonderful. I only wish there was a Kenyan restaurant in town, so I could do the same for you. You'll have to settle for some photographs I have of my homeland. I'll bring them with me."

They chatted a few more minutes before hanging up. Caitlyn decided she'd give one last ditch effort to persuade the adoption agency to give up some more information before calling it a night.

The receptionist put her call through to Evelyn and, once more, she pleaded her case. She told the receptionist that she'd been able to ascertain that Rachel's biological mother and father were engaged in some sort of altercation that led to her death and his imprisonment. She simply wanted to know if she were on the right track or if she should switch gears.

"I'm afraid I'm not at liberty to say. I have not heard from any of the family members to date, but I will tell you that none of them are still in the area. Really, Miss Woodbridge, that is all I'm willing to do for you. I am putting my career and my business on the line for you as it is. You'll have to be content with that. Good day." With that, she hung up the phone.

Great. Do I even continue with the courthouse in Bayfield? What's the point now?

Then Caitlyn did something she had never done in her life. She prayed that God would show her which direction to take. She was at a loss and frustrated and felt as though every door she opened was being slammed shut in her face. She had finally come to the knowledge that God was trying to slow her down for some reason, and she needed to be okay with that.

Alright, Lord, she prayed, *I can take a hint. Just show me what to do next, please?*

While she waited for direction, she decided that she could use the time she was stranded here to work on her other case. She needed to tie up some loose ends in finding the family of Kevin Monacucci.

Caitlyn had located his family in a matter of days, as they hadn't traveled far from where they originally lived in

Manhattan. Kevin's wife, Cathy, was living with their grown children in upstate New York. She just needed to call her and see if she was interested in speaking with her husband at this point in her life.

She picked up the phone and dialed the number she had for Cathy. Crossing her fingers out of habit, she suddenly realized what she was doing and stopped, saying a prayer instead.

"Hello?" a sweet, gentle voice answered the phone.

Caitlyn let out her breath and replied, "Hello, is this Cathy Monacucci?"

"Yes, this is Cathy. May I help you?"

"Hi, my name is Caitlyn, and I'm an investigator working with Thomas Allen and Associates in New York City." Before she could say any more, Cathy cut her off.

"Oh no! It's Kevin isn't it? Is he okay? He's not dead, tell me he's not dead!" she wailed, terrified.

"No, no he's not dead," Caitlyn assured her quickly, "but I've been hired to find you *for* him. One of our clients befriended him and wanted to see him reunited with his family. May I be frank with you, Cathy?"

"Of course, please."

"Kevin is a new man. He has cleaned up his life and is working now. He is at the Veterans Administration helping people who have been through the same kind of traumatic events that he has endured. He is attending a local church regularly and living with a friend, until he can afford to move into his own place, which shouldn't be much longer."

Cathy broke down then and wept. Caitlyn could hear her thanking God that her prayers had been answered. She did not hear even a hint of unforgiveness or bitterness in her voice.

"You have no idea what this means to me and the kids. Please, tell me how I can get hold of him? It's been years since I've seen him, and I've never given up hope that he would come back to us," she responded.

The ladies spoke for nearly an hour, and when Caitlyn hung up the phone, she had the beginnings of a plan in place. She tried to call Thomas again, this time with success.

"Thomas! I'm so glad I caught you. I have so much to tell you!" She was speaking so fast that he told her to take a deep breath and start at the beginning.

She told him of her conversation with Cathy and how the family wanted very much to be reunited with Kevin. They made plans for her to fly in to New York in about a month, and in the meantime, they would contact Kevin and make sure he was ready to see them. They were both overjoyed that at least this mission was being accomplished.

She next told him about meeting Afrika, and how she had given her life to Christ because of him. She had always known he was a believer; he was quite open in his faith. He was overjoyed at the news and told her so.

She then reluctantly told him of her budding relationship with Afrika, nervous because she knew what his reaction might be. He was an intelligent man to be sure, and he would immediately know what the implications of a long distance relationship were.

He was quiet for a moment, and when he spoke, his words lifted her heart.

"Caitlyn, if this is the man you feel God has given you, I say go for it! Go slowly, but if you feel led to relocate, go with my blessings. You are a smart, dedicated, talented investigator, and I have full confidence that you can find work anywhere. I will do whatever I can to help you succeed. I would be happy to write you a letter of reference or whatever you need. I don't want you to feel like you owe me anything. You are free to pursue your dreams." He spoke kindly to her, and she knew he meant it.

Her thoughts drifted back to the flat in the city that she had never had the desire to decorate or even unpack in. Strange, she'd been so excited when she found it, but it had never felt like home for some reason. Had God been calling her even then?

****

Thomas picked up the phone and called Rachel at home that night. He told her of the good news that Caitlyn had shared with him, and she was delighted. She couldn't wait to tell Kevin and she made plans to pick him up early for church and take him to breakfast. She sincerely hoped that he would respond the same way. She was nervous that she had overstepped the boundaries between them, but she gave it all to God and prayed that she hadn't been mistaken in hearing Him.

The two of them finished their conversation on the phone by lifting the matter in prayer. Thomas led them, and as they prayed for Kevin, he also silently prayed for Rachel, knowing that her time of reckoning was coming quickly as well. How would she react to the news that her own family had been found?

Kevin was preparing for bed on Saturday night, when his roommate appeared in his room and told him he had a phone call.

"Hello?" he answered.

"Hey, Kevo, it's Rachel. I was wondering if I could take you to breakfast before church tomorrow? I sort of have something I'd like to talk with you about," she asked, with hesitation clear in her voice.

"Sure, that'd be great. Is everything ok?" He picked up on her unease and was instantly concerned. He had come to care a great deal for this young lady, thinking of her as a daughter he'd never had.

"Oh yeah, I just want to ask you to be in prayer tonight. I have something pretty huge to tell you, and I really feel like God's hand is in it. Just be open to what he wants to do in your life," she replied.

His curiosity was piqued now, and he wanted to ask more questions but restrained himself. He promised he'd pray and that he'd be ready to go at eight the next morning.

He hung up with her and spent the majority of the night in his bed, seeking the face of God.

Lord, you have changed my life, and I trust you. I don't know what you have planned for me tomorrow, but whatever it is, I pray my heart will remain open. If I am harboring any unforgiveness toward anyone, I pray you will show it to me. If I have fear in my life, show me that too. I want only whatever it is that you want for my life. Thank you for saving me and setting me free. And thank you Lord, for Rachel and what she has meant to me. I ask that

you bless her like she has blessed me. In your perfect and beautiful
name I pray, Jesus, AMEN.
He turned over and eventually found sleep. He found
himself in a dream surrounded by his lovely wife and three
handsome grown boys. They embraced him and in their
arms he found forgiveness, acceptance, and love. When he
woke in the morning, his pillow was wet with his own tears.

****

Caitlyn was thoroughly enjoying the church service that
Sunday morning. Word had spread quickly amongst the
believers that Pastor Afrika was courting her, and they had
warmly welcomed her in their midst. She wasn't sure how
she would be accepted and all of it was so unfamiliar to her,
but her fears were allayed after the first hug. She knew she
was one of them now.

Worship was loud and boisterous, as the people of God sang
from their heart and soul. Peace invaded her soul, and she
suddenly realized that she felt like she'd finally come home.

Home. This was where she was meant to be. A thrill shot
through her and joy began to bubble up. She knew what
she had to do, and as she shook hands with her new friends
and said her goodbyes at the end of the service, she was
beginning to make her plans for a move to Iowa.

Afrika smiled warmly at her over their shared lunch of
shepherd's pie. Their time together had become so precious
in light of her leaving soon to go back to New York. She
hadn't yet told him of her decision to move here, certain he
would see it as too early in her relationship with him. His
next words stunned her.

"Caitlyn, have you decided to move here yet? You have
nothing to keep you in New York other than a job, and I

know you can find work here. Tell me, how do you feel about me? Do you think I am worth the sacrifice?" he asked her bluntly, his words softened by the lilting African accent and the emotion shining in his chocolate eyes.

Goosebumps raced up her arms as she stared at him. She'd been trying to think of a way to tell him that she wanted to move here, without seeming like she was pushing things too quickly. She choked the tears back and took a deep breath before speaking.

"As a matter of fact, I was wondering how to tell you that I have pretty much decided to move. I thought you might think me too forward or presumptuous."

"My dear, let there not be any artifice between us. I want you to always feel free to talk to me about anything. We are on God's time table not our own. If things are heading in that direction, who are we to tell the very One that brought us together that the timing isn't right or that we are rushing things. It seems as though that is the way He wants it to be. We have everything that is important in common. We are doing it the right way. We are not rushing into marriage for the wrong reasons, but there is no way for us to get to know one another with you in another state. It is not logical," he explained.

She constantly had to change the way that she thought about things. Courting was so different from what she expected. Truthfully, she could see herself married to him, and it didn't scare her like she thought it might.

"Give me your hand. I want to pray together, and I want both of us to be certain we are doing what God wants us to do. There should be a peace for both of us in this."

They prayed together quietly so as not to disturb the other guests in the restaurant. In the end, they both felt confident that the decision for her to move was the right one. She would call Thomas and let him know that she was coming back in a week, only to pack her things and move to Iowa. She would finish the final project she was in the midst of, and then she would be busy finding work for herself here.

****

Rachel and Kevin sat together in the small coffee shop, eating eggs and pancakes, and discussing the latest Bible study that they were each involved in. She shared with him the courtship that was evolving between herself and Greg, and he was delighted to hear that she had found a man of God who genuinely cared for her.

He told her of the dream he had the night before, and she dropped her coffee mug, spilling hot coffee everywhere. Rachel apologized profusely and began to wipe it up with the extra napkins on the table.

Flustered, she explained that the reason she wanted to bring him to lunch was to discuss his family. His eyebrows rose at that, and he looked questioningly at her.

"Kevin, I found them, and they are eager to see you."

He was clearly shocked and at first didn't respond.

"I . . . uh . . . what do you mean you found them?!"

"They have been living in upstate New York, in a small town called Williamsburg. Your boys never left home, Kevin. They have all been praying for you for years and didn't want to stray too far in the hopes that you would all be together again one day as a family. Cathy is coming to see you, with the boys, in about a month. That is, of course, if you want to see them," she explained quietly, with compassion in her voice.

He began to cry. He just couldn't hold it in any longer. He was so overwhelmed with emotion that he couldn't even begin to understand what he was feeling. Hope, fear, and shame were filling him now. How could he ever make up for the years he had lost? He had missed seeing his boys grow to become men. He had simply withdrawn into himself and shut out the rest of society; his own family included.

"She really wants to see me? After all I've done to her? And to the boys?" he rasped out, with pain and regret in his voice.

"Yes! She still loves you, and she wants to reconcile. You'll see. The whole family is thrilled that they are coming to see you."

They finished up their breakfast and prepared to head out to church. He stopped her and thanked her for what she'd done, giving her a long hug. When they entered the church twenty minutes later he had so much to be thankful for, and the tears started again as he sang his heart out for the Lord.

Chapter Twenty

Dr. Terry Cobb had devoted his life to the practice of medicine. At the age of 42, he had never married or had children and had no social life to speak of. He was an attractive man, nearly 6'2", with blue eyes that crinkled at the corners when he smiled, dark hair generously peppered with silver, and had a lean, rangy body. He tended to downplay his looks, however, and wore conservative button down shirts and thick black horn-rimmed glasses.

He took a much different approach with his patients than most physicians he knew. They were like extended family for him. He checked in on them at home and sent them Christmas or birthday cards. He sat by their bedsides, when they were in pain and comforted them, and sometimes when he was unfortunate enough to lose one, he sat with them as they passed on. They, likewise, adored him, and he had garnered for himself a reputation as a doctor who actually *cared.*

His first patient of the day was here for a second opinion on a brain cancer diagnosis that she had recently received. His heart grieved, as he looked over her biopsy results, x-rays, and MRI. There was no doubt that the first opinion had been accurate. He sighed heavily and reached for his phone.

Dr. Cobb buzzed his head nurse and asked her if she would please send Theresa Wakefield-Anderson in to his office. It was important to him that he get to know his patients on a more personal level, before he started poking and prodding their bodies, so he always met with them one-on-one for a consultation before a physical examination.

He didn't know what he had expected to find, when she walked in his office door, but when he stood to shake her hand, he found himself staring at the most beautiful woman he'd ever seen. She literally stole words from him, along with his breath, and for a moment he couldn't speak. She stared curiously at him, and he finally remembered himself.

"Hello, Theresa, I'm Dr. Cobb. Please, have a seat."

He put her x-rays up on the light box, along with her various MRI scans. He began to explain to her in layman's terms what she had to look forward to.

"I would like to get you started on chemotherapy and radiation as soon as possible. The tumor is rather large, and we now run the risk of the cancer spreading to the rest of your body. I understand, after discussing your case with your first physician, that he gave you six months?" he asked gently.

She nodded stiffly, obviously still unwilling to accept his words.

"Theresa, I work a little differently. I have never given a patient a number like that. I believe that anything is possible, and I never give up without a fight. I am going to ask you to have that same attitude. This is a war, and you will need all the soldiers standing beside you to fight it, as you can get!" he said confidently.

For the first time since receiving her diagnosis, she felt a glimmer of hope. She believed him, and now that the denial had begun to lift, she was ready for the battle of her life.

"Since we are about a week out from Christmas, I think we should set it up for after the 25th. I would hate to see your holiday ruined by trips to the hospital and all the unfortunate side effects that go along with chemotherapy. Why don't I set something up for after the first of the year for you?"

"No. That won't be necessary. I assure you. I have no family, no husband, not even a close friend to celebrate the holiday with. I'm not a religious person either, so Christmas has no significance for me, other than an increase in sales," she replied with a smirk.

"Let's just go ahead and get started now. I have a trustworthy assistant that can hold down the fort for a while in my absence. You can make the first appointment for tomorrow. Now, tell me about the side effects. I want to know what I'm getting myself into."

Dr. Cobb paused for a moment, uncertain how to take this headstrong woman. Was she really this straightforward and fearless? Or was it all an act of a woman in denial and only trying desperately to appear strong?

"The side effects of chemo can vary. Some patients experience one or two of them, while others have all. It is going to depend on your overall health and the lifestyle that you lead.

Stress does have an impact on how you will feel, so if your job or other things in your life are wearing you out, I'm going to ask you to make your health a priority and start slowing things down a bit. You will most likely experience some nausea and vomiting, and also some hair loss. Those are the two most common symptoms." He paused here, seeing her face pale a bit. She did have the most amazing hair, and it would be tragic to see her lose those thick gorgeous auburn locks.

"Other symptoms that may occur are gastrointestinal disturbances, such as diarrhea, constipation, or gas. You will most likely feel more fatigued and have dryer skin than you are used to. I have some informational pamphlets I will give you before you leave today. Let's not focus on all this right now, though. I want to think about getting you better, not the cost of what that will mean. Do you have any questions for me?"

She thought for a moment and shook her head. It was all so much to take in. She was sure that once she got home and had time to think, she would have a lot of questions for him.

"Let's get you into a room so that I can get an examination started. I'll have my nurse give you one of those lovely paper gowns to put on and get your blood pressure. While she attends to that, I'm going to call the hospital and set up an appointment for the morning. I know a really amazing nurse that I'm going to request for you. You will be in good hands with her, I promise."

****

Rachel had begun spending every spare moment she had with Greg. They had started alternating Sundays at one another's churches, until they could agree which one they should both attend. They joined a class at her church on biblical courtships, and they were learning a lot about each other and what God expected from them as a couple.

Rachel introduced Greg to Kevin and the two were instant friends. He even asked Greg if he would be there, when he was reunited with his wife and children. He was obviously nervous for the big event and needed the extra moral support. With the event looming in just a week, Kevin spent extra time in prayer every day, asking God that he would keep his hand on his family, give him wisdom to handle the situation, and that, in the end His will would be done.

Rachel called and made a reservation at the Four Seasons Hotel for a suite for the following week, under Cathy Monacucci's name. She wanted everything to be perfect for her friend who had already been through so much. She made arrangements for a lovely brunch of crepes, croissants, and fresh fruit to be delivered to the suite, along with a bright bouquet of flowers. She didn't tell Kevo any of this, because she wanted to surprise him and, more than that, she wanted to bless him.

She got a call the next morning from Theresa, asking if she would please swing by her apartment on her way in to the office that morning. She grabbed a coffee for both of them, headed up the elevator to the top floor, and rang the doorbell.

She hadn't seen Theresa in two weeks and was shocked at her pale, gaunt appearance. It was if she had aged ten years and lost twenty pounds. Dark circles rimmed her bloodshot eyes, and the makeup she wore didn't cover the fact that all the color had washed out of her face. Her thick hair was held back in a simple ponytail, and she was wearing a plain, but trendy, white tracksuit. As long as she'd known Theresa, she'd never seen her in anything less than haute couture. Sweats were completely out of the question.

"Hi," Rachel began tentatively. "How are you? Is everything okay?"

"Come in and sit down, won't you? I have a lot to tell you, and you are about to find your commitment to the company challenged. We'll see what you are capable of," she said with a weary voice.

They sat in the overstuffed chairs in the living room and sipped on their lattes. Rachel waited patiently for her to begin, not wanting to rush what was obviously going to be a difficult conversation.

"I've been diagnosed with stage three brain cancer. It is incurable, and inoperable, and chances are I won't be here this time next year." She held a hand up to stop the words of protest she could see forming on Rachel's lips.

"I am going to fight it, rest assured. I've never given up without a fight, and I'm not about to start now, when my own life is on the line. I began chemotherapy and radiation treatments this week, and it is already starting to take a toll on me. This is where you come in.

I will need your help running *Her Wicked Ways* for me for a few months, until I see how things are going to go. I will be available by phone to you at all times for conferences, but I trust you implicitly. You know my vision for the future of this company, and everyone who works for me understands that your word is as good as mine. I do not want any of the employees to know why I am taking a leave of absence, and I -" her words were cut off by an outraged Rachel.

"You have to tell them! They love you! They are going to know something is going on, and I can't lie to them. Can't I at least tell them you are out on medical leave? I need to give them *something*," she protested.

"No, you don't. Frankly, it's none of their business. I am a paycheck to them, nothing more," she said bluntly.

Rachel didn't understand Theresa's inability to accept love. There were almost 75 employees in the offices of *Her Wicked Ways* and any one of them would have said that they adored her. She was universally respected and admired, and all of her dedicated workers were thrilled to be where they were. It broke her heart that she couldn't seem to communicate that to her.

"As I was saying, I will be undergoing some treatments and unable to work for the time being. I put together a portfolio for you of what is coming up over the next six months. We have a fashion show in Paris in February for the new Spring line, a cover for Vogue and Cosmopolitan in March, and a new catalog that needs to be put together before June. That should keep you pretty busy. I don't expect you to do all of this without proper compensation, so I've instructed Marsha in HR to give you a 30% raise, as well as an expense account for all of the traveling you will need to do.

The company jet is available at all times for you, so you needn't bother with commercial travel. Inside the portfolio you will find various credit cards that have no spending limit. All I ask is that you submit an expense report every six weeks to accounting.

Also, my privacy is of the utmost importance, Rachel. I do not want even a hint of this reaching the press or anyone else. If anyone asks about my absence, please tell them I am taking a prolonged vacation around the world and that I do not have an expected date of return. Any questions?"

Of course she had questions! Like how on earth was she supposed to do all of this alone?! Was Theresa going to be okay? What could she do to help her personally? What was God doing here?

"I'm sure questions will arise once all of this sinks in, but I will call you when that happens. Please, tell me what I can do to help you with your recovery? Do you need someone to come in and clean or cook for you? Something, please . . . I feel so helpless," she pleaded.

"Already taken care of. I have hired a housekeeper to come in several times a week, and an organic chef to cook meals and deliver them. I'm going to be fine, really."

They talked for another hour regarding various business matters that needed attending to. Rachel could see that Theresa was becoming exhausted, and she gathered her things to leave. She hesitated for a moment and asked Theresa, if she could pray for her. She saw the shimmer of tears in her mentor's eyes, as she nodded, and the two women held hands.

"Lord, I lift up my dear friend to you and ask that you would carry her through this journey. I know that while she acts strong, she must be terrified of what lies ahead. If it is in your will, please heal her body. I ask that you would make the treatments she must have bearable. Most of all Lord, I pray that she would know that you are with her through this entire ordeal, that you love her desperately, and that your heart breaks right along side of hers. We thank you, Jesus, for what you are doing in her life even now, knowing that you want only what is best for her. In your beautiful name we pray, Jesus, AMEN."

After Theresa closed the door, she went back to bed and crawled under the covers. Her expensive Egyptian cotton sheets and fluffy down pillows brought her no comfort, as she contemplated Rachel's words. She had slowly, over the past year, begun to listen a little more carefully, when she talked of God. Perhaps He was worth considering after all. She wondered about all of the Christians that had been in her life and couldn't help but think that it couldn't be a coincidence.

Her parents had been amazing examples of what believers were supposed to live out. Then, just as they passed away, her husband who had been nothing but faithful and loving to her in spite of the way she treated him, and had become a Christian. Thomas and Jenna had been good friends to her as well, reaching out to her during the various crises in her life and showing her kindness and compassion.

Finally, there was Rachel. Fiercely loyal, always dependable, kind as they come, Rachel. She could find no hypocrisy, no unforgiveness, no pride or arrogance in this girl. She was pure sweetness and love, and she continually reached out to Theresa on behalf of Jesus.

There just had to be a catch, of that she was certain. Why would a holy and righteous God want anything to do with someone like her? She had always been driven by her goals, obsessed with power and money, selfish and prideful. She had belittled her employees, driven away her husband, and killed her only child. She would be the first to admit she had lived her life for herself, and now she was paying the price. God would never accept her, not until she made amends and cleaned up her life.

She had kept her appointment with Thomas, after she had received her results from Dr. Cobb. He helped to draw up a will and make some final arrangements. She had been honest with him in telling him about her prognosis, and he asked her if he could tell Jenna. She agreed and spent some time in prayer with him before leaving.

It was curious, but she had to admit that she felt a measure of peace, after they had prayed. Was God real after all? Did he love her in spite of her unworthiness? Could He take away her pain?

On her way back to the apartment, she stopped off at a Christian bookstore and bought herself a Bible. She asked the clerk behind the counter for a recommendation, since they all looked the same to her, and she knew she'd never be able to understand King James English. She recommended an easy to read version that was written in modern every day English and had common questions that people ask about God written in the side margins.

That Bible sat on her bedside table for several days, before she finally had the courage to open it. But there came a night when the anxiety wouldn't let her sleep, and she took hold of the word, only to find it had taken hold of her. She didn't know where she was supposed to start reading, so she just opened it to a random page in the back and read.

For everyone has sinned; we all fall short of God's glorious standard. Yet God, with undeserved kindness, declares that we are righteous. He did this through Christ Jesus when He freed us from the penalty for our sins. For God presented Jesus as the sacrifice for sin. People are made right with God when they believe that Jesus sacrificed His life, shedding His blood. This sacrifice shows that God was being fair when He held back and did not punish those who sinned in times past, for He was looking ahead and including them in what He would do in this present time. God did this to demonstrate His righteousness, for He himself is fair and just, and He declares sinners to be right in His sight when they believe in Jesus.

That couldn't be right. It almost seemed like it was saying that everyone sinned, but God was still willing to forgive them, as long as they believed in His son who died for their sin. That was way too easy. Surely there was more to it than that!

So, she read a little further, certain she would find the catch somewhere in the following chapters.

When people work, their wages are not a gift, but something they have earned. But people are counted as righteous, not because of their work, but because of their faith in God who forgives sinners.

Now he was speaking her language. She knew the value of hard work and the reward of a big paycheck. There was a big difference between a wage and a gift, so he is saying that God gives forgiveness as a gift for people who simply have faith in Him?

This was a revelation for her. She'd always thought of Christians as holier-than-thou people who thought they were perfect, but if she was reading this accurately, that wasn't the case at all! They were not better or worse than anyone else, they only admitted their fault to a God who forgives without question.

She set the book down, closed her eyes, and for the first time in many, many, years she said a prayer.

God, if you are real, I need to know it! I don't understand most of this and reading the Bible is a completely new experience for me. Will you please show me the truth? I don't know if this is the proper thing to ask or not, but if you still do this sort of thing, will you give me a sign? And will you make it something unmistakable? I admit it, I don't want to die. I don't know what waits for me on the other side, and I don't want to find out too late that I have been wrong about you all along. Thank you for listening, if you are there. Amen.

Chapter Twenty One

Caitlyn knew that she should have gone home to get started on her packing and moving arrangements, but she couldn't bear to be parted from Afrika over the holidays, so she made flight arrangements for a trip home on the 26th, and in the meantime, she planned to enjoy every minute with him for the next three days. She found a huge shopping mall not far from her hotel and went in search of the perfect gift.

As she arrived in the tightly packed lot, she started to worry. What on earth did one buy an African Pastor for Christmas? She browsed the stores but nothing was popping out at her. Caitlyn thought she must have walked seven miles and was exhausted, when she finally stumbled into a tiny boutique in a corner of the mall called Traditions. Taking note of the large tribal masks hanging in the window, she entered, curious to see what they carried.

A deep rich voice, heavily accented and eerily familiar, greeted her.

"Hello, how may I help you today?" he asked. She looked up to see a large African man wearing a traditional tribal tunic over blue jeans. He smiled widely at her, and she felt like she had just met Afrika's twin.

"Hi, I am looking for a gift for a dear friend for Christmas. He is a Pastor here, and he is from Kenya." But before she could say another word, he began to laugh. He had a hearty, earthy chuckle that warmed her down to the depths of her soul. She liked him instantly and wondered about that.

"You must be speaking of Pastor Afrika! Yes, yes, I know him. We come from the same area of Kenya, and, in fact, lived in villages only twenty miles apart. I did not know him then. I only met him recently here in my store. He is a frequent visitor, and we have gotten to know one another. Wonderful man of God! My name is Chizoba, which means God Protect Us. It is so nice to meet you! I can show you something that Afrika has had his eye on if you like?"

She agreed quickly and was shown a large plaque hanging prominently on one wall. He explained the piece to her. There had lived a family of Christian missionaries that came to his country 80 years earlier to share the gospel. They had come up against a severe language barrier. Even so they found the African people to be warm and friendly, and very open to hear what they were teaching, so they rewrote what is commonly called the Apostle's Creed in a language that was more easily understood to the villagers. It made such an impact on them that eventually nearly everyone in the village had given their lives to Christ, and it had eventually led to his own salvation. Chizoba could recite it from memory himself, but even so he wanted to commemorate it with this plaque, which he had commissioned by an elder in the tribe.

It was a massive piece of olive wood, intricately carved with images of the cross, the resurrection, and angels. She was immediately taken with it and began to read the words engraved prominently in the center.

We believe in the one high God, who out of love created the beautiful earth and everything in it. He created people and wanted them to be happy in the world. God loves the world and every nation and tribe on the earth. We have known this high God in the darkness and now we know him in the light.

God promised in the book of His Word, the Bible, that he would save the world and all the nations and tribes. We believe that God made good his promise by sending his only son, Jesus Christ, a man of flesh, a Jew by tribe. Born poor in a little village, he left his home and was always on safari doing good, curing people by the power of God, teaching them about God and humanity and showing them that the meaning of religion is love.

But he was rejected by his people, tortured and nailed hands and feet to a cross and died. He was buried in a grave but the hyenas did not dare touch him. On the 3rd day, he rose from that grave and ascended to the sky. He is the Lord. We are waiting for him. He is alive! In this we believe, AMEN.

Gooseflesh rose on her skin, as she read the words, and she felt tears come into her eyes. It was *beautiful!* She knew that God had brought her here and that she had finally found the perfect gift for Afrika. She didn't even ask how much the piece was; she knew she had to have it.

Chizoba wrapped it quickly for her and asked if he could say a prayer over her, before she left. She was surprised, but agreed, and the two bowed their heads in prayer.

"Lord God, you are mighty! Thank you for bringing a new friend and sister in Christ into my life. I pray now for her, and for the courtship, which you have instigated between her and my brother, Afrika. I ask that you would keep your hand upon them and that they would walk by faith, not by sight. Keep them in the palm of your hand, and guide them by your Spirit. These things I pray, knowing you are good, and you love us. AMEN."

Caitlyn looked up at him stunned. She had not told him they were courting! He smiled knowingly at her and said simply, "God told me. You didn't have to." He gave her a warm hug and asked her to come see him again.

****

Thomas Allen had been fighting a tug at his spirit for some time now. Practicing the law with all of its elements and intricacies, which had in the past fascinated him, had suddenly begun to lose its hold on him. Slowly, he was starting to realize that God was calling him to a different path. It was one he didn't want to walk.

Something had shaken loose inside of him one day several years previous with words spoken to him in anger by a client. He sat, sipping his tea, and recalled that day with a knot in his stomach.

"You missed your calling, Thomas! You should have been a Pastor!"

What was it about the thought of leaving his practice to go to seminary that scared him so? He had enough money by now, more in fact than he could ever spend in a lifetime. He didn't even have to work if he chose not to. His wife would support him, and he knew that his church would as well.

Was it the loss of the security he had in knowing what he was supposed to do, day in and day out, with no guesswork on his part? He would be leaving a life of comfort and rules for one in which he would have to walk by faith, trusting God for every single decision he made or word he spoke. It frankly terrified him.

But then, he thought with a chuckle, *God does like to move us out of our comfort zone doesn't he? I should be happy He isn't calling me as a missionary to Afghanistan!*

He sighed heavily, knowing this was a battle he'd never win and also knowing that he would never truly find peace in a life that wasn't ordered by God. He put his glasses on and reached for the power button on his laptop. He said a silent prayer in the hopes that he could find a reputable school not too far from home.

****

Caitlyn had still not been able to make a trip back to Bayfield to resume her research. The snow had made it impossible for her to make the trip in her rented mid-size sedan, which was not made for winter travel. When she had inquired with the rental company about renting an SUV or pickup truck with four-wheel drive, she'd been informed that they were sold out.

She had discussed the situation with Afrika, intent on getting some godly advice. He'd simply said, "It appears that God is thwarting your efforts, my dear. I suggest you pray and wait for him to answer. The solution you are seeking is not going anywhere. It will wait for you to find it."

So she waited, trying to be patient and explaining to Thomas that doors were being consistently closed in her face. In the end, he agreed with Afrika.

"God always answers prayers, Caitlyn. Sometimes He says 'Yes,' sometimes it's 'No,' and sometimes the answer is 'Not yet, be patient.' You will have to be okay with that."

Christmas morning dawned clear and bright, the snow sparkling in the morning sun. Caitlyn donned a bright red sweater with matching hat, knee high black boots, and a thick, fluffy black scarf and headed out for an early breakfast before the Christmas service with Afrika. He took her to his favorite pancake house, and the two were like children, excitedly ordering a huge breakfast accompanied by hot chocolate. They chattered away eagerly about the gifts they had purchased for one another and made plans to go caroling that night at a retirement home with a group of people from the church.

Caitlyn couldn't remember ever being so happy or carefree in her life. The only dark cloud that had tried her dampen her sunshine had been her parents. She had called them the night before to tell them about her budding relationship with Afrika and had been met with dead silence over the phone line.

When they finally spoke, it was with disapproval heavy in their voices. They completely objected to the whole thing on many levels. Her mother was shocked at her decision to become a born again Christian. It was rather unseemly in her mind. After all, they had been raised in the Church of England and that was the right and proper way to live their lives. For Caitlyn to say that she *knew* she was going to heaven seemed downright presumptuous and arrogant.

As for her father, his objection had been to her rushed decision to move to Iowa of all places, in order to continue in a relationship with a man she barely knew! She was leaving behind a good job in a big city with a fat paycheck to go to an uncertain future. It made no sense.

She tried in vain to reason with them, but she knew they wouldn't be persuaded, and she would have to live with their disapproval. Caitlyn made a decision to be okay with how they felt, and to love them, and pray for them anyway. She knew that the only one who could change a person's heart was God himself, so she would leave it to him.

For now, she would be content to enjoy Afrika's company and see how things played out between them. She was happy, and she knew that God was blessing their time together. She was growing in Christ, falling in love with a good man who loved Jesus as she did, and was looking forward to a future filled with His mercies. What more could she possibly ask for?

What Caitlyn didn't know what that Afrika was dealing with opposition in his own life, when it came to their relationship. What he was experiencing, however, was considerably uglier. He had been approached by several members of the congregation under the guise of concern for his well-being.

"Pastor, we are worried that you might be entering into a relationship that is not good for you. Surely, God would prefer to see you with someone of your own race?" one rather blunt congregant had said.

Stunned at the malice behind the words, he had to reign in his own anger at the ignorance of such a statement. He took a deep breath and spoke slowly so as not to raise his voice.

"Does God not say we are all created in his image? Is God black, or is He white?" he had asked plainly.

Chastened at the tone, the man turned red and apologized profusely, walking off in a rush. Unfortunately, two others with similar concerns had approached Afrika, and he had finally decided that perhaps a sermon on the topic was in order.

He hadn't spoken of any this to Caitlyn, knowing that she was new in the faith and not wanting her to have to face this kind of attack so soon. He prepared to deliver the message, after she left for New York. He hoped that the arrows would hit their target before she returned, but it had broken his heart and he knew that the heart of his Savior would be grieved by the actions of His children. He saw it as an opportunity for the church to grow, however, and decided that he would invite several other members of the African community to the service.

Yes, God was good! If He chose to use Afrika to stretch his people and get them out of their comfort zone, so be it. He was up to the challenge.

In the meantime, he was becoming more and more enamored by the lovely young English girl that God had brought into his life. He made an appointment with a jeweler in town and spent a good deal of time picking out the perfect ring for her. It was a delicate diamond solitaire in a silver setting, and it sparkled under the light. On a Pastor's salary he couldn't afford anything extravagant, but he knew that Caitlyn wouldn't have wanted anything like that. She didn't wear much jewelry, and she didn't need to. She was beautiful without the extra adornment.

His plan was to propose to her on Valentine's Day. He wanted it to be perfect and so he made arrangements to have dinner at the nicest steak house in town, followed by a horse-drawn carriage ride in the park, which he would have draped in lights. He was certain by now that she felt the same way he did. He simply couldn't imagine his life without her, and he wanted to make her his wife.

The main question in his mind now was who would perform his wedding ceremony? After all, he was the Pastor! Like a flash of lightening, it came to him suddenly. He knew the perfect man to ask. He reached for the phone and dialed the number he had long ago committed to memory.

****

Thomas had sat Jenna and his eight-year-old daughter, Kiersten, down for a family talk. It had taken him a week to get up the courage to tell them of his plans, and he wasn't 100% sure they would be happy to hear what he had to say.

He ordered pizza and sodas delivered to the house, along with roses for Jenna and a Disney movie for Kiersten. A little bribery never hurt.

"There is something that I have wanted to discuss with the two of you for some time, and frankly, I've been too scared to do it. I just can't put it off any longer. God is calling me to become a Pastor," he blurted out before he lost his courage.

His wife shrieked and raced around the table to embrace him, followed immediately by his daughter. They both began talking over the top of each other, asking question after question, clearly delighted by the news.

He laughed and said, "Alright, alright! One at a time, please!"

"When did all of this happen? Where will you go to school? What about your practice and your clients?" Jenna asked excitedly.

"I've found a nearby seminary, where I can go to school part time, until I finish up a couple of projects I am working on for several clients. Then, I am going to sell my share of the firm to one of my partners and focus on going to school full time."

"Daddy, does this mean we get to go to church more?" Kiersten asked. She loved Sunday school and always resisted going home at the end of service.

He laughed, relieved that this was going so well, "Sure thing honey."

They talked for hours as they ate their pizza, and the burden that he had been carrying for so long began to lift from his shoulders. He knew that he had a long road ahead of him and that he had a lot of loose ends at work that would need to be tied up, but he was excited by the prospect and looking forward to it.

They spent the rest of the evening watching cartoon characters frolic on the television screen while curled up on the couch together under a big cozy blanket. Thomas couldn't help but think about how blessed he truly was.

****

It was time to say goodbye for a little while, and Caitlyn's heart was broken. She cried on Afrika's shoulder, and he reassured her that they would talk every day on the phone, and, before long, she would be back with him. She planned to be back in one month and in the meantime, Afrika would be looking for a short-term lease on an apartment for her.

They sat in the airport on a hard plastic chair, holding hands and talking quietly about their future together. He told her that he wanted to take her to Kenya one day, so that she could see where he had grown up and experience the passion that his people had for God. He spoke almost poetically about his homeland, and she was fully aware of how he longed for home.

She confessed to him that her parents were not exactly thrilled about what she was doing and asked him to pray for them. He talked to her about a passage in the Bible from the book of Ephesians, where God talks about our battle not being against flesh and blood but rather against the principalities and powers of this earth. He explained that it meant we needed to be aware of a spiritual battle for our hearts, being fought against the enemy of our souls. He gave her the address where she could find the passage and asked her to study it.

One thing that she loved about Afrika was that he never wanted her to take his words at face value. He continually challenged her to make sure that they lined up with what the word of God said. In doing so, she knew she could trust him. He was humble in heart, something she struggled with herself, and she wanted to be more like that.

Finally, the last boarding call was made, and they knew they had to say their goodbyes. He gave her a fierce hug and made her promise to call him the moment her plane landed in New York. With a last wave goodbye, she walked away from him and took a little piece of his heart, as she went.

****

Afrika heard the crackle over the phone lines, as his call was placed, and he said a prayer that it go through. Kenya was not the telecommunications giant America was, and often his calls would be cut off, if they went through at all. Finally, after ten rings, a man with a gruff voice picked up the call.

"Hello?" he asked.

"Father! It is your long lost son, Afrika! I miss you and mother so. How is everything back home?" he asked, eager for word of his extended family and church.

"Oh son, it is so good to hear your voice! It is well here, as we celebrate the birth of our Messiah. The church is growing, son! We have almost two thousand each Sunday in services and have built a small orphanage to help the children who have lost their parents to AIDS. I am most excited to see what God is doing in our little village. Tell me though, how is your own church coming along?"

Abdu, translated as 'worshiper of God', had been aptly named. He had become Pastor of a tiny church of 45 people some twenty years earlier. He had been most satisfied to see God raise their church up to a force to be reckoned with.

"Actually, that's why I am calling. I've met a most amazing woman, and I plan to ask for her hand. I am calling to ask you to come and perform the ceremony. There is no one I would trust more, and it would mean so much to both of us," he said.

He told his father in great detail of how he met Caitlyn and led her to the Lord, before beginning their courtship. Abdu was thrilled to hear that his son had finally found love. It was the greatest gift to come down from the Creator and was priceless in his eyes.

"Let me speak to your mother, and we will make some arrangements. Do you have a date in mind?" he asked.

"I am going to propose in February, but I do not think it wise to wait too long after that. We want to avoid the temptation to sin, so I think within three or four months. Perhaps in May? It is lovely here that time of year. We could have the reception in the park next to the church."

They talked for another twenty minutes, discussing plans for the ceremony and their trip. He hoped they would stay with him in the parsonage, as he hadn't seen them in almost ten years. Abdu said he would come a week early to give them time to get to know the bride. As Afrika hung up the phone, he felt a deep satisfaction in his soul. It felt *right* somehow. He knew that the Lord was smiling down on them and that they had a huge adventure ahead.

Chapter Twenty Two

Dr. Cobb was nervous. He had made the decision and now was regretting it. Was this completely inappropriate? Probably. Spinning on his heel to leave, he heard her door open, and he winced, realizing he wouldn't make his getaway after all.

"Dr. Cobb?" Theresa asked, surprised to see him there.

"Oh, uh . . . hi. I was just going to drop this off on your doorstep," he said self-consciously, shuffling his feet.

She noticed then that he was holding a bottle of wine, a potted poinsettia, and a small wrapped gift. Shock registered on her features, but she quickly recovered.

"Please, come in."

He followed her into an apartment that could only be described as magnificent. It was decorated in warm, rich browns and golds, filled with expensive antiques as well as modern furniture and artwork. He couldn't help but notice the massive spa-like bathroom, as he passed, but the most amazing one to behold in the entire room was Theresa.

He could see the paleness of her skin and the circles forming under her eyes, and even so, she was still the most beautiful woman he'd ever met. She had dressed up for Christmas in spite of having nobody to celebrate with and was stunning in a black lace gown, with her auburn hair flowing freely around her bare shoulders.

"Don't you have a wife or family you should be with today?" she asked him.

"Oh, not really. I mean, I am not married, and my family is all out of state. I normally just work on the holidays, but you said you were going to be alone today, so I thought maybe we could be alone together," he said with a chuckle.

"How about I open that wine for us?" she offered.

Walking into the kitchen, Theresa couldn't help but think that he was kind of cute, in a nerdy sort of way. He certainly was the last person she expected to find on her doorstep, and the look on his face when she startled him was that of a guilty boy who had been caught doing something wrong. She grinned. This could be fun.

Bringing the wine back into the living room, she asked him how long he had been practicing medicine. She was hoping to get him to warm up a little. He was clearly ill at ease.

"Well, I was about 25, when I finished my residency and went into oncology. Both of my parents died of cancer so I understand what my patients are enduring. I want to be there for them and help them if I can," he said simply.

Sitting this close, she could see the cobalt blue of his eyes, and the tiny smile lines at the corners of them. He smelled really good, and the nearness of him was making her heart beat a little faster. *Uh, oh,* she thought, *am I in trouble here? I can't be attracted to my doctor!* Thinking quickly, she changed the subject.

"I wanted to thank you for setting up the treatments for me and especially for introducing me to Lacey. She's a wonderful nurse, very compassionate."

"Yes, I've worked with her for years. She does have a huge heart. So, how have you been feeling?"

"Oh, a little sick here and there. Mostly I'm just really tired, and the headaches are awful, but let's not talk shop tonight, ok? Tell you what, since neither of us have plans for today, why don't we go out to dinner? I know of a wonderful Chinese restaurant just a few blocks over," she suggested.

"Chinese food for Christmas dinner? Sounds traditional enough for me. I'm not really dressed . . ." he trailed off.

"You look very nice. It's not a very fancy place anyway, and it's never really busy, so we can probably get right in. Let me get my coat."

They left the apartment and decided to walk the few blocks. It had snowed the night before, and the city looked like a Christmas card. As they walked in the snow, Theresa found that he was very easy to talk to, once he felt comfortable with her. She wondered if he had ever done this with any of his other patients. Somehow she doubted it.

She told him that she had met with her attorney and set up a will. He looked sharply at her, and she held her hand up. She explained that she just wanted to cover her bases and wasn't giving up yet. He said he was glad that she was willing to fight.

"I've seen so many of my patients who get this diagnosis, and they just lay down and die. They don't even try. It's just too much for them. I have to say that I admire your courage and your spunk. I think you really stand a better chance if you choose life, and you don't let the negative thoughts take over."

The Chinese restaurant was tiny and charming, and the older woman who owned it recognized her immediately. Theresa surprised him by responding to the woman in

Cantonese. She shrugged sheepishly and said that she ate here so often that it helped to speak a little of the language.

As the evening progressed, Theresa found herself telling him things she hadn't talked about in years. She told him about her ex-husband, and how they had come to divorce. He asked her if she missed him or still had feelings for him.

"Sometimes I miss his friendship and his support, but I had to put some distance between the two of us, because the pain was too great. I wish him only good things though. He was a wonderful man, and I didn't deserve him. I hope that he has moved on and found happiness with someone else," she said, and he believed her.

"What about you? Why is a handsome, eligible doctor, such as yourself still single?" she teased.

"Well, I guess I never really had time for a relationship. I was always so driven by my career. Now that I'm in my 40's, I regret that. I'm feeling my age these days and wishing I had someone to share life with," he looked at her meaningfully, and she actually felt herself blush.

She quickly changed the subject, talking about how good the food was, how beautiful the weather, and any other mundane thing she could think of. It was ironic that she should meet this wonderful man only due to the fact that she was dying. It would be irresponsible of her to see him after this. She wasn't planning to go anywhere, but what if she did die? She couldn't put him through that.

"Tell me, where do you stand when it comes to religion?" she looked him directly in the eye, but for the first time she wasn't challenging someone. She sincerely wanted to know what he thought. She had this hunger building inside of her, and she had no idea where to go with it.

His eyes met hers, and he said simply, "I believe in God. I don't know about Jesus or the Bible or how any of that works, but you don't see the things that I see day-in and day-out as a doctor and not believe in God.

It's not uncommon for someone who receives the news that you have to suddenly start questioning how things are supposed to go, when they die. I am certainly open to it. I guess I just never gave it a whole lot of thought."

She leaned back in her chair and studied him. He was so different from any man she had ever met. He was humble, and she wasn't even a little intimidated by him like she was with a lot of doctors she'd known. He didn't seem to have anything to prove. Clearly there was no God complex to deal with, like so many other doctors she'd met. He was just a really nice man.

"I have been thinking about it lately, I must confess. You have to understand that I've always considered myself a staunch atheist, or, at the very least, an agnostic. I've always hated God for taking away so much from me. My family, my husband, and now maybe my life, yet there is a side of me that wonders if these things break His heart too, and if He has been calling out to me in the midst of my pain, but I just wouldn't hear him."

She was feeling very contemplative, and she didn't know if it was the holiday or the company. She couldn't get over the fact that she was discussing things that she had hidden deep in her heart for so long with a man she barely knew. Theresa just felt safe with him somehow.

"I don't know the answers for any of that. I want to be your friend, Theresa, and I want to be there for you. If God is what you are searching for, I will go with you to find Him. It's crazy, but I have this feeling we were supposed to meet. I don't understand any of it, and I want you to know that I've never spent time outside of my office or the hospital with a patient like this, but I am so drawn to you. I haven't been able to stop thinking about you, since you first came into see me."

As much as she wanted someone to go through all of this with her, she thought it was a bad idea. She opened her mouth to object, and he interrupted her, taking her hands in his across the table.

"Just give me a chance. I know what you are thinking, before you even say it. You're scared and you don't want to drag me through it. Let me prove to you that I can handle it. I want to take you out tomorrow night. I will come and pick you up, and it will be a real date. Ok? One night, that's all I ask. If afterward you still only want to keep that doctor/patient relationship, then I won't ask you for more."

She saw the sincerity in his eyes, the eagerness, and she caved. Nodding her head hesitantly, she squeezed his fingers and smiled.

****

Greg picked Rachel up that morning and they went to the Christmas morning service at her church. The two had slowly gravitated toward her church and eventually decided they would make it their home.

She was chattering away about the big reunion that had taken place the night before. Kevin had wanted them both there, when he saw his wife and kids for the first time in so many years. He was a nervous wreck, but it had been beautiful. The hotel staff had decorated the room with a tree and lots of lights and candles. It glowed with warmth and had relaxed him a bit.

Then they had finally arrived, and after hugs all around, the crying began in earnest. They had years to catch up on, and Rachel and Greg discreetly made their exits, so the family could have some time in private. They all planned to be at the service this morning, and they had so much to be thankful for.

The choir sang Christmas carols, as well as the traditional worship music. During their favorite song, Greg took Rachel's hand and led her to the altar for prayer. While they were on their knees, he gently reached again for her hand and said, "Rachel, these last few months together have been amazing. You have shown me what the love of Christ looks like, you have made me want to be a better man, and I can't see myself without you standing beside me. I love you so much. Will you marry me?"

He held out a small ring box to her and opened it carefully. Shining in the velvet depths was a gorgeous antique diamond ring surrounded by emeralds. She gasped softly and nodded her head vigorously. Throwing her arms around him she said, "Yes, oh yes! I love you!"

Behind them the congregation was on their feet loudly applauding, cheering, and whistling. They had completely forgotten themselves and turned to face their brothers and sisters in Christ with tears on their cheeks.

Kevin and Cathy, along with their boys, were the first to congratulate them with hugs all around. They were followed by Thomas and Jenna Allen who shared their own good news. The festiveness in the room was contagious and tears flowed freely. It was the best Christmas any of them could remember, and they all made plans to go to the Allen's house for dinner.

****

Theresa called Thomas the next day and asked him if his investigator had made any more progress on the hunt for Rachel's family. He explained to her that there had been a huge snowstorm in Iowa, and although Caitlyn had been close to finding answers, they would have to wait a little while longer.

"I do have some news that I'd like to share with you, if you have a moment," he said tentatively.

"Of course."

"I am going to be leaving the practice of law to become a Minister. I have a few projects that I will need to finish up, but I'm hoping that by the end of the New Year I will be a full time theological student."

She hadn't seen that one coming. He had been her lawyer for almost twenty years, and more than that, he and his wife were good friends. She hoped that wouldn't change.

"Well, if that's what you feel like you need to do, I am happy for you, Thomas. I hope that doesn't mean you'll be moving out of town?" she asked worriedly.

"No, there is a seminary nearby, so I can commute for awhile," he responded.

She was happy to hear it and tempted to tell him about her change of heart regarding God, but once again, her pride got in the way. They set up an appointment for her to come in and sign some final paperwork before getting off the phone.

Theresa gathered her coat, purse, and Bible and headed out the door for her next treatment. She had become friendly with the chemotherapy nurse at the hospital and was looking forward to seeing her if not to the therapy itself.

"Theresa! Hi, how are you feeling today?" Lacey McHenry asked. She was a tall brunette with chocolate brown eyes and a bright smile. She had worked in the cancer ward for ten years, and she loved her patients. They each felt like they were the only patients she had, and they adored her as well.

"I'm a little tired, but ok. Let's get this over with, shall we?" She sat in the large comfortable chair and allowed Lacey to hook up the I.V. Once she was settled in, the nurse asked her if there was anything she needed. She declined the offer and reached for her Bible.

Theresa had found that reading the Bible was coming easier to her. She just decided that if God was really God, he wouldn't be afraid of her questions and so she prayed that way. If she didn't understand something, she said so, and she felt deep within her that He was listening.

Her favorite book was the Gospel of John. Reading the story of how Jesus was born, lived, and ministered to people around him, even the untouchable people, surprised her. The account of his death took her breath away and brought tears to her eyes, which surprised her. When Lacey returned to the room to tell her she was done and unhook her I.V., she was amazed at how fast the time had gone.

As she rode back to her apartment, she decided to call Rachel and ask her to tell her more about how the God thing worked. She hated the thought of swallowing her pride, but she trusted Rachel and knew that she would be honest with her. She put her coat and purse away, but before she could reach for the phone, it rang.

"Theresa, it's Rachel. I was just checking on you to see how you are feeling."

Theresa held the phone out from her ear and stared at it. That was weird. It was almost as if Rachel had known she was going to call.

"Actually I was about to call you. Can you come over tomorrow? There's something I'd like to talk to you about."

"Sure, I have something to tell you too! But I'll wait and tell you when I see you. Get some rest, and I'll come by, when I close up tomorrow after work."

She hung up the phone and ran to the bathroom to vomit. It hit her so fast that she almost didn't make it. She didn't think she'd ever get used to this. She had already lost ten pounds and was thin to begin with. The worst thing was that after only ten days of treatment, she noticed that her hairbrush was filling up much faster than normal. She thought she could handle the fatigue, the nausea, and the headaches, but losing her hair terrified her.

She stared at herself in the mirror and asked herself once again if she was making a huge mistake by agreeing to see Terry, but she was scared, and she really didn't want to go through this alone. She was reaching out and grasping at his offer like a drowning woman would a life raft. For once, she admitted that she wasn't strong enough, and she needed a friend.

Chapter Twenty Three

Caitlyn had finally managed to convince the Bayfield courthouse to fax over a copy of the documents she had been trying to get her hands on for weeks now. It had taken numerous phone calls, a great deal of pestering, and finally a substantial 'donation' to the county to get them. She poured herself a hot cup of tea and sat on her folding chair at her makeshift table to read.

When she finished reading an hour later, she typed up a report for Thomas and faxed it over along with the paperwork from the courthouse. Now she could finally concentrate on packing. She dug into it with vigor, excited to think of her new life to come.

She hadn't unpacked a lot of her things from the trip here from England six months earlier, so it didn't take much. She thought she could probably be ready to go in about ten days. She grinned to think of how surprised Afrika would be to see her early.

Caitlyn grabbed her purse and headed out to run a few errands. She went to the bank to close out her account, the post office for a change of address form, and finally Thomas' office to say her goodbyes. She was unprepared for his strange attitude, when she saw him. He was reading her report, and his face had gone white.

"Thomas, what is it?" she asked, concerned for him.

"Oh. Hi, Caitlyn. Um, this report you sent me. Are you sure it's accurate?" he asked carefully.

She was a little put off by that. After all, she was a professional known for double and triple checking her sources to make sure what she reported was precise in every way.

"Yes, of course it is. You have no idea the lengths I had to go to in order to get that information. Believe me when I tell you that it's all true. Why?"

"I can't really get into it with you, without betraying my client's confidentiality, but let me just say this is going to stir up quite a hornet's nest. Thank you so much for all your hard work. We are really going to miss you around here. Actually, I should say that *they* are going to miss you at the firm. I am resigning to go back to school. I've been called to be a Pastor, so I'm stepping down here."

"Oh, that's wonderful! I'm so happy for you!" she exclaimed.

"Thanks. I just have to tie up a few loose ends. I would like to have you out for dinner before you leave for Iowa, if you can make it. Say Friday night?" he asked.

"Sure, sounds good. I'll call you later in the week to get the details. Let me know if I can bring anything." She said goodbye and left the office, wondering what in the report could have worked him up so much.

Thomas held the report, reading and re-reading it several times, before the gravity of it finally sank in for him. God's timing never failed to amaze him. He closed up his office for the day. There was no way he could work now. All he wanted to do was go home and be with his family.

****

Afrika was drawing on the passage from the Book of Acts chapter ten for his upcoming sermon. He read aloud verse 34 and 35:

Then Peter began to speak: "I now realize how true it is that God does not show favoritism but accepts from every nation the one who fears him and does what is right.

Thank you Jesus, Afrika whispered, as he always did when he read scripture. It truly was God breathed and answered every question mankind could have. He wanted to express the heart of God to his congregation this Sunday. God was no respecter of persons, and in His eyes, we are all loved. The kind of questions that had been asked of him lately really reflected that some in his midst didn't have a true grasp of how deep and how wide and how high the love of God really was. He looked at the heart of a man, not the color of his skin.

He missed Caitlyn. He couldn't wait for her to come back, and he had been diligently trying to find her an apartment. He had a couple of leads that he was planning to go check out this afternoon, and he knew a couple of local attorneys that were looking for an investigator as well.

He finished up his notes, and as was his custom, he prayed over them. *Father God, I ask that when I deliver your word this weekend, it will not be my words but your own. Use me, Lord, as a tool in your hands. I want to feel your heartbeat, and more than that, I want your people to know how great your love for them is. Help me to impart it to them somehow. Thank you for your grace and your mercy, which is new every day. I give this day to you, Lord, to do with as you wish. In your perfect name I pray, AMEN.*

He closed his Bible and put his notes away to type up later. He was fully aware that his relationship with Caitlyn might be too much for a few Christians to handle and that was ok.

He lived to please God, not man. Lord help him if that ever changed.

****

Thomas had explained to Jenna that Caitlyn would be moving to Iowa in the next week and that he wanted to have a farewell dinner for her. As usual she had created a gourmet feast and had Kiersten setting the table just as the doorbell rang.

He answered the door and hugged her in greeting. They followed their noses into the kitchen to find Jenna pulling a large prime rib and baked potatoes from the oven. She had mushrooms sautéing on the stovetop next to a large pot of steamed artichokes.

"That smells so good, and I'm starving!" Caitlyn confessed.

"Great, let's go sit. I can't wait to hear all about how things are going for you. It sounds like God is doing big things in your life," Jenna said.

They held hands around the table and prayed over their meal before digging in heartily. Groans of appreciation were heard all around, and Jenna basked in the praise of a job well done.

"So tell me all about your new man," she said.

"Well, he is a Pastor from Kenya, and he has a small church in Des Moines. I met him while I was out doing some research for Thomas. He is beautiful, and he loves God so much. He is the one who led me to the Lord. I have learned so much from him! We began courting about two weeks after we met. I am moving out there soon. It's the craziest thing I've ever done. It just feels right somehow." She knew she was babbling, but she couldn't help it. She was so happy and had been dying to share it all with them.

They spent an enjoyable evening together, and finally at ten she said that she needed to get home. She thanked them and headed out the door, thinking that she couldn't wait to get home and call Afrika.

****

Rachel had arrived at Theresa's apartment at seven that night, exhausted after a long day of work, but still riding high on the heels of her proposal. She couldn't wait to tell Theresa all about it. She rang the doorbell, and she tried to hide her dismay at Theresa's appearance, when she opened the door.

"C'mon in. I just made a pot of coffee, would you like some?" she asked.

"No, thank you. I just had a cup at the office," she replied. She took in Theresa's gaunt appearance and tried to think of a tactful way to bring it up.

Finally she just came out with it.

"How have you been feeling? Are the treatments helping you at all?" she asked gently, scared of the answer.

Theresa sighed and set her mug on the coffee table. She didn't want to admit how bad she was really feeling, so she changed the subject.

"Actually, there is something else that I would much rather discuss with you if that's ok. This might come as a shock, but I have been reading the Bible. I have some questions, and I don't really know who else to ask," she said.

Rachel tried to remain calm, but inside she was screaming, "*Yes!*"

"From what I am reading in Romans, it seems like God is saying that all you have to do is ask for forgiveness, trust in Him for salvation, and live for Him the rest of your life. I'm sorry, but it seems too easy. What about all the bad things I've done in this life? Will I have to pay for them in the next life or what?"

Rachel shook her head, a smile on her face. "That's a pretty common misconception. That's why Jesus died on the cross: to pay for your sins because you *can't* pay for them yourself. We do sometimes have to deal with the consequences of our sin. Imagine yourself as a child, playing ball in your front yard. You hit one, and it goes straight through your neighbor's window. You go running home to tell your mother, terrified of all the trouble you'll get into. She realizes it was an accident, so she doesn't punish you, but you still need to pay to get that window repaired.

The same is true of God. He knows that we are human and that we will sometimes fall. He doesn't punish us, but there are times when we have to deal with the results our sin can cause, not only in our own lives, but also in the lives of others.

As to your other question, the plan of salvation is simple, but it's not easy. We have to put aside our own pride and accept that we were never meant to carry the burden of this life alone. We need Jesus."

Theresa thought about what she said, meditating on her words. "What if you have done something truly awful? I mean, aren't there some sins that are too big for Him to forgive?" She wasn't about to tell her of the one big mistake she'd made; the one that had haunted her for so many years.

"There is nothing so big that God won't forgive it. The Bible says that the only unforgiveable thing is to die apart from Him. In fact, I believe He will pursue you relentlessly until you take your last breath. He loves you so much, Theresa, of that, you can be sure. Sometimes we just don't see it, until we come to a place of complete brokenness."

It was too much for her to take in all at once. She needed time to think and process everything. She just couldn't wrap her mind around the idea that she could actually be set free from her demons. Why couldn't this have happened to her years ago, when she still had lots of life left?

"God is doing a work in your heart, Theresa. Be open to it. He wants you to seek Him out. In fact He says in the Bible to seek Him with all your heart. He isn't afraid of your questions. I will be praying for you, my friend. Now you have been avoiding my other question. I want to know how you have been feeling. Please, be honest with me."

"Honestly? Not great. The headaches are getting worse, and the chemo has made me feel pretty sick most of the time," she admitted. "The good news is that my doctor is handsome and charming, and he likes me," she grinned impishly and Rachel laughed with her.

"You know what, it's been nice having you here. Thank you for answering all my questions. I'll probably have more if that's ok."

"Any time, you know that. Oh! I almost forgot, I have some exciting news to share. Greg and I are getting married!" she chirped excitedly.

Theresa shrieked like a schoolgirl and hugged her friend hard. "That's wonderful news! I'm so happy for you! Will you let me help you plan it?"

"That would be awesome, if you are feeling up to it. We haven't set a date yet, but I will let you know. I'd better be getting home. Poor Henry is probably dancing around with his legs crossed by now." She stood to leave, and Theresa gave her a tight hug, whispering her thanks.

She walked her to the door and waved goodbye, then retreated to her bathroom to get ready. She had a date tonight!

****

Rachel had invited Greg over that night to discuss wedding plans. She told him that she was really worried about Theresa and wanted to have the wedding soon. It was really important to her that she was able to come. She had no idea where things would go with her, and she wanted to make sure that she was still well enough to stand by her side. She was the closest thing she had to family now, and she had come to a place where her approval was paramount in her life.

"That's fine with me, honey. I am ready to get married today!" he laughed.

"Seriously, let's pick a date. Do you think we could pull it together by the end of February?" she asked.

"I don't need a fancy wedding. All I need is you. We can have a small, simple wedding and spend the money on a nice honeymoon. Anywhere you want to go."

She threw her arms around him, still over the moon about him and convinced it was all a dream. They spent the next few hours talking over what they wanted in the ceremony, and where they would host the reception. As the hour grew late, Greg regretfully said he had to get home, as he had an early client. He kissed her on the cheek and headed home.

As she laid her head down on her pillow, she said a prayer for Theresa. *Lord, I lift my friend to you and ask that you would heal her body and also her soul. I see you lifting the veil from her eyes, and I'm so thankful that she is beginning to respond to you. I pray that you would bring other godly people into her life that will speak truth to her. Thank you for all you are doing in her life, Lord. I pray these things in your name, knowing you are faithful and true. Amen.*

****

Theresa woke with a smile on her face, even as the nausea sent her running to the bathroom. The previous evening with Terry had been glorious. He had taken her to the Russian Tea Room for dinner. Then they had gone ice skating in Central Park and finished the night snuggled under a fur blanket, watching the children on the ice while sipping hot chocolate.

He was the most amazing man. He was sweet, considerate, and romantic. It was so insane that at a time in her life, when she was facing a deadly illness, all she could think about was this tall, dark, and handsome man in a lab coat. She felt like a teenager with her first crush. He was consuming her thoughts. She had plans to go out with him again tonight, and she was excited to see what they would do.

She was so tired though. She would have to rest for the day, or she'd never make it. She reached over and started the hot water in her bathtub, adding in her favorite vanilla scented oil and lighting some candles. While it filled, she made a light breakfast of dry toast and green tea and flipped through her calendar.

She had that appointment with Thomas this afternoon. She couldn't wait to hear what he had found out about Rachel's parents. At least if she *were* going to die, she could do one good deed before she went. She finished her breakfast and padded into the bathroom, adding some soft saxophone music to the CD player.

Sinking into the tub with a sigh, she thought again about her evening with the good doctor. She dozed in her magnificent tub, a big grin on her face.

Chapter Twenty Four

Caitlyn was having second thoughts. Was she crazy?! She was giving up everything to move halfway across the country for a man she'd known only a few weeks. What if she got there only to find out that he was a pathological liar, or that he had six other wives back in Kenya, or that he was secretly a crack addicted pyromaniac shoplifter?

She took a moment to get on her knees before God and ask for some direction.

Lord, I am terrified that I am making a big mistake here. I don't know if it's just last minute jitters now that the flat has sold and my job is gone. I don't know if you are trying to warn me or it is just my imagination. Please show me what to do before it's too late. I trust you Jesus and I only want to live in your perfect will for my life. I am going to go, but if I am not supposed to, please stop me. I lift my relationship with Afrika and lay it at the foot of the cross. Guide us where you want us to go, in Jesus name I pray, AMEN.

She felt a little bit better, if for no other reason than she had spoken it all out loud. Where was this trepidation coming from? She was normally a confident woman, not afraid of taking risks. She had felt good about her decision until this morning, as she prepared to ship the remainder of her boxes at the post office and pick up her plane tickets from the travel agent.

She tried to put these thoughts out of her mind and get on with the business of moving. Three suitcases lined up next to her front door alongside her briefcase and laptop computer. She headed downstairs to turn her key over to the landlord and was completely oblivious to the dark presence that hovered over her, in a dimension undetectable to the human eye.

****

Afrika put the finishing touches on his sermon notes for the next morning. After a solid 45 minutes of fumbling through it, he finally put it away. He simply could not concentrate today. He was experiencing something in his spirit that he couldn't quite put his finger on. He felt . . . uneasy.

There was a knot in his stomach, and he couldn't explain away. It was almost as if he knew something bad was about to happen, but he had no idea what it was or how to stop it.

As a Pastor he was certain that there was a whole world beyond what we could experience. A supernatural dimension that was more real than anything we could conjure up in our current realm. Having spent the majority of his life in Africa, he had seen things that nobody could explain outside of demonic forces.

In a village not far from his own, for instance, a so-called medicine man placed curses on the people who refused to bow down to him, and one by one they died of a horrific flesh eating disease that nobody could explain. He had also seen a man of God go into that same village and rebuke the enemy, bringing about a great revival and setting the people free from witchcraft.

Yes, spiritual forces were real. There was no such thing as good magic or white magic, as many supposed. It simply boiled down to going down the path of righteousness in following Christ or being deceived into following the enemy. Most people didn't even know how the devil worked, with wily schemes and beautiful deception.

It broke his heart to think of the millions in this country who unknowingly opened doors to evil in their own lives by visiting fortune tellers, reading tarot cards, playing with Ouija boards. All in the vain hopes of knowing how their future would turn out. If only they would turn to the One who loved them, died for them, and knows the rest of their story as only He can.

Afrika registered that this uncomfortable feeling was not of God. He felt it specifically in regard to his relationship with Caitlyn, and he recognized the ugly whispers in his ear as demonic.

In a way, he praised God for this. He knew that the enemy would only try to attack those who are a threat to his way of life. He and Caitlyn had a relationship that glorified God and he knew that they would be used by Him to bring others into His kingdom. Even so, he knew he couldn't allow this attack to continue.

He bowed his head in prayer. *Almighty God, creator of the heavens and the earth, I come before you now asking that you would cover me in the blood of the Lamb as I address the enemy of my soul. Remind him that I am more than a conqueror in Christ Jesus our Lord and that I stand against him only be your power and your authority. AMEN.*

Satan, I rebuke you in the name of Jesus Christ. You have no place in my life or that of the one I love. You will leave now, taking with you any of your dark angels that have attached themselves to Caitlyn or me. We are spoken for by the one true God and you will not come between us or our relationship with Him. I command these things in the name of Jesus Christ, the risen one!

Instantly the knot dissolved in his stomach, replaced by that sweet peace that passes all understanding. He thanked the

Lord for his goodness and pulled his notes back out, finally able to concentrate on his work.

****

Caitlyn boarded the plane at 6:15 that evening and was a little bit more clear-headed about the whole thing. She didn't understand what had happened since this morning but could only attribute it to prayer. Her anxiety had completely dissipated and she was once again deliriously happy and on her way to her beloved.

She had been so busy during the previous week that she hadn't taken the time to read the passage Afrika had told her about. The four-hour plane ride would give her some time to read. She pulled out her Bible, which was becoming well-worn and marked up with pen and highlighter. Caitlyn turned to the Book of Ephesians, chapter six.

Finally, be strong in the Lord and in his mighty power. Put on the full armor of God, so that you can take your stand against the devil's schemes. For our struggle is not against flesh and blood, but against the rulers, against the authorities, against the powers of this dark world and against the spiritual forces of evil in the heavenly realms. Therefore put on the full armor of God, so that when the day of evil comes, you may be able to stand your ground, and after you have done everything, to stand. Stand firm then, with the belt of truth buckled around your waist, with the breastplate of righteousness in place, and with your feet fitted with the readiness that comes from the gospel of peace. In addition to all this, take up the shield of faith, with which you can extinguish all the flaming arrows of the evil one. Take the helmet of salvation and the sword of the Spirit, which is the word of God. And pray in the Spirit on all occasions with all kinds of prayers and requests. With this in mind, be alert and always keep on praying for all the Lord's people.

As she read this, Caitlyn could feel a small prickle at the base of her neck. Since meeting Afrika and becoming a believer, she no longer called them goose bumps. They were God Bumps! She could feel His whisper across her skin, hear His love in her ear, and sense His presence by her side. She never would have considered herself a spiritual person or even one attuned to the supernatural, until now.

God was telling her something here, she was certain of it. *Be strong in the Lord and in his mighty power.* She reflected on that first verse. She knew that the Bible was the inspired word of God and that every single sentence in it was there for a purpose. She also believed that she read what God wanted her to read, *when* He wanted her to read it.

The question became *why* was he telling her to be strong in Him now, at this particular time. She thought back to the fear that had swamped her this morning. Her certainty that Afrika was the one she was meant to be with had disintegrated in a flash, and she had been overwhelmed with indecision. Then, upon spending some time in prayer, the fear had left her. Was it really possible that the enemy had come in to try and dissuade her?

Again that feeling of dread tried to creep in, but this time, she squashed it. She picked up her Bible and continued to read. She thanked God with everything she had in her, for His goodness and mercy.

Caitlyn's plane landed right on time, and she hailed a taxi to take her to the hotel. She settled in and ordered room service for dinner. She planned to surprise Afrika in the morning at church. He had no idea that she was on her way here, and she couldn't wait to see the look on his face!

****

Afrika had spent the remainder of Saturday running a few errands that he had been neglecting. He met with an apartment manager to check out an apartment for Caitlyn, in a complex not far from the church. It was a tiny studio apartment but it had a month-to-month lease that was perfect, and it came fully furnished.

He then drove out to the mall to meet with his friend, Chizoba. He wanted to gather as many of his African friends as he could and invite them to the service tomorrow. In his heart, he knew that tension between races was mutual at times. It was important to him that he was the one to bridge the gap and help to bring about healing in their community.

Chizoba was finishing up with a customer, when he walked in, so he stood to the side and politely waited, admiring all of the remarkable artwork.

"Pastor Afrika!" he exclaimed upon seeing his friend. "So good to see you. Tell me what brings you in today? Are you here to find a gift equally beautiful to the one Caitlyn bought you?" his deep, hearty chuckle reverberated in the tiny shop.

"No, although I appreciate the help you gave her. The piece is exquisite. I am here to invite you to church tomorrow. My message is one you may be interested in hearing," he replied with an enigmatic smile.

"Really? May I have a hint?"

"No, I don't want to ruin what must be unbearable anticipation for you. Please do come, and bring your friends and family."

"Certainly I will be there. Thank you for the invitation. Now, I want to hear all about you and your lovely young lady," he teased.

The two men spent some time talking and sharing stories of their homes in Kenya. Finally Afrika begged off, saying he needed to go and that he had an appointment in town. They hugged each other fiercely, in a way that only brothers can, and said goodbye.

His next stop was at the law offices of Baker and Baker. He had an appointment with the senior partner, George Baker, and was buzzed in promptly. George came out with his hand extended to the man who had been his Pastor for the last five years.

"Pastor! So good to see you. Please, have a seat," he exclaimed.

"Hello, George. I really appreciate you making time to see me this afternoon. As we discussed on Sunday, my friend Caitlyn is relocating to Des Moines and is an excellent private investigator. She prefers to work with a law firm as opposed to freelance work. You said that you may have an opening for her?" Afrika asked politely.

"As a matter of fact, I made a few phone calls since our discussion. I spoke with her former employer, Thomas Allen, and it sounds like she is the perfect candidate. I would love to meet with her. And, unless someone else snatches her up first, I do believe she has a job with us if she wants it," he responded, smiling widely.

The men shook hands and Pastor Afrika got a promise from George that he would be in service the next morning.

****

Caitlyn dressed carefully for church in a striking grey pinstriped suit with a teal silk blouse and high-heeled boots. She wanted to look especially pretty for Afrika today. She took a little more time than she was accustomed to styling her hair and applying her makeup. Almost an hour later she felt spectacular when she looked in the mirror and judged herself ready to go.

Grabbing her purse, coat, and Bible, she headed out the door and took a taxi to the church. She slipped into the back pew just as the worship team took its place and began to play. Several members of the congregation noticed her and came over to give her hugs and welcome her back, but a few others gave her a cold stare that unnerved her greatly.

What on earth is that all about, she wondered? Thirty minutes later, she had her answer.

Pastor Afrika took walked to the pulpit and set his Bible down on the podium. He greeted the congregation and shared a few announcements before plunging headlong into his sermon.

"As many of you are aware, I have entered into a courtship with a lovely young lady that God was kind enough to bring into my life. I am thrilled to see where He is leading us and how He will use us for his glory. Unfortunately my excitement is not shared by all. I have been approached by a small handful of people, who will remain nameless, that expressed concern over the relationship. It seems that they are uncomfortable with the fact that we are of different races. God has laid on my heart that this is an issue He wants addressed.

Turn with me, if you will, in your Bible to the Book of Genesis, Chapter One. As you are turning there, I'm going to warn you that we are going to be tracking down quite a few verses, in quite a few books, so I hope you have come prepared with your sword for battle." There was a smattering of laughter in the crowd, as the pages rustled.

Caitlyn felt herself turning pink as the gazes of those around her lingered on her face. She'd had no idea this was the topic of the morning's sermon.

"Most of you are familiar with this book of the Bible, but for those who aren't, this is where it all started. This is the account of creation, and it tells in beautiful detail how God created the heavens and the earth. Let's start in Verse 26. *Then God said, "Let us make mankind in our image, in our likeness, so that they may rule over the fish in the sea and the birds in the sky, over the livestock and all the wild animals, and over all the creatures that move along the ground."* *So God created mankind in his own image, in the image of God he created them; male and female he created them.* *God blessed them and said to them, "Be fruitful and increase in number; fill the earth and subdue it. Rule over the fish in the sea and the birds in the sky and over every living creature that moves on the ground."*

I'd like to begin by pointing out that God created man in his own image. Our earth is populated by a wonderful abundance of all walks of life. We have people with every skin color: black, white, red, brown, yellow. And we all come in different sizes, shapes, heights, with different hair types and colors. We are tall, short, thin, fat, muscular, or scrawny. Some of us have brown eyes, others have blue or green.

So tell me this, with the wide variety and endless combinations of physical attributes in the world today, which of us looks exactly like God himself? Is it the Caucasian? Or the Asian man? What about Native Americans, or South Americans? Is God European, or is He Canadian?" Now the laughter was full-blown, but he could see his point was getting across.

"No, we understand that when God said we were created in His image, he is not implying that a physical likeness, although that is also partially true. When God created us in His image, He gave us a distinctive nature and place in creation. According to First Corinthians, we are the image and glory of God. The Psalms and the Book of Hebrews proclaims that we are made a little lower than the angels, and that God crowned us with glory and honor. As sovereign among the creatures of creation, man has dominion over everything on earth.

Being in God's image means we can do things God does, we talk, rest, sit, walk, hear, smell, reason, think, and even have some features that God has like, a face and back, a mouth, and hands. I do not have the time this morning to reference all of the verses where this information can be found, but if you read the Bible at all, you will recognize these attributes. This does not mean God has the same physical features man has, but that man can function, in part, like God does.

Then in Chapter Two Verse Seven, God "breathed into his nostrils the breath of life; and man became a living soul." This is where we see the image of God in man. We have a soul which animates us and a spirit that connects us to God.

In this we are all created equal, the very image and likeness of God. If you go back and look at Verse Twenty-Eight, it says '*Be fruitful and increase in number; fill the earth and subdue it. Marry only someone of your own race and only have children with people of the same color.*

Again good-natured laughter filled the room.

"What?! This is not what your Bible says?" he asked, feigning shock.

"Alright," he said laughing, "I think the point I am attempting to make here is that in God's eyes, we are all on equal footing. You needn't turn there now, but in the Book of Acts, Peter says something very profound. He was taken down a peg or two when God showed him that Gentiles and Jews were not to be segregated in their worship of Him. He said, 'I now realize how true it is that God does not show favoritism.'

Let's turn to the Book of James, Chapter Three Verse Nine and read along with me.

With the tongue we praise our Lord and Father, and with it we curse human beings, who have been made in God's likeness. Out of the same mouth come praise and cursing. My brothers and sisters, this should not be.

"Well, now. That almost sounds like a warning doesn't it? How can we say we love the Lord our God in one breathe, and in the other, curse someone who is created in his very image? James is correct in saying that this should not be!

Let me say that one reason many well-meaning believers have said that we should not marry out of our race can be traced back to the Old Testament teaching that we should not marry foreigners. You have to understand that God forbade that type of marriage because He was concerned with the worship of false gods and knowing that his people were easily led astray did not want them to bow down to an idol. Yes, God is a jealous God and will not stand for us allowing another to take His place in our hearts.

But when we, as followers of Jesus Christ, find that same love for Him in another person, God will bless that union. In His word we see that he does not want us to marry an unbeliever. Turn with me now, back to the Book of Second Corinthians."

Out of the corner of his eye, Afrika saw two men get up from their chairs and walk out the back door. It broke his heart, and he said a quick prayer for them as they left.

"Let's go to Chapter Six and begin in Verse Fourteen. Read with me now:

Do not be yoked together with unbelievers. For what do righteousness and wickedness have in common? Or what fellowship can light have with darkness? What harmony is there between Christ and Belial? Or what does a believer have in common with an unbeliever? What agreement is there between the temple of God and idols? For we are the temple of the living God, as God has said, "I will live with them and walk among them, and I will be their God, and they will be my people."

Clearly God is more concerned with what is in our heart than the color of the skin that He himself created. One more passage I want to read with you in closing. Please open your Bibles to the Book of John Chapter Thirteen. Let's pick it up in Verse 34:

"A new command I give you: Love one another. As I have loved you, so you must love one another. By this, everyone will know that you are my disciples, if you love one another."

It all boils down to this, *love*. God doesn't politely ask us to love one another. He commands it! And he doesn't say for the white people to love the other white people or for black people to love black people. He says **YOU MUST LOVE ONE ANOTHER.** Listen, please brothers and sisters in Christ, to what he says next. *By this everyone will know that you are my disciples, if you love one another.* Did you hear that? How is the world going to know that we are any different than they are, if we act the same way that they do?!

I want to share a quote by the great Martin Luther King Jr. He said, 'Darkness cannot drive out darkness; only light can do that. Hate cannot drive out hate; only love can do that.' Jesus called us to be the light in this dark world. This week as you go about your Father's business, I challenge you to be that light. Thank you."

He closed in prayer, and the hearts of his people *had* been challenged. They came to him to apologize, one by one, and found forgiveness there. Many others came and thanked him for his words of wisdom, to which he simply replied, "It was not me. It was Him."

And standing at the edge of the crowd was Caitlyn, eyes red and puffy from weeping. She embraced him tightly and told him how proud she was of him. But in another realm, the dark forces were stirred again, preparing to do battle.

Chapter Twenty Five

Rachel had a secret. She had been holding on to it for years now, and nobody in her life knew of it. Now that she was engaged to Greg, it was eating at her and she wasn't quite sure what to do about it. It wasn't necessarily a bad thing either. Most people would, in fact, call it wonderful.

She had by now been working for *Her Wicked Ways* for over ten years. Her original plan had been to apprentice for Theresa for a couple of years before breaking out on her own and designing a clothing line for the full figured woman. Over the years, she had gotten comfortable in life, and although she still thought about her plan from time to time, for the most part she was content to remain where she was.

If she were honest with herself, she would have admitted that the money and prestige that went along with working for the most famous clothing designer in the world were what kept her where she was. Her salary had over the years increased to the top end of a six-figure income. As her needs were small and her apartment modest (and paid for by the company), she had saved quite a fortune.

This was her great secret. She was, unbeknownst to anyone else but her banker, a multi-millionaire. With an expense account, paid living quarters, free clothing from the company, a hired driver and anything else she could possibly need taken care of, she had no need to spend her money, and the money terrified her.

Rachel was a small town girl who had grown up in a modest home. Her parents were never extravagant by any stretch of the imagination. Her mother was a coupon-clipper who sewed her own and Rachel's clothing. Her father drove the same car for twenty-five years and was proud of it. Every spare dime they had ever had was given to the church for missions; aside from the small amount they had given her for college.

She had no idea what to do about her money. It earned a large amount of interest each year, and her banker had advised her many years before to invest some of it, which had paid off well for her. She was so frightened that someone would steal it from her in a scam of some sort, or that she would fritter it away on something useless in the grand scheme of eternity, or worse yet, that someone pretending to care would use her for the money, that she had never spent a single penny.

Now, she was engaged to a wonderful man, and the fear of that large bank account lurked in the back of her mind. How would she tell him? How would he react to it? What if he wanted to spend it on something that she wouldn't approve of? Did she even have to tell him about it?

If only she knew where her parents were, she would happily give it all to them to advance the gospel in China. She missed them so much. Periodically she called the Pastor that had taken over their church in Iowa, but he still hadn't heard anything from them. Her phone calls to him became fewer and fewer, as she couldn't face the news he gave her.

She made plans to discuss it with Thomas. Perhaps he could recommend a worthy charity or ministry in need that she could give to. Then she wouldn't *have* to tell Greg anything.

****

Theresa was preparing for her meeting with Thomas. She was so excited to be able to finally reunite Rachel with her family. How wonderful it would be if she could get them here for the wedding! It would make the perfect gift. She sighed happily and finished applying her makeup.

She planned to meet up with Terry for lunch after her appointment at the law firm. Things had been going so well with them. They had spent nearly every spare moment together, and she found herself growing attached to him in a way that scared her a little. Since her divorce from Stephen, Theresa had made it a point to focus on her career. She didn't want or need the complications of another relationship in her life.

Yet, she knew that she needed him right now. Slowly but surely God was chipping away at her pride. She was completely defenseless before Him and thought that for the first time in her life, she couldn't do any of this alone.

Her driver knocked on her door, and she grabbed her coat and purse before hurrying out the door. In spite of her illness, she felt that she actually had so much to look forward to. *Don't take it all from me God. I'm not ready!*

She was ushered into Thomas' office twenty minutes later, so excited and nervous to hear his report that she could barely contain herself. She wanted to shake him by his lapels and shout, *"JUST SPIT IT OUT!!"*

He began slowly, "I apologize for the length of time it took us to get the answers you were seeking. It wasn't an easy task, I assure you. Before I get into all of this, I must ask, how are you feeling?"

What?! She didn't have time for this. Everyone was always asking her how she was feeling. Frankly she'd feel a lot better if people would quit asking her how she was feeling!

"I'm fine. Can we get on with this please?" she said abruptly.

"Theresa, I'm sorry. It's just that this is going to come as a bit of a shock for you, and I want to make sure you are physically able to handle what I'm about to tell you."

"What do you mean?"

"Let me start at the beginning. Caitlyn, our investigator, went back to Iowa where Rachel was raised and did some research. The first thing she learned was that her biological parents are both deceased."

At this, Theresa's heart sank. It was the last thing she had expected to hear, and it was just one more devastation in a long life full of them. She had built up this fantasy in her mind of both of her birth parents arriving at the wedding and of a beautiful, sweet reunion. How desperately she had wanted that for her dear friend!

"The adoption agency told her, however, how the parents died and that there was some remaining family. She wouldn't disclose who that was but assured her that she would contact them. Caitlyn next went to the public library to research small town newspaper articles and came across an article written about a young couple. It seems that the young lady was about seven months pregnant when her boyfriend beat her to death."

He paused for a moment, watching the facts penetrate her brain. The look on her face as she started to connect the dots was one he would never forget. She seemed at first confused, then terrified, and finally she turned white as a sheet.

"The baby girl was saved and sent to a local hospital for several months to undergo medical treatment. Her father went to prison for murder and was killed many years later by a fellow inmate. She had an uncle, but he was killed in the Vietnam War. Her grandparents followed a few years later in a car accident. The only remaining blood relative of Rachel Jenkins sits in front of me now," he finished softly.

Theresa sat shaking her head back and forth and began to hyperventilate. She stood to her feet and told him in broken, fragmented words that he was wrong. It couldn't be. Thomas watched as her face went paler, and she began to sway on her feet, but before he could reach her, she slipped to the floor in a faint.

****

Terry was paged to Theresa's hospital room and raced there as fast as he could in a full-blown panic. He arrived to find a tall, handsome, bespectacled man standing by her side. She had finally regained consciousness and was talking quietly with the man, color high in her cheeks.

When he saw him approach, Thomas extended his hand and introduced himself. He explained that Theresa was fine and that she had just received some rather disturbing news, which caused her to faint. He excused himself to head back to his office.

"I'm sorry, if I worried you. I guess I'm in a bit of shock right now. Please, sit. You make me nervous, hovering over me like that," she ordered.

He did as he was told, concerned for her evident in his eyes.

"I've told you that I made it my personal mission to find Rachel's birth family? Well, it seems that would be me," she said bluntly and tears began in her eyes.

She explained the whole back-story to him, and as she spoke, something truly magnificent occurred to her. She sat straight up in bed, her eyes wide, and she started talking faster.

"Terry! I just realized something. Several weeks ago I prayed to God that if he was real to show me a sign. I asked him for something I couldn't miss, something truly obvious, to show me he really loves me. This is the answer to that prayer! I have family!" she shrieked and jumped out of bed to hug him.

He was happy for her but cautioned her to settle down. Her health was precarious, and he didn't want her to relapse and collapse again.

"No, I most certainly will not settle down. It all makes sense now. He is real! Don't you get it? God is real, and He answers the prayers of a fool like me!" she laughed delightedly, and he joined her. Her enthusiasm was contagious, and her joy palpable.

The two of them would later look back at this as the defining moment, when they would turn their hearts to God. It was a long process, and for Theresa especially, there was much baggage that had to be dumped. But they had hope at last.

He helped her get discharged quickly and accompanied her home, walking her to her apartment in spite of her protests. He wouldn't be at ease, until he knew she was home safe and sound and resting comfortably.

Terry told her that he had set up another round of treatments for her the following week and that he was impressed with how she was holding up so far. She was a fighter and now, thank God, she had even more to fight for. He said goodbye and tucked her into bed with a cup of tea.

After he left, she lay in bed still high on the adrenaline rush of finding out that someone she already loved dearly was actually her own flesh and blood. Her first instinct was to call her and tell her right away. Then she thought about it and decided to wait for a little while. Rachel had a new man in her life, was running the business in Theresa's absence, and had a wedding to plan. Dumping something this huge on her now would be a lot for her to take in. There was plenty of time for that. For now, she was going to bask in the secret that was wholly her own.

****

Rachel and Greg were watching a movie, curled up on her couch eating popcorn and talking about the wedding.

"Have you ever thought about having children?" he asked her suddenly.

She was taken aback at that. It was something that hadn't crossed her mind in years. Having never dated or even thought about marriage for most of her adult life, children were far from her mind. This was all so new to her, and she had to learn as she went.

"No, honestly I haven't. I always thought I would die an old maid," she joked with him.

"Really? I think you would make a wonderful mother. You have so much patience, and so much love to give. I would like to give you about six children," he said confidently.

Rachel started to choke on her popcorn. He jumped up and started to pound her on the back. It finally dislodged itself, and she looked at him in astonishment, her face nearly purple from the exertion.

"Six?! Really? That's uh, a lot of kids," she said nervously. This was a conversation that she didn't think she was ready for. They weren't even married yet, and he was already talking about a half a dozen children.

"I don't think so. I think children are a blessing from God," he said stubbornly.

"Oh, I agree completely, but there's plenty of time for that. Right now I have a career that I love, and I have plans to one day start my own line of clothing. I don't know how I could do that and raise a bunch of kids."

"I see. I guess I just thought that after we got married you would be ready to stay home and raise kids with me. I make decent money doing what I do, so you wouldn't really need to work."

Her mind flashed to the large bank account sitting untouched and thought it wouldn't be a good time to bring that up. She had no idea he was so old-fashioned when it came to the roles of husband and wife. She needed to tread carefully here.

"Honey, I understand what you are saying, but this is my dream. I worked hard in college and in the business to get to where I am, and I'm just not ready to give that up yet. If and when children come along, can't we talk about all of this then?"

She could see his jaw muscles bunching and could almost hear the grinding of his teeth. She had to give him credit, though. He kept his temper in check and finally said, "You know, we haven't given any thought to premarital counseling. There are probably other issues lurking that we aren't even aware of. Maybe we should contact the Pastor to sign up for some classes."

She agreed and told him that she loved him. There was nothing that they couldn't work through together with God's help. She knew that the time to discuss her money was coming soon, and there was no possible way she would be able to avoid it. Now he would throw it in her face as evidence that she didn't need to work.

She made a mental note to spend some time in prayer tonight seeking God's direction and to study the Bible. Long ago she decided that all of her decisions needed to be brought before her Savior. She simply couldn't navigate these treacherous waters without Him.

****

Theresa woke to another blinding headache. She whimpered and carefully made her way to the bathroom for her pills. She tossed them back with a glass of water and filled her tub nearly to overflowing before shedding her clothes and sinking gratefully into its depths.

She had been able to hide the worst of her symptoms from Terry, but the truth was she felt worse every day. It seemed like the treatments were only making her feel worse. On top of the horrible nausea and burns on her skin from radiation, she was slowly losing her hair. She dropped her face into her hands and wept.

Lord, set me free from this! You say you love me, how can you allow me to suffer so? I have the love of a good man, family that I adore, and a good life now. Please Lord, please heal my body. Give me another chance to do it right.

Tears dripped off her face, and she sobbed out her fear and agony. Happiness was within her grasp and yet she was fighting for her life. It all seemed so unfair! She soaked for an hour in her tub, replenishing the hot water periodically, until she was a shriveled prune.

Her headache finally subsided somewhat, and she rose gingerly to put on her robe and make a cup of chamomile

tea. She hoped she would be able to get back to sleep.
Her day ahead was full with plans to meet florists,
photographers, and reception halls with Rachel. The thought
made her smile, and she drifted off to sleep.

God on His throne watch his beloved slumber. He
dispatched angels to stand guard over her while she slept.
He whispered words of love in her ear and held her in his
arms, bringing her the sweetest of dreams. He smiled down
on her, thrilled beyond words that she had finally come to
Him.

He knew the battle that lay before her, and He knew its
outcome. He had prepared her heart and mind for it, and He
was well pleased with His precious daughter.

Kissing her on the cheek, He reminded her once again that
He loved her beyond all measure and that He had prepared
a place for her where there would be no more pain, no more
suffering, and where finally all her tears would be wiped
away.

Chapter Twenty Six

Afrika and Caitlyn said goodbye to the last of the members of church following that Sunday service. They were both famished and even though it had only been two weeks since they had last seen one another, they felt like they had so much to catch up on.

While he drove them to a nearby café for lunch, Afrika filled her in on everything that had happened in her absence. He explained the opposition he had come up against that had inspired him to write the sermon he had just given. He said that while most of the congregation had been very supportive and excited for him, a handful of individuals were almost hostile to the idea. He knew that meant that there were probably more who were simply to reserved to say it directly to his face.

"I thought it was very insightful, Afrika. These are things that I had never really thought about before meeting you. I have to confess that when I look at you, I simply see a beautiful man who loves God. The color of your skin has never mattered to me. I'm sorry for what you have had to go through. It's probably a good thing I wasn't here to hear all of that, because I probably would have punched first and asked questions later!" she admitted.

They both laughed and Afrika told her that his initial reaction was one of anger, too. "But once I allowed God to minister to my heart and help me to forgive, I realized it was just another opportunity to minister to people. Caitlyn, we live in a fallen world and unfortunately racism is alive and well today. We just never think that it will infect the body. Surely you saw the two men in the congregation get up and leave during the message?" he asked.

She nodded, and the sadness in her eyes reflected his own feelings.

"It breaks my heart that they were not open to what God was trying to show them today, but I shall continue to pray for them. Perhaps a seed was planted today that will take root and grow. I know that I have been obedient. I think that this is something that you and I will have to learn to overcome together. Not everyone is going to be accepting of our relationship."

"It's ok. As long as God blesses our union that's all I really care about," she grinned up at him.

"Let's talk about happier things shall we? I have some exciting news for you! I have found you an apartment, fully furnished, that will do a six-month lease for you. I also have found you a job at a local law firm." Afrika was quite pleased with himself and couldn't wait to hear her response.

"You did what?!" she demanded. Her face had gone alarmingly red, and he could almost see the steam rising off of it. Clearly she was not pleased.

"I found you a job and an apartment. What is wrong? I thought you would be happy." He was completely baffled by her reaction.

"Afrika, I am a grown woman capable of making my own decisions. What if I go in there and don't like the people I am to work for? I don't know anything about the company, or what they expect of me. Now I won't be able to get out of it tactfully! Not only that, but you picked out an apartment for me that I've never set foot in. You don't have to live there, I do! What on earth were you thinking?" she asked.

He was so certain she would be thrilled to have everything taken care of. It had never occurred to him that she would get angry as his presumption. His own anger started to rise, as he felt rejection take hold. Couldn't she see that he had done it out of a heart of love for her?

"I'll tell you what I was thinking. I was thinking that you were moving your entire life here, and you had plenty to worry about as it is. I thought I would try to make the transition easier on you and that you would be thankful for the help!" he blurted out, hurt evident on his face.

Caitlyn took a deep steadying breath before continuing. "Afrika, I know you meant well. I'm sorry, if I snapped at you. You must understand that I have always been an independent woman. It's probably why I have never had a serious relationship with anyone before now. I like to do things my own way without anyone else's interference. You need to allow me to make my own decisions, or this is never going to work!" she said as gently as she could. Her anger was still under the surface, although it had started to dim.

"I am sorry. I didn't mean to take anything for granted. Honestly, I was just trying to help. From now on, let's decide to make decisions together as a couple. I know you are a confident woman and that you are used to doing things your own way. That is going to have to change though. God brought us together to complete one another. Our lives will begin to interlace and our decisions will impact one another. Let us bring this matter to the Lord and ask Him to help us learn to trust each other."

She agreed and they prayed together. The afternoon was ruined, however, and the conversation grew stilted. Caitlyn had a sick feeling in the pit of her stomach that she had just made the biggest mistake of her life.

Mara Monahan

****

Rachel was running late to her appointment to meet with Greg and their Pastor for their second pre-marital counseling session. Kevin and Cathy had just stopped by to say their goodbyes, and it was a bittersweet moment for her. She was really going to miss her dear friend. Kevin had managed a transfer to Warrensburg and was moving to be with his family. Their reunion had gone perfectly, better than they could have possibly hoped for. They still had a lot of healing to do, but the couple was as giddy as teenagers in love and couldn't wait to start over.

She raced for the elevator and ran to the waiting car and driver. She told him that she was late for her appointment and to please hurry. In her purse was the questionnaire the Pastor had given her to complete the week before. There were so many questions put to her that she had never even considered before she had gotten engaged. Did she want to have a joint bank account? What were her thoughts on working outside of the home? Did she want children, and if so, how many? Would she recognize her husband as head of the household?

It had taken her three full hours to complete, as she agonized over each question. She had to keep checking herself, because she was answering them in a way that she thought Greg would want to hear. Thank God for whiteout! She had gone back to each question two or three times to try to answer honestly from her heart.

She surprised herself with how much her career meant to her. When she was a little girl, she had idolized her mother and wanted nothing more than to be a mother herself. Then, as she grew into adulthood, she never really thought there was a chance she could have a husband and children, so she had focused whole-heartedly on her career, and it had paid off for her.

Then there was the whole issue of money. God had been speaking to her heart on this issue, and she finally realized that she had been putting it before Him. It wasn't even that she loved money before God; it was that it terrified her and had a hold on her. She finally, painfully decided that today was the day she would tell Greg and let the chips fall where they may.

She arrived twenty minutes late and flew into the office in full apologetic mode.

"I am so sorry, Greg! Kevin came by, just as I was leaving, to say goodbye. He is moving upstate to be with his wife and kids. I had no idea he was coming, and I had to spend some time with him before he left," she explained in a rush.

"It's no problem. Pastor and I have had some time to get to know one another a little better, and it's been really nice," he smiled at her. She was so thankful for his easygoing manner.

Pastor Robert Thompson had been doing premarital counseling with the church for over thirty years. He enjoyed watching young couples in love, but it came with its drawbacks, too. Sometimes in the course of counseling, they discovered issues that were simply to big for them to overcome. Other times he met with couples in which one person was saved and the other wasn't. He hated it, when he had to advise them not to marry. He had to be honest though and save them pain further down the line. Unfortunately most of the time they didn't listen to him, and he ended up doing counseling with them later in the vain attempt to keep them from divorce.

He wasn't worried about Rachel and Greg. They kept God firmly in the center of their relationship, and although they clearly had an issue or two that would need some open communication, he knew they would get through it and be stronger in the end.

"Did you both bring your questionnaires back with you today?" he asked.

They nodded in the affirmative and produced their copies. Rachel's own test was considerably worn and wrinkled. Pastor Robert raised his eyebrows in concern.

"Oh, I had to redo it several times," she admitted with a chuckle. "I realized at one point that I was answering with what I thought Greg would want to hear, and not what was necessarily true."

That perked the Pastor's interest, and they got started going over the answers. As they compared notes, it was suddenly clear that they were on the same page with most everything, until it came to the issues of work, children, and money.

"Greg, what would you like to see as far as Rachel's role in your home?" Pastor Robert asked.

"Well, I have always wanted to be the provider. I want to take care of my wife and cherish her. I want to come home to her and not have her stressed out from working all day. I guess I'm sort of old-fashioned in that regard. It doesn't matter to me as much as when we start having kids. I suppose I can compromise on her working, until the children start coming, but I feel pretty strongly that I want the mother of my kids to be at home with them and eventually for them to be homeschooled," he said.

"And you, Rachel?" The Pastor had been watching her fidget, since the subject first came up. This was something that they had obviously discussed once before.

"I love what I do. I can't imagine giving it up for anything. I love the people I work with, the mission field I work in, and the satisfaction I get out of seeing the hard work I put in paying off. Yes, I can agree with Greg that when the children start to arrive, I would want to be with them as much as possible. I just don't know if I could give it up entirely."

Pastor Robert discussed with both of them the importance of communication in all things. It was okay for them to disagree on things, as long as they continued to talk about them. He felt that with the two of them following Christ, they could overcome anything. They needed to remain in the word of God, in prayer and in fellowship with other believers. They were human after all and living in a fallen world. They were bound to make mistakes, to argue, and to have issues. Marriage is hard work, but it's even harder apart from Christ.

They moved onto the subject of money, and once again, Rachel became a bit squirmy. Greg was at ease and talked about having a joint bank account. He knew that Rachel made more money than he did, but he was secure, and it really didn't bother him. He loved what he did, and he did it out of a genuine love for people and not for the paycheck.

"Rachel, it looks like you have something you'd like to share?" the Pastor suggested gently.

"Umm . . . Yeah. Greg, I have a confession to make to you. I have been struggling with something that I have kept hidden from you, since we began courting. At first, I justified it because we barely knew each other, and I didn't want it to have an impact in any way on us getting to know one another. Then I just kept putting it off out of fear of how you would react. Finally, God called me on it and told me that if I couldn't be honest with the man I'm about to marry, what chance do we have?"

Greg was watching her with blatant fear on his face. He had no idea what she was about to say, but he was sure he didn't want to hear it.

"I am, well . . . rich. I mean, really rich. I'm sorry I haven't told you before now. Please understand that it doesn't have anything to do with not trusting you. I just, well, I guess I just wanted to make sure you loved me for me. I have no emotional attachment to this money. We can give it all away if you want. I just live simply and so over the years it has added up." She was speaking so fast that she was tripping over her words and fear of his reaction was starting to creep up on her.

Greg stared at her in shock. He didn't even know what to say to that. He had expected her to say something truly awful. He had expected a secret gambling problem, or shopping addiction, or maybe that she had gone bankrupt, but this? This was good news! He thought carefully about how to respond. The last thing he wanted to do was allow her to think in any way that the money would change how he felt about her.

"Rachel, of course I'm not mad about that. It doesn't change how I feel about you. I would love you, if you were dirt poor, and I had to take on a second and third job to support you. I'm proud of you for not squandering away God's blessings! And I don't want to tell you want to do, but don't you think that since God has blessed you with that kind of money, that perhaps we should use it to bless others? We could give it to a ministry or missions or start a foundation to help the homeless in the city? It shouldn't scare you, it should excite you!"

She wept with relief and ran to him, throwing her arms around his neck. She whispered her love to him, and he responded in kind. They heard the gentle clearing of a throat and broke apart, slightly embarrassed. In the moment, they had completely forgotten the presence of the Pastor.

The rest of the session was a complete loss, as Greg and Rachel in their excitement talked over the top of each other. The Pastor attempted to interrupt them a couple of times and finally gave up. He was content that at least one issue had been ironed out for them and made an appointment for the following week.

They decided to go for a long walk and Rachel instructed her driver to meet up with them at Central Park in an hour. As they strode, hand in hand, she confessed how nervous she had been to tell him about the money. He gripped her hand tighter and told her that he never wanted her to be scared to tell him anything. He was in this for the long haul.

They had finalized a date for the wedding and they continued to pray that Theresa would hold up. It had become so important to her that her friend and mentor would be by her side. The wedding would be small and simple, with an Asian-inspired theme in homage to her parents in China.
She picked orchids and cherry blossoms for her bouquet, purchased dozens of Chinese lanterns to decorate the sanctuary, and planned to have sushi and teriyaki chicken at the reception.

The hardest decision so far had been where to honeymoon. Greg was an outdoorsy sort who enjoyed hiking and mountain climbing, and he wanted to take a trip to Colorado or Montana to go camping and fishing. Rachel was more interested in a tropical locale for snorkeling and maybe a spa experience. Ultimately they decided to wait and see how Theresa was faring physically, because Rachel couldn't leave the company for a long period of time, if she weren't doing well.

Greg had secretly met with a travel agent to plan the ultimate honeymoon for his new bride. They would be going first to Colorado for some hiking and fresh air. He had booked them in the nicest spa hotel he could find. Then, after a week, they were jetting off for another two weeks in the Bahamas. He knew she had no idea, and he played up the idea of just going camping. He felt like a kid at Christmas, knowing that the surprise would completely overwhelm her.

With just weeks to go before the ceremony, Greg had been left to do much of the planning himself. Rachel was just too busy running Her Wicked Ways. She was typically working fourteen-hour days, and she literally dropped into bed each night, completely exhausted. He didn't mind though. He actually enjoyed the process of planning the ceremony that would forever unite them. He poured himself into the tiniest of details and ran everything by Rachel first.

He found an acoustic guitarist to play their favorite song as she walked up the aisle, a caterer with an excellent reputation, and a band that was available on short notice. He booked a suite at the Plaza for their first night together as husband and wife, and most nights that was all he could think of.

****

Caitlyn was troubled. She and Afrika had their first argument, and she was feeling out of sorts. She couldn't help but have some trepidation about the decision she had made to come to Iowa and she wondered if she had jumped the gun. She had felt a peace about it, when she had boarded that plane, and she thought back to the scripture she had read. We wrestle not against flesh *and blood* . . . .

Sensing that something dark in the spiritual realm was moving against her and Afrika, she knelt on the floor and prayed.

Lord God, I feel that something is trying to come between Afrika and I, and I ask for your intervention. I know that you are responsible for bringing us together and I trust you. I pray that you will remain in the center of our relationship no matter what the enemy tries to throw our way. Thank you for your goodness and your love, which is never ending. I pray these things in your beautiful name, Jesus. AMEN.

She was exhausted from her long journey and the day's emotional events and fell asleep almost the instant her head hit the pillow. She awoke a moment later in a foreign land, where the heat was as oppressive as the landscape was striking in its beauty. She saw elephants and lions, a massive sun setting over the safari, and hundreds upon hundreds of African children singing with their hands lifted high. She saw Afrika on a platform, speaking the word of God, and the conviction falling upon the people. She saw the sick healed and blind men gain their sight. Then she saw herself, again surrounded by children. This time they listened to her, as she told them stories about Jesus. They were enraptured, and asked her question after question.

The scene before her, as powerful as it was, faded to black in an instant. It was replaced by a lone figure, robed in white, with sandals on his dusty feet. He spoke to her, and his words were drenched in love, "My child, I am calling you. Come."

She sat straight up in bed, her heart pounding and tears soaked her face. She glanced at the clock. 3:14 a.m. Without hesitation, she picked up her phone and dialed Afrika. He answered on the first ring and said, "I know. He called me too."

Chapter Twenty Seven

Theresa and Terry had grown extremely close in the months since they started seeing each other. She confided so much to him, things that she didn't like to talk about, guilt over the loss of her sister and parents, heartache over the loss of her brother, her child, her husband. They talked a lot about God and what having a relationship with him meant.

She confessed that while she was finally starting to believe, she wasn't sure if she was ready to surrender. She still struggled with thoughts of needing to clean herself up before going to Him. Theresa knew that she was a sinner, through and through. There were so many things that she wished she could take back. She felt small and ugly in the presence of Almighty God and wanted to try and make things right in her life, before going to Him. She simply couldn't wrap her mind around the idea that he had died for her, warts and all.

They decided to start reading the Bible together as a couple. She loved that they were experiencing all of this together, learning new things that neither of them had ever known. They began in the Book of Romans, as it had answered so many of Theresa's concerns right off the bat.

He would ask her questions, and when she didn't know the answer, she called Rachel. Many times the two couples would get together for a time of fellowship, and the older couple gleaned so much from the younger. Her pride that she held so fiercely to for so many years had all but dissipated. Where once she would have felt foolish asking something that she thought she should have known, she now blurted it out without thinking twice.

They also spent a good deal of time helping Rachel and Greg with the planning of the wedding. Theresa wanted to do something really big for Rachel; she just hadn't decided what that was yet. The girl simply didn't require much in life. Greg had told her of their honeymoon plans, and it was already paid for. She already had an apartment she loved, a car and driver, an expense account, and all of her needs were fully met, so she decided to devote the matter to prayer. She truly believed that God was in the business of answering prayers, and that He would tell her what the perfect gift was.

After one wonderful evening spent with Terry, she was exhausted and lay in bed ruminating on the things that she regretted. Stephen always came to mind, when she was feeling this way. She had treated him abominably, putting her own selfish desires ahead of him and the child they should have had together. She wondered how he was doing, and suddenly was aware of a still small voice in her heart.

Call him.

No, that couldn't be right. She had kept tabs on him to a certain extent, over the years. He still held a piece of her heart and always would. She hated herself for what she had done to destroy the love they once had, but in spite of all that, there was no way she was going to contact him.

Call him.

She must be imagining things. Even so, her heart started to beat a little faster, and she felt her hands grow clammy. What would she even say to him after all this time? What if a woman answered his phone?

Call him. Now.

Alright, alright! Apparently *He* wasn't going to let this go. With trembling fingers, she dialed the number she had long ago memorized.

"Hello?" an achingly familiar voice answered on the second ring. It was all Theresa could do not to hang up. Time to put on your big girl pants she thought.

"Stephen? It's me, Theresa," she managed.

Silence. Maybe she made a huge mistake. Maybe that hadn't been the voice of God encouraging her to call. Maybe it was just the remainder of the fully loaded pizza she had eaten for dinner.

"Theresa? Wow. I never thought I'd hear from you again. How are you?" he said, actually sounding like he wanted to know.

"I'm ok." She lied.

"It's so good to hear from you. I pray for you all the time, you know."

"You do?" she choked back tears. She so desperately wanted to tell him how things in her life had changed so dramatically, but that wasn't why she was supposed to call him, and she knew it.

"Yeah. I only wanted the best for you."

"Stephen, I wanted to call you and say . . . well, say how sorry I am for the way I treated you. I'm sorry for everything, the abortion, the divorce, all of it. If I could go back and do it all differently, I would. I want you to know that God has started to open my eyes about some things, and I know that you praying for me had everything to do with that, so thank you." She was openly sobbing now and it felt . . . good.

As she spoke the words, a little crack broke open in the wall around her heart. She felt the burden start to lift. She confessed so much to him: the drive for power and prestige, the love of money, and the hunger to make more and more at the expense of their marriage. She admitted that she had even put her future career ahead of her own child.

"Theresa, I forgave you long ago. The one you need to confess all of this to is God. Only He can bring you the healing and forgiveness you are seeking. Give it all to him, lay it at the foot of the cross, and allow Him to carry your burdens. The Bible says to taste and see that He is good. He came not to condemn you, but to forgive you. He loves you, Theresa, more than you can possibly know.

I sense that you are holding back from Him. Don't wait, please. None of us have the promise of even one more day. What if He decided to take your life tomorrow? Would you be ready to face eternity?" he asked her plainly.

Oh, if only you knew, she thought, stunned at his words. *You are so right. I certainly don't have the promise of too many more days.*

"I just don't see how He will take me as I am. I am filthy before Him, and I know that," she said, pleading in her voice. She wanted what he was offering her, but she was terrified to take it.

"Listen to me. Jesus died on that cross for you, just as you are. He knows all, and He forgives all. He forgives the sins you know you have committed, and He forgives the ones you aren't even aware of. He is like a parachute. You can believe in Him all you like, but until you put Him on, He can't save you."

"What do I need to do?" she was completely, finally, utterly broken. After years of heartache, disappointment and pain, she was at rock bottom. There was nobody who could save her now but Christ himself.

"If you read the Book of Romans, you will see that He says we must admit that we are sinners, believe Jesus died on the cross for us, and confess Him as our Savior. So pray that now, Theresa, and make sure you *mean it*."

She did. Right then, on the phone with her ex-husband, who by all rights should hate her. She laid her life out, before the One who knew all and loved her anyway. She repented of every evil thing she had ever done, she asked forgiveness, and pleaded with Jesus to make her whole again. She poured out her heart to Him and gave him everything she had, asking Him to take control. She needed Him desperately.

The heavens rejoiced and the angels celebrated, as they had on countless other occasions. Eugene and Mary Wakefield led the celebration that followed, worshiping the Lord with all they had, for setting their daughter free. God smiled, for He knew that He was just getting started.

****

The final weeks leading up to the wedding fled away quickly. Rachel and Greg began to panic that they didn't have everything covered. They planned to have a rehearsal dinner with Theresa and Terry the night before the ceremony. Only a few weeks previous, the two of them had asked them to stand up for them as Best Man and Maid of Honor.

They wholeheartedly agreed and were truly honored. As they gathered that night for the simple dinner Theresa had cooked, they sat around the table, laughing and enjoying each other's company. Theresa raised her glass for a toast, and the mood quickly turned serious, and she said that she had finally come to a decision on a wedding gift for the couple.

"I struggled for a couple of months on finding the *perfect* gift for you. I realized pretty quickly that you have everything you could possibly want, and are the only person I know who is truly content in life, so I thought 'What would Rachel do?' The answer was simple. I prayed and asked God to show me what I should give you.

I have wanted to tell you something for a long time now, and the moment has never seemed right. You have been so busy taking care of the company and doing my job for me. Then you had your wedding to plan. I wanted the timing to be perfect, and since I have given my life to Jesus, I hear Him speak to me. It's as plain as day! He has told me that the time is now."

Rachel looked at her curiously, obviously without a clue at all as to what she was about to say. Theresa took a deep breath and plunged in.

"I know it was never important to you, but I thought it should be. I hired a private investigator to track down your biological parents."

Rachel started to object, and Theresa quickly cut her off.

"I'm afraid that your mother and father have passed away. I will give you the details, if you want to hear them. Your grandparents are gone too, as is an uncle who died a brave soldier, saving a little girl in the Vietnam War. You do, however, have an aunt who is still alive," she finished quietly, stalling for a moment to see her reaction.

Rachel had been holding her breath. She had known about her birth parents, but had always wondered if she had any extended family. It had never been something she wanted to pursue, because she was happy in the knowledge that her adoptive parents had chosen her and raised her in a loving home, serving the Lord. Now, she felt a sudden thrill of excitement. She had an aunt! What was she like? Where was she? Did she want to meet her? She felt Greg hold her close and loved the security he gave her.

"Rachel, it's me. I'm your aunt," Theresa finished, with tears in her eyes.

It took a full thirty seconds for the words to penetrate her consciousness. Theresa? That couldn't be! She had been right there all along. She had been her friend, her mentor, and was now her sister in Christ.

Joy flooded her heart, and she leapt from her chair and raced to Theresa's side, hugging her gently. Emotion poured out of her, as the two women held tightly to one another. They cried and repeated over and over words of thanksgiving to God.

It was a night of celebration in the elaborate kitchen in New York and in the throne room of God. He poured out His love on His children and stirred their hearts toward Him. He looked back on the intricate plan He had put into action so many years before and was pleased.

****

The acoustic guitar began to play its exquisite music, as the door opened and Theresa walked slowly up the aisle. She found herself staring across at Terry, and she saw the love he had for her plain in his eyes. Would she one day find herself in this spot, standing across from him? She turned

327

her attention back to the bride, who was making her way down the aisle on the arm of Thomas Allen, who had been humbled to give her away.

She was breath taking in a simple but elegant gown of ivory that showed off her new figure to perfection. Her hair had been swept up in a complicated chignon by chopsticks, and the ambient light set off by the Chinese lanterns glowed on her skin.

Greg felt his heart stop in his chest, when he saw her, and he had to remind himself to breathe. He didn't want to be one of those grooms who fainted at his own wedding. As he watched her walk toward him, he said a silent but heartfelt prayer of thanksgiving to his God.

The wedding was perfect. It hadn't been expensive or ornate, but the love that was shared by the young couple was palpable, and there wasn't a dry eye in the room. Tissues were passed around with wild abandon, and even the Pastor admitted to getting choked up. When they were pronounced husband and wife, the applause had been deafening, and they knew that an angelic host had joined them in their enthusiasm.

They lingered for the photographs and eventually met up with the small group of people invited to the reception. Theresa and Terry danced many slow dances together that night, enjoying the feeling of being in each other's arms.

"Theresa, there are some things I have been meaning to talk to you about," he began.

"Mmmm," she mumbled, her head on his chest, soaking in the feeling of contentment.

"Theresa, I have watched your life change, since the moment I met you. God has softened you so much and brought about a peace I never would have thought possible for a woman with your diagnosis. I have to admit that it's real. Once I admitted that to myself, I knew the next step I had to take. I committed my life to Him."

"That's wonderful!" she said, still not moving her head. She didn't want this moment to end. The man she loved had given his life to Christ. Her own flesh and blood, the only one left, had gotten married today to a man she was clearly head over heels in love with. Here she was, dancing the night away with the man of her dreams.

"There is one other thing. I know we don't know what the future holds for you, or for us, for that matter, I just know that I want that future to have both of us in it, for as long as it lasts. Theresa, I love you so much. I can't get over how quickly I fell for you, but it's true. Will you marry me?" he asked her, his words heavy with emotion.

Her head lifted from his chest, and she looked into his eyes. She felt that thrill go through her and wondered if she was being selfish to say yes. She might leave him. She didn't want to. She wanted to stay, but it could happen, and they both knew it.

Terry watched the emotions play over her face and knew what she had been thinking, as clearly as if she had said the words out loud.

"I know. I don't care. I want to be with you, for as long as God allows. I want every moment that is left to us! Maybe I am being greedy, but I don't care. I love you!"

She couldn't deny him. She loved him, and she wanted to be with him too. Slowly, she nodded her head. He swung her up off her feet and spun her in a circle, as she giggled.

He kissed her neck and told her over and over again that he loved her.

"I am ready now if you are," he said, eager to be on with it.

"Silly man, we need a license and a minister. We can't just get married at the drop of a hat!" she teased.

"The minister is still here. Let me make a couple of phone calls. I will be right back." With that, he was gone.

She found Rachel and Greg and shared the good news with them. They were thrilled, and when she confessed that he was determined to do the deed *today*, they encouraged her to go for it.

Terry came back ten minutes later with a triumphant grin on his face.

"I have a patient who works for the justice of the peace. He is bringing over a marriage license. Pastor Robert said he would be happy to perform the ceremony tonight."

She was stunned at how fast he worked, but readily agreed to it. Her head was spinning, and she forgot her exhaustion and was excited that she would be married tonight. It was all happening so quickly, but if felt *right, a*s if it had been predetermined by God.

Before the evening was over, Rachel and Greg stood up for Theresa and Terry. Each of them left for their wedding night, filled with joy and excited to begin their new journey together. One couple, young, healthy, and full of vigor; the other couple, eagerly clinging to the few precious moments they had left.

Chapter Twenty Eight

Caitlyn and Afrika were meeting with their caterer in an hour to pick out the menu for the wedding reception. They both loved food and knew it would be hard to narrow it down to just a few items but were excited to taste everything together.

She was putting the final touches on her makeup, as her mind drifted back to the day he had proposed to her three months previously. He had taken her out for the most romantic night of her life, and she could see that a lot of thought and effort had gone into the proposal. They ate dinner in a quiet bistro with candlelight and a strolling violinist, which was followed by a horse drawn carriage ride, where they sipped hot cider while snuggled under a warm blanket. The evening ended with a walk through the park that had been lit by thousands of twinkling lights.

Afrika had taken her hands in his own and said, "Each morning when I rise, I give thanks to the One who brought you into my life. I never thought I would find the kind of joy that He has brought me. When I came to this country, my only mission was the serve Him with my whole heart. I never thought I would be blessed to find a woman who is as beautiful on the inside, as she is on the outside, and who loves Him as much as I do. I love you, Caitlyn, so much. Will you do the honor of becoming my wife?"

She had hoped that was what this night was about, and when he said the words to her, her heart melted. How good God was!

"Yes! Yes! Of course I'll marry you! I love you Afrika, and I am so thankful that God brought us together. Wherever He takes us, I will be content with you by my side."

They had spent the following weeks planning the wedding for the middle of May. All was set, and the only thing that concerned her was that they didn't have a minister to perform the ceremony. Each time she broached the subject with him, he would tell her not to worry about it, that he had it under control. She loved his mysterious side, but sometimes it drove her a little nuts.

She arrived at the caterers on time and sat next to her handsome fiancée. He was eagerly looking over the menu with a huge smile on his face.

They ordered a variety of items to taste and finally decided on coconut chicken with fresh mango sauce, grilled vegetable skewers with lemon garlic zest, mini New Hampshire crab cakes with jalapeno dip, artichokes parmesan, gruyere quiche tartlets, beef fennel kabobs, and warm brie puffs.

It was an extensive and elaborate menu, but they were willing to skimp in other areas to have good food. Each had been to many weddings, where the food was bland or downright awful.

Their next stop was to a local bakery that specialized in wedding cakes. Afrika did not have much of a sweet tooth. Growing up in Kenya, as he did, he hadn't been exposed to sweets on a regular basis and had the beautiful teeth to prove it. He left the cake choice entirely up to Caitlyn.

She chose a traditional British cake for them. There weren't many English wedding traditions that she felt overly fond of, but the cake was one that she had always adored. She

was still holding out hope that her own parents would
attend, and that the cake would help to pacify them as well.

They chose a small wedding cake for them, made of
fruitcake, with a top layer traditionally known as the
"christening cake." The christening cake was kept for the
first child's christening. Knowing that most American's
abhorred fruitcake, Caitlyn also ordered a traditional vanilla
cake with white frosting for their guests.

The couple rounded out the day with a visit to their
photographer for some last minute arrangements. They
wanted to have entirely black and white photographs, as
each felt they were more dramatic. They like the vintage
romantic feel that they carried and knew that would not be
changed by future trends.

They found a little café in town to have dinner and sat
reminiscing over their brief courtship. They snickered over
the enemy's vain attempts to break them up in the beginning
and marveled at how God had gotten them through. Caitlyn
had ended up taking the apartment and job after all. She
loved working for Baker and Baker; the managing partner
was a devout Christian who had always treated her with
deference and respect.

Afrika also shared a wedding tradition from his own
homeland with her that he wanted to have for their
ceremony. Couples in Africa would bind their hands
together with rope to symbolize their joining forever as
husband and wife, in a tradition called "tying the knot."

She loved the idea, and it was settled. They were content with
adding in a few simple touches that represented both cultures.

They had often talked of *the dream*. It amazed them that they
had the same dream that night, and yet they were learning

333

that with God, nothing is impossible. Clearly He was calling them to Africa, but for now, they did not know when or in what capacity. No matter how many times they discussed the dream, they never failed to break out in tears and goose bumps.

"I do have a surprise for you, little one. I hope you will be happy with it, but I made the arrangements through a travel agency, so if you decide you want to go somewhere else, we can change our plans. I bought two tickets for us to go to Kenya for our honeymoon. There is a really nice resort there, a spa actually, and I booked us a suite, as well as a Safari with a local tour guide. It has been on my heart, since we began courting, to take you to my homeland. I want you to see the beauty of Africa, the majesty, and splendor."

Caitlyn was floored. She had no idea he had been cooking this surprise up for her, but she was ecstatic!

"Oh, that is wonderful! I cannot wait! Do we need to get immunizations or anything before we go? I hear the insects there are the size of city buses."

He laughed his rich, deep, hearty laugh that she had come to love.

"You are such a girl! Yes, it would be wise to get a few vaccinations, before we go. The diseases in Africa can take you down quickly. Don't worry about the bugs. They only take a few American tourists a year as sacrifice to their Gods. You should be fine."

They both laughed then, delighting in one another, and never failing to find endless topics to discuss. Coming from two such diverse backgrounds and cultures, learning about each other was going to take a lifetime. They looked forward to it.

****

It was May 14, and the wedding was in one week. Afrika made one last ditch effort to convince Caitlyn's parents to come for the wedding, even offering to pay for the plane tickets and hotel accommodations. He wasn't a wealthy man, but had lived simply for many years, and he had accumulated a small nest egg. He and Caitlyn had shared the expenses of the wedding amicably and would even have quite a bit left over to begin their new life.

The Woodhouses had been adamant, however, that they didn't approve of her marriage and wouldn't be attending. They were so proper and so polite that it almost didn't seem like an outright rejection of *him*, but that's exactly what it was. Afrika could handle it; he just worried about how it would affect his bride. It broke his heart for her, knowing how much she loved her parents. Perhaps in time they would come to know and love him.

He hung up the phone and said a prayer for them, asking God to soften their hearts. He then gathered his coat and car keys with a spring in his step and headed for the door. His parent's flight was coming in about thirty minutes. It had been almost ten years, since he had last seen them and his heart was nearly bursting with anticipation.

His mother and father had been born again Christians for over twenty years now. They were warm and loving people, and he had no concerns whatsoever that they would adore Caitlyn, and she them. He planned to cook a big dinner for them and invite her over to eat.

It had taken Afrika several trips into town to find the things he needed to make a traditional Kenyan meal for his parents, but he had also learned from Caitlyn how to make a kidney pie and scones for dessert. He wanted to introduce them to some of her culture as well.

He made *Ugali*, a porridge from maize, and *Nyama choma*, which was roasted goat meat. He was interested to see Caitlyn's reaction to the food. He thought that if he could eat kidney pie, she could certainly try goat meat.

His parents walked off the plane and ran straight into his arms. He never ceased to be amazed at their energy level. Considering that they were well into their sixties and had just spent twelve hours on a plane, they should by all rights be exhausted. Still, they chattered away excitedly, asking questions about his church and his fiancée, the city of Des Moines, and American customs. He was worn out just answering them.

Abdu and his wife, Adila, had never been to the United States. They were in awe of the technology they saw, the friendliness of the people, but mostly at how available food was. Afrika had stopped at a grocery store on the way back to the parsonage, and they marveled at the massive quantities of food. They asked their son if the people in this country were thankful for the bounty.

"Some, perhaps, but I would say for the most part, Americans are spoiled and take much for granted," he responded sadly.

They were clearly perplexed by this but said no more on the subject. He brought them home and allowed them a bit of time to relax, after their long journey. They unpacked their meager belongings, as he put the meal in the oven to warm, and then drove over to pick up Caitlyn.

She opened her door to him with a welcoming smile, dressed casually in jeans and a sweater. On the drive over he said, "I have a surprise for you. Prepare yourself, my dear."

She was intrigued, but assumed it was a special meal he had prepared or perhaps a small wedding gift. When she walked through the door of the parsonage, two strikingly handsome African strangers met her. They were dressed in traditional garb, he in a colorful tunic, and she in a headdress. They held their arms open to her, and she naturally went into them. She instantly knew who they were and felt as if she were coming home.

The evening was spent getting to know each other and the older couple asked so many questions of Caitlyn that her head was spinning. Their main concern appeared to be how she had given her life to Christ and what it had been like for her since. They were clearly very spiritual people and told stories of seeing people healed and raised from the dead in Kenya.

She was enthralled with them. She later confessed to Afrika that she wished they were her own parents. He replied with a smile that they soon would be.

The greatest surprise for her, however, had been the announcement that Abdu would be performing their ceremony. She punched Afrika in the arm and asked how he could have withheld the information from her.

"It wouldn't have been a surprise, if I had told you!" he laughed playfully and held her arms at her side to avoid further abuse.

Several hours later, he returned her to her apartment.

"They love you, you know. I could see it in their eyes. They will be happy to call you daughter."

"Really? That's a huge relief. I have to admit, I didn't know how they would take the idea of you marrying a Brit," she laughed.

"All my parents ever asked of me was that I marry someone who loves God. That is where their heart lies, and I know that they are pleased with my choice."

They sat in the car talking quietly, not wanting the evening to end. Each one was thinking the same thing. They couldn't wait for the wedding night. Temptation was a difficult thing, and they had battled it for months now. They wanted to enter this marriage pure, and they had managed to remain celibate. They weren't fools, however, and knew that it had been wise to make the courtship fairly short.

He said goodnight and gave her a chaste kiss on the cheek, but he certainly wanted more. Less than a week to go. He could hold out.

She waved at him, as she let herself into her apartment. Once on the other side of the door, she leaned into it for support. Less than a week to go. Could she make it?

****

The wedding day had finally arrived, and Caitlyn was an emotional wreck. She had asked her close friends, the Allens, to come and stand by her. Jenna would be her only attendant, and Thomas would give her away. She was devastated by her parents' disapproval and had hoped in vain right up until today that they would surprise her and show up.

She kept tearing up, as Jenna fastened the dozens of tiny buttons at her back. She wore an elegant strapless champagne gown with a small train that trailed in her wake. She had decided on a tiara in lieu of a veil, and her long hair had been curled and fell over her shoulders in silky waves. She completed the look with tiny pearls in her ears and at her throat. It was simple yet chic, and she felt like a princess.

She wondered how Afrika was holding up and smiled when she thought of him. For all his bold confidence, she knew him well enough to know he was probably as nervous as she was.

The entire congregation had turned out, as well as many friends and well-wishers from the African community. They were surprised to see over three hundred guests in attendance, filling their small sanctuary to capacity.

Afrika stood stiffly near the altar of the church with Chizoba by his side. He could see how nervous his friend was, so he laid a hand on his shoulder and said, "Brother, why don't we pray?" He took his hands and said, *"Father God, we are so thankful this day is finally here! I ask that you would bring your peace to my friend and allow him to bask in your goodness today. I pray that you would take away his feelings of anxiety and replace them with joy. Today he will be joined with his love, and I thank you for bringing them together. You are a good God who loves us beyond measure, and we are so grateful! We pray these things, knowing your presence is here, and that you are faithful to answer our prayers. In Jesus name we pray, AMEN."*

Afrika took a deep breath and thanked his friend. He relaxed a little and focused on the door that his bride would emerge from. Just then the music started up, and he felt a jolt to his heart.

Jenna started down the aisle and made her way to the altar. A hush fell over the crowd, and Afrika was quite certain that all in attendance could hear the pounding of his heart, as his stunning bride made her appearance. His knees went weak, and he could feel the strong, sure hand of his father on his shoulder, steadying him.

She smiled up at him, and he felt his heart pound faster. What had he done to deserve her? She fairly took his breath away!

Thomas gave her hand to him and took his seat. Abdu began the ceremony and asked the maid of honor and the best man to tie their hands together with the rope, thereby symbolizing their unity in life.

Finally, they were pronounced husband and wife. They hesitantly leaned in toward one another and shared their first kiss. Applause exploded in the sanctuary and eventually Abdu was forced to break them up. They may otherwise have spent the rest of the day at the altar.

The reception went by in a moment, and they begged off to head to their hotel room. Many hours later, as they lay in each other's arms, they gave thanks to their God. Overwhelmed with love for Him and emotionally spent, they drifted off to sleep.

****

One week later, Afrika and Caitlyn stepped off the plane in Kenya. They bid goodbye to Abdu and Adila, who had flown with them, and drove to their hotel. Their room was no less than extravagant.

Their bed was draped in mosquito netting, and the room was lit with candles and overflowing with tropical flowers. They had a four-room suite that included a dining area, a living room, and a massive bathroom with a jetted tub. Their balcony had an incredible view of the African landscape that caused Caitlyn to gape in astonishment. She'd had no idea it was so beautiful.

They had arrived just as the sun was setting over the safari, and they stood, arms around each other, and watched it go down. She sighed contentedly and thought that she could actually live here.

They spent a week traveling and seeing the wildlife. Their tour guide was amazing and brought them to little known spots to see lions and gazelles, elephants and hyenas, and to see all of it from the safety of the jeep.

They had only one week left to them, when they received the phone call. They had been lounging on their balcony sipping iced tea, and Afrika reached for the phone. It was Abdu.

"Son, we have had a tragedy occur in a nearby village. A Pastor who had come from America for a weeklong revival has fallen ill and passed away. Thousands of pilgrims have made their way here to listen to him speak and will have to leave disappointed. God has laid it on my heart to call you. Will you come?" With those last words, Afrika felt the goose bumps start up again.

Will you come?

He promised to discuss it with Caitlyn, but was quite sure what her response would be.

They arrived the next day and set up the platform for him to speak. Everything else had been prepared already. They had thousands of Bibles translated into Swahili to give out, cases of fresh bottled water, speakers set up so that his voice could reach the masses, and food prepared to feed them all.

When he took the stage, he hadn't even been sure what he would say. He hadn't the time to prepare a message, yet this didn't trouble him. It was obvious that God had prepared him ahead of time for this, and he knew that the words would come.

Afrika spoke for hours on the love of God, the death and resurrection of Christ, and how He came to take away our sin. A small worship band had been assembled, and together they prayed for hours for the thousands of people who accepted the Lord that day. They saw many healed of sickness, vision and hearing was restored to them, and the lame walked. Caitlyn watched in stunned amazement, as even the tiniest details of her dream were coming to pass.

She saw a multitude of hands raised in the air in complete surrender and adoration. As she stood watching, she became aware of a group of children that had gathered around her. The group was growing quickly and one determined child was yanking on her shorts.

"Will you tell us about Him?" she asked with a slight lisp.

She looked out at a group of at least a hundred children and felt the whisper of God on her skin. Tears were flowing now without reserve, and she told them the greatest story ever told. By the end of the night, every single one of those children had given their lives to Christ and were standing at their feet with their arms raised in praise.

Caitlyn was on the ground. Face first in the dirt, she praised God with every fiber in her being and sobbed out her love for Him. She had never known such joy and fulfillment, and she knew that their fate was sealed. She didn't even have to ask her husband, she simply knew they were moving to Africa.

Chapter Twenty Nine

Five months passed with Theresa and Terry living in pure wedded bliss. They saw each day as a gift from God, one to be treasured and never taken for granted. Their days were spent cuddling up in bed, reading the Bible, doing crossword puzzles, or watching old romantic movies. Terry was an excellent chef and enjoyed cooking for her and pampering her. He gave up his practice, with the exception of remaining on call, so that he could spend as much time as possible with her.

She was, however, hiding much of her pain and nausea from him to the best of her ability. Theresa's dizzy spells were intensifying, and she had begun to lose her equilibrium to the point where she fell at least once a day. Thankfully it hadn't happened in front of anyone yet. She struggled to hold onto some dignity, but with the hair loss, the clumsiness and fatigue, and the nearly paralyzing headaches, it wasn't easy. She chose to remain home most of the time.

Rachel was doing a fantastic job overseeing the company in her absence, but even she couldn't keep up. Reluctantly Theresa chose to hire two more assistants for the office. Once again she went back to the Pratt Institute, her alma mater, in search of help. She left her contact information with the administrator, along with a vivid job description, and what she was looking for in an assistant for Rachel.

Three days later, she received via fax in her apartment, two excellent resumes. With some curiosity, she noted that the two applicants were probably related, as they had the same last name. Sisters most likely, she thought. Well, no matter, she intended to interview them promptly. If they were as

343

talented as their resumes led her to believe, she hit pay dirt on the first try.

The next morning, she took extra care with her appearance. She planned their interviews to take place in her office. Theresa hadn't been well enough to visit *Her Wicked Ways* in over six months. She knew how she looked, and it wasn't good. To date she had lost almost forty pounds, had dark circles under her eyes, and pale skin. Her hair had dwindled away dramatically.

She spent an hour with her hair and makeup and finally decided on a classic chignon topped off with a cloche style hat that had a long peacock feather trailing to one side.

She donned an indigo silk blouse under an elegant dark grey suit, hoping that the color would accentuate her eyes and not the smudges under them. She took a deep breath, said a fast prayer, and walked briskly into her offices.

The stunned look on the receptionist's face said it all. She stammered out a quick hello and looked away, trying desperately not to betray her astonishment. Theresa made a fast getaway to her office and closed the door. She was trembling, as she picked up her phone and buzzed Rachel.

This was the most difficult thing she'd had to do in a long time, and she knew that word would move like wildfire through the building. Rachel slipped in discreetly to ask how she was doing.

"I'm okay, really. As you know, I have been trying to find you a little bit of help around here, and I've narrowed it down to the best two candidates. I thought perhaps you could help me interview them. I seem to tire easily these days."

As she spoke, she dug in her brief case and handed the two resumes over to Rachel. Rachel glanced over them quickly, and her eyebrows rose in surprise.

"Yes, I know. I think they must be sisters. As long as they are professional, I don't think it will be a problem, but, since you have been holding down the fort, and doing an excellent job I might add, I will leave the final decision to you."

They discussed briefly what they wanted to ask during the interview, as well as the compensation package and benefits being offered. Five minutes later the receptionist buzzed Theresa to let her know the applicants had arrived, and Rachel went to bring the first one in.

"Hello, Melody. My name is Theresa. Please have a seat and tell us a little about yourself." She smiled warmly at the girl and took note of her impeccable fashion sense and stunning beauty. The only drawback might be the pack of star struck men following her around!

"Well, as you know from my resume, my name is Melody Andersen. I am sure you took note of the same last name I share with your other applicant. That's my sister, Harmony, and just to warn you, we are identical twins. You will learn to be able to tell us apart. We come from a musical background, our mother sings and writes music, and our father plays the drums. Music and art have always been a big part of my life, as if my name itself were prophetic.

I've loved fashion for as long as I can remember, and it was always my lifelong dream to work for you.

You were my inspiration to get into this business, and I've followed your career, since I was twelve years old. I am so honored to finally meet you in person!"

The interview went on for another thirty minutes, but Theresa loved her after the first thirty seconds. She was ready to hire her on the spot. Melody was a breath of fresh air, open and honest, dedicated to her craft, and full of energy. She had talent; Theresa could tell that by the poetic way she spoke, and the flare with her own clothing. She could hardly wait to meet the second twin!

Rachel walked her back to the foyer and asked her to wait for a few minutes, while she conferred with her boss. The moment she walked back into the office, she knew that Theresa felt the same way about Melody that she did!

They agreed to offer her the position, but wanted to interview Harmony first. Rachel went to retrieve her from the front and when she stepped out Theresa took the time to take several deep breaths and sip on some mineral water. She was fading quickly and knew she needed to get home and into bed soon.

When Harmony walked through her door, she almost fell out of her chair. She could swear that Melody slipped into the restroom and changed clothes. They were, beyond doubt, identical!

The girls had waist length honey blonde hair and pale green eyes. Their unique features were only magnified by the deep olive complexion and tiny perfect figures. Truly, they could have been models, if they had chosen, and Theresa was further intrigued by how well spoken and polite they were. It was her experience that girls this beautiful were arrogant and crass. She was utterly smitten with them. It wouldn't surprise her to learn in the future that they were both solid Christians.

After the interview ended, she and Rachel agreed to let them know together that they had been hired. By the end of the morning, she was entirely exhausted, but she felt like she had just accomplished something huge. She saw big potential for her new girls and couldn't wait to see what they would do for the company.

She went back to her apartment and was just about to tuck herself in for a long nap, when her husband called.

"Hi, sweetheart. How are you feeling this morning?" he asked her gently.

Oh how she loved this man! He was so compassionate with her and completely devoted to meeting every need she had, even before she knew she had it.

"I'm really tired, but otherwise alright. I was just getting ready to go back to bed for a little nap. Where are you?"

"I got called in to work. They need me to pull a twelve-hour shift at the hospital. Will you be okay, until I can get home? It will most likely be the middle of the night . . ." he trailed off uncertainly.

"Of course. I'll probably just sleep the whole time. At least I won't feel guilty, since you won't be home anyway," she smiled into the phone.

"Good. I promise, when I get home to give you a nice long backrub. How does that sound?"

"Like heaven," she laughed.

They hung up, and she was asleep almost instantly.

****

She woke, alone to the familiar, searing pain of what she wished was only a migraine. Moaning softly, she reached for the Japanese silk kimono hanging by the side of her bed and gingerly made her way to the bathroom.

Sighing, she reached for the first bottle, then the second. When she had what she thought was just enough to take the edge off her pain, she tossed them back with a glass of water. Gazing into the empty glass, she thought about how simple and happy her life used to be.

Now that she was a believer, she gave these worries over to God. Still, they haunted her most days, and she longed for the day, when He would wipe the tears from her eyes, and she would finally see her Savior. For now, when she hurt like this, it seemed like the recriminations haunted her.

She missed Sara with her twinkling aqua marine eyes and devilish sense of humor, and Coleman, the gentle giant always willing to rescue a damsel in distress. Tears running freely now, she thought about how that had literally been the death of him.

Sliding to the cold stone floor of her bathroom, she allowed the memories to come flooding back, one by one . . . .

****

Rachel sat straight up in bed, heart pounding, and tears soaking her face. She had just been thrust from the most vivid dream she ever remembered having in her life. She had seen people that she didn't know but who had somehow seemed familiar. She saw a very beautiful and young pregnant woman fighting for the life of her child and being beaten viciously by an angry young man.

His snarling, rage-filled face then morphed into a kind gentle one with dimples, sea-green eyes and a wide smile. He was very handsome and muscular, wearing a freshly pressed military uniform. She saw him run into a jungle and jump in front of a frightened young girl, beating off her attackers. Then he died too.

The next scene that filled her mind was that of a woman scared and trembling on the floor, with tears falling from her eyes. She recognized her at the same moment that she saw her fall unconscious.

Rachel shook Greg awake and told him that he needed to call 911 and send paramedics to Theresa's apartment. She threw on some clothes and ran out the door to the elevator.

Thankfully, Theresa had given her a spare set of keys years before, and she wasted no time opening the door to her apartment. She raced to the bathroom and flipped on the lights. Just as she feared, she found Theresa in a slump on the floor, unconscious and cold. She quickly felt for a pulse. It was there, but it was weak and unsteady.

She gently patted her face, trying to wake her. "Theresa, wake up! It's me, it's Rachel! Don't you dare die on me!" Over and over she shook her and tried to wake her, but to no avail. Finally, after what seemed like an eternity, the paramedics arrived.

They managed to resuscitate a clearly confused and disoriented Theresa and brought her to the hospital. Rachel used her phone to call Greg, then a car and driver, and finally Terry to warn him of what had taken place.

She didn't even realize how hard she had been crying, until she looked down and saw that the front of her shirt was soaking wet.

****

Rachel paced nervously in the waiting room, anxious for news of her beloved aunt. She had made no friends among the nursing staff, whom she had pestered to the point of angering them. They had finally firmly told her that she would have to be patient and that the doctor would come out to see her when they knew something.

Greg had held her hand and prayed for her, but the peace they were seeking was not to be found . . . not yet anyway. Rachel just couldn't sit there and do nothing. She was filled with anxiety and needed something to occupy her. She went to the cafeteria for a cup of coffee and some change. She found a phone booth, and called Thomas and Jenna Allen. They told her they would be there right away.

When she finally made her way back to the waiting room, she found Terry sitting with Greg and weeping. She ran the last few steps and begged him to tell her everything.

"It's not good. I don't think she has much longer. She is in and out of consciousness, but we had another CAT scan done on her, and the tumor has more than doubled in size. I don't know if she has been hiding from me how sick she really is, or if I was just too much in love and didn't want to admit the truth. I don't want to lose her!"

He was sobbing now, not caring who saw, and Rachel and Greg began to cry too. They laid their hands on his shoulder and prayed fervently for Theresa, for him, and for God's presence during this gut-wrenching time. They were at a complete loss and had no idea how they would ever get through this.

The doctor appeared and told them they could go back and see her. She was sitting up in bed, attached to several monitors with an I.V. tube snaking from one arm and an oxygen mask over her face. She was deathly pale, but she smiled weakly at them, as they entered the room, trying to communicate to them that she was going to be all right, but she wasn't, and they all knew it.

They gathered on each side of her bed, and just as they were about to pray for her, Thomas and Jenna arrived to join them. They prayed long and hard and the tears ran freely. At one point, Rachel opened her eyes to look at Theresa and found she had fallen asleep again. She prayed that wherever she was, God would meet her there and comfort her.

The last six hours of Theresa Cobb's life were spent in the loving arms of her husband, surrounded by the five people who had come to mean the most to her. They poured out their love extravagantly on her and didn't leave her side for a moment.

She took her oxygen mask off at 7:15 a.m., and looked at each of them individually, and told them what they meant to her. She spoke in a voice barely above a whisper, hoarse and weak, but determined to speak her mind.

"Thomas, there were many times that you drove me crazy over the years. You always stubbornly insisted in believing that there was a God who loved me and died to save me. For years, I butted heads with you about that. Now I want to thank you, because you planted a seed in my heart that refused to die. Because of you and your stubborn insistence, I get to go home to Him. Thank you.

Jenna, that day that you came to see me after I had the abortion is one I will never forget. I know now that God sent you to me to help me heal. You are so full of kindness and grace, and I pray you never change. Thank you for always being my friend, even when I felt like I didn't deserve one." At this, she asked for a glass of water for her dry throat. She took a small sip and continued.

"Greg, from the first time I met Rachel, I always hoped she would find a man to treat her like the priceless gift that she is. You have never failed to do that. I see in you a desire to shower her with love and to make her always believe that she deserves it. Thank you for loving her like you do, and thank you for your friendship.

Rachel. Oh Rachel, how can I ever begin to say what I have in my heart for you? You are the daughter I never had! You filled a hole in my life; one I put there myself so many years ago. You are absolutely precious in my eyes, and I can never thank God enough for you. I love you so very much! I know that He has huge plans for you, and I will be cheering you on from the other side. I assure you! Praise God that I will see you again one day in eternity."

The sniffling, blowing noses, and weeping could be heard around that floor of the hospital. The nurses had taken a moment to stop and listen at the door, discreetly. They were used to seeing death here, but even they knew something special was happening. There was a profound sense of the eternal happening and a hush had fallen over them all.

"Terry, my dearest husband. You are proof that God loves me. At a time when even the most devoted loved ones might abandon a woman as sick as I was, you came into my life and brought what I needed the most: love, support, beauty, and hope. Thank you for helping me through this, for being my home. I love you so very much, and I am going to ask you not to mourn for me.

I know that we both hoped I'd miraculously come through this, but you know what? I am going to be okay! I'm going to go home and be with Him, and honestly, as much as I'm going to miss all of you, *I can't wait.* My heart longs for home.

I promise you that after you see Jesus, I will be the second person to meet you in heaven. I will be watching and praying for all of you, I swear. You are going to be okay, because God is going to carry you through this, and we aren't saying goodbye. We are saying *until we meet again."*

Her farewell speech had cost her greatly and with those last words, she fell unconscious again. Her loved ones cried harder and held onto to one another. Terry fell across her bed and begged her not to go. Even the nurses outside the door were crying.

Thomas and Jenna, Greg and Rachel, and Terry had all seen her transform from a bitter angry woman with a grudge against a God she thought had ruined her life, to a gentle meek spirit who had embraced Him to the fullest, relying on Him for her very breath. It was so hard to believe they were losing her now, when she had come to mean so much to all of them.

They lingered in her room for another hour, hoping against hope that she would regain consciousness. At about 9:00 that morning, all but Terry had finally, regretfully decided it was time to go. Just as they gathered their belongings to leave, however, she sat straight up in bed and yanked her oxygen mask off.

"Oh!" she exclaimed with a strength in her voice that none had thought her capable of. "Do you see Him?! Oh, He is *so beautiful!* I am coming Lord!" she laughed delightedly like a small child, and her face shone with an indescribable light. The group of mourners in the room felt goose bumps stand up on their arms, and they gaped at one another in astonishment.

"The music, can you hear it? He is calling me to Him!" The joy that emanated from her in that moment was contagious and by now the nurses had rushed into the room. There was an electrical charge that raced through them, and they felt the very presence of God Almighty. Theresa raised her arms to Him as if in a dance, closed her eyes, and stepped from this world into the next.

The mood in the room had changed from one of total and utter sorrow, to one of exhilaration, and the tears became happy ones. What an incredible once-in-a-lifetime gift they had received. They had just watched the woman who had loved and inspired them, challenged and amazed them, and ultimately leave them, walk away hand in hand with her Savior.

Epilogue

Rachel and Greg arrived at the home of Thomas and Jenna Allen, two weeks from the date of Theresa's passing. Terry had already arrived and appeared to be doing well. He smiled in greeting and stood to hug them fiercely. A peace had invaded his life, since knowing and loving Theresa, and it was a peace that he could only attribute to God.

"Now that we are all here, let's go ahead and get on with the will. I'm sure that none of you want to hear my impressive, but boring, legal-ese, so I'm going to just tell you in plain old American English what her final wishes were.

Terry, Theresa left you her apartment and her most treasured possession, her Bible. She said that she knew you weren't concerned with money and that you would be happy to have the home that you lived in together and loved each other. She left you a letter. I have it here in an envelope." He handed it over to Terry and watched the man struggle to maintain composure. He took the letter and held it reverently, clearly anxious to be alone to read it. Rachel reached over and squeezed his hand in support.

"Rachel, Theresa wanted you to take full control of her business, and in giving it over to you, she wanted to make sure you were well taken care of. She gave you her entire remaining estate, which is estimated to date at 78.5 million dollars. There were a couple of stipulations, however, and at this point, I'm instructed to read the following letter to you:

My dearest Rachel,

You are by far more talented than I ever was. I believe you could do great things with my company and that's why I am giving it to you. There are, however, a few things that I would like you to do. Ultimately, it will be your decision of course, but I think you will agree with me on this.

I want you to change the name of the company to <u>Redemption</u>, as I no longer believe that anything called Wicked can be good. Add a scripture to each clothing tag, under the name, from John 3:16. If even one person is saved because of this, I will be over the moon!

Next, I would really like to see the clothing itself change to something more demure. Show the world that a woman doesn't have to reveal her body in order to be considered beautiful. There are plenty of companies out there that will show cleavage and belly buttons. You can be the exception. Make a stand for God!

And pursue your dreams Rachel! You always wanted a clothing line for full figured women. I say go for it! People need to know that God's creation comes in all shapes and sizes.

Finally, I want you to take 20% of all future earnings from the company and give it to missionaries. Let's continue working together, this time in seeing the Word of God go to the four corners of the earth. There are people dying all around us who have never once heard the name of Jesus Christ.

As for you, my sweet girl, I want to offer you some encouragement. In honor of your parents, whom I admire tremendously for raising you the way that they did, go to China! Take some time off, and go look for your parents. They deserve to know what a wonderful woman you turned out to be.

We hired those two talented young women. You thought it was for a little extra help in the office, but I knew that day I was leaving you soon, and I wanted you to have someone you can trust to take over so that you could have a break. As talented as you are, you can't do it all Rachel. Take a vacation with Greg and relax for a while. Enjoy being young and in love. Life goes by so fast.

I'll be watching for you at the gates, my dear. You'll know who I am, because I'll be the one jumping up and down for joy!

All my love and prayers,
Theresa

Rachel wiped at the tears on her face and smiled. It was as if Theresa were here in the room again with her. She knew that the words of wisdom were ones that she would live by. Her once all-consuming need to have her own company no longer seemed as important. She had it now, but she knew it wouldn't fulfill her needs. God was the only one who could do that, and He in His infinite wisdom had given her Greg.

She would take the advice offered and run with it. She would leave the company in the trustworthy hands of Harmony and Melody for a few weeks and travel with Greg to China. When she returned, she would start a new life. Her company would thrive to raise money for missions, and she and Greg could start a family.

She looked towards the heavens and whispered a thank you.

God, she prayed silently, *take care of her 'til I get there ok? And tell her I love her!*

He smiled down at her and said, "Done!"